VAMPIRE'S LOVE 1: *Blood Curse*

Rina paced restlessly around the perimeters of the house, smiling to herself - lucky thing it was only a superstition that vampires couldn't enter a house without invitation. All she needed was a broken window, perhaps, or cellar door. She spotted the tree that grew near the house, its branches stretching to the height of the lighted room upstairs. She scaled it as easily as a cat and perched on a branch, her weight scarcely stirring its leaves. As she watched the boy get into bed her mouth fell open in fascination. Through the open window, she could smell the dust of the grave that clung to him. She watched for a long time as he tossed under the sheets. Finally he grew still...

A cold breath of air stirred the curtains as Rina found herself standing beside the boy's bed trying to remember who she was. Rina. A vampire. She was two hundred years old...

Also written by Janice Harrell:

The Secret Diaries

1: Temptation
2: Betrayal
3: Escape

Point Horror

VAMPIRE'S LOVE

1: BLOOD CURSE

Janice Harrell

■SCHOLASTIC

Scholastic Children's Books,
Commonwealth House, 1-19 New Oxford Street,
London, WC1A 1NU, UK
a division of Scholastic Publications Ltd
London ~ New York ~ Toronto ~ Sydney ~ Auckland

First published in the US by Scholastic Inc., 1995
First published in the UK by Scholastic Ltd, 1996

Copyright © Janice Harrell, 1995

ISBN: 0 590 13981 9

Printed by Cox & Wyman, Reading, Berks

10 9 8 7 6 5 4 3 2 1

1

It was late but a light still burned in a big house on Netherwood Lane. In an upstairs bedroom, James Ryder lay sprawled on his stomach on his bed scowling at an old sketch pad he had found in his closet. Inside its cardboard cover was printed, in block letters—

JAMES CHAMBLESS RYDER
TYLER FALLS, NORTH CAROLINA
PLANET EARTH
AT THE EDGE OF A MINOR GALAXY

James smiled wryly. Back in the seventh grade he'd been awfully certain of his place in the universe, hadn't he? Things made sense to him back then. It must have been nice.

The phone by the bed rang and James reached for it. He knew only one person inconsiderate enough to call this late. "Hi, Chelsea," he said, settling back against his pillow.

"How did you know it was me?" she cried.

James smiled. "Who else calls at one A.M.?"

"Did I wake you up?"

"No," James admitted.

"Good. We just got back from the Outer Banks and I had to tell you right this minute that I love, love, love you! I missed you so much. My aunt was staying with us at the beach cottage with her four bratty kids, and I'm still sticky from them slobbering all over me."

"With competition like that I had to look good," he said. He flipped back to the last few empty pages of the old sketch pad. "Really, Chels, you ought not to call at this time of night. You could have woken up the whole family."

"Aren't you glad to hear from me?"

"Sure," said James. "Of course I am," he added more firmly. He was holding the receiver with his chin against his shoulder, and as he spoke he sketched a cartoon of Chelsea. She was easy to draw. With her broad-jawed face and tiny nose she reminded James of a cat. One of the aristocratic kind—Siamese, maybe. He gave her a slender cat's body and a long expressive tail that curled into a question mark. He could hear her muffled voice as she said something to her mother.

"My mother is nagging me to hang up," she said, returning to the receiver. "Like I don't remember that tomorrow is a school day? Am I stupid or what? Of course I remember. I'm just not going to let school ruin my life. I cannot wait to get away to college. Then it's good-bye forever to this dinky town, this family, the whole bit. Once I'm away from home, I can do anything I want and Mom can't do a thing about it. *Just a minute!* I have to go, James. My mother is going to kill me if I don't hang up. See you tomorrow."

James's nerves were jangled when he hung up, and he knew there wasn't a chance he was going to fall asleep. He tossed the dog-eared sketchbook to the floor. He had been on edge even before Chelsea called, he realized. He put on his sneakers and moved silently downstairs and out of the house.

Rina Cargiale's black cape brushed the grass as she walked in Oak Level Cemetery. It swung open with every step, showing the gleam of its black satin lining. Though the night was warm, eddies of cold air rolled off her, and in the moonlight her face looked ashen. Her footsteps were silent and neither the cape nor her tiny, slippered feet left any trail on the dew-frosted grass.

She went to the oldest part of the cemetery where an iron fence threw barred shadows against the gravestones. A huge oak stood at the edge of the old cemetery, and its mighty roots heaved the tombstones drunkenly askew. A marble angel leaned precariously to one side. On another grave, a marble lion slept on a marble cushion that slanted downward sharply.

Rina inhaled the scent of mildew that clung to the ancient tombstones and the still-fainter scent of old bones. She often visited these old graves, fascinated by the way the big oak made the ground heave and buckle, as if it sought to wake the dead. It stirred a hope in her that she didn't dare acknowledge even to herself.

The moon shone bright as a searchlight overhead and her shadow leapt to meet her as she walked. Suddenly she sensed that someone else was in the graveyard. She grew still and then quit breathing altogether. The vibration of heavy footsteps traveled through the thin soles of her slippers, and the night breeze brought an unfamiliar scent. Her sensitive nostrils quivered.

Slipping swiftly from shadow to shadow, she crept close to the iron fence and peeked through its bars to the lawn outside. There were no gravestones in the newer part of the cemetery, only brass plaques that lay flat in the grass. A solitary figure stood some yards from Rina, head bent. He sank to one knee, his back to her. She noticed under his feet the cross-hatched lines that showed the grass had been recently sodded. It was a new grave he was visiting, then. But why at this time of night? Rina's interest quickened. The boy had no shovel, so he couldn't be planning to dig up the corpse. Perhaps he needed only a small amount of dirt. As much grave dirt as would fill a flowerpot would be enough for rites of black magic.

In her black cape Rina looked like a shadow under the overreaching oak tree, so she knew the boy would not see her spying on him. Her amber eyes glowed like a cat's as she watched, and when at last he stood up, she knew she had been wrong about his stealing grave dirt. The newly planted squares of sod lay undisturbed.

The boy turned around and looked at her a long time, as if he were a deer caught in the glare of her gaze. Either the moon or deep emotion had drained his face of color and his blond hair looked silken and insubstantial. Rina was so stunned by his beauty that she gasped. She wondered if he were some spectral prince come to take her to the underworld. It took her several moments to realize that he hadn't seen her though he seemed to be looking right at her. Perhaps he was only struck by the picturesqueness of the old cemetery with its marble monuments standing like misshapen bones in the moonlight.

The boy turned and walked away down the gravel path. He was wearing sneakers, Rina noticed, a prosaic detail that told her he was no visitor from the underworld.

She slipped silently out the iron gate and followed him. Though he had much longer legs and was walking fast, it was easy for her to keep him in sight. Her entranced gaze fastened on his pale hair in the darkness ahead of her, and she let herself fall into a state in which she was as much shadow as substance. She drifted after him fluidly, sliding along the dark edges of the sidewalk, her white fingers trailing along a crumbling wall. A shifting pattern of light and darkness, she moved silently. Her small feet moved over a bunchy mint plant without crushing its aromatic leaves.

The boy let himself in the front door of a two-story frame house. A light flicked on inside. Rina peered hungrily through an open window and saw a grand piano, a splash of flowers in a vase on a gleaming table, and brightly colored chintz furniture. The living room spoke of home and happiness and her heart felt a familiar stab of envy. But then the light downstairs flickered out and she heard the boy walking up the stairs. Pricking her ears, she heard running water in the bathroom. A light came on in an upstairs bedroom.

Rina paced restlessly around the perimeters of the house, smiling to herself—lucky thing it was only a superstition that vampires couldn't enter a house without an invitation. All she needed was a broken window, perhaps, or cellar door. She spotted the tree that grew near the house, its branches stretching to the height of the lighted room upstairs. She scaled it as easily as a cat and perched on a branch, her weight scarcely stirring its leaves. As she watched the boy get into bed her mouth fell open in fascination. Through the open window, she could smell the dust of the grave that clung to him. She watched for a long time as he tossed under the sheets. Finally he grew still, his breathing measured. When she was sure that he was asleep, she let her concentration scatter to that muddled state that comes just before unconsciousness. Her molecules drifted and became a mist that hovered for a moment like a cloud before the open window.

Suddenly, like a magnifying glass in the sun, her wavering consciousness managed to focus the scattered molecules onto the rug beside his bed. A cold breath of air stirred the curtains as Rina found herself standing beside the boy's bed trying to remember who she was. Rina. A vampire. She was two hundred years old. She lived on Oak Lane in the home of an old lady who died several months before.

Reassured that she could remember that much, she touched herself gingerly, letting her fingers slide down her body. She was relieved to be solid once more. Changing into a mist frightened her. She was afraid she would someday let herself scatter into the shadows and be unable to collect herself. But tonight she had been forced to take the risk. She hadn't sorted out the reasons in her own mind, but she knew it had something to do with her need to get close to this boy.

Rina bent over him and inhaled his scent. Her cape shielded him from the moonlight and, as if sensing the change in the light, the boy frowned in his sleep and mumbled something she couldn't catch. Afraid he might wake, she held a hand close to his face, her fingers splayed out like starfish over his closed eyes. She focused her concentration, willing him to sleep. At last he grew still.

Her hand was so close to him then that she could feel the heat of his blood pulsing through his veins. At the thought of the blood her fangs slid out of their sheaths and glinted white in the moonlight. Her mouth watered and suddenly she bent her dark head and sank her fangs into his neck. His legs jerked reflexively. As she drank his blood, he did not struggle. Instead he sighed in satisfaction as if it were he who were feeding. The spell she had cast had held.

After a moment, she pushed away from him and licked the blood off her lips. She folded her arms across her chest and smiled down on him. If she had enchanted him, she thought, then it was only fair because he had caught her in a web of enchantment as well. She stared at him, wanting to drink up his beauty as she had drunk his blood. Though he was blond, dark lashes lay against his cheeks and he had black eyebrows.

He looked sleekly muscled and his body pressed heavily against the wrinkled sheets. Rina was surprised that she had earlier mistaken him for a visitor from the spirit world. Now that she saw him up close, he was so poignantly human. His helplessness in sleep struck a chord of tenderness in her.

She glided around the room, fingering his belongings and humming softly to herself. His blood, warm inside her, had banished the icy chill that often troubled her at night. Glancing around, she saw a couple of posters of rock groups and a few charcoal sketches that had been taped to the wall. By the window was a bookcase that held both books and CDs. A few athletic trophies were pushed up against them, like bookends. One showed a gilt figure mounted on horseback. Rina's sharp eyes made out a name etched on it—James Ryder. Another trophy seemed to be some sort of award for the hundred-yard dash.

Rina paused a moment before a somber painting that hung beside the bureau. Painted in blues, greens, and browns, it showed four people gazing at a burning candle. One was James himself, she realized, a good likeness. The others in the picture must be members of his family. The initials J.R. were neatly written in the lower right-hand corner. James must be the artist.

She looked with renewed interest at the

charcoal sketches taped to the walls. He must have drawn them as well. They were lively and drawn with sure strokes. One showed a girl with a pie-shaped face, blond hair, and a demure smile. The fluid style of the sketch reminded Rina of the work of an artist she had met in Paris in the last century who had wanted to draw her, but she had refused. It was unwise for vampires to risk the glare of publicity.

Rina opened the high school yearbook lying on the desk and leafed through it until she found James's picture. Gazing at it, she felt her heart turn over. The intensity of her passion frightened her and she closed the book abruptly. Behind her, James snorted. Then, to her surprise, he sat up.

In a movement quicker than thought, Rina folded herself into the knee well of the desk and crouched there, holding the yearbook clutched to her chest. James struggled free of the sheets and staggered to the window. Standing there, leaning against the windowsill, he rubbed his fingers against the fang marks she had made in his neck. He stared out the window a moment, puzzled, as if he were wondering what had woken him. Then he groaned a little and stumbled back to bed. The bedsprings creaked as he threw himself down and jerked the sheet over him. Perhaps, she thought, he was faint from the loss of blood.

Rina waited until she could hear the heavy breathing that meant he was asleep before she emerged from under his desk. Then she laid the yearbook back down and flitted to the window. Opening the window a bit wider, she put a slender foot out of it and slid out onto the roof. Her cape billowed behind her like a sail as she ran down the sloped roof and then leapt lightly to the ground. "James," she whispered. She liked the feel of his name wrapped around her tongue. Her fangs gleamed in the moonlight when she smiled. His smell and taste intoxicated her. She hadn't had such a powerful feeling since—since she couldn't really recall when. Two hundred years of memories had proved to be a heavy burden, so she had grown in the habit of letting memories slip through her fingers like sand. She thought little about the past and less of the future. Only small threads of recollections tugged at her now and then.

But tonight, with a passion that frightened her, she knew she must have James. A future without him was unimaginable. She wanted to drink him up and pour her own blood down his throat. That would be bliss, she thought with a sharp intake of her breath, and the end of all her loneliness. She drew her cape tightly around her as she slipped into the shadows and her sudden embarrassed giggle rang out from the darkness.

2

It was the first day of classes and it looked as if everyone had shown up early. A group of kids James didn't know had gathered under an oak by the street. The girls had masses of curly hair and wore astonishing numbers of rings. The boys wore short-cropped hair and sullen looks. A cloud of black smoke hovered over them. Several were gloomily puffing on cigarettes. Their gazes were faintly hostile as he passed. He was just as glad to draw close to the building's entrance and into more familiar social territory. He noticed that the low retaining wall near the entrance had been staked out by the Band Mafia—a tight group. During the summer they practiced together at band camp and during the fall he knew they conducted hot romances on the buses that took them to band competitions. They ran to messy hair and some had a habit of tucking drumsticks under their belts. Hanging out with them were a bunch of kids who did drama and constructed sets for school plays. "Yo, James!" Mike Hanson called.

James grinned and waved. He liked Mike but hadn't seen much of him lately. When Mike got serious about trumpet, he had pretty much disappeared into the band.

James's own bunch usually gathered near the railing that was at the top of the steps, running along the edge of the cement porch in front of the main building. It was a good place to see and be seen. "The top crowd gets the top steps," Chelsea had once pointed out. But her image of kids as blocks on a social pyramid made James squirm. He wondered if the reason it made him uncomfortable was that he could see there was a tiny germ of truth in it.

Some of Chelsea's buddies—Molly Haggerty, Laura Blalock, and Candi Alston—were perched on the top steps now, their hair gleaming in the morning sun. Tom Schwartzkoff was explaining something to them but they didn't seem to be paying much attention. Molly and Laura were touching each other, giggling, sneaking glimpses at other people out of the corners of their eyes. Ross Morgan and Brice Hanson stood with their thumbs hooked in their belt loops. James had the feeling they had been practicing how to stand all summer. He shook his head impatiently. What was the matter with him? He had known these kids most of his life, had run track and studied for tests with them, and all of a sudden he found himself looking at them as if they were strangers.

They called out to him and he flashed them a smile as he passed. He took a deep breath when he reached the railing. Last year, he remembered he had felt like king of all he surveyed from up at the top of the steps. Today he just felt tired. He wondered if he was coming down with something. The quick climb up the steps had left him feeling vaguely light-headed. He wished Chelsea would show up. He tried to avoid noticing the clumps of frightened freshmen, clinging together at the foot of the steps. He had enough problems without taking forlorn freshmen under his wing.

"Jim-bo," boomed a familiar voice, and James grinned as he saw Trip Davis bounding toward him. Trip was so big that basic survival instincts made others step aside to let him gallop up the stairs. The crowd parted before him as if he were an ocean liner. "Jeez, can you believe this heat?" Reaching James's side, Trip sagged heavily against the railing. "Three guys passed out at practice Friday and Coach had to pour cold water on their heads. Brutal, man." Trip's hair, cut short on top, bunched out below his ears. He had a heavy chin, blue eyes, and his grin showed strong white teeth. "Hey, what's that, man?" he exclaimed. "A hickey on your neck? Woo-oo!"

James pushed his friend's hand away and turned his collar up to hide the mark. When he was getting dressed that morning, he had noticed the yellowish bruise above the collarbone. In the middle of the bruise were two neat puncture marks.

"Does Chelsea know about this?" asked Trip. "Watch out, man, here she comes, Chelsea the Terminator."

"Will you cut it out, Trip?" snapped James. He didn't like to admit it, but since his sister's death he worried about his health. He had woken up that morning feeling weak and his heart had fluttered in alarm. He had examined himself closely in the bathroom mirror, looking for some clue that he would die young the way his sister had. That was when he had spotted the sinister little bruise. A dismal conviction had caught hold of him that he was doomed.

All his chilling fears vanished, though, as he watched Chelsea walking up the steps toward them. She was nodding and smiling as she went, as if she were in some sort of royal procession. She didn't seem to be aware that James was impatiently waiting for her. But she knew it all right. He could tell by the way she moved. Her skimpy purple skirt clung to slender hips and revealed a perfect expanse of tanned leg. James caught his breath in admiration. She had scooped her blond hair up on her head with a handful of wrapping paper bows and was wearing earrings made out of matching crimped ribbon. More than anything, she reminded James of the summer carousel at the park—she was fun. And fun was just what he needed.

She reached him at last and flashed him an amused grin.

"Lookey, lookey, James has got a hickey!" crowed Trip.

James felt himself redden.

Chelsea sidled up close to James and let her fingers walk up the back of his neck. He noticed that her smile did not reach her eyes.

"Yuck! It looks like something bit you, James! What happened?" Chelsea drew away from him and looked at him in surprise.

"I expect it must have been some bug," he said uncomfortably. "I was out walking late last night. Maybe that's when I got it."

Trip danced around them and bared his teeth in a snarl. "A vampire!" he cried, cupping his fingers over his head. "I want to drink your blood!"

Chelsea laughed.

Trip gnawed noisily on his wrist. "Ah, zee good red blood," he said. "Zis will help me kill on football field."

"You are disgusting." James wanted to join in the joking, but he felt his mouth twist in distaste. Trip and Chelsea were getting on his nerves, but it was his problem, not theirs. He'd better pull himself together or he was going to end up driving away all his friends.

Everybody expected him to be over his sister's

death by now. It had been two months since she died, and already the others acted as if she had never existed. Nobody so much as mentioned her name.

What did he expect? he asked himself. Naturally, his friends didn't want to keep thinking about Susan's death. They wanted to have a good time. He wouldn't have minded having a good time himself. It was just that he'd practically forgotten how.

Late that night the school buildings were dark except where glimmers of moonlight cast uneasy shadows into the rooms. Rina wafted her way through the main building, following James's trail—faint now since he had left so many hours before. Confusing and unfamiliar scents filled the halls, but she knew his locker at once when she found it, and she ran her fingers lovingly over the slotted metal front of the locker. She could smell his sneakers inside.

Glancing around, she recognized the place from pictures in James's yearbook. In bland brick buildings like this James took academic subjects and joined clubs. She had seen the clubs in the yearbook, their members squinting at the camera. She wished now that she had stolen it. It would have been useful for studying the school's unfamiliar rituals.

During her girlhood in Transylvania, over two

hundred years ago, it had been the custom for girls to learn only simple skills from their mothers at home. The vampire who had lured her from her family, however, was of noble birth and had been educated by the finest tutors. It had amused him to teach Rina something of what he knew. His family's decaying castle had been full of books. Tucked away at window seats and strewn all over the cobwebbed library, Rina had found books about what then passed for science—alchemy, astrology, Newton's works on mathematics and on light and gravity. In the desperate days when she had been trapped in Vlad's power, she had comforted herself with books. She loved them. But she had never been to school. The world pictured in James's yearbook was alien and frightening to her.

A plastic sign at a doorway read OFFICE. Rina thought it would be best to know her way around a little before she presented herself here as a student, and it was helpful having the rooms neatly labeled.

Behind the counter in the office, she found a filing cabinet. At once she began flipping through the student files. She lifted James's schedule out of his folder and swiftly committed it to memory.

She saw no reason why she couldn't easily pass as a student. After two hundred years of existence, she still looked like the sixteen-year-old she had been when her mortal life ended. She would have the usual problem of not having the necessary documents—no birth certificate, no driver's license, no social security number, no school records. But she was accustomed to finding ways around the modern world's obsession with documents, and she didn't let that trouble her.

A sudden tinkle of glass made her lift her head sharply. She heard raucous laughter. Slipping out of the office, she glided down the hall toward the noise. She heard footsteps inside a room labeled COMPUTER LAB. Rina wrinkled her nose as the whiff of stale sweat wafted out to her from the half-open door. She silently slid into the room. Inside, she saw rows of computers standing on tables looking like large ivory teeth in the darkness. Then she realized where the smell was coming from. A boy with long, stringy hair stood with his back to her, close to the windows. He was sliding a computer monitor over the waist-high cabinet that was beneath the windows to a dark shape outside—another boy presumably. He had reached in and was taking the machine from the first boy. Thieves, she decided.

The long-haired boy turned around. When he saw her standing by the door, his eyes bugged in astonishment. "Run, Ricky!" he yelled. But then he registered a double take. "No, wait," he added in a different voice. "Hold on. It's just a girl."

The boy outside the window cried, "What's a

girl doing there? Where is she? It's so dark in there I can't see."

The long-haired boy scrutinized Rina with narrowed eyes. "Is somebody with you?"

"No," Rina said. "I'm alone." Slowly, she walked toward him. Already she was thinking of this creature not as a boy, but as food.

"What's your game?" asked the boy uneasily as she drew close to him. He had a thin stubble on his chin and pale, watery eyes.

Suddenly, she grabbed his shoulders and sank her teeth into his neck. She felt him go limp from the shock, but her firm grip held him standing.

"Hey, what's going on?" cried the boy outside. "This ain't no time to make out! Oh, jeez, I see a blue light. Somebody must have spotted us and called the cops."

Rina sensed movement behind her and released her victim suddenly, spinning around to face the new threat.

A burly boy stood silhouetted in the open doorway. "What are you doing to him?" he cried.

He lunged at her then, but Rina grabbed his wrist and threw him to the floor. The floor shuddered as he fell and Rina heard him gasp. He fumbled clumsily at his pocket. Rina caught a glimmer of light on steel as his knife slashed at her leg. She cried out in pain when the blade struck her. Her flesh felt slick and cold with blood and she could feel its dampness in her shoe. Glancing down, she saw that a puddle of her dark blood had formed at her foot. She kicked the boy with her injured leg and a spray of blood droplets spattered the floor. He grunted and rolled out of her reach.

Rina heard the other boy stirring behind her. He had regained consciousness and staggered to his feet. Towering over her, his face contorted, he tackled her. She ripped herself free of his grasp and threw him hard against the cabinet. The blow stunned him and he slid to the floor. He sat propped against the cabinet, his eyes closed.

The cut in her flesh was already healing. Turning to see the other boy coming at her, she swiftly snatched the knife out of his hand. The movement was so fast, her white hand was a blur.

The boy stared a moment in amazement at his suddenly empty hand. Then, uttering a cry of rage, he rushed at her. Rina slashed a quick Z with the knife. His hot blood gushed onto her hand as his shrill scream split the silence. The boy gazed down at his blood-darkened shirt and his eyes went blank.

In the distance Rina heard a motor roar to life, which meant the third boy was getting away. A flashing blue light reflected ominously on the windows, but even the arrival of the police could not distract her from the blood-soaked shirt before her. Suddenly, his knees folded and he fell to the floor. She sank to the floor and straddled him. Then she put her arms around him and lifted him in a tender embrace as she bit his neck. The ecstasy of blood lust took her and she rocked with the rhythm of his surging blood. She could feel warmth spreading to her fingers and toes, a blissful heat close to numbness. It was as if she were floating on a bloodred river as warm as bathwater, and she sighed with contentment.

When at last she stood up, she glanced at the boy who was slumped against the cabinet and saw that his face was pale with shock.

"Don't hurt me!" he whispered. "I won't tell anybody."

Rina picked up the pocketknife and cut her victim's throat to disguise the mark of her fangs. With so much blood splattered on the floor, no one would notice that some of it was unaccounted for, drunk up by a vampire.

She sat down next to the other boy and leaned against the cabinet, weighed down with heavy feeding.

"S'okay," he whispered. "S'awright. I don't know a thing. You can trust me."

She took his hand in hers and stroked the palm, noticing that his flesh felt clammy and almost as cool as her own. Sweat shone on his forehead and his lips trembled. She laughed. The boy was a fool. Why should he imagine that she would trust him? He was a thief.

"I think I'd like to go to this school," said Rina.

"If you were me, what subjects would you take?"

The boy's Adam's apple moved convulsively. He tried to speak but nothing came out.

"Should I be a cheerleader?" Rina looked into his watery blue eyes. "Would that be good, do you think?" She could feel blood drying on her cheeks, puckering the skin a little.

The boy stared at her in horror. When he parted his lips to speak, he produced bubbles of spit.

"Police!" a gruff voice called from outside. "Come out with your hands up."

"Help!" the boy shrieked suddenly. "Help me!"

Rina buried her fangs in the boy's neck and his scream ended in a gurgle. She placed her hand on his chest and sucked until she felt the pounding of his heart stop.

She heard footsteps and low voices in the hall outside. The police had entered the building. It was time to leave. The small puddle of her own blood had already evaporated, leaving a dark stain on the tile.

She grabbed the edge of the open window, lifted herself up over the cabinet, and slipped out, lithe as an acrobat. She scarcely made a sound as she dropped lightly to the ground. Standing below, she could hear exclamations of horror. The police had found the bodies.

Rina let herself grow vague and loose. She slipped from shadow to shadow in the moonlit school yard feeling euphoric. A thin alley cat rubbed against her ankle. Suddenly it arched its back and screamed. In a flash it disappeared into the bushes. It was odd how cats knew what she was. Cats and horses both. Stupid creatures, but strongly intuitive. Glancing around, she took care to avoid the street where the flashing blue light rotated. She didn't want to meet up with the police when she had blood all over her face.

School life would agree with her very well, she thought. She would enjoy being a part of the throngs of students. It struck her that she was lonely.

3

The next morning during first period two police cruisers were parked outside the entrance of the high school, and even a casual observer could have seen that something was wrong. In the school office, Mrs. Spraggens, the assistant principal, looked harassed. Her hair, normally swept in a neat bun, had come out of its hairpins and trailed down in forlorn wisps. "When do you think we can have the computer lab back?" she asked the police officer anxiously.

The officer murmured something Chelsea couldn't hear though she strained her ears. When she had volunteered to help out in the office first period, her only thought had been to get out of study hall. She had never dreamed it would turn out to be exciting.

Mrs. Spraggens ran her fingers through her hair. "Of course, we can manage without the lab. We'll do something. But if you could just say *when* we could have it back, I could plan.

It will have to be put to rights first, of course."
She hesitated. "Was there a lot of blood?"

The dark girl at the counter dropped her pen
with a clatter. Chelsea glanced at her in irritation,
wishing she would go away. But the girl fixed
Chelsea with a level gaze that commanded her
attention. "I need to register," she said.

"Mrs. Spraggens," Chelsea raised her voice,
"we've got a new student here."

Mrs. Spraggens buried her fingers in her hair.
"Mrs. Holland will have to handle it, Chelsea. I
simply can't right now. I've got my hands full."

"Hang on," Chelsea told the girl.

Chelsea went down the passageway to where
the counseling offices were clustered. Glancing in
the first door, she saw that Mrs. Holland, too, was
talking to a police officer. Chelsea already knew
the basic facts about the double murder that had
brought the police to the school, but she couldn't
resist standing quietly a moment and eavesdrop-
ping, in case Mrs. Holland and the police officer
should let drop a juicy tidbit of information.

"His name is in our computer." Mrs. Holland
pulled some papers out of a manila folder. "But
he isn't a student here now. I've pulled his perma-
nent record and I see that he was held back in
the eighth grade and was suspended three
times." She sighed. "A born troublemaker, but he
did finally graduate last year." She glanced up
and saw Chelsea.

"Sorry to interrupt, Mrs. H.," said Chelsea, "but we've got a new student who's trying to register."

The counselor pulled some forms out of her desk drawer and handed them to Chelsea. "Let her sign up for whatever she wants, Chelsea, and I'll straighten it out later. Tell her she needs to come in and see me next week when things have settled down."

Chelsea nodded. Although she would have liked to linger a while longer listening to what Mrs. Holland and the police officer were saying to each other, she didn't want to be too obvious about it, so she left.

When she got back to the main office, she pushed the forms and a list of classes over the counter to the new girl. "Here, fill these out and sign up for whatever you want. You're going to have to get your old school to send your records," she explained. "Then Mrs. Holland can see what you need to take. You'd better come in next week and talk to her."

"My records may be hard to get," said the girl. "There was a fire at my old school."

"Where was your old school?"

The dark girl blinked. After a slight pause she said, "San Francisco." She bent her head over the form. Without checking the course titles against the list in a pamphlet Chelsea had given her, she filled in the courses she wanted to take. Her handwriting looked like calligraphy.

Chelsea took the sheet from her. "Incredible," she said. "You've got exactly the same courses as my boyfriend James."

A slow hiss escaped the girl's lips. Chelsea glanced at her in surprise.

"Your boyfriend?" the new girl repeated, as if she was having trouble taking it in. For the first time, Chelsea noticed the weird yellowish color of the girl's eyes and she shivered. A chill blast seemed to have hit the back of her neck. She glanced over at the air-conditioning vent. Odd. She wasn't standing at all close to it.

"Yeah, my boyfriend," Chelsea said. "You're bound to get to meet him. I mean, after all, you're in all the same classes. He is so cool." She picked up the form the new girl had filled out. "That makes it easy, come to think of it. Since your schedule matches up with his, we know for sure that you won't have any conflicts. Mrs. H. will be amazed that I registered you without messing up."

Chelsea turned the form around so she could read it. "Larina Cargiale—what kind of name is that? Italian?"

"Romanian," said Rina.

Chelsea grinned. "Hey, Romania's where Transylvania is, isn't it? Know any vampires?"

"No," Rina said meekly. "Do you?"

No sense of humor, decided Chelsea. The bell rang with a muffled clangor outside the office.

"That's second period starting," explained Chelsea. "So you'll go right to your second-period class and skip going to first period." She glanced around the office. Mrs. Spraggens and the police officer had stepped into the principal's office. "I'm finished here, so I can show you the way to your class if you want," she said. "With the crazy layout we have around here, you'd never find your class. This place is a zoo."

"Thank you," said Larina.

Chelsea studied the new girl out of the corner of her eye as they walked. She stirred in Chelsea an uncomfortable sense of competitiveness. Undoubtedly pretty in an exotic, offbeat way, she had pronounced cheekbones, light, almost golden eyes, and dark hair that fell in wild curls to her shoulders. She was wearing brand-new jeans and a loose T-shirt with a swirling depiction of a caterpillar smoking a hookah. The smoke from the caterpillar's pipe spelled out the message, *Whoo are you?* A very good question, thought Chelsea. Something about the girl was strange. She couldn't quite put her finger on it, but it was as if she radiated a magnetic field. Chelsea wanted to ignore her, but it was hard. Her gaze was drawn to the girl in spite of herself.

"I'm called Rina," the dark girl offered in a timid voice.

"So was your school in San Francisco big, Rina?" asked Chelsea.

"I guess." Rina glanced at her. "Most American high schools are, aren't they?"

"So about how many students?" Chelsea asked.

"About the usual number," Rina murmured.

Chelsea sighed. Helpless people brought out the worst in her. A person ought to have some backbone. She supposed the girl was one of those shy types who wrote poetry. You only had to look at her to realize she didn't do sports—she looked as if the first stiff wind would bowl her over. A total zero. A mouse. In a way, Chelsea was relieved that the girl had so little personality. Not that she really imagined Rina was James's type.

"Why is a police car out front?" asked Rina. "Are the police here at the school every day?"

"Oh, no!" cried Chelsea. "This isn't the kind of school where they have metal detectors, if that's what you're thinking. The only reason the cops came is because something truly bizarre happened last night. It looks like two guys broke into the computer lab. Anyway, when the police went in to arrest them, they found out they were dead!"

"How awful!" murmured Rina.

"They hadn't been dead long when the police got there, either. That's what's so weird. The police just missed catching the murderer. I figure one of the gang must have gone berserk—maybe he panicked when the cops showed up—and he killed the other two." She shrugged. "Anyway, whatever happened, it doesn't have anything to do with us."

"No, of course not," agreed Rina.

At least the girl showed no sign of having a mind of her own, Chelsea thought. The important thing was to impress on her from the beginning that James was already taken. Suddenly Chelsea realized she hadn't given Rina the new student packet. She snapped her fingers in irritation. "I should have given you the freshman orientation booklet," Chelsea said. "I forgot."

Rina looked alarmed. "But I'm not a freshman. I'm in James's class."

"Yeah, but it's got the school rules in it and a list of all the clubs and stuff. You ought to stop by the office tomorrow and get it. It gives the meeting times and all."

Chelsea spotted James leaning against the wall. He straightened up when he saw them and walked toward them smiling.

"This is Rina," Chelsea told him. "She's new." She slipped her arm around his waist. "Did you hear? They've got the computer lab locked up and a big sign on the door because they found *two dead people in there*. Isn't that incredible? I mean, it gives me the creeps just to think about it."

"Yeah, I know," said James. "It's all anybody could talk about in English class. Mrs. Kimbro looked like she was going to have a heart attack. Somebody told me they had a cop standing by

the door of the computer lab." James smiled.
"We'd better watch out or we're going to scare
Rina to death. First day at a new school is bad
enough without walking in on two murders."

"I'm not scared," said Rina softly.

"Good," said James. "Because it's just some
weird thing that doesn't have anything to do with
us. Where are you from?"

"She's from California." When he shot his
dazzling smile at the new girl, Chelsea felt like
grabbing him and shaking him hard. It drove her
nuts how he had to go out of his way to be nice
to everybody. Once or twice she had tried to
point out to him that a person's social life ought
not to be charity work, but he just gave her that
smile and kept on doing whatever he wanted, not
paying the slightest attention.

"Okay, let's see who you have." James took
Rina's schedule from her. "You've got Butler for
history—he's good. You'll like him. Whitfield is
the only one that teaches calculus, but they say
he's okay. Good at explaining stuff." James
frowned. "Hey, how about this? Your schedule is
exactly the same as mine! I mean exactly. That's
weird." James's brow cleared. "Tell you what.
Since we've got the same schedule, why don't you
go to lunch with Chelsea and me. Until you get to
know some people around here, lunch in the cafeteria can be pretty awful."

"I am getting to know people already." Rina

smiled shyly. "I know you and I know Chelsea."

The girl is a leech, thought Chelsea grimly. And as long as James kept being friendly, it was going to be very hard to get rid of her.

Kids began to file into the classroom. Chelsea pulled James aside and planted an accusing finger on his chest. "Please notice that your social worker hang-up is kicking in again," she said. "Did you *have* to ask that girl to have lunch with us? I promise you she has *no* personality. Zip. Let her get to know other clueless types, James. You aren't doing her any favors letting her think we're going to be her best friends."

James' eyes crinkled at the corners. "It's okay, Chels," he said. "I'm not adopting her. It's only lunch."

Chelsea heaved a sigh as James turned and disappeared into the classroom. It was infuriating that even as long as she had been going out with him, she still couldn't get him to do what she wanted.

Rina wanted to sit next to James during class, but he stood over in a corner with some other boys, talking. She saw a shaft of sunlight slanting through the windows near them, spotlighting a pencil sharpener, and she shuddered. She was convinced that the direct sun rays drained her of her supernatural strength. She always felt heavy and slow once the sun came up and her senses were dulled.

Deciding that the back of the class would be a good spot for observation, she settled into a seat there. Then she did her best to tune in and decipher the buzzing chatter around her.

"He got a DWI and the company jerked his policy. His dad was freaked out."

"I got four thirty on the verbal and four fifty on the math. I may kill myself."

"—looked at me like I was a slug. So I said I don't need that. Forget it, babe. I'm out of here."

"It was twenty-four valve, two-point-five liter, V-six. I want the turbo. For the power. But the suspension's squishy."

"—felt practically married. Never again. Free agent and going to stay that way."

"So sad. I mean, just really sad. I hate to even mention it to him. I don't know him that well, and I can't figure out what to say, you know? I'd probably burst into tears and humiliate myself. Don't *look* at him, Alicia. What if he looks over here and sees us looking at him? But honestly, isn't he the best thing you've ever *seen*?"

"—used to go to school here, believe it or not. Kind of a career criminal, I guess, but small potatoes."

"No computer class tomorrow, either, I'll bet. Cops are all over the place."

Rina's head was spinning. She understood most of the words but she didn't always get the drift. What was a DWI? And what about the numbers 430 and 450 was so important? Perhaps they had mystic ritual significance, like the number 7 or the number 5, which was found in pentagons.

She was relieved when class began and the chatter stilled. It seemed the meaning of it was always just out of her grasp. The world of these kids seemed attractive, but it was maddeningly elusive.

James walked with Rina to the next class. "It takes a while to find your way around," he said. "This place is a maze."

"A zoo," she suggested. It seemed safe to echo Chelsea.

He laughed. "That, too. But don't worry. You'll get used to it. I was lost my entire first week, but finally things start to make sense."

Rina noticed that James was not as pale as she had thought when she first saw him by moonlight. His was not the sort of skin that tanned easily, but the summer sun had given him a dusky blush. And though his hair was streaked with platinum, underneath it was the color of honey.

When he became a vampire, his skin would whiten and his eyes would change color. She thought he might not like that. But if she could bind him tightly to her with spells, he might not mind so very much. She must bring him along gently, weaving enchantment in the moonlight, until he came to her with eagerness, hungry for her blood.

"You're kind of shy, aren't you?" James said, startling her. Rina gulped and took a step away from him. Had he already noticed that she was different?

"I used to be shy, too, when I was little." James grinned. "But just remember what they always say—imagine everyone with their clothes off. It helps."

Rina's ears grew hot. She did not find James's suggestion helpful at all. He had embarrassed her.

"Here we are," he said. Taking her elbow, he guided her into the classroom door. Somehow before she quite knew how, he had gone off in another direction and was talking to some guys. He seemed to know lots of people.

Rina took a seat at the back of the classroom and waited hopefully for calculus class to begin. She was sure she would enjoy it. She didn't recall precisely when she had learned calculus, but she had always enjoyed abstract number systems. Fiddling with figures was something for her to do on the long winter nights, which had seemed all the longer since she had forgotten how to sleep.

When the class had ended, Rina heard the kids around her muttering anxiously about what would be covered on the test. She realized that she would make an easy *A* if she stayed. How long she remained a student, of course, depended on how long it took to ensnare James with her spells.

He appeared suddenly at her side. "Lunchtime," he said. "Let's go."

As they walked to the cafeteria, he said, "I can't get over it—we've got all the same classes. No one's ever been in all my classes since I came to this school. I wonder what the odds of that are."

Rina thought a moment. "About two million to one, but that assumes none of the classes are linked. Since some are a prerequisite for the others and all students are not equally likely to take each class, that would throw off a simple calculation."

"You must like math." He gave her a curious look.

She nodded, blushing a little. "Abstract number systems aren't slippery the way language is."

James blinked. "Huh?"

"Language changes."

"You mean like with slang? The way my parents say *neat* and we say *cool*?"

She nodded. "And it's different in different countries. But calculus is the same everywhere. It hasn't changed a bit since Isaac Newton invented it in the eighteenth century."

James looked amused. "I'll take your word for it."

When they got to the cafeteria, Chelsea appeared before them. She grabbed James's hand and pulled his arm around her waist. "Kiss, kiss," she demanded.

James brushed a light kiss on her cheek.

Rina felt as if a knife were twisting inside her when she saw the genuine affection in his eyes, but she carefully made her face blank to hide her feelings.

The noise and the smells of the cafeteria made her ill. As she filed with the others into the cafeteria line she saw that a blue haze hovered over the grill. Women wearing hair nets slapped thin hamburger patties on the sizzling, metal surface. A stack of frozen burgers was on the counter just within her reach. The burgers were separated by flimsy sheets of paper. When Rina was sure no one was looking, she deftly lifted a frozen patty out of the stack and slipped it into a bun.

"Trip!" screeched Chelsea only inches from Rina's ear. Rina jumped in alarm. She was afraid Chelsea had seen her pilfering the raw burger.

A huge boy elbowed his way past the others in line and plopped his tray down behind Chelsea's. No one challenged his right to barge ahead in line, Rina noticed. She wondered if the others were afraid of him. He was big and had a fierce face. He banged his hand suddenly on his tray, making all the other trays on the line rattle. "I'll have it *my* way!" he thundered. "Raw!"

Rina was startled. That was the way she liked her hamburgers, too. But the boy did not look like a vampire.

Chelsea giggled. "Animal!"

"Go ahead—flatter me," Trip exclaimed, smacking his lips. "I eat it up." He pinched Chelsea.

"Cut it out, Trip," she said.

"Do you know there are people in this school—and I'm not making this up, folks—who think 'Cut-it-out' is my first name?"

"Well, move it, Cut-it-out," said James. "I'm starving."

They emerged from the cafeteria line. Rina was stunned by the noise and confusion of the main room. "Let's eat outside," suggested Chelsea.

Rina was relieved. Even the sun of the out-of-doors would be better than the blare of hundreds of shrill voices and the stench of sweaty sneakers and overcooked food. She meekly followed the others to some picnic tables set up outside the cafeteria on the grass. The light was brighter outside, but at least it was an escape from the sickening smells. A fly buzzed around her head and she watched its progress curiously. Vampires sometimes turned into flies—it was an advanced and complicated maneuver, but she knew that it could be done. The fly lit on the table and its iridescent back gleamed. Perched on a crumb it rubbed its front legs together, and Rina lost interest. Only ordinary flies liked the taste of crumbs. Vampire flies preferred blood.

The kids already at the tables made room for them. Rina was careful to choose a seat in the shade.

"Oh, yuck!" cried Chelsea. "Look at that! Your burger is dripping blood."

Rina was surprised to see that the frozen meat had already melted. Reddish juice dripped down the bun. Her fangs unsheathed, crowding her mouth uncomfortably, and her mouth watered. She felt self-conscious. "I like them rare," she mumbled, biting into the bun quickly. She felt moisture trickle down her chin and licked it off. Suddenly, she realized that the others were regarding her with fascination. Had they caught a glimpse of her fangs? she thought, freezing. Her eyes darted anxiously from one face to the next. "Haven't you ever heard of steak tartare?" she said faintly. "Some people like beef raw."

"I'll take it back for you," offered James. "There's no call for you to be embarrassed. It's the kitchen staff that messed up, not you."

"No, it's fine, really," Rina insisted. She gulped the rest down hastily. She didn't usually eat much solid food, and as soon as she had downed it, the heavy burger lay in her stomach like lead.

She could see James eyeing her with concern. Chelsea had entwined her arm around his neck, and now she whispered something in his ear. She knew Rina was watching and without doubt the hugs and giggles were a show put on for Rina's benefit. Chelsea was warning her off. The maneuver was transparent, and Rina was not sure that James was enjoying it. His ears were turning pink with embarrassment.

Rina studied her rival carefully. Chelsea was wearing a skimpy skirt and simple black sandals, both deliberately chosen, probably, to emphasize the length of her tanned legs. Rina felt a pang of envy when she noticed how often the boys sitting at the picnic table let their gazes fall on those outstretched legs.

Smugness radiated from Chelsea like heat waves, and Rina could feel hate stirring in her. It would be too bad if she had to kill Chelsea, she thought, glancing down at her sharp fingernails. Humiliating her would be so much more fully satisfying.

4

By the time Rina returned home, the setting sun had bronzed the house's windows and made it look secretive. When she turned her key in the lock and stepped inside, only the black ormolu clock sounded in the gloom.

When she reached the second floor, away from the ticking, silence pressed painfully against her eardrums. She longed for the comforting murmur of human voices. The emptiness and isolation of the old house wore on her nerves constantly, but she knew she could not afford to risk the inquiring eyes of neighbors. One of them might notice that she never slept or bought groceries. Someone might even catch sight of her coming in one night with her mouth stained with blood.

She went into her bedroom and pulled a worn suitcase from under her bed. It was of cracked leather, its brass studs tarnished beyond polishing. In places, the black leather had taken on a copper color with age.

She opened the bag on her bed. She wasn't sure what had moved her to reach for it. Flitting from one night to the next like a ray of shifting darkness, she lived so much from moment to moment that her own motives were sometimes obscure to her.

Lifting fragile ribbons out of the bag, she laid them on one pale hand, scarcely breathing for fear their brittle fabric would tumble into dust. Only a blush of the original tints remained, but she knew they had once been brave red and green streamers. She had loved to braid them into her hair. She was a little surprised that they still had the power to please her. They seemed like fragile ghosts of a long-dead joy. She replaced them carefully in the bag, took out a cameo, yellowed with age, and turned it over in her palm. The miniature painted on the back was amateurish. But it showed clearly enough the features of a snub-nosed, brunette woman, her hair pulled back severely from her face. Mother. Suddenly, like a strong flavor bursting against the top of the mouth, Rina remembered the warmth of human love, and tears stung her eyes. Always in her childhood there had been the smell of her mother's bread baking in the kitchen. A pot of soup had simmered on the fender of the stove, with turnips, meaty bones, and greens. Nearby, in the taproom of her father's inn, the smell was of beer and the earthy stink of manure that clung to the men's boots as they tromped in from the fields. At night the tavern's walls rang with sad songs. *"Frum za verde de hemei*—like the hopvine in green leaf. Women have weak minds, but men's are weaker still."* It was a cynical sort of song, she supposed, and reflected a low opinion of human nature, but in her memory it was sweet. She could hear in her mind the background clatter of horses' hooves tapping a drumbeat against the cobblestones in the courtyard. She remembered herself as a small girl, peering at the blurred shapes of the horses through the narrow window in the dark passageway that separated the taproom from the stairwell.

Rina sighed and groped again in the leather bag until her fingers touched something smooth. She pulled out a bracelet made of rubies and slipped it on. Her heart shriveled. Vlad had given her these rubies the night he asked her to go away with him. He was a highwayman, though not many years older than herself, with the smooth face of youth. He had stolen the bracelet from a noble lady. No wonder Rina had never dared tell her father that she often slipped out to see him. Many warm nights he had kissed her under the walnut tree while his black horse stomped and ruffled her hair with his steamy breath.

She had been sixteen, grown up enough for love, she decided. One night she had said she would go away with Vlad and be his wife. Her heart had pounded when he had lifted her up behind him in the saddle, because she had been afraid that her father would hear them. Far better it would have been for her if her father had heard and dashed out with his knife drawn, but they had slipped silently away, her heart sounding louder than the horses' hoofbeats.

Vlad's big horse was named Devil. Vlad had tied Rina's leather bag to the horse's saddle and it had flapped against his shining flanks as they galloped down the coach road. His hooves thundered and struck sparks off the road's hard surface.

After a while the branches of the deep forest arched overhead. They grew thicker, almost impenetrable, and Rina could no longer see the lights of the inn. "Why did we leave the road?" she had cried.

"Be quiet," Vlad had said shortly.

She heard twigs break against the horse's flanks. A branch swept her kerchief off her head, and an owl screamed in the darkness. As she clung desperately to her sweetheart, her mouth was dry from fear.

Suddenly, Vlad had turned in the saddle and laughed. Even in the darkness she could see the long white lines of his fangs. She knew with a sudden shrinking of her flesh that he was one of the *nosferatu*, the undead. "Take me home," she had sobbed. "I won't tell anybody what you are. Please! I beg you!" But he had pulled Devil up sharply and dismounted. Rina had grabbed the reins in her hands and kicked the horse with her heels. But the horse had not moved except to turn his head to look at her, and she saw that his eyes glowed phosphorescent. A devil horse. No ordinary horse would have carried a vampire.

Vlad had lifted her squirming out of the saddle and clasped her in his icy arms. She had beat on his chest with her fists and wept. "How can you do this to me?" she had screamed. "All I ever did wrong was to fall in love with you!" Then he bent his head suddenly as if to kiss her, and she felt his fangs sink into her flesh like a burning iron. She gasped with the pain. The darkness swam with red and suddenly she could hear a pounding drum in her ears, louder than the devil horse's hoofbeats. She longed to die so that her pain would end, and at last blackness closed over her consciousness.

When she opened her eyes, she saw stars like holes of brightness in the sky and knew that she was no longer in the forest. Air was caught in the damp grass, making it feel puffy under her fingertips. Rolling over, she saw the wide arch of the starry sky overhead. She was in a meadow, perhaps. Some open, grassy place. She could hear the devil horse snorting and stomping not far away. Perhaps she could creep away unseen.

If only she could find the coach road, some kind passerby might be persuaded to take her to her father's inn. Slowly, and with great care, she lifted herself a little and crawled on her hands and knees.

Vlad's laughter rang out in the darkness, chilling her. "Where do you think you are going, my pretty one?" he cried. "You are bound to stay with me forever now."

"No!" she cried. "You lied to me." She struggled to her feet.

"I always lie." His fangs flashed white. "It's so much easier when it comes to getting what I want. And, my pretty, I want you."

He unbuttoned the lace ruffle at his wrist and pushed up the sleeve. She could see then a wicked long red line on the flesh. "I opened my arm, you see." He smiled. "And let my blood drip down your throat. You know what that means." He lowered his voice to a whisper. "You have drunk the blood of the undead."

She understood then why her feet and hands felt light and why she could see in the dark and hear the small voles and mice scurrying to hide in the forest. She had become a vampire.

Vlad had drawn closer to her and folded his arms around her and laughed. She had wept until her head ached, but it was no use. She knew she could never return to her father's inn.

Though it had happened long ago, the memory

was like a sour taste in her mouth. She tore the ruby bracelet off her wrist and threw it back in the bag. The lesson she had learned came back to her powerfully—love is dangerous. Love had made her trust Vlad, and he had bitterly betrayed her.

She hastily pushed the black leather bag back under the bed, but the memories it had wakened were not so easily put away. She leapt up and paced the floor quickly, her heels tapping on the bare oak. She had escaped from Vlad by means of her own cleverness and strength, she reminded herself. There was no reason for her heart to be fluttering under her ribs like a trapped bird. She was no longer the frightened girl Vlad had stolen from the protection of her family. She was a vampire. She was strong.

She gazed out the window and saw that night was gathering under the trees. Already she could feel her strength growing. The tapping heels of her shoes sounded lighter on the floor. It was 7:34 by the ormolu clock—her clock. It was all hers—the clock, the house, the three-corner cupboard filled with delicate china teacups. One day a lawyer had come to the house with a mysterious document that, as it turned out, had been the old lady's will. After the old lady's death, the house, the car, a small income, the ormolu clock, had all passed in due course to Rina. She had found a security she had never dared dream of. No longer did she need to wander from town to town eking out a bare living by putting up shingles that claimed she was a "palm reader" or "herbal counselor." Odd to think that a change in the weather had proved to be the hinge of her fate. She had taken shelter here from a driving rain. Then somehow she had stayed on for months. She remembered being content sitting on the edge of the bed, listening to the old lady's stories about her youth. It had become the usual thing for Rina to read to her and stroke her hair tenderly as she fell asleep. Then, every night, when the old lady lay limp on the pillow, her breath rattling in her throat, Rina pierced the flesh at the base of the neck very delicately and sipped her blood. The old lady had been frail, and yet such was Rina's delicacy that the life had ebbed out of her by slow degrees. No one, not even the attending physician, had doubted that the death was natural.

The strange thing was that the old lady had loved her even when she knew that Rina was slowly killing her. Perhaps she had been ready to die. Once she had said that she had already outlived everyone she cared about.

Rina watched the last sliver of the sun's disk slip below the horizon. *It is good to be loved,* she told herself. *It can be profitable. But falling in love is bad.*

Darkness lay thick on the streets now. She opened the door and slipped out, letting her essence unwind a little in the breeze so that her body was light and airy. The white flowers of nicotiana bloomed beside the walk, poison sleeping in their thick leaves. Rina snapped off a flower and sucked on its stalk as she glided to the cemetery.

Spells and moon magic filled her imagination. Vlad had torn her life from her throat painfully, she remembered, and she had hated him. But death did not have to be cruel. Rina had made the old lady die gently. And that was how she wanted to kill James, slowly and sweetly. She could not bear for him to hate her the way she had hated Vlad.

She remembered the ruined castle where Vlad had taken her after that terrible night in the meadow. The castle had been grim and desolate since villagers had set it afire years before, but Vlad continued to live there secretly. When Rina saw it, its gardens were overgrown with nettles, its roof was shattered, and the rotting tapestries hung in tatters on walls that were black with mildew. "This is where you will stay," he had announced with authority. And she had been too afraid to answer him.

But as days turned into months, she grew accustomed to the cold and dark rooms, so different from the cheerful comfort of her father's inn. After a while she could scarcely remember what it was like to sit by a warm fire. Wind whistled mournfully in the chimneys as Vlad tutored her in vampire lore. Nights he took her hunting, sharing his kill until she learned to strike a death blow. She remembered the shock the first night she became a murderer. The moon was shining bright overhead and a peasant lay under her, his coarse smock dark with spilled blood. She touched his hand and realized with a shock that it was growing cold. She had killed him. Bewildered sheep bleated plaintively around her, moving like white ghosts in the darkness. "Hurry up," Vlad had snapped. "You must have drunk your fill by now. Let's go." *No*, a voice in her mind had shrieked. *I don't want this. I don't have the heart of a murderer.*

Always they had returned to the ruined castle. She remembered rain dripping monotonously through its broken roof as she crouched in its decayed library, searching for a spell that might undo the harm Vlad had done to her. She had pored over old books, growing almost faint from their musty smell. Silverfish, their dwelling places in the binding disturbed, had slipped under her white fingers. Bloodless creatures, they seemed to know they had nothing to fear from her, their fellow creature of the darkness.

In the vampire's dark library, she had found spells for the full moon, spells that when murmured only in her mind would leak out of her white fingers and leave her prey with glazed eyes,

happy to die. But the one spell she most wanted
she could not find—the spell to make her human
again. Perhaps, she thought bitterly, it did not
exist.

Living in darkness, as she did it, was better to
let minutes slip away. It was better to cling to
nothing when nothing mattered anymore. It was
better to forget being human.

What chord had twanged inside her tonight
that moved her to pull out her souvenirs of life?
The boy—James. The beautiful one with the
scent of grave dust clinging to him. When she
first saw him she had thought he was of her
world, but soon realized that he was human. She
felt a pang of regret for her own lost life. No matter. She had learned spells enough, she thought,
to steal James's soul and make him a vampire.

Rina slid along the iron fence of the old cemetery, her fingers like threads of moonlight in the
shadows. She had become a vague wispiness and
scarcely more than a shadow, when suddenly she
caught her breath sharply. Terror made her body
heavy and solid and the rush of the violent
change made her head ring. She gasped. James
was walking not ten feet ahead of her. "James!"
she cried.

Instinctively James spun around, knees bent
and hands open as if to defend himself. He felt
foolish when a small figure detached itself from

the shadows. "Rina!" he cried. "You just about scared me to death. What are you doing out here?"

Her light-colored eyes were luminous in the dark. "I'm taking a walk," she said. "Do you come here a lot?"

"When I can't sleep," he admitted. He saw her glance at Susan's grave. He knew what the brass plate said—SUSAN AMANDA RYDER. And somehow he felt that Rina knew what it said, too. He had the uneasy sensation that she was reading his mind.

"It's quiet here at night," said Rina. "And I love the old cemetery—it's my favorite place to walk."

When she stood next to him, her head barely came up to his shoulder. She had a faint scent he couldn't place, some sort of herb, maybe, the sort of thing girls bought at weird shops that had beaded curtains. James felt he was losing the train of his thought as he looked into her eyes, and he suddenly jerked himself back to attention. "Walking out here at night is a bad idea," he said.

"You walk here," protested Rina. "You told me yourself that you come here when you can't sleep."

"It's different with guys." In spite of his words, James found himself remembering the two boys killed during the burglary at the school. One of them had been the kind who would push in your face if you looked at him the wrong way, yet somebody had murdered him just the same.

Maybe it wasn't so different for boys. He took a deep breath. "I'll bet your parents would have a fit if they knew where you were."

"My parents are dead," said Rina.

"I'm sorry," he said gruffly.

The silence in the graveyard seemed to press against him and a bitter lump rose in his throat. He imagined himself picketing the graveyard with a placard, DEATH UNFAIR TO LIVING THINGS. A smile twisted his lips. *This is the way it is,* he told himself. *There aren't any guarantees. You'd better get used to it.*

He glanced down at Rina. "I'd better walk with you to your car. Where are you parked?"

She shook her dark curls. "I didn't drive. I walked. I don't live far from here."

They were standing by Susan's grave, but James was careful not to look at it again. Until Susan died he had never realized how intensely private grief was. In fact, he had never thought about grief at all before. Now it was practically all he did think about. Yet anytime anybody tried to be sympathetic, they always sounded stupid and out of touch, as if they had stepped off a pastel greeting card.

He felt a painful constriction over his breastbone and his hip ached, as they walked away from the grave. The bone stung where they had put in the needle to get his bone marrow to try to save Susan. He knew the incision had healed; the pain was all in his mind, he told himself, but he couldn't quell the uneasy feeling that he was coming apart.

James's hand brushed lightly against Rina's. She felt like ice. He had to quell the impulse to take her hands in his to warm them. Maybe she was so cold because he had scared her with his warning about walking alone at night. But what he had said was true. Anybody would have agreed with him that the world was full of crazies and criminals. You couldn't be too careful.

"Who do you live with now?" he asked.

"Nobody."

James was jolted. "You live by yourself?"

"Lots of people live alone."

"Not people our age. When did your parents—" He couldn't make himself say the word.

"I'd rather not talk about it," said Rina in a small voice.

"Sure," he said. "That's cool. I understand."

"I turn here," said Rina at last. "Oak Street."

When James saw Rina's dark house, he was staggered. It lay at the end of the cul-de-sac and looked like a ghostly ship floating in the moonlight. He gazed at its tall windows and the gingerbread cutwork along the eaves. It was the sort of place that should have been a haunted house. "How did you end up here?" he asked, amazed. "You'd be a lot better off in an apartment where there are other people and a swimming pool and stuff like that."

"I inherited it," she said. "It does get a little lonely."

"I'll bet!" he breathed. He hesitated. "Isn't anybody looking out after you, Rina?" he asked. Bad as things were at his house, he simply couldn't imagine how it would be to be new in town and living all by himself. He was certain he would go stark, staring nuts.

"I can take care of myself," she said. "You don't have to worry about me."

"I can't help worrying about you. You ought to sell this place and move. Look, I tell you what. My mother knows some real estate agents. I'll get one of them to give you a call."

"No," said Rina. "Don't do that. I like it here. I like the privacy."

It's got too much privacy, James thought, glancing at the house uneasily. It had everything a person didn't need—a gazebo, a big detached garage, wide lawns, and plenty of trees. More important, not a soul lived within screaming distance. He started to say that, but what held him back was the thought that if he wasn't careful he was going to end up like Chelsea, telling other people what to do all the time. He couldn't erase the worried frown that he could feel forming between his brows. The setup seemed crazy. "Promise me that you won't go walking alone at night," he insisted.

She shook her head. "I can't promise that. Night is my favorite time."

James was uncomfortably aware that he was being a hypocrite. He was out until all hours himself, and lately he walked a lot in the cemetery. One night he had stood on Susan's grave in the rain and screamed her name. He had been choking on the driving rain and even his underwear had been plastered to his skin, but none of that had been enough to make him straighten up and act normal. Who knew better than he did that sometimes you had to do insane things just so you didn't feel the pain inside? "Well, promise me you'll take a knife or something with you, anyway," he said at last.

"Would you like to come inside for a minute?" she asked.

"You can't afford to ask strange guys in when you're living by yourself," James said. "They might misunderstand."

"You're not a strange guy," said Rina. "I know you."

"Not that well," grumbled James. He realized with horror that he was sounding just like his father. What was happening to him? "The truth is," he went on, "it's late. I've got to be getting on home."

Rina's shoulders drooped. She was obviously disappointed. Lonely probably. The whole setup stank—she shouldn't be living in that mausoleum by herself. He really was going to have to persuade her to move.

He reached out and patted her on the back. "Take care of yourself." As he walked away, he thought ruefully that Chelsea was right—he did have a social worker complex. A chill breeze raised goose bumps on his bare arms and he reluctantly headed home.

He cringed at the thought of getting back to his family. They all spoke so softly these days, as if Susan were still sick upstairs. They were behaving as if they were in a play and everybody had to be line perfect in their parts, or somebody would take them out back and shoot them. He couldn't remember the last time any of them had laughed.

James heard a flutter of wings as he passed a low tree. "Susan!" he exclaimed involuntarily. Then he was overcome by a feeling that he was an idiot. But sometimes he had the eerie sense that she was still around. A flickering candle or a sudden noise would make him turn around, expecting to see her.

She hadn't even said good-bye the night his parents rushed her off to the hospital for the last time. She had been out of sorts and irritable for months, not even interested in him. It was as if someone had stolen her away and put a withered sick person in her place who did nothing but wince and talk about doctors and injections. He had been angry at her for being like that. But now he wanted to dig up her wasted body with his bare hands and try to breathe his own life into it. Nobody at school had any idea what he was feeling. It was too sick to talk about.

5

When James got back to the house, the phone was ringing. "I'll get it!" he called. He picked up the receiver. "Hello?"

"Let's go get pizza," said Trip. "I'm ravenous. I already got hold of Chelsea and she's all for it."

"Okay, I'll meet you there," said James. Relief swept over him that he wouldn't have to go upstairs, after all, and pass by Susan's empty room.

His mother stepped into the living room and smiled. "Are you going out with your friends, dear? That's nice."

I can't help you, James thought, staring at his mother's wan face. *I can't even help myself.* "Yeah, we're going to get pizza," he said aloud. "I'm not sure when I'll be back."

A couple of years ago she would have reminded him that it was a school night and he had homework, but it had been a long time since anyone in his family had worried about when he got in or whether he did his homework.

James fled.

Pizzeria Speciale was noisy and crowded. The jukebox blared an unfamiliar tune with a heavy drumbeat. James could feel it thudding in his bones and his teeth. Chelsea and Trip had already gotten there. He spotted them over in a corner booth and threaded his way through crowded tables to get to them. He slid in beside Chelsea. "Where's Rachel?" he asked. "I thought she'd be here."

"Rachel's dumped me," said Trip, pulling a long face.

"Poor Trip." Chelsea leaned over the table and patted his hand.

"She said I liked football better than I liked her," growled Trip.

James grinned. "Well, no argument about that—you do."

"That's not the point!" Trip banged on the table. "Girls and football are different!"

"He's sharp," said Chelsea. "Want to run that by us again, Trip? Now, what is the difference between a girl and a football?" The waitress put a pizza on the metal pedestal before them. "We went ahead and ordered before you got here," Chelsea said with a shrug. "Since we always order the same thing anyway, there didn't seem to be any point in waiting."

"Rachel didn't like it that I had to spend so much time at practice," Trip went on. "She said she hardly ever saw me. Does that make sense? I mean, she knew I played football when we started going together. What'd she expect?"

James grinned. "You could give up football, I guess."

"Very funny." Trip banged his fist into his hand. "I'll never give it up, man. I love that feeling when I tackle guys and they sort of crunch underneath me."

As Chelsea picked up a pizza slice the mozzarella stretched and then broke loose from its moorings. She adeptly snagged it with one finger and plastered the wayward strand of mozzarella back onto the pizza with her pinkie. "I want to ask you a serious question, Trip. Didn't you feel kind of funny when you broke Ron's arm?"

"How do you mean 'funny'?" Trip asked.

"She means guilty," suggested James.

"Heck, no! It was a good play."

"Did you hear the bone snap?" asked Chelsea.

"You're ruining my appetite, Chels," said James. "Lay off. It's not like Trip did it on purpose."

"Poor Ron's going to have to have surgery, you know," said Chelsea. "The break's a funny V-shape or in a funny place or something like that. I'm not too sure about the details. Allison was explaining it to me, but I can't remember."

"Now, you don't hear Allison complaining about the time Ron's at practice, do you?" said

Trip. "That's the way a girlfriend ought to be."

"Ron's not going to practice for the rest of the season," Chelsea pointed out. "So she'll be seeing a lot of him. She's pretty mad at you, by the way."

Trip grinned. "You can't make an omelet without breaking legs."

"Oh, come on, Trip," said James. "You know you felt bad."

"It wasn't my fault, man. I was only doing what I was supposed to be doing."

The waitress plopped three plastic glasses down before them. "Medium diet cola, large cola, large iced tea," she announced.

"We're in a rut," complained Chelsea as the waitress left. "We come here too much. The waitress knew our order before I even told her. I will be so glad when I get away from this town where you never run into a thing that's new and exciting."

"What about that girl you showed up with at lunch today?" asked Trip.

"Rina?" asked Chelsea.

"Yeah."

"She's not exciting. She's not even *interesting*," said Chelsea.

"Oh, come on," said James. "You haven't even gotten to know her yet."

"No," said Chelsea, "and I don't want to."

James considered telling them about Rina's odd living setup, but he decided against it.

Chances were they'd only crack some joke. They didn't mean any harm, but he was in no mood for jokes. He figured he had a little better idea what Rina was up against than they did. His mind wandered as he traced a pattern on his napkin with a fork. Rina's eyes were an unusual color, almost golden. He had never seen eyes quite like that. She didn't say much, but those eyes were drenched with feeling. And for such a little bit of a thing, she was amazingly fearless. The trouble with Chelsea and Trip was they couldn't appreciate somebody who was out of the ordinary.

James was startled to see Trip's paw waving in his face.

"He's conscious," Trip growled. "We don't have to call nine-one-one after all."

James brushed Trip's hand aside, irritated.

"We asked you twice if you want to go get yogurt after," said Chelsea. "Are you completely out of it, or what?"

"Sometimes I get lost in my thoughts," snapped James. "So sue me."

Trip's and Chelsea's eyes met in a meaningful glance. James hated the idea that his friends were talking behind his back. He supposed they were telling each other what bad shape he was in and how they had to make allowances. Unreasonably, he felt angry at both of them. "Okay," he said abruptly. "Let's go get yogurt."

Chelsea lifted another slice of pizza. "Not yet. Let me finish."

"You're gonna get big as a house if you keep up like that," Trip said.

"You *are* big as a house," Chelsea said sweetly. "And we like you anyway."

Lately, James had noticed that Chelsea and Trip were always sparring. It had made him wonder once or twice if there was some kind of attraction there. *Would he care,* he wondered, *if they paired off?*

He felt Chelsea's bare instep rubbing against his leg. She wiggled her toes, and he felt the warm tickling at his ankle. She flashed him a smile and he found himself melting. James reached for her hand and squeezed it. *Was he out of his mind?* he wondered. Sure, he would care. He put his arm around her, pulled her close, and kissed her.

"Mmm," she said. "That's more like it."

"You guys are disgusting," said Trip.

"You're just jealous," said Chelsea. "You need to line up another girlfriend."

"Like it's that easy," grumbled Trip.

"James and I will help, won't we, James?"

"No," said James firmly. "We will stay out of it."

Chelsea grinned. "*So* bossy." She ruffled his hair.

In spite of himself, James grinned.

* * *

The house was silent when James got home.
Someone had left the light on in the hall and he
switched it off as he went upstairs. He was so
tired, he didn't even bother to brush his teeth. He
simply stripped down to his shorts and climbed
into bed. An unexpectedly chill breeze swept in
the half-open window and a branch creaked outside, but his arms and legs were already heavy
with sleep and it seemed too much trouble to get
out of bed and close the window.

The moon rose and made dark shadows in
the room. Suddenly he awoke with a start. Rina
was standing by the window, the moon painting
her hair silver. Hastily James grabbed his robe
and slid out of bed, wrapping the robe around
him. "Jeez," he whispered, stunned. "What are
you *doing* here? How did you get in?"

"Through the window," she explained. "I
climbed the tree, ran along the roof, and here
I am!"

James shivered. He supposed the cold chill
was from shock. It wasn't every night that he
woke up to find a girl in his room. He could see
Rina's face, a pale oval in the moonlight, but
there was a curious unreality to her presence.
She was the last girl he would expect to come
shinnying up a tree and into his bedroom.
Chelsea might have done something like that as a
joke, but Rina had struck him as delicate, even a
bit shy. "You've got to leave," he said abruptly.

His pulse was racing as if he had been running.

Her eyes glistened with tears. "Can't I stay even for a little while?"

"No!" James's vehemence astonished him. His heart was pounding so hard, he felt dizzy. The crazy thing was he wanted her to stay. But he knew he'd better make her get out of his room right away. The whole business was entirely too strange to suit him.

She drew closer, her gaze holding his almost hypnotically. James wanted to kiss her, but the wild pounding at his temples told him he'd be better off not to touch her at all. A rush of excitement made his stomach feel tight. Suddenly his life had become intensely interesting.

As if the question of her leaving had been settled in her favor, Rina sat down on his bed. "I'll leave in a minute," she promised, glancing around the room. "What are the trophies for?"

That was a harmless question, and James felt himself relax a little. Tying the sash of his robe tightly, he cautiously perched on the edge of his desk. It seemed needlessly cruel to push her out the window by force, and the truth was, he didn't even want to. "Mostly track. I had to give it up last year, but I'm thinking of—maybe taking it up again. I guess I'll train with the team for a while, anyway, until I make up my mind."

Rina glanced around the room, and James saw she was staring blankly at the Smashing

Pumpkins poster behind his bed. Next to it was a kind of abstract poster for Nine Inch Nails.

"Those must be your favorite music groups," said Rina. She eyed him anxiously, as if wondering whether she had said the right thing.

James smiled. "Yeah." He noticed she was wearing jeans and a T-shirt, which was one thing that made him sure he wasn't dreaming. In his dreams when girls showed up in his bedroom, they were usually wearing considerably less.

"Tell me about the painting," said Rina, pointing to it.

In the dim light, the painting was little more than a gleam in the darkness. He wondered how it had happened to catch Rina's attention. "It's a portrait I did of my family," he explained. "My mom and dad, my brother and me."

"Why is everybody looking at a candle?"

James hesitated. "The candle stands for my sister Susan. She had just died when I painted it. That's why everybody in the painting looks sad. I mean, you can't see it that well from here, but if you could—well, that's what it's about."

"You loved her, didn't you?" asked Rina.

James felt his throat close off painfully. He shut his eyes and suddenly Rina was beside him. A cold chill made the hair on the back of his neck lift as he felt her stroke his hair. Suddenly he slid his arm around her and pulled her close. He felt hot and his heart seemed to be beating in his ears. He was unsure what he was going to do next, when suddenly a sharp pain made him shudder. A feeling like warm water lapping over him, swept him, and he seemed to be drifting—not caring what happened next. He could feel the strain in the muscles of his neck as his head fell to one side, but it didn't seem to matter. He was floating, powerless as a drifting balloon, slipping through the darkness. A drifting spirit. All grief was behind him and he felt only the sharp, true pain that set him free, a pain that was close to ecstasy.

Slowly he became conscious of the weight of his arms and legs. The plush of his bathrobe was slipping a little under him and he remembered that he was not flying through the night sky. Instead, he was perched precariously on the edge of his desk and he had an uneasy feeling that something was wrong. His eyes opened in alarm, and he saw Rina standing close by him, close enough that he could feel her breath. Her lips looked damp and her amber eyes were glazed and vacant. Fear fluttered in his stomach, but she stroked his neck gently and he felt his pulse slow down. "It's all right," she whispered. "I'm finished."

James shook the hair out of his face impatiently and stumbled to his feet. Finished? With what? But before he could follow up that thought, he felt himself grabbing hold of the bedpost to keep from falling. His body felt thick and heavy in a pleasant sort of way. Somehow he was too weak to move as Rina walked away. She darkened the room with shadow as she stood at the window. "*À bientôt*," she whispered. He heard her lift the window open and felt the stirrings of a breeze. His pulse thumped in his throat as he watched her slip out the window.

The full strangeness of what had happened had hit him suddenly as he stared at the window. He wasn't sure, but it seemed almost as if she had *bit* him. James frowned a little, mildly surprised that he couldn't hear her footsteps on the roof. Usually, even something as small as a squirrel made a terrific racket on the shingles.

A high singing sound in his ears made him wonder if he were about to pass out, and he fell into the bed. *À bientôt*, she had said. His French was pretty shaky, but that didn't exactly mean good-bye, did it? It was more like "see you soon." A smile touched his lips as he let himself slip into unconsciousness.

6

![ornamental divider]

The next morning when he was checking himself in the mirror, James noticed another yellowish bruise on his neck. He remembered quite clearly the sharp pain he felt when he had embraced Rina the night before, a pain at the base of his neck as if she had nipped him. He remembered, too, with some guilt, that he had enjoyed it.

Kinky—the word sprung to his mind like an accusation. He wasn't at all clear about what happened. There was just that little bite, sharp and dark like a black secret. But somehow it had cut his mind free from pain.

He shook his head, reminding himself that he and Rina didn't *do* anything, really. He was clear enough about that. It wasn't as if he was going to come down with one of those gruesome diseases they'd been lectured about at school since the sixth grade. Why did he feel so guilty? It was kinky—that was the problem.

But the other thing bugging him was that he knew what Chelsea would think if she found out Rina had slipped into his room last night. She'd be at Rina's eyes with her fingernails. He shivered at the thought. With any luck, Chelsea wouldn't find out. He wasn't going to tell her, that was for sure. He wasn't that crazy.

When James got to school, he found Trip and Chelsea leaning against the railing by the entrance. They were so involved in what they were saying that at first they didn't notice that he had come up.

"But who else could have done it?" Chelsea asked. Seeing James suddenly, she grabbed his hand. "Guess what? One of the burglars has turned himself in."

"The burglars?" repeated James stupidly. His mind was still focused on the night before, and he found himself growing warm with self-consciousness at the thought of Rina's visit.

"The guys who broke into the school," explained Chelsea. "It was all over the newspaper this morning. My dad read it to us at breakfast. A guy came into the police station with his lawyer and he brought the missing computer with him, so they knew he wasn't making up the story."

"They locked him up, natch," said Trip. "I mean, they had those two dead bodies, right?"

"They locked him up only because of the burglary. He claims he didn't do the murders," said Chelsea.

"They always say that," said Trip scornfully.

"You should read the story in the paper," Chelsea insisted. "It sounds to me like the cops believe him. He's passed a lie-detector test."

"Chelsea's excited because the guy says a girl was in the room," Trip explained.

James shook his head in bewilderment. "A girl was in on the robbery with them?"

"No, *a different* girl," said Chelsea. "Somebody they didn't know. She was already at the school when they broke in."

"So have the police let this guy go?" asked James.

"Not exactly," Chelsea admitted.

"I'll bet he's the one who did it," said Trip.

"Maybe they're holding him for his own protection!" argued Chelsea. "Because he's a witness and there's a murderer still at large! A girl!"

"Oh, come on!" Trip laughed.

"It's a well-known fact that the female is deadlier than the male," said Chelsea. "I don't see what's so funny about that."

"What Chelsea likes," said Trip, "is that this Ricky guy says the girl kissed Mark before she killed him."

James stared.

"It's strange," Chelsea admitted. "Ricky said he couldn't see too well, but it looked like this strange girl was kissing Mark. Do you remember Mark, James? A big, tough-looking guy. He graduated last year."

"Sure I remember him," said James. "I tried to stay out of his way."

"The girl seemed to like him okay." Trip smirked.

"I keep trying to figure out where she fits in," Chelsea said. "Aren't you curious?"

James propped a foot up on the railing. "Let me get this straight," he said. "Ricky the burglar saw this girl kissing Mark and then some other guys came in and killed him?"

"Jealous, maybe," observed Trip.

"Ricky wasn't too clear about the other guys," explained Chelsea. "Of course, he was scared out of his mind, which may explain it. It seems like there were three guys who broke into the school—Ricky and the two guys who got killed. What happened is that while this girl was kissing Mark, somebody else came in and the next thing Ricky knows all hell breaks loose and he sees the cops so he gets out of there."

"So nobody really knows what happened," suggested James.

"Two boys got murdered," said Chelsea. "We know that much. And a girl was in there with them!"

"It's the black widow stuff that you like, isn't it?" said Trip, shooting her a look. "Love and then—kaboom, the female spider eats him up."

"You've got to admit it's interesting," said Chelsea. "After all, it's possible, if Ricky is telling the truth, that a girl killed those two guys!"

"The Barbie doll murder! I can see the headlines!" cried Trip.

"Sexist!" Chelsea punched him lightly in the stomach. "This isn't funny, Trip. It's serious. Two guys have been murdered!"

"A knife is a woman's weapon anyway," put in James. "Don't you think?"

"Maybe this girl didn't like the way Mark kissed. So—whoa, curtains," suggested Trip.

"You know, whatever way you look at it, it sounds kinky," said James.

Kinky. There was that word again. It was stark in James's brain. He saw Rina walking toward them and sweat trickled between his shoulder blades. What if she said something about what happened last night? The sunlight showed fiery highlights in her hair as she approached. She had dramatic black and white coloring— dark hair, milky white skin. James was not surprised when she edged into the shadow cast by the building. Her pallor made it obvious that she had a habit of avoiding the sun.

"Hi," she said.

"Hi," said James. For a paranoid instant he had the sensation that everyone in school guessed what had happened last night. He felt morbidly conspicious, as if a big red marker were drawing a circle around him and Rina, and everyone had turned to stare at them.

"So, how are you liking your classes so far, Rina?" asked Trip.

Rina brightened. "I like them."

James glanced at Rina briefly, then his eyes flicked away. He fingered the base of his neck uneasily, feeling the tender spot there. He began to wonder if he had only dreamed what happened. Was it remotely possible that he had been bitten by a strange beetle and had had a weird allergic reaction? Hallucinations, maybe? The whole thing was beginning to seem unreal. Nothing in Rina's face gave away the strange closeness they had shared the night before.

"Have you stopped by the office and gotten that list of clubs I told you about, Rina?" Chelsea asked pointedly. "If you want to get to know people, you're going to have to make an effort."

"Don't worry about me, Chelsea," Rina said. "I'm doing fine."

James was embarrassed. Why did Chelsea have to get her needle into Rina today of all days? He admitted, a little shamefaced, that it worried him that Chelsea might get Rina mad, and that if she did, Rina might drop a hint about what happened last night. Or even tell Chelsea outright. He could feel cold sweat dampening his shirt at the thought. What would he do if that happened? Chelsea had been known to give him a hard time even for looking at another girl. Intuitively he sensed that breaking up with her was going to be a nightmare. Now that he considered the question in the cold light of day, he was sure Rina wasn't worth it.

"Somebody told me the computer lab is going to be open today," Rina said.

"Zat so?" said Trip. "Guess the police must be finished with the lab work. That was fast."

"So I guess that means we'll have computer class now. I've never taken a computer class before," Rina said, frowning. "I don't think I'm going to like it."

James stared at her, stupefied. Her matter-of-fact words were so far from what he was thinking that he felt as if he were having some out-of-body experience.

"There's no homework in a computer class," put in Trip. "That's one good thing."

The bell went off like a bomb over their heads, and relief flooded James. At least he didn't have to stand around anymore waiting to see if Rina was going to spill the truth. He took Chelsea's arm and headed in the direction of her first class. "I wish you would lay off Rina," he said in a low voice.

"I don't know what you're talking about," she said.

James sighed. The ways that girls got at each

other was subtle, but he knew it when he saw it. "That stuff about how she ought to join clubs so she could get to know people," he suggested.

"Well, she should," said Chelsea. "She can't hang out with us, James!"

"She only just got here, Chels," he pointed out patiently. "She doesn't know anybody else but us."

"Bet you anything that she manages to have lunch with us again today."

"So what?" He shrugged. "It's no big deal."

"Yeah, but you watch—it *starts* with having lunch with us, and the next thing you know we won't be able to get rid of her. She's starting to latch on to us."

"I don't see why she gets to you so much." James's skin was crawling with uneasiness. The way Chelsea was freaking out over Rina, it had to mean something. He wondered if somehow she had guessed that something had gone on between him and Rina.

"There's something weird about her," said Chelsea, frowning. "When I look her right in the eye, it's like I can't look away."

James himself had noticed the hypnotic quality of Rina's gaze, but he was afraid that talking about it might lead to dangerous territory. The last thing he wanted was to find himself confessing to Chelsea that he felt magnetically drawn to Rina. "Her eyes are a kind of unusual color," he said cautiously.

"She scares me."

"Oh, come on!"

"Doesn't she give you a kind of funny feeling in the pit of your stomach?" asked Chelsea. "Be honest now."

"I don't know what you're talking about." Rina had a powerful effect on him all right, but chills didn't quite describe it. It was more like he wanted to kiss her. He was squirming with guilt every minute they talked about her.

"She doesn't even quite look like other people," Chelsea said.

James shrugged. "Well, she's not from around here. Aren't you getting kind of carried away, Chels?"

"If you tell me to 'get a grip,'" said Chelsea evenly, "I will *scream*. I am very cool. I'm only trying to explain a gut reaction kind of thing." Her eyes widened. "I just thought of something— now that Rachel and Trip have broken up, he's looking for a new girl. What if he takes up with Rina? I mean, she *is* pretty. Even I have to admit that. And didn't you think he was being awfully nice to her this morning? Asking her about how she liked her courses and all?"

James choked on sudden laughter. "Oh, come on," he said helplessly. "Get real."

"I don't see what's so funny."

James shook his head. "I just don't think Trip is Rina's type, that's all."

"He's male, she's female," said Chelsea acidly.
"That's all it takes."

Doesn't it matter whether or not you like each other? James wondered. He started to say it, but Chelsea was already looking at him funny. Maybe she was already wondering whether Rina was after him instead of Trip. He wished he hadn't said anything. "Well," he said. "At least she doesn't seem like the sort who'd give him grief about football practice."

"She probably doesn't even know what football is," said Chelsea. "She's strange."

Privately, James had to agree. Rina was strange. But the problem was she was also strangely attractive. He glanced at his watch. "I've got to get to class."

"Say hello to Rina for me," said Chelsea sweetly.

James grinned a farewell and plunged into the crowd that clogged the hallway.

He slid into class just as the last bell rang. His eyes fell on Rina and a chill went down his spine as if a piece of ice had slipped down his back. Perhaps it was because he had run into her in the cemetery last night, but now, looking at her, he felt as if he'd been touched by death.

He took a seat as far from her as he could, near the door. He hardly heard a word of what Mrs. Kimbro said. English literature was the last thing on his mind. As soon as the final bell rang, he shot out into the hall. A cold tingling made his skin seem as if it didn't belong to him. He felt like one of those jerks who makes out with a girl and then acts as if he can't remember her name. Not that he had made out with Rina. Not exactly. He wiped his damp palms hastily on his jeans.

Glancing over his shoulder, he saw Rina. He looked away at once. Just catching a glimpse of her made him feel weak at the knees. A strange desire he hardly understood seemed to buzz in his blood. He wanted to draw her close to him, and at the same time she scared him. *What was going on with him?* he wondered miserably.

Rina edged into the computer lab. She could smell the stench of disinfectant, and her attention was drawn to the darkened spot on the floor where the boys' blood had spilled. She saw the wide swath of tile that had been scrubbed when the police had cleaned up after their investigation. A dark stain remained where her own blood had evaporated. She smiled. A laboratory test of that tile would not show hemoglobin, since vampire blood had a different, supernatural essence. Even if the police had been able to scrape up a trace of her blood, which was unlikely, a laboratory test would show nothing. The lab workers could only imagine that something had gone wrong with their slide.

She glanced around the room with distaste,

remembering that she loathed computers. It had
been hard enough for her to give up writing with
a quill pen when fountain pens were invented.
The pace of change seemed dizzying, and she
was not ready yet to deal with the mysteries of
this new machine. She stared at the textbook
that lay beside it. "Get to know your computer!"
She didn't want to get to know her computer. She
wanted to kill her computer.

It did not help that she was anxious about
whether her spells were working on James.
Doubt nagged at her when she remembered
other spells that had failed. Vlad had worked
spells on her and yet it had not been enough to
bind her to him. Maybe the heart could not be
bound by spells. Rina found herself wondering
miserably why she had ever thought that it
could. When James refused to meet her eyes, she
was afraid that maybe he didn't like her.

She was edgy, and suddenly she felt she could
not stand the aggravation of dealing with the stupid computer on top of everything else. She
stood up and went over to the teacher's desk.
"May I be excused?" she asked.

Mrs. Healy nodded distractedly and Rina
stepped out into the silent hall. She looked in
both directions, instinctively cautious. No one
was coming. She didn't have to go far down the
hall before she spotted what she was looking
for—the door marked JANITOR. She opened the

door and the sour smell of damp mops hit her. A large, rusty sink was low on one wall, draped with dirty dust cloths. On the other wall she saw a small metal door at shoulder height. She opened it, relieved to see that each circuit was clearly labeled. She flipped the switch labeled COMPUTER LAB and a faint smile lit her face. That should shut off the stupid computers for a while at least.

"Hey!" a hoarse voice cried. "What are you doing in here? Why are you monkeying around with the breaker box?"

Rina spun round and saw that an angry, gray-haired man had barged in behind her. Small red veins showed in his nose and his jowls were blotched. At once, Rina reached out and laid her cool hands on either side of his neck. He was dazed by her touch, and when her fangs slid out of their sheaths he did not even blink. She bit his throat and let his hot blood flow into her mouth. She could feel the rhythm of his heart forcing the blood into her, and warmth seeped into her fingers and her toes until she felt numb.

Time seemed to move slowly. She wasn't sure whether seconds or minutes had passed when she forced herself to pull away from the limp body that lay crumpled on the cement floor. The janitor's mouth was agape, showing uneven yellow teeth. Rina's hands and feet tingled pleasantly, but she realized with a sudden sinking of her heart that this attack had not been worth the risk. It was broad daylight and the building was full of people. James was in a classroom only yards away. How could she have been so stupid?

Anxiously, Rina peeked out the door. At least no one was coming. She dashed into the nearby rest room. There she checked herself in the mirror for signs of blood, her anxiety growing every second as she thought of what she had done. What if she had ruined everything!

Taking a deep breath, Rina pushed open the swinging door and crept into the hallway. Even from here she could see the janitor's foot sticking out from the open door. Anyone might have passed by and seen it! Rina nudged the foot back in the utility closet and forced the door closed. Her pulse was pounding painfully with nervousness, but she straightened her back in resolution and returned to class. All she had to do was act innocent, she told herself. There was no reason for anyone to suspect her. It might be a long time before the janitor's body was found, and the longer it took the less likely it was that anyone would connect the attack on him with her brief absence from the classroom.

It was dim when she went back in the room, and its machines were silent. The incessant hum of twenty computers had been stilled the instant she had tripped the circuit breaker.

"Maybe we ought to check the circuit breaker box," suggested James.

"Right," said Neil Hubbard, getting up to go with him.

Rina tensed. She wished she had been quick-witted enough to flip the power back on after she had attacked the man. Now his body would be found!

James knew the circuit breaker box was in the nearby janitor's closet, because for a while last year he had run an ancient film projector that made the circuit kick out practically every time he used it. He pulled the door of the closet and jumped back suddenly when a heavy, booted foot fell out. An involuntary cry escaped him. He opened the door and spotted the janitor awkwardly sprawled on the cement floor.

"Is he dead?" Neil whispered.

James bent to one knee and reached his hand out to hold it before the man's mouth and nose. "He's still breathing. Run to the office," he said. "Get them to send an ambulance!"

Neil turned at once and fled. James could hear his running footsteps.

"What's wrong?" somebody yelled.

Kids were streaming out of the computer classroom, their faces alive with curiosity.

"James?" Mrs. Healy stepped out into the hall.

"Something's happened to the janitor," James said. "Neil's calling the rescue squad."

Mrs. Healy shooed the kids back in the

classroom. "We'll only be in the way, people. Help is on the way. You heard. Now back to your desks, please."

But Rina lingered at the door after the others had gone in, her eyes burning with a strange and mournful brilliance. James could not tear his gaze away from her.

"He's going to be all right," James repeated, hoping he was speaking the truth.

He didn't see how she could have heard. He was speaking softly, almost to himself, but she nodded and disappeared into the classroom.

James knelt at the janitor's side, his heart racing. The man couldn't be dead already, could he? He was very pale. Suddenly James saw a ruby bead of blood. James leaned forward and unbuttoned the janitor's shirt. He could see the blue line that marked the passage of the carotid artery under the skin, and at its base, just above the collarbone, were two pinholes, one of them specked with blood. The flesh was an unnatural white around each puncture mark, as if he had been stung.

James rocked back on his heels, dizzy with shock. He was vaguely conscious of running footsteps. He looked up and saw the principal and Neil standing at the door. Kids were peeking out of the computer lab, trying to see what was happening.

"H-his neck," James stuttered. "Something's happened to him."

Mrs. Spraggens clasped her hands and stared wide-eyed into the little room. "We've called the rescue squad. They'll be here in a minute."

Neil gave James a hand and he lurched to his feet. His knees were unsteady, he realized, and he sat down abruptly on the floor.

"Are you all right, James?" Mrs. Spraggens said quickly. "You look pale. No, don't get up! Put your head between your knees."

Neil peered curiously at the janitor. "Do you think he broke his neck?" he asked. "He's lying there kind of funny."

"Don't say that, Neil," whimpered Mrs. Spraggens. "Even when people are unconscious they can hear what you say, and it can have a very negative effect on them. I'm certain he'll be perfectly fine. Help is on the way. You boys had better get back to class. James, if you want to go home, just come to the office and get a pass. I can see this has been a terrible shock to you."

James shook his head numbly. "I'm okay," he said. He got up.

Neil put his arm around James's shoulder as they walked back to the classroom. "You sure, man? You look awful."

James shook him off. "I'm fine." He glanced over his shoulder. "Did you see the blood on his neck?"

Neil gave him a look. "Are you sure you're okay? I didn't see any blood."

"It was just a drop," said James. "Right above the collarbone. You were looking right at him. Didn't you see it?"

Neil shrugged. "I just saw a kind of a bruise there, is that what you mean?"

"A bruise?"

"Yeah, a little yellow bruise. That's all."

James shivered.

"I think you'd better go get yourself that pass and go home," said Neil. "No kidding."

"Leave me alone, will you?" snapped James. "I'm okay."

When the boys got back to class, kids crowded around them asking questions. They all heard the ambulance siren and caught a glimpse of paramedics racing past the open doorway. Rina was in an agony of apprehension. How could she have been so stupid as to attack someone at school? James looked pale and shaken, and she couldn't get him to meet her eyes. She had the horrible feeling that he suspected something.

Suddenly the lights went on. Rina's computer shot out sparks.

Mrs. Healy ran to her side. "What happened? Are you all right, Rina?" Her trembling hand touched Rina's shoulder.

"I think the computer has some problems," Rina said. While everyone was watching the emergency medics run by, she had busied herself with switching all the connections at the back of her computer. But now she could take no pleasure in the destruction of her machine. She was too worried.

All around the room she could hear the chuckling sound of computers "booting up." It sounded as if they were laughing at her.

"Dear me," said Mrs. Healy, gazing in dismay at Rina's blank screen. "What else can possibly go wrong?" She snatched the plug out of the surge protector strip. "We're already a computer short. The police are holding the stolen one as evidence, and there's simply no telling when it will be released. Rina, you'll have to look on with James for the time being and do the best you can."

Beseechingly, Rina touched James's hand. He jerked it away. Looking into his eyes, she saw that he was frightened.

"Are you okay?" she asked anxiously.

"I'm fine."

Rina felt her heart squeeze in fear. What if James had already guessed that she was a vampire?

7

After school the next day, James stopped by the office. "I thought you might have heard how the janitor is getting along," he said to Mrs. Spraggens.

She invited him into her office and closed the door. "We're trying not to make too much of a deal out of Mr. Brown's collapse," she said in a low voice, "because everyone is still so upset by the—the previous unpleasantness." Her voice sank to a whisper. "You know, the burglary."

"Is Mr. Brown going to be okay?" asked James. He ran his finger around the inside of his shirt collar, uncomfortably aware of the tender spot at the base of his neck. His bruise matched the one he had seen on the janitor's neck—he was sure of that.

"They think he'll pull through." Mrs. Spraggens smiled. "It is so like you to be concerned, James."

James felt himself growing uncomfortably

hot. He wished now that he had not come by. All he could think of was the strange and dark pleasure Rina had given him when she had visited his room. His knees felt weak and he had to sit down in the chair across from Mrs. Spraggens's desk, uncomfortably conscious of the thudding of his heart. "D-did they say anything about what his trouble was?"

"Probably anemia," said Mrs. Spraggens. "His hemoglobin count was abnormally low. They're still doing tests. I'm thankful to say, though, it was nothing having to do with our circuit breaker box. You know how safety conscious I try to be." She laughed nervously. "I'll admit when I found the poor man passed out on a cement floor near the electric box, I was afraid we might be in for a lawsuit. But it turned out not to be electrocution after all, but just a run-of-the-mill health problem."

"A run-of-the-mill health problem," James repeated numbly.

"We think the rest of the staff can cover for him until he's back on the job."

James stumbled to his feet.

"I appreciate your concern," Mrs. Spraggens said. "And I'll try to keep you posted on his condition, but at this point, that's all we know." Mrs. Spraggens's eyes softened behind her glasses. "Tell your mother hello for me, James. I know she hasn't gotten out much since poor

Susan became ill. But she's so often in my thoughts."

James nodded, unable to speak. He wasn't even sure how he got out of the office. Somehow he managed to stagger to the rest room and dash cold water on his face. When he stared at himself in the mirror, it seemed to him that his eyes looked blurred and strange. Blank, like a doll's eyes. He fingered the tender place at the base of his neck. The bruise was not healing this time as quickly as before.

He rested his hands on the sink, biting his lip until he winced with the pain. A tiny bead of blood formed on his lower lip and he stared at it. A tiny bead of blood. He had seen one on the janitor's neck. He must be going out of his mind. What possible connection could there be between him and what had happened to the janitor?

James took to avoiding Rina. He told himself he needed time to figure things out, and the next day he avoided her reproachful eyes as he hurried past her on the way to the cafeteria. He took Chelsea's arm when he ran into her and suggested hastily, "Let's eat with Tom and Molly and the bunch."

When he and Chelsea had filled their trays, he guided her firmly to the table where their friends sat. James felt as if these kids he had known most of his life were a kind of armor. Armor against what? He wasn't sure. He couldn't think straight with Trip telling dumb jokes and trying to balance an olive on his nose. The girls were checking out how Candi was looking at Andy across the cafeteria. "I think she's going to dump Chad," offered Molly. "She's definitely giving Andy the look."

Who cared? James was amazed anybody could work up an interest in Candi's love life. James had the weary sensation that he would always be able to predict everything that his friends were going to say and do.

"Snell is really a tough grader," Tom reported gloomily. "I hope I don't get a *C* in his class. It could really hurt my chances of getting into Carolina."

Trip did not seem to be particularly worried about getting into college. He sliced his olive in half and put one half on each eye. "Duh," he said, "you think I can put this talent on my college aps?"

Chelsea threw a napkin at him. He grinned, and the olives fell onto his tray.

James remembered that Trip used to play with his food way back in grade school. He liked to stir chocolate milk and peas into his mashed potatoes. Just sitting next to him was enough to ruin a guy's appetite.

In spite of himself, James found his eyes

drawn to Rina. He saw her sitting by herself at a distant table and felt an ache of longing. Rina was different. He would have loved to bury his fingers in that wild raven hair of hers. She seemed to touch some deep chord inside him. She looked up suddenly and caught his eye, and James found himself imagining the cool and windy plain of death and eternity. He shivered and looked away.

He managed to stay clear of her at school, but it hit him that he had gotten in the habit of leaving his bedroom window open. One night he watched the curtains fluttering at the open window and he finally admitted to himself that he was hoping Rina would return.

A couple of days later he ran into her at her locker. "Hi," he said.

"Hi," she said shyly.

They stood in silence then and James felt tension crackle between them, like lightning skipping along an electric wire.

"I haven't seen you much lately," said Rina at last. "I only see you in class, I mean. Are you— are you avoiding me?" Her eyes met his pleadingly.

James shook his head. He felt himself going hot.

"Oh, good." Rina sighed. "I was kind of worried about that." She looked at him anxiously.

"I was thinking I might come see you sometime. Like I did before. If you think that'd be okay, I mean."

"Sure," gulped James. "Why not?"

The bell rang suddenly and James was relieved. He was glad of an excuse to escape the magnetic spell of Rina's eyes, and he practically ran toward his next class. His heart seemed to be swelling inside him, filling up his chest, and he stopped a minute and leaned against a wall to catch his breath.

"Hey, man, you okay?" It was Bill Grant from the track team. He had stopped suddenly and was facing James expectantly as if he was considering administering first aid.

"Sure." James shrugged. "I'm fine. Just realized I left my chem homework at home is all." He smiled. "Panic attack."

"Hey, no problem. I'm always forgetting mine. Dixon only takes off a letter grade."

James nodded and watched Bill walk away, the laces of his untied tennis shoes flopping so loosely it was a wonder he didn't trip.

A panic attack, James thought. That part was true, anyhow. Why had he told Rina he wanted her to come visit him? It must be because he hungered for her touch. That was why he had been leaving his window open, wasn't it?

8

That night James didn't put on pajamas. He left his jeans on as he crawled into bed. Sleeping fully clothed marked his own acknowledgment to himself that he expected Rina to come. At midnight, when there was still no sign of her, he switched off the bedside lamp and slipped under the sheets, weak with relief. *I'm just glad she didn't take me seriously,* he told himself, pounding the pillow into submission. *This thing with Rina— whatever it is—is crazy. I don't need it, that's for sure.* At the same time he was conscious of a twinge of disappointment as he drifted off to sleep.

He wasn't sure what time it was when he felt something tickle him and drowsily stirred awake. He woke suddenly with a jerk and realized that Rina's pale fingers were touching his throat. "Nice," she murmured softly. She was standing beside his bed, a dark shadow with amber cat's eyes. James rolled over and leapt out of the bed. His heart was pounding so hard, he felt sick.

She gazed at him curiously. "Do you always sleep in your clothes like that?"

James felt heat rush to his face. He glanced uneasily at the half-open window. If he hadn't wanted her to come, he wondered, then why had he more or less invited her?

"Are you afraid of me?" she asked.

"No!" he said a little too loudly.

She smiled. "Then come here."

James found himself drawing close to her. He had the oddest sense that he had rehearsed this, as if he had woken up from dreaming of it only to find himself doing it.

She put her hands on his shoulders and made him sit down on the bed. "This is nice, isn't it?" she breathed softly as her lips touched the fine hairs of his skin. He squirmed uneasily. He wanted to get away, but when she kissed his neck his body responded to her in spite of himself. Already his blood was stirring and he felt excitement pounding in his throat.

She pressed her hand against his face and slowly pushed his head to the side. Suddenly she bit. He heard himself utter a weak cry like a bird and he tried to push her away, but the strength ebbed out of him. Her arm was around him, holding him, as she stroked his throat. "I won't hurt you," she murmured. "Only a tiny sharp pain. I don't want to hurt you. I only want your heart and soul."

His breath was coming fast now and he felt a tender pleasure sweep him up. He was lost in it, light-headed and dizzy. Even his bones were light and his hands clutched at empty air as he reeled, cartwheeling in black space. Suddenly he felt he was floating above the earth, riding on the hot wind that blew between stars. He caught a glimpse over his shoulder at Orion, a bright bracelet of diamonds in the sky. Somehow Mr. Dixon, his teacher, was there, sitting in a chair, as if the galaxy were his living room. James was trying hard to understand what he was saying but he couldn't quite catch it. Then he had the sense of falling, but instead of being afraid, he was wildly exhilarated by the freedom of his fall, as if this were what he had been waiting for.

Suddenly it occurred to him that he couldn't remember his name. Yet he felt a deep certainty that his name no longer mattered. He could have burst with the ecstasy of his soaring flight.

He spread his arms and lifted himself up effortlessly over the trees. Then it occurred to him that he had never seen shaggy trees like these. Lichens grew in their trunks and he could make out a wild boar, his tusks white in the moonlight, rooting noisily under a low branch. This was no forest he had ever seen. It was as if he had entered someone else's memory!

In a sudden panic, he diminished into a tiny point of hot consciousness and felt himself

plummeting like a stone past unfamiliar land-
scapes. His speed was startling and the sinking
feeling in his stomach left him terrified. He had
forgotten how to fly!

To his relief, he realized the dream was ending. It was as if sleep had become a thin curtain
that he could see through. He made out the familiar gleam of the trophies on his bookcase. His
eyes were closed, but he could see through the
veil of veins in his eyelids. He felt the wrinkled
bedspread under his fingers. His own room.
Safe!

His eyes flew open and he saw Rina. Her face
had a strange fixed look and he felt a flutter of fear
as she stroked his cheek. He gasped for breath.
"We've got to stop doing this," he whispered.
"Whatever it is." He glanced uneasily at the door,
conscious that his parents were just down the hall.
Sweat was dripping down his back and he felt
dizzy. "What if my family heard something?" he
gasped. All around the room were reminders of
who he was—track and horseback riding trophies,
sketches, books, pictures of his family. He felt
himself stiffen. What Rina was doing to him felt
dangerous. He realized he could never put his obscure feeling into words. "Chelsea'd kill me if she
knew you were here," he gulped.

Rina traced a figure on his cheek with her
sharp nail. "Tell Chelsea I'm your girlfriend now,"
she suggested.

"I can't!" he protested.

Rina looked hurt. "You don't like what I do to you?"

James pushed the damp hair out of his face. "I don't even want to *think* about what you do to me," he said feelingly.

A tear glistened in her eye.

"It's nothing against you." James struggled to his feet. He felt an overwhelming need to get out of her reach. Intuitively he felt he could be stronger if she weren't touching him. He staggered to his desk and sank to the chair, exhausted. "I *like* you, Rina," he protested. "You're a sweet girl. But you knew I had something going with Chelsea. Chelsea and me have been together for over a year." He wished Rina would just disappear from his life without making him feel like more of a creep than he felt already. "We've even bought a page in the yearbook together," he said.

Rina looked puzzled. "Is that like being married?"

James was uncomfortably aware that most of the couples who swore their undying love on the pages of the yearbook had broken up by the time the book actually came out in the spring, but he didn't think he'd better mention that to Rina. "I can't just drop Chelsea all of a sudden like she's an outdated carton of milk or something," he said.

"You're nice," said Rina simply. "I like you."

"I like you, too," said James, closing his eyes so he didn't have to look at her beautiful and oddly frightening face. "But you and me, it just can't be. Understand?"

"I think so," said Rina slowly. "It's because of Chelsea."

"Yes," said James. He felt weak with relief that she was taking it so well. But when he opened his eyes and saw her, he found himself losing his train of thought.

"I'm glad you like me," Rina said softly. "We can still be friends, can't we?"

"Sure," said James. He realized suddenly that Rina touched his heart in a dark place that he didn't share with anyone else. When he had walked with her by Susan's grave, he had seen a sadness in her eyes that echoed his own. It seemed as if she understood the crazy things he was going through. No wonder he was having trouble brushing her off. In some way, he must not even want to. He had retreated beyond her reach, but she came over to him and stroked his hair. It tickled, and he felt himself stretching like a cat. He flexed his toes luxuriously.

"I would never laugh at you or tease you," Rina said. "I would never treat you the way Trip and Chelsea do."

An explosive laugh escaped James. What Rina did to him was so much kinkier than anything he had ever done with Chelsea that the sick humor of it nearly blew him away.

"Trip and Chelsea are not nice," Rina said.

James brushed her hand away, smiling a little. "Maybe they aren't always nice, Rina. Nobody's nice all the time. But most of the time they're just kidding around. They don't mean anything by it."

Rina traced a pattern on his chest with her nail, and for minute or two James had trouble collecting his thoughts. "Trip and Chelsea are jealous of you because you're beautiful and good," she murmured.

"Guys aren't beautiful," he protested. "You have such a funny way of talking." Seeing the hurt in her eyes, he added quickly, "I mean, it's not bad, you know, but different."

"My parents were from Romania," Rina explained. A flush darkened her cheeks. "And for a long time I was home schooled."

"Well, it's okay not to be just like everybody else." His gaze fell on her and suddenly he couldn't pull his eyes away. He felt almost limp— it was that floating sensation again, he realized. With just a little effort, he felt he could have lifted himself into the air. Her skin was pale and flawless, like porcelain in its perfection, and tonight it was stained with a beautiful warmth he hadn't noticed before. Just looking at her gave him an odd sense of peace. She was as cool as moonlight.

"So it's all right if I say you're beautiful?" she suggested.

"No!" he cried, stiffening suddenly. The idea that Rina might go around school telling people he was beautiful horrified him. "I'm not," he said. "And I'm no better than Chelsea or Trip, either." His voice softened a little as he gazed at her. "Now you—you're beautiful."

"You think so?" she asked shyly.

"Absolutely," he said. He realized that he'd be better off not to look at her. He had to be firm about her leaving, and it would be a lot easier if he weren't looking into her eyes. "Believe me," he said, "pretty soon you'll find some guy who'll be crazy about you."

"But not you?" She was plaintive.

"Not me," he said. "Because of Chelsea." It was not the whole truth, but his experience told him that with girls the whole truth was seldom a good idea.

"I'm leaving now," said Rina.

With a fluidity that astonished him, she turned away and slipped out the window. He hardly had time to feel relieved that she was going before she was gone!

James took a deep breath. It was a relief that she was gone, and yet at the same time he felt a little let down. He shut the window after her and locked it tight. Then he climbed into bed and in the darkness listened to his heart beat. He could hardly lift his head off the pillow, he was so weak. It was almost as if he had become unraveled by the overwhelming loss of self Rina had brought to him. Yet he could not feel sorry about what had happened. In the moments they were together a dark peace and pleasure had sifted into his heart. He could hardly believe that he had told her to get out of his life when she had brought him the only quiet he had been able to find in weeks. He pulled his pillow over his head and fell into a dreamless sleep.

For the next few days, even though he had resolved not to think about Rina, James found his attention drawn magnetically to the window that she had used to get into his room. At last, he was forced to pull the curtains closed over the locked window so he could concentrate on his homework.

What he had done with Rina was sick, he reminded himself. Whatever it was, it wasn't normal. But then his thoughts did an about-face. Maybe he was merely getting hung up on labels. What if it turned out that Rina and the dark forgetfulness she offered him was what he really yearned for in his deepest, truest self?

At school he felt like a wild animal during hunting season. It wasn't easy to avoid Rina when she was in all his classes, but he took care to come to class a minute late and to dash out the second the bell rang. During every class period he looked straight at the teacher and the board, terrified that he might accidentally turn around and meet Rina's eyes.

He knew he wasn't taking time to be friendly to the kids he knew, but he ignored the hurt glances that followed him as he hurried past. It was as if his classes and his friends were only a painted backdrop to the real drama that was what was going on between him and Rina.

When he closed his eyes he found himself tensing expectantly, waiting for her touch. Remembering the last strange night that she had crept into his room, he was amazed he had found the strength to tell her not to come back. If she did come again, he couldn't be sure he would be able to tell her to leave. But what if he left the window to his room open, and she came every night? He was afraid to imagine what would happen then.

He pulled books out of his locker, and when he turned around, he nearly choked. Rina was standing facing him, and he realized with a gasp that he had forgotten how good she looked. That detail had simply slipped his mind. His memory of her was of a touch, a scent, and a sharp pain that brought cold peace sifting through his blood. Now that she was standing before him he saw with a fresh shock the beauty of her ivory face with its high cheekbones and odd-colored eyes.

"Hi." She smiled.

He wanted to reach out and crush her close to him, but he was conscious that kids were looking at them curiously. Everybody knew Chelsea was his girlfriend, and he sensed that even a casual glance must pick up the odd intensity that crackled between him and Rina.

"Hi," he said. The greeting seemed comically inadequate and he could hear harsh, derisive laughter sounding in his brain.

Rina touched his cheek and James flinched, then gave himself up to the peace he felt flowing through her fingers. He closed his eyes, conscious only of her faint scent.

"We're still friends, aren't we?" she asked.

He gulped. "Sure." He gently removed her hand from his face and held it a moment in his own. Her fingers were limp and cold and he wondered if she was frightened.

"I've been walking in the cemetery a couple of times late at night," she said, "but I haven't seen you there." She smiled. "Maybe that means your heart is quiet. You are content and you have sweet dreams about your girlfriend Chelsea."

James didn't answer. He didn't have to. He saw by the change in her expression that she knew the truth. He wasn't dreaming of Chelsea, or of anything else for that matter. The slate of his mind had been wiped clean. The past few days he had had trouble focusing on anything but this strange thing going on with Rina.

"Have you studied for the calculus test?" asked Rina.

James stared at her incredulously. He supposed this was an example of her subtle sense of humor. As if he could concentrate on calculus at a time like this!

"I don't think it will be hard," Rina went on, as if she had not noticed his shock. "I suppose you and Chelsea and Trip are going out someplace together tonight."

He shook his head. "No," he croaked hoarsely. "I'm going with my folks to an opening at the art museum in the city. It's a big deal. Everybody gets dressed up." There was a strange unreality to everything he said. Was he actually going to go eat canapés with a bunch of art lovers when a storm of emotion was scouring his brain clean of everything but Rina? Her name sounded in his mind like the wind, full of promise and danger.

The second bell sounded over their heads. James lifted both hands and ran his fingers through his hair desperately. "Gotta go," he said. "We're going to be late. I mean really late!" He took off running, his sneakers squeaking in the empty halls. He knew that Rina must be going to chemistry class, too, but it never occurred to him to wait for her. He ran hard, sensing that she was behind him and feeling somehow that he was running for his life.

He skidded into the chemistry lab gasping for breath. Everyone else had already arrived, and several kids looked up in surprise. In the far corner of the lab, a girl's dark and gleaming head was bent over a lab notebook. He felt a sick sinking feeling in the pit of his stomach. He knew who it must be—but it was impossible! He *must* have beat her to class. He had run the whole way! But then she looked up at him. It was Rina, all right. He gulped painfully.

"Are you okay, James?" asked Mr. Dixon. "Sit down! Put your head between your knees."

James felt dark laughter welling up inside him. People seemed to be constantly telling him to put his head between his knees these days. He rested his head on the table, on his folded arms. The stainless-steel sink and spigot gleamed beside him looking detached from reality, as if they were museum exhibits taken from a world that had vanished from the earth.

He felt the teacher's hand on his shoulder and winced. "Next time don't try to run the hundred-yard dash just because you're a little late," said Mr. Dixon.

How could Rina already be here in the classroom? James wondered. It just didn't make sense.

9

"There's something weird about Rina," Chelsea told Trip.

Trip cracked his knuckles as he surveyed the kids moving toward school buses and the student parking lot. "Her name is foreign," he pointed out. "That probably accounts for it."

"That's not so!" said Chelsea impatiently. "You never hear me saying that Dipika Shah or Ed Wu are weird."

Trip thought about it. "Well, they aren't, that's why," he said.

"Right. So it doesn't have anything to do with her name. It's only that I have a very bad feeling about her," insisted Chelsea. "Don't you think it's funny that she showed up when she did? I mean right after those two boys were murdered?"

"Lots of people were showing up then," Trip pointed out. "It was the second day of school." He gazed at a meek-looking blond girl. Skinny legs but nice face. Freckles. He wasn't sure whether freckles were a plus or a minus. "Do you think people would figure I was desperate if I went out with a freshman?" he asked.

"Depends on which freshman," said Chelsea crisply. "Quit trolling for girls, Trip, and pay attention. Remember that fellow Ricky's story that a girl was in the computer lab?" She lowered her voice. "What if the girl he saw in there was Rina?"

Trip grinned. "Sure. You're telling me that a little tiny thing like Rina murdered two big thugs? Dream on."

"It's possible," insisted Chelsea.

"What does James say about your nutty theory?"

"I haven't mentioned it to him yet," Chelsea admitted. "He always sticks up for Rina. Like at lunch. For the past few days we've managed to duck her, for a change, and eat lunch by ourselves. But even though we haven't been sitting with her, I can tell he's always looking at her. And when I made some crack about her dippy clothes, he practically bit my head off. It's like she's cast some spell on him."

"You couldn't be a little bit jealous?" teased Trip.

"No! It's not that," snapped Chelsea. "Look at his eyes! Ever since she started hanging around, he's changed. Half the time he seems out of it.

How many times have you had to snap your fingers in his face just to get his attention?"

"He's got a lot on his mind, Chels." Trip shrugged uncomfortably. "You know—Susan."

"No!" she exploded. "It's not that. It's Rina! I'm sure of it."

"I expect you'll take care of her," said Trip, his eyes following the progress of the willowy blond girl as she walked to where the buses were waiting. "Good old Chelsea the Terminator."

"That's not funny anymore," snapped Chelsea.

Trip had called her "the Terminator" since the seventh grade when she had somehow organized a giggling campaign against Jennifer Griffith. She had driven Jennifer out of the school, but he knew she hated for him to mention it.

"It's not my fault Jennifer got so freaked out that she transferred to a private school!" Chelsea said heatedly. "Besides, she was *much* happier there. I did her a favor."

"Sure, you did," he said.

"Besides, it's ancient history. You wouldn't want me bringing up every stupid thing you did way back in the seventh grade."

"The way I remember it I was an angel." Trip cracked his knuckles.

Chelsea glanced around impatiently. "Where on earth can James be?" She covered her eyes suddenly with her hand. "Don't look now," she said between clenched teeth, "but it's Rina, the

Dragon Lady. She's coming over here."

Rina sailed toward them. Something about the way she moved made her seem almost as if she were floating, thought Trip. She didn't barge around the way other kids did but glided and held her head high, like a dancer. She looked good, he admitted, if you liked them midget sized. Even the slightly out-of-it clothes could not detract from her beauty.

She planted herself squarely before them. "Hi!" she said.

"Hi," said Chelsea without enthusiasm.

"How's it going, Rina?" asked Trip. "Did you ever get a new computer? Somebody told me yours exploded."

"They got me another one, thank you," said Rina.

An awkward silence fell. Chelsea was wishing hotly that Rina would drop dead and, she reflected, that wasn't a thought that could be expressed in light conversation.

"I don't have much homework tonight," Rina said. "Do you?"

Trip snorted. "I get mine done in study hall and Chelsea never bothers."

Looking down, Rina dug the toe of her shoe into the grass self-consciously. "I was thinking I might take in a movie." She looked up suddenly. "Maybe you'd like to go with me, Chelsea."

Chelsea was obviously startled. Trip saw her blink and take a step back.

"You aren't busy, are you?" asked Rina. "I thought this would be a good time for you because I knew James would be driving over to that art exhibit in Raleigh tonight."

Chelsea's eyes flashed. "Oh, you did, did you?" She didn't like it that Rina was so up on what James was doing, but she recovered quickly and flashed her teeth in a rigid smile. "Thanks, Rina," she said, "I'd just love to go to a movie. What's playing?"

Rina made a vague gesture. "Oh, I don't know. I thought we'd go see whatever's on at the mall."

"Then you've got your choice between a cartoon, a karate movie, and a vampire movie," said Trip. "Have fun, girls."

"I'll meet you there," said Chelsea, glaring at Trip. "Let's plan to get there a little early so we'll have time to have a snack and a good talk."

"Okay," said Rina. Her eyes were already wandering, as if she had lost interest in Chelsea. Trip wondered what the natural color of Rina's eyes was. She must be wearing contact lenses—almost had to be. He'd never seen real eyes that color.

"Well, see you—tonight around seven," she said. As she walked away from them, her black hair gleamed like silk in the sunshine.

Trip's eyes followed her until she turned the corner of the building. As soon as she was out of sight, he punched Chelsea lightly in the ribs. "I can't believe you're going to a movie with her! I thought you hated her guts."

"Stop it!" hissed Chelsea. "Going to the movie with her is a part of my plan."

"Ooo, excuse me, Miss Terminator," said Trip. "I didn't realize you had a plan."

"Honestly," she said, stomping her foot. "I can see why Rachel ditched you. You can be so dense."

"No fair, Chelsea," he said, hurt. "That's a low blow. I'm still trying to get over Rachel."

"You are over her," said Chelsea. "I noticed it days ago. So quit asking for sympathy." She tapped her toe. "I plan to draw Rina out and find out exactly what she was doing the night of the burglary."

"James already told us she lives alone, so what's she going to say. You ain't going to get an alibi, sweetheart. In fact, I'll bet you don't get anything out of this except a boring night at the movies. She'd have to be pretty dumb to come right out and confess to you, and I don't think she's dumb. James told me she aced the first calculus quiz."

"There are different kinds of dumb." Chelsea's puzzled eyes met Trip's. "Did you see how she just came up and asked me to go to the movie as if she were ordering a hamburger? The girl has no social skills. I don't understand why James can't see that."

Trip smiled. "Maybe he sees it, all right. Maybe he just doesn't care."

"Thanks, Trip. Thanks a lot."

"All I'm saying is that looks count," Trip argued. He could feel a surge of emotion propelling him to say what he knew he shouldn't say. "Why else do you go out with James instead of me, huh?" He stared at her challengingly.

"I go out with James because he is utterly cool and I am in love with him." Chelsea returned his long look. "And you are supposed to be his friend, in case you've forgotten."

"All I said was James looks good," Trip protested, backpedaling swiftly in a panic. "Does that make me his enemy?"

Chelsea smiled. "You know you and me are alike in a funny kind of way."

"Yeah, we are." He grinned, relaxing a little. "We both have that little mean streak that gives us an edge." He socked his fist in his hand, enjoying the feel of his own strength. "You'd never catch James playing football," he added between clenched teeth.

"Of course not," said Chelsea. "James won't risk anything that might ruin his hands because he's an artist. All of which means he needs us to take care of him." She spun around and waved energetically. James had stepped out of the building and was squinting into the sunshine. As he walked toward them, he looked, Trip noticed, the way guys looked who'd been tackled and ended up with a concussion. The eyes were kind of unfocused.

Chelsea's short skirt flounced as she ran to James and threw herself into his arms. He looked down at her, stunned, as if she had dropped suddenly from the sky. Trip, watching them, found he couldn't take his eyes off Chelsea's legs. They seemed to go on for miles and he would have loved to touch them. *Crazy idea,* he thought, trying to put it out of his mind. Chelsea would clobber him if he touched her. Not to mention James . . . his buddy.

As James turned his head, the sun picked out the platinum highlights in his blond hair and cast his eyes in deep shadow. He gave Trip a careless wave but didn't bother to come over, which was kind of funny. Usually he did. James could have been voted "guy most likely to stand around and pass the time of day." But today he and Chelsea turned away at once and headed together toward the parking lot.

Trip smiled a little as they disappeared around the corner of the building. "Okay, so he's my best friend," he murmured to himself. "It doesn't count. All's fair in love and war."

10

~

That evening Rina and Chelsea sat at a small table under one of the mall's ficus trees. Near them sat a couple of skinny preteens in skimpy kilts. Their legs were festooned with Band-Aids, and they were sharing an ice-cream sundae. A tired woman in a wraparound pink apron propelled a push broom across the tile floor.

"So exactly when did you move to town?" asked Chelsea abruptly.

"I've been here a while." Rina shrugged. "I'm not sure exactly. Why?"

"You must know when you came to town," said Chelsea. "How can you not know that?"

Rina had already decided that Chelsea had to die. It seemed to be James's loyalty to her that stiffened his will and kept him from giving himself up to the spells.

"I was just wondering why you didn't show up the first day of school," said Chelsea. "Why did you wait until the second day?"

"First day, second day, what difference does it make?" Rina felt her gums tingle as her fangs stirred.

Chelsea's gaze was insistent, as if she were trying to bore inside Rina's mind. "Can you remember what you were doing the night before you came to school?" she demanded.

Rina burst into sudden laughter. "I killed them both with my little nail file!" she cried gaily.

Chelsea recoiled and went pale. But when Rina's smile didn't fade, uncertainty slowly crept into Chelsea's eyes.

"Oh, don't be stupid, Chelsea," Rina went on impatiently. "Can't you see that I'm only kidding? Why would I kill those two boys? I don't want to steal any computers. I hate computers. Why, I even sabotaged my own computer at school just so I wouldn't have to mess with it." She narrowed her eyes. "Anyway, if you were so sure I was a murderer, why did you agree to go to the movie with me tonight?"

"I didn't say you were a murderer." Chelsea irritably rattled her ice in its cup. "Look, I only agreed to go to the movie with you because I felt sorry for you. You don't have to jump down my throat just for asking a simple question."

Rina tested the sharpness of her fingernail against her palm. "It's nice of you to take an interest."

"I know it's tough coming to a new school,"

Chelsea said, "and like I said, I want to help out."

Rina had decided to kill Chelsea during the movie. All attention would be on the screen then and Chelsea would be sitting very close at hand. Rina felt her mouth water with anticipation.

"You need to find some kids who are more like you to hang out with." Chelsea had fixed Rina in a relentless stare. "I promise you you'd be happier in the long run with a crowd where you fit in."

Rina felt her laughter threatening to brim over, and she raised a napkin to her mouth to hide her amusement. A crowd of vampires, perhaps? Was that the kind of group Chelsea had in mind? That was where she would fit in.

"Have you met any of the kids in the computer club?" Chelsea asked.

"I hate computers," said Rina. "I told you."

"Okay, maybe not the computer club," Chelsea conceded. "But that's the *type* of kid you need, sort of quiet and clue . . . well, quiet. And there's this very nice girl in my English class I could introduce you to, Martha. She makes all her own clothes and she breeds parakeets in her spare time. You two would get along great. I want to help you find your niche."

Rina saw what Chelsea was up to. She wanted to pry Rina away from James and persuade her that she would fit in better with kids who were, in Chelsea's view, clueless, colorless, and hopeless. "It's nice of you to be concerned about my social life." Rina lowered her eyes. "But you don't need to worry about me, Chelsea. I'm fine."

"I guess you're thinking you're friends with James," snapped Chelsea. "I'm afraid I have to be blunt here, Rina. James is nice to *everybody*. All you have to do is make him feel sorry for you and he's all over you, but like I'm always telling him, he's not doing anybody any favors that way. He makes people think he likes them for themselves, when really it's just pity."

Rina could feel her temples pounding with suppressed rage. Normally she did not particularly enjoy killing. But she realized that it would be a pleasure to kill Chelsea. How she would love to dig her teeth into that white neck and choke off the insults!

"You might want to rethink the way you dress," Chelsea went on. "I know these things are different in different schools, but around here not even the biggest geeks in school wear the kind of blue jeans you do. You look like a retired farmer. Now, if you're hard up and I can help out by lending you some clothes, just holler. Of course, we're nothing like the same size, are we? I guess you probably have to buy your clothes in the kiddie department."

Rina glanced at her watch and stood up abruptly. The stupid girl had made her angrier than she would have thought possible. "We're going to be late for the movie. We'd better go."

Chelsea glanced up at the theater marquee. "I don't want to see *Revenge of the Kung-Fu*. All they'd do is kick each other in the face all night."

Rina smiled. She knew she would enjoy giving a good swift kick to Chelsea's chin. "Let's go see *Blood Feast*, then, huh?" she agreed.

They filed into the theater with a few other stragglers. Only a thin crowd was seated in the theater. The feature had begun and a white light beamed through the darkness overhead to the big screen. Its erratic flashing illuminated the rows of plush seats, and Rina saw at once that the theater was not a good place for the kill. An unexpected burst of bright light from the projector might flash just as she attacked. She settled down in her seat, resigned to seeing the movie.

The actor playing the vampire wore white pancake makeup. Rina yawned during the early graveyard scenes as he struggled out of his coffin and stepped groaning into clouds formed by tins of dry ice. But much later she sat up sharply, her attention drawn by what was happening on screen. The actor had sprung on a defenseless passerby and the camera switched to a closeup. Blood ran down the vampire's white cheeks—six-foot-high streams of blood in glowing color. Rina's eyes widened, and she gulped.

"Want some popcorn?" Chelsea hissed in her ear.

Rina shook her head mutely. She was afraid to speak. What if Chelsea spotted her fangs?

Chelsea stumbled over her knees and came back a bit later with a tub of buttered popcorn in one hand and an iced drink in the other. She spilled some drink on Rina as she squeezed back in her seat. "Boy, there's a draft in here," she said, shivering. "I feel like I'm sitting next to a block of ice."

Rina reflected that it had been days since she had fed. No wonder she was cold. She felt embarrassed, too, that her mouth had watered at the unreal image that flickered on the screen before her. "The film is so unrealistic," she whispered.

"Of course it's unrealistic," hissed Chelsea. "It's about vampires. What did you expect? A documentary?"

"All that stuff about coffins," Rina whispered. "Why would anyone want to sleep in a coffin? It would be such a tight squeeze."

"I guess you'd have to be a vampire to understand." Chelsea stuffed a handful of popcorn into her mouth.

"Supernatural beings don't sleep," Rina argued. "They don't need to breathe, either!" She paused a moment. She herself went through the motions of breathing, of course, but purely out of habit. She could stop anytime she wanted.

"You can't expect actors to hold their breath

for an hour and a half," said Chelsea. "Would you be quiet, Rina? I want to see this movie even if you don't."

On screen a girl in a white nightgown screamed and ran away. The vampire's huge figure stood out of focus close to the camera. Rina knew it would only be seconds before there would be another bloodbath, and she covered her eyes with her hands and tried not to think about what was happening on screen.

"You *aren't* closing your eyes, are you? Don't be such a wuss." Chelsea laughed. "What's the use of coming to a movie if you aren't going to watch it?" She pulled Rina's hands away from her eyes.

Blood seemed to be raining over the screen as Rina stared at it, mesmerized. She could feel her fangs razor sharp against her tongue. She struggled to her feet. "Excuse me," she mumbled. Doing her best to keep her mouth shut, she scooted down the row of empty seats.

As she glided up the aisle, she glanced at the moviegoers. Their faces were pink with reflected light from the screen, and from the glazed fascination in their eyes, anyone might have thought they were all vampires.

She ran to the ladies' room and leaned against the blow dryer, breathing heavily. She felt chilled to the bone. Punching the steel button on the blow dryer, she rotated the stainless nozzle so that the hot air blew onto her face, then down onto her cold hands and feet. She caught a glimpse of herself in the mirror and was dismayed to see that her mouth looked slack with desire. Her fangs glowed long and blue in the strange fluorescent light. She reminded herself that however much she wanted to kill Chelsea, she had to force herself to be careful. *It will do me no good to kill Chelsea if I do it so clumsily that the police come after me and I have to get out of town without taking James.*

She pressed her hand to her chest. When she could feel that her heart was quiet, and when she was sure that her fangs had retracted, she left the ladies' room and slipped back into the theater. People were getting up and screen credits had begun to roll. Suddenly Chelsea grabbed her arm. "You missed the best part," Chelsea said. "They drove a stake through the vampire's heart." She pushed open the doors to the lobby. "Wouldn't you love to see a movie just once where the vampire got away with it?"

"Oh, yes," Rina murmured. "I love happy endings."

"I don't know if you'd call that a happy ending," said Chelsea, "but at least it would be different. Sometimes I could shriek from boredom. I mean, nothing ever happens around here!"

The two girls stepped out of the lobby into the parking lot.

"Well, here's my car," said Chelsea.

Rina glanced at the little car. A school parking decal was on the bumper and beside it was a sticker that said, LIFE'S A BEACH.

People were milling about everywhere, and Rina felt opportunity slipping away from her. A butterfly of panic stirred in her stomach.

"See ya," said Chelsea, reaching for her door.

"Wait!" Rina said abruptly. "I've got something I want to show you."

"What?" Chelsea spun around, her eyes narrowed suspiciously. "Is it something about James?"

Rina nodded. "It's in my car." She jerked her head to indicate where she was parked.

Grimly, Chelsea followed her along the sidewalk that skirted the mall. The two girls walked past a Dumpster and some parked vans with a department store logo on their side panels.

"Why did you park so far away?" asked Chelsea.

"It's just a bit farther down now," said Rina.

After they rounded the fleet of vans, Rina could see the car she had inherited from the old lady. The gray Lincoln was parked almost out of reach of the tall light, and in the uncertain illumination at the back of the parking lot, it looked like a ghost car. Behind it grew wild undergrowth that came up to the curb and farther back stood the heavy dark presence of brooding trees.

"There it is," said Rina.

"It looks like an old lady's car!" hooted Chelsea.

"It runs well."

"I'll bet," snorted Chelsea. "Just the thing for going to funerals."

"I hope so," said Rina softly.

"So what is this big surprise of yours?" asked Chelsea.

"You have to see it. I can't explain."

The two girls walked over to the car. Chelsea folded her arms obstinately as Rina unlocked the door. "Are you going to show me? Or am I supposed to get it out of the car for you, too?"

"Take a peek," suggested Rina.

Chelsea hesitated, but curiosity got the best of her and she bent to peer in. At once Rina pulled her to the ground.

"Hey, what—?" cried Chelsea.

Rina felt her sharp fingernails digging into Chelsea's flesh as she wrestled the other girl to the ground.

Suddenly Chelsea bit her viciously. Rina, surprised, loosened her grip and shook her injured arm. The neat curve of Chelsea's teeth marks showed on the flesh and blood welled darkly from the wound. Chelsea rolled over swiftly and scrambled to her feet, her lips dark with Rina's blood. Off balance and half stunned, she staggered into the undergrowth. Chelsea gasped. "Are you out of your mind?" she said. "You are acting like a maniac. What's your problem?"

Rina leapt on her and threw her arms around the larger girl's neck in a death embrace, gripping her tightly. Her fangs slid instantly out of their sheaths as she tore at Chelsea's neck.

The taller girl jerked and fell. Rina was scarcely conscious that they had fallen into the thick underbrush. She could feel Chelsea's blood flowing into her throat, and after the long tantalizing preamble of the movie, she was so excited that her vision was clouded by the bloom of red.

Suddenly Rina heard the low hum of an engine and froze. She wrested her fangs free of Chelsea's throat and lifted her head attentively. She held her breath as the engine drew closer. Throbbing softly, it paused nearby. She could hear the crackle of a two-way radio. Headlights were focused on a patch of vegetation only a few feet ahead. Rina strained to see through the bushes and succeeded in making out the emblem of the police department on the vehicle's door.

She felt chilled. Had they noticed the struggle in the bushes?

Then she heard the engine thrum a retreat in the darkness. The police had driven on. She realized that the cruiser must have been making a routine circuit of the mall. Her solitary car had drawn their attention, but they had not seen the struggle in the undergrowth. The trouble was, if they were making routine checks, then they might return. Rina stood up. The night air stung the gash Chelsea had made in the tender flesh of her arm. She was frantic to get away before the police returned. She staggered to her car and slid in behind the wheel. With a trembling hand she fit the key into the ignition. Blood dripped from her torn arm—the bite had been vicious. Chelsea had fought her hard, and Rina felt drained from the exertion of the kill. Her head was buzzing with panic as she stepped on the gas and sped out of the parking lot. She was so close to having James in her grasp that having the police car show up unexpectedly at the wrong time seemed a bad omen, as if a raven had flown overhead.

11

Chelsea could feel herself wavering in and out of consciousness. She moaned, and when at last she came to, she felt sick to her stomach. The stars shone with unnatural brightness overhead, but she had no eye for their beauty.

She licked her parched lips and was startled by their taste. Her eyes flew open and she uttered a weak cry. She ached all over and was horribly thirsty. She licked her lips again and a sudden electric charge of energy made her shiver.

Her vision seemed to grow sharper as she struggled to her hands and knees. But then a tremor shook her and she had to sit down and grab hold of her knees to keep from falling. The insects buzzing around her ears sounded loud as an orchestra. Near her a brown moth browsed among the bushes. As she watched it in bewilderment, she heard the scales of its wings rub against each other with a noise like folding venetian blinds. She shook her head. It was impossible! Moths didn't sound like venetian blinds. Trembling, she covered her ears with her hands.

When at last she dared to take a fearful peek at the sky overhead, she saw that the stars looked like Christmas decorations wreathed in spun glass. As she watched they swelled as big as plates, then receded to tiny bright pinpoints.

Chelsea held her aching head in her hands. The earth seemed to be whirling. She knew suddenly that she was on a spinning ball in the blackness of outer space. She would have to be careful not to lose her footing. Turning her head toward a soft whooshing sound, she saw the large black shape of a bird settle in a distant tree. The owl blinked, showing round yellow eyes with slit-shaped pupils. She shivered when she heard his small bill click ominously. He must be too far away for her to hear his bill click. She was hallucinating!

Suddenly she remembered Rina's attack on her. Could these strange sensations she was suffering be the aftereffects of shock? She remembered now that she had been pulled down to the pavement and that they had struggled. Gingerly she felt the place on her neck where she remembered feeling a blinding pain. It was only a little tender.

Now James would have to believe her—he

couldn't deny after this that Rina was strange. More than strange—actually psycho. With any luck she'd soon be carried off to the loony bin.

Chelsea's knees felt wobbly, but she managed to struggle to her feet and was relieved to find that she could stand up. She ran her fingers through her tangled hair and pulled out bits of leaves and broken twigs. Taking a barrette out of her pocket, she pulled her long hair up and gathered it on top of her head.

She took a deep breath. Funny—in spite of everything she had been through, she was beginning to feel great. Maybe it was the delightful prospect of getting Rina locked up that had given her such a charge. Really, it was almost worth going through all this if she could get rid of Rina for good.

She picked her way through the bushes and retrieved her purse. At least nothing had been stolen, she thought, checking the contents carefully.

There was no sign of Rina's car, she noticed. It was just as well. Chelsea felt like slapping her till her ears bled, but she didn't think she'd better do that. It would only weaken her case when she went to the police station to press assault charges.

She had the sensation that cold was rolling off of her as if she were a package of frozen vegetables. She hugged herself and shivered. Chills were a symptom of shock, she recalled. She had learned that once in a first-aid class. At least she could walk okay. Staggering a little, she made her way around at the corner of the mall and headed back to her car.

Her car was still parked in front of the theater, but it was the only car parked there now. The theater marquee had gone dark and only a low light burned in the lobby.

Chelsea slid in behind the wheel and peeked at herself in the rearview mirror. She could make out a faint yellow bruise at the base of her neck and she touched it tentatively. That was where she had felt the pain. Suddenly she noticed the two small puncture marks in the middle of the bruise and her eyes widened. She recalled the fang marks of the vampire in the movie! When she thought of the blood that had gushed from his victim's torn throat, something tingled at the roof of her mouth, and Chelsea felt her lips opening against her will as if a fan were unfolding inside her mouth. Her lips parted and white teeth like slender tusks protruded from her mouth, their points resting against her lower lip. Gasping, she covered her mouth hastily with her hands. No! But when she cautiously stuck her index finger in her mouth, she could feel the razor-sharp points of the strange new teeth. She went rigid with horror and suddenly the night was split by her scream.

* * *

Rina sat at the kitchen table doing her homework. She was hoping the routine would help calm her nerves. She supposed she was more than usually on edge because so much depended on getting rid of Chelsea. She drummed her fingers on the kitchen table and stared sightlessly at her class notes. Having that police car show up had seemed uncannily bad luck. The cruiser had glided up like a silent bird of prey, and she was sure it boded no good. The kitchen phone rang and she picked up the receiver at once.

"Rina? Did I wake you up?" James's voice asked.

"N-no," said Rina. She felt herself growing warm with embarrassment when she realized how appalled James would be if he knew that she never slept. "I had trouble sleeping and got up to drink some warm milk," she said quickly.

"Chelsea's mom just called me," he said. "Chelsea never got home tonight, and they wanted to know if she was with me. Of course, I didn't know anything about it. My folks and I were off all night at that opening at the art museum. But when I called Trip he told me you and Chelsea went to the movie together, so I thought I'd better check with you. What time did the movie let out?"

"About ten," said Rina.

"Did she say anything about where she was going afterward?" asked James.

"No," said Rina. "We were parked in different parts of the parking lot, so we said good-bye in the lobby. Do you think something might have happened to her?"

"I hope not. Her folks are thinking maybe she went over to somebody's house to listen to records or something and forgot to call them. Maybe a bunch of them were watching TV and they all fell asleep." His voice trailed off. Perhaps he himself saw how unlikely that was. "Her folks are going to check with the hospitals and call the police, too. The truth is we're afraid that maybe she got carjacked." James paused. "Look, Rina, do you have your windows and doors locked? Make sure. It gives me the creeps thinking of you in that big house alone."

"I'll check them," she said in a small voice. "I promise."

"Maybe she ran out of gas or had car trouble and couldn't get to a phone. I have half a mind to get in the car and go out looking myself. Sitting around here waiting for word is driving me crazy. Her folks promised they'd call me if they got any news."

"Poor Chelsea, I hope—" Rina's voice trailed off.

"Yeah," said James gruffly. "Me, too."

Rina felt a little sick when she remembered Chelsea's crumpled body lying in the bushes. How long would it take the police to discover it?

Her anger at Chelsea had disappeared and she felt appalled at what she had done.

When James had hung up, she stared at the silent phone for a long time. She could feel herself shriveling with guilt. She had hated Chelsea, but now that Chelsea was dead she felt awful about killing her. It was as if her feelings had been colored by James's response. Was that possible? What was happening to her?

Rina trudged upstairs. When she stepped into her room, the white curtain billowed out like a living thing and she cried out and clutched her hand to her throat. The pages of the book on the bed slowly leafed over one by one, as if a ghost were reading. Rina leapt to the window and slammed it shut. What was wrong with her? Over the years her crimes had always slipped through her fingers like sand without leaving a mark on her conscience. She pressed her fingertips to her temples. Crimes! Where had that word come from? It wasn't even a vampire word. Vampires did not commit crimes; they fed.

Rina gulped painfully. This was one of those times when she longed to sleep, to let unconsciousness close over her, but she could not sleep and the night stretched out endlessly before her. She felt like a dumb animal pinned to an operating table awaiting a probing knife. Soon the police would find Chelsea's car. Then they would search the area and come upon the dead body. Rina knew that she was sure to be questioned. She had been the last person to see Chelsea alive.

She pulled the old leather bag out from the bed and tossed its contents on the white bedspread. The jeweled bracelet fell to the floor with a loose clatter, but she did not stoop to pick it up. She clutched the old cameo and pressed it to her lips, wishing with all her heart that she could become again the innocent girl she had been when she had worn it.

12

Chelsea drove aimlessly—she felt too confused to be sure what she should do next. On either side of the street neon lights made bright scribbles in the night, but she scarcely glanced at them. The vampire movie had infected her life, she decided. It had leaked off of the movie screen and stained the ordinary stuff of reality. Somehow she had become a vampire. But wait a minute—that was impossible! Vampires didn't exist.

She felt at the roof of her mouth with her finger. Behind her perfect teeth bulged two unfamiliar ridges. She shivered.

Whatever had happened to her, it must be Rina's fault. Who else but Rina could have left the fang marks in her neck? Chelsea touched the tender spot. Rina must be a vampire. Nothing else made sense. And somehow her attack had made Chelsea into a vampire as well. Maybe being a vampire was contagious, like catching cold.

Chelsea decided to find Rina's house. Hadn't
James said she lived on Oak Street? If only she
could shake Rina hard, perhaps she could make
her cough up a spell that would undo the dam-
age. Then she could drive a stake through Rina's
heart the way the vampire's pursuers had done in
the movie, wedging a sharpened stake between
the ribs and hammering it in with hard sure
blows.

She felt herself tingle with pleasurable anticipation. But Chelsea remembered suddenly that
Rina was far from helpless. For such a small person, her strength had been startling. Of course,
the reason she was so strong was probably because she was a vampire. Superhuman, Chelsea
reminded herself. In her grip Chelsea had felt as
light as balsa wood.

She knew she was in no shape to confront
Rina tonight when she was still reeling from the
shock of what had happened. Her knees trembled and her hands felt icy cold. What strength
she had was wavering and uncertain. Revenge
would have to wait.

A huge tractor trailer passed her, spraying her
windshield with diesel exhaust. She turned on
the windshield wipers, but succeeded only in
smearing the glass. Frowning, she strained to see
the dark highway. Perhaps she could find a dis-
creet dentist in Raleigh who would grind down
the fangs. No one would have to know what had

happened—except Rina, and she wouldn't dare tell. Chelsea decided that she was same as before, really, only she felt lighter somehow, as if with only a little effort she could become the wind and blow away.

Thinking of Rina, Chelsea writhed in hatred. She felt a tingling at the roof of her mouth as her fangs stirred and she thought how she would love to dig them into Rina's throat. Perhaps she would not get the dentist to file them down until after she had confronted Rina.

Chelsea's foot was heavy on the accelerator, and the little Mazda ate up the miles. The car passed exits lit up with golden arches, exits with gas station signs. At last Chelsea realized that she must be almost to Raleigh. Exits had given way to cross streets. She was forced to stop for a traffic light.

A wave of nausea swept over her suddenly and she pulled the car over to the side of the road, clutching at her convulsed stomach. The sick feeling left her feeling damp and weak, and it was some moments before she glanced out the car window and realized that she had pulled up before a seedy-looking bar at the edge of town. The place was evidently open for business, because a dispirited-looking man got out of his car and went in. Jukebox music sounded thinly when Chelsea rolled down her car window.

Next to it stood a pawnshop that looked to

Chelsea like a front for selling stolen goods. The bar and the pawnshop shared the same gravel parking lot, but between them ran a dark space, a narrow alley, as if they shrank from admitting any close association.

Chelsea was startled to see a movement in the alley. A shadow, moving in fits and starts, seemed to be coming toward her. Glancing upward, she realized the parking lot light could not have cast that shadow. As she returned her fascinated gaze to the alley, the thin shadow's borders shifted and changed. *The blob*, she thought uneasily. Then she made out in its depths the slowly coalescing image of a tall, dark boy. The hair at the back of her neck stood on end.

She felt she had to get a closer look at the strange creature. Something close to hunger stirred inside her and before she had a chance to think it over, she leapt out of her car and began walking toward him. "Hi," she said, feeling a little foolish. Funny to think how many times she had said "Unreal!" not meaning anything in particular. But this time it was true—the boy was unreal!

In the darkness she saw his teeth flash white in a sudden smile.

As she edged into the alley, discarded candy wrappers rustled under her feet. Now that she was close to him he seemed real, and she wondered if his emergence from a shifting shadow

had been some sort of optical illusion. He was a dark boy not much older than she was and his hair was pulled back in a ponytail. An antique-looking earring dangled from one earlobe. His eyes were an opaque green, as if they were made of semiprecious stones. She could hear the soft sound of his breathing.

"What's your name?" she demanded. "Mine's Chelsea."

"My name is Vlad, little vampire."

Chelsea glanced guiltily toward the open parking lot. Luckily no one was there who might overhear. "How did you know I was a vampire?" she whispered. "Do I look any different?" Uneasily, she touched her front teeth with her finger. She knew there was the matter of the fangs—but she could take care of those.

"You look wonderful," the boy said, smiling. "But I know my own kind by the smell and the look of them. Just as you knew me. You did know me, didn't you?"

Chelsea wondered if it had been some recognition of likeness that had made her jump out of the car and move toward him. She preferred to think she had been prompted by her sense of adventure. "I only just turned into a vampire," she explained. "I'm going to have it undone as fast as I can."

Vlad bent over, and Chelsea saw in surprise that he was convulsed with silent laughter.

"That's rude," she said sternly. "I don't see what's so funny."

He wiped his eyes and spoke in a stifled voice. "I'm sorry. Indeed it is true that there are old tales about vampires turning back into human beings."

"Well, then—" said Chelsea.

"I am only amazed that anyone would *want* to turn back into a human being," he went on. "To be one of the undead is to rule the dark world as one of the immortals! We stride through the centuries and hold power in our hand—all fear the vampire. Have you considered that we can kill our enemies with no risk? I've killed many, many of mine." He made a sweeping gesture to indicate vast armies of murdered enemies. "And as for sweethearts . . ." he gave her a sly sideways glance, "I make them into vampires and if I wish they can be at my side, young and beautiful, forever. What could be better?"

Chelsea frowned. "It does sound like a good deal when you put it that way."

"Vampires never get fat," Vlad added.

Chelsea patted her concave stomach uneasily. "I never have to worry about my weight," she said. "I play soccer, I ride and swim."

"Ah, but vampires never die, either, little one!"

"I'm not going to die for years and years anyway," said Chelsea. "I'm not worried about something that isn't going to happen until I'm old." But she remembered James's sister's funeral, and a chill seized her. Young people did die. In car accidents and of diseases. It would be terrible to die when she was still young and beautiful. There were so many fun things she hadn't done yet.

"But *never* to die, young one," he said silkily. *"Never!"*

"I don't know why you keep calling me 'young one,'" she said irritably. "I'm seventeen. I'll bet you aren't much older than me."

His lips twitched. "Perhaps not. But I am, as they say, old in sin."

Chelsea laughed suddenly. He looked good, she thought, and he had a certain charm. But the trace of foreign accent turned her off.

"Shall we take a walk together?" he suggested, extending his crooked arm.

Chelsea glanced over her shoulder at the parking lot. "Why walk?" she said. "I've got my car."

Vlad rolled his eyes. "Americans! Slaves to the automobile. No, no, we will walk together along a country road, you and I, so that we may get better acquainted." A long hiss escaped his lips and she was surprised to see that his greenish eyes glowed. "There is much," he said, "that I can teach you."

A gurgle of laughter bubbled from Chelsea's throat as she took his hand. A date with a vampire. At last, something different had happened to her.

The bar and the pawnshop were the only tawdry bits of strip development along the highway. Behind them stood land as it had existed before the highway was cut through. A plain dirt road bisected the substantial tract of pine woods that ran along the highway. They walked deep into the pine woods, and Chelsea, still uncertain of her strength, was glad to lean on Vlad's arm. A slender moon rode overhead in a yellowish glow cast by the lights of the nearby city. "I don't know what's the matter with me." Chelsea sighed. "I try to keep in shape, but since this happened, sometimes I feel great and then all of a sudden I feel awful. It comes and goes."

"It's because you're new." Vlad smiled and bent close to her. She could feel his breath tickling her neck. "I love the taste of new vampires."

"Whoa!" Chelsea jerked away. "I don't want anybody to bite me, thank you very much. I've had enough of that for one night. If you're going to try any funny business I'll go back to my car right now."

He sat down at the side of the road and smiled up at her. "No problem. You go first."

Chelsea backed away from him uneasily. "What are you talking about?"

"Don't you want to taste my blood?" he asked.

To her horror Chelsea felt her fangs slide out of their sheaths.

"You do!" Vlad laughed. "I can tell." He patted the ground beside him. "Come to me, little one. Bite into my flesh and drink."

"But that's so sick!" gulped Chelsea.

He smiled. "Sounds good, though, eh?"

"I won't do it," said Chelsea. "I don't want to get into this stuff. It might be hard to break the habit."

"I'm sure you can stop anytime you want." He smiled. "Wouldn't you like to suck up my supernatural strength? Don't you want to feel your head floating with the delicious pleasure of a vampire blood feast, little one?"

Chelsea wondered if his blood really would make her stronger. She was used to having a lot more energy, and his offer was tempting. She sank to the damp grass. "I don't believe in drinking blood," she said. "I don't want to be judgmental or anything. I mean, I don't care if you want to do it. But it's just not for me. I like kissing and I think I'll just stick with that."

"Kiss me, then," said Vlad. He took the band out of his hair and let it flow free. His hair was dark and wild, unlike any hair Chelsea had ever seen before. She could not take her eyes off his pale face with its strong chin and chiseled cheekbones, framed by the mass of wiry hair. He leaned back, propping himself up with his hands, and tilted his head back. His shirt was unbuttoned at the neck and she could see the arch of his neck and the pulse flickering under the skin. "Kiss me," he said softly. "Kiss me here." He touched his throat.

Chelsea hesitated and then, as if she were moving in a dream, she brushed her lips against his skin.

"Now!" he commanded. "Bite me!"

She felt her lips stretch, as almost against her will her mouth opened wide and her fangs were bared. She drew away from him skittishly. "I don't want to do this," she whimpered.

"Oh, yes, you do." He smiled.

Angrily she grabbed him suddenly and bit hard. As her fangs bit into the flesh, she heard his mocking laughter roaring in her ears. Something wet was flowing into her mouth, filling her cheeks until she was forced to gulp it down. His blood affected her like nothing she had ever drunk before. Her nose grew numb and she felt oddly light-headed. Soon she found herself gulping it down greedily.

At last she fell away from him, a little dizzy.

"Now," he whispered, "it's my turn."

She licked her lips. "Okay," she said, "but watch it. If you hurt me too much I'll make you sorry." She winced when he nipped her skin, drawing blood. The length of his fangs was scary, and she shivered when she caught a glimpse of them.

"Don't look," he suggested, and she turned her face away. It was like giving blood at the blood bank, she decided. Unpleasant if she looked at the huge needles and the slack plastic bag filling up with blood, but not so bad if she thought about something else. What she thought about was how she was going to get back at Rina if it was the last thing she did.

Chelsea was so engrossed in revenge fantasies that she was startled to hear Vlad say something she didn't understand.

"Speak English," she snapped. She touched her neck gingerly where his fangs had punctured the skin. She wondered if makeup would cover the marks.

"I'm sorry," he said thickly. "For a moment I forgot where I was."

"Shouldn't we be looking for a coffin or something?" She buttoned her shirt's top button and glanced anxiously at the sky, no longer certain that the yellowish glow in the sky came from the glow of city lights. "It looks as if the sun might be coming up."

He leaned back on his elbows, completely at ease, and laughed. Already she had learned to hate his easy laughter. "Coffins are for the superstitious," he cried. "And as for dawn—pah!" He snapped his fingers. "I sneer at it." He leapt lightly to his feet. "It is true that new vampires should stay clear of the sun until they are well hardened. At first, they are tender and uncertain, like a new bud. But a vampire as well seasoned as I need never worry about daylight. I dislike the sun, but I do not fear it."

Chelsea frowned. "Well, since I'm new, I think we'd better find a place out of the sun. I don't want to take any chances."

He dusted off his pants, which she noticed were a good deal too tight. "You're welcome to share my humble abode," he said. To her surprise, he turned and began thrashing through the woods. Chelsea hurried after him, feeling springy pine needles under her feet. She had to shield her face with her arms from the branches that snapped in her face. "Why don't the branches hit you?" she cried.

"Because I'm loose," he called over his shoulder. "I don't fight them. Let yourself go."

To her horror, Chelsea saw that Vlad was fading into a shadow. She had almost forgotten that the substantial boy at her side had first appeared to her as a formless apparition. "Don't leave me alone!" she cried.

"You aren't alone. I'm here," he whispered. His voice was scarcely distinguishable from the wind stirring in the branches overhead. Her skin prickled with alarm when a damp tendril of darkness brushed against her cheek. She cried out.

"Try it yourself!" said a voice behind her. "It's not difficult. Remember that you're not flesh and blood anymore. Let yourself go! Let your mind wander."

She spun around, and as he spoke he grew solid before her eyes. She blinked at him unbelievingly. It's some kind of trick, she thought, shivering.

"I can't both explain and fade out at the same time," he said. "I don't know how it is, but when I collect my thoughts and start making sense, the next thing I know I'm solid and stubbing my toe against a tree."

"You are *weird*!" Chelsea cried. "You are truly strange."

"So are you, my little cabbage leaf—now." He smiled and gestured ahead grandly. "Here we are. My humble abode!"

Chelsea gazed in dismay at the tumbledown unpainted shack she glimpsed through the trees. The disused road it stood on was no more than a dirt path. The shack's windows stared back at her blankly. It was completely boarded up. The narrow wooden porch bore a tacked sign that said CONDEMNED BY ORDER OF THE CITY.

"We can't go in there!" she cried. "The floor might cave in. Can't you see the place has been condemned?"

"Suit yourself." He shrugged. "But a fall can't hurt you, you know. You're already dead."

"I am not!" protested Chelsea.

"You're one of the *nosferatu*," he amended. "The living dead."

Chelsea heard the trill of a bird and she

shivered. Daylight would burst on them any minute; she was in no position to be choosy. Gritting her teeth, she walked up to the shack and put one foot hesitantly on the step. She glanced over her shoulder at Vlad. "I hope the wood doesn't give way," she said. "I might break a leg."

"You're lighter than you think," he replied. "Remember, you aren't human."

The way he kept harping on her being a vampire made her so angry that she stomped up the stairs and pushed the door open roughly. It banged against the wall like a pistol shot. Whirlwinds and eddies of dust stirred when she threw the door open, but the rotting wood held her weight. An empty tin can lay in one corner and torn wallpaper hung in strips from the stained walls. A plastic doll lay on the floor on a heap of rubbish and rags. "Couldn't you find a better place to live than this?" she demanded.

Vlad tossed the can aside and sat down in a corner. "I had to take what I could find." He frowned. "Nobody that I've killed lately seemed to carry much cash."

"You need to size them up first," said Chelsea, wrinkling her nose distastefully as she glanced around at the filthy room. "You want to go after somebody driving a Mercedes or maybe a guy that's a runner for the numbers racket."

He smiled. "Clearly, we have much to learn

from each other. I can teach you how to be a vampire and you can teach me how to be an American."

"I noticed right away that you had a funny accent." She glanced at him. "Where are you from?"

"Romania."

Chelsea rolled her eyes. "Why do I ask?" she groaned.

"Deteriorating economic conditions in my own country made it desirable that I move on," he explained, "so I stowed away in the baggage compartment of a plane." He examined his sharp-looking fingernails. Chelsea had never seen a boy with such long, pointed nails.

"You took a big risk stowing away like that," she said. "People die that way."

"Not those of us who are vampires." He smiled. "The thin air at the high altitudes is no problem. I don't need air and I'm quite indifferent to temperature." He pressed his hand to his flat stomach. "My only problem with stowing away is that I suffer horribly from motion sickness. Back in the days when I was human, mortals traveled by foot or on horseback—I liked that better."

"You must be a hundred!" cried Chelsea.

"At least."

She sat down, put her hands behind her head, and leaned back against the wall. It was a dump, but for now, she decided, it would have to do.

"I guess we'd better get some shut-eye," she said.

His eyes crinkled with amusement. "Vampires don't sleep, my pretty."

"You're kidding me!" she cried. "What am I supposed to do all day, then. It's not like we've got any video games. We don't even have a television!"

"I could teach you a thing or two about being a vampire," he suggested, glancing at her under his lashes.

Before Chelsea's horrified eyes, Vlad's flesh grew glossy and green. His eyes bulged and became large blank jellies that threatened to pop out of his skull. It dawned on her that his hair was gone. She could see the gleaming of his bare greenish scalp. He had become bald with only sparse dark hairs standing out from his skull! His face was rubbery and strangely distorted. It grew expressionless as his mouth pursed into a tight O and then contracted to a dot. At the same time she heard a loud buzzing that sounded so strange and directionless that she wondered if it came from inside her head. She pressed her hands tightly over her ears to shut out the noise. "Stop that!" she screamed. "What's happening to you?" His arms and legs had shrunk to black hairy sticks that twitched oddly. He fell to his belly, balancing precariously on the twitching sticks, and she realized he was shrinking. "No!" Chelsea screamed, shutting her eyes tight.

"Don't!" She drummed with her fists and heels on the dusty floor until the buzzing sound grew softer.

When she opened her eyes, he was gone. She leapt to her feet. He had left her alone! She needed someone to teach her how to be a vampire and he had gone!

Choking on a sob, she started to run after him, but then she saw that the sun had leaked in through a broken board over the window. The pale beam of light highlighted dust motes in the air. She froze. The sun was up. Now she didn't dare to go outside. What had Vlad told her? New vampires needed to stay in the dark until they hardened. For all she knew, the sun might burn her or even kill her.

A large green fly perched on the can, its buzz loud and monotonous. Suddenly, Chelsea felt a chill of misgiving. The fly was so large, its hard carapace so strikingly green that it made her ill wondering what it must eat. She was sure it was something horrible. She stared at it, unable to take her eyes off of it. "Vlad!" she shrieked. "It's you!"

The fly buzzed an answer and Chelsea found herself sinking to the floor, doubled over in hysterical laughter as she clutched her hands to her head.

13

"Are you sure Chelsea's car hasn't been found?" Rina asked.

James shook his head. He rested his foot on the railing in front of the school and stared out at the crowd of kids. His face was blank, and Rina wondered what he was thinking. He seemed hardly conscious of her, and she wondered if he remembered she was standing beside him. Then he glanced at her and she saw the sharp light of intelligence in his eyes. That meant that her spell had weakened, and she felt a painful twist of her heart at the knowledge that he was drifting away from her.

"The police put out an all-points bulletin," James said. "The highway patrol in three states are looking for the car. If they could just find it, at least it'd narrow down the search area some. It'd give us something to go on."

"I suppose they looked at the shopping center," suggested Rina, glancing at him anxiously.

James gripped the railing. "I looked there myself. About four this morning, after I talked to you, I went over there and drove over the entire lot. Nothing. Not a trace."

Rina felt goose bumps rise on her arms. James hadn't seen Chelsea's car at the mall? Who would have moved it?

Trip collapsed suddenly on the step at their feet. "I can't believe it," he cried. "Chelsea!"

James swallowed. "For all we know she could turn up all right, Trip. Maybe she's got amnesia or something."

Trip laughed harshly. "You don't believe that any more than I do. Chelsea wandering around in a highway rest stop not able to remember her name or phone number?" Trip shook his head. "I just can't picture it. It's not true." He looked up at them, his eyes glistened with tears. "I'll tell you one thing, whoever did this would never get Chelsea without a fight. Never."

James glanced despairingly at the school building. "I don't see how we can go all day listening to junk about chemistry and computers. I'm about to go out of my mind." He fingered the base of his neck, and the unconscious gesture made Rina wince.

A petite blond girl ran up and threw her arms around James. "I just heard!" she cried. "Poor Chelsea."

A group of kids stood awkwardly aside.

"Maybe it'll be all right," one of them suggested timidly. "If she's been kidnapped, I mean, it's not like they've found a body or anything. We've got to hope for the best."

Trip's face looked shiny and red. "I don't know how much of this I can take," he said, standing up abruptly. They all watched as he lurched away, heading toward the parking lot.

"He ought not to be driving in the shape he's in," one of the girls said.

A guy wearing low-slung jeans weighted down with pockets came over. "Any word from the police?" he asked.

James shook his head.

"I'm going home," murmured Rina. Hoisting her book bag over her shoulder, she walked away. When she glanced back over her shoulder, James was standing in the middle of a growing crowd. Even from the distance, Rina could see his unguarded expression of grief. It seemed fitting somehow that at this time James should be mobbed by his friends while she went to her car alone.

Rina felt heavy and numb as she made her way to her car and drove away. She knew that she couldn't sit through a long day at school with so much uncertainty churning in her mind. She drove to the mall and pulled her car around to the back of the parking lot. It troubled her to think that the police might catch her revisiting the scene of the crime, but her anxiety was so strong she couldn't stop herself. She got out of the car and gazed around at the thick undergrowth that pressed up to the curb. In the harsh light of morning the bushes looked dry and weedy. Perhaps she had come to the wrong place, she told herself, but then, standing on the curb, she saw broken twigs and crushed leaves. This must have been where Chelsea's body had lain hidden. If so, it was gone. Nothing remained at all—neither Chelsea's purse nor any shred of torn clothing. Rina tried to tell herself that this couldn't be the right place. One blackberry patch by a featureless long curb looked much like another, she told herself. Someone else might have trampled the underbrush in this spot. But as she turned to go a glimmer of light made her turn her head sharply. She caught her breath as she spied several long blond hairs clinging to a bush. Chelsea had been here, but now she was gone. Rina felt dizzy with the sudden implication. *Chelsea bit me and I was bleeding*, she thought. *What if Chelsea drank some of my blood?*

Rina was stiff with fear as she drove back to her house. Chelsea as a vampire was a terrifying thought. Rina had wanted to put Chelsea out of the picture, but what if instead she had only made her adversary far more powerful?

When she pulled up into her driveway, it took her a moment to notice that James's car was parked at the curb. Then she saw that he was at her front door, pounding on it. She jumped out of her car and shouted his name.

He spun around. As she ran up the steps he looked visibly relieved. "Am I glad to see you," he cried. "I was getting ready to break into the house."

"What's happened?" she cried. "Have they found Chelsea?" For a split second she allowed herself to think that the police had recovered Chelsea's body and that was the reason she had not found it in the underbrush.

"I don't know. I haven't heard a thing. They've got all these crisis counselors coming in at school, and I couldn't face it. I don't know where Trip has got himself to, but when I came over and you weren't here, my imagination started doing overtime. I was thinking I'd find your battered body inside."

She unlocked the door. "Come on in. I'll fix you some tea."

He looked around as they went in. "This reminds me of my great-grandmother's house."

"I haven't done much to it," admitted Rina. "This is the way it was when I inherited it."

James smiled. "I think you're picking up the local accent, Rina. You're starting to sound like you come from around here."

She flushed. "Languages come easily to me. I have a good ear." She realized that after only a few weeks of going to high school she was starting to sound more like the others. Odd. She had hoped to change James to be like her. But instead she was becoming more like him.

She went into the kitchen and reached in the cupboard for a kettle. Her head was whirling and she needed time away from James to think. *If Chelsea is a vampire now,* she told herself, *the first thing she will want to do, probably, is to make James into a vampire, too, so they can be close again.* James would have to be warned. But how?

To Rina's dismay, James followed her into the kitchen. "It sure is clean in here," he observed. "We've always got jam out on the counter, notes stuck to the fridge, newspapers all over the place. This looks as if no one ever uses it."

Rina smiled weakly. If he only knew. She put the kettle on, then turned around to face him.

"You know why I came over here, Rina?" he said quietly.

"No!" she cried, not wanting suddenly to hear what he had to say.

He put his hands on her shoulders and regarded her seriously. "Those nights when you were in my room I don't know what it is you did to me, but I want you to do it again. I can't stand going on this way. It hurts too much. When I think about poor Chelsea—" He broke off and turned away from her. "She's dead, Rina. She's got to be. And when somebody finds her body rotting in the woods somewhere, I don't want to be around."

"You loved her," cried Rina. The words seemed to be wrenched from her painfully.

James looked away. "Maybe. In a way. But once or twice I thought I wouldn't care if she disappeared." He looked at Rina blankly. "And now that she has, I feel so guilty I can't stand it."

The kettle emitted a piercing shriek. Rina took it off the burner with shaking hands and poured hot water into a cup. The tea bag darkened and grew limp underwater. She shook some stale cookies out and bore the tray into the living room.

James plopped down on the couch. "You won't help me out, will you?" he said in an expressionless voice. "Is it because I said I loved Chelsea? Are you mad at me?"

Rina regarded him helplessly. Sun was streaming in the kitchen window and she realized suddenly that she loved the clarity in James's eyes. The light hairs on the backs of his arms, the ink-stained fingers, his slow and easy smile, seemed individually his and heartbreakingly precious. She had wanted James to come to her willingly, and now that he had, she discovered she no longer wanted him to be a vampire. It was as if she had taken a sweet morsel into her mouth and found that it had lost its flavor. "I can't do it—I don't want you to change," she said sadly.

James leapt to his feet. "Heck no, why

change," he asked bitterly, "when things are so good the way they are?"

He slammed the door behind him as he stormed out, and Rina regarded the door in despair.

The shard of sunshine that had leaked in where the shack's boards were cracked had disappeared. Night must be falling, but it seemed to Chelsea that several lifetimes had passed instead of only one day. All day, Vlad had dazzled her by showing her the fascinating array of existences possible to her now that she was a vampire—she could change shape at will and could come close to disappearing if she turned into a mist. Incredible. She could feel herself swelling with her new power.

"You have a natural aptitude for being a vampire," Vlad conceded. "We'll make a great team."

Chelsea did not answer. She had no intention of being a "team" with Vlad, but she figured it was smarter not to say so. Having seen all he could do, she was slightly afraid of him. She had decided that as soon as she had learned everything she could from him, she would get rid of him. She didn't want to spend an eternity with some cheap guy with a foreign accent and a superior-sounding laugh. She wanted to get back together with her own friends from school. But intuitively she felt it would be safer to slip away

without announcing it. She hadn't told Vlad
where she lived or even her last name. Once she
got away from him she was okay. He would
never know how to find her.

"I'm stronger now," she said, stretching.
"Tomorrow I need to get back to school. I don't
want to get too far behind with my work.
Besides, my parents are probably fit to be tied by
now."

"Why bother with school?" Vlad shrugged.

"Everybody's got to go to school," said
Chelsea. But she wondered suddenly why this
should be true. Compared to turning into a bat,
school seemed dull.

"You've got all the time in the world to learn
anything you're interested in," Vlad pointed out.
"I myself am learning constantly. Until I mislaid
my paperback during a scuffle last night, I was
reading *The Remembrance of Things Past* in
French." He rolled the can next to him gently
with his finger. "Human passions fascinate me."
He glanced up at her. "And it's not as if you wish
to prepare for a career, is it?"

"I might," said Chelsea. But she remembered
suddenly how she hated the rinky-dink rules at
school and the stultifying boredom of sitting in
classrooms on hot afternoons. She remembered
the air thick with chalk dust, the creaking of
desks—it wasn't as if she had ever cared much
for studying. She would have done a lot less of it

if her parents hadn't kept nagging her—they were sort of fixated on the subject of school. They might not notice that she had become a vampire—they weren't all that observant. But they would certainly notice if she dropped out of school.

Vlad reached into the tin can and tugged out a thick envelope that had lain curled inside it. Chelsea's sharp eyes made out that its return address was an airline. Vlad fanned two airline tickets out in his hand and smiled. "Tickets to Las Vegas," he said. "I took them from someone just the other day. Have you ever visited Las Vegas?"

Chelsea found herself leaning closer to him, eyeing the tickets hungrily. "No," she said. "I hear they have great shows there. It would be lots of fun."

Vlad smiled. "Let's go together," he suggested.

Chelsea hesitated. She could always ditch Vlad later. After she had seen Las Vegas. "Why not?" She smiled at him.

14

Rina left her jeans soaking in bleach in the bathtub upstairs. Chelsea's gibe about her clothes had stung and she had decided she wanted to make her jeans look faded and old like the other kids'. In the parlor she threw back the heavy draperies, but the sheer curtains under them still gave the light in the room an eerie undersea quality. On the mantel dried flowers stood stiffly under a glass dome as if to underscore that life had stopped inside the house. The loud tick of the ormolu clock seemed to sound behind Rina's eyes. She felt she couldn't stand it anymore. Suddenly she ran upstairs and pulled pillows off the bed. Hugging the pillows tightly, she ran back down to the parlor. She tottered precariously on a chair as she put the pillows up on the shelf and heaped them around the clock to muffle the sound.

Breathless, she scrambled down from the chair, snatched up the phone, and punched the redial button.

"Browning's Building Supply," said a nasal voice.

"This is Larina Cargiale. Those workmen you promised to send still haven't arrived."

"They ought to be there any minute, hon. They must have got held up on the last job."

Rina hung up. She felt as if she were trembling, but when she held her hands out in front of her she saw that they were steady. Suddenly the doorbell sounded. When she opened the door, a small slight man with faded blond hair stood before her. "You the lady that needs the new door?"

Rina nodded.

"This it?" The man ran his fingers down the smooth painted surface of the door and glanced up at its impressive height. "Nothing wrong with this door," he said, rapping it smartly with his knuckles. "Solid oak—they don't make 'em like this anymore."

"I know, but the mail slot has got to go," said Rina.

He shrugged. "I guess you're worried about security."

She was relieved to put such a harmless-sounding label to her fears. "That's it," she said.

"I never heard of a burglar running a wire through a mail slot," he said. "I mean, sure it could be done. But it's a heck of a lot easier for them just to break a window."

"All the same," said Rina, "I don't want the mail slot." She knew that a determined vampire would be able to slip through it in minutes. *Even if Chelsea is a vampire, she won't have the first idea how to go about making herself into a mist. She has no one to teach her. Chances are she is stumbling around somewhere in a state of confusion, wondering what has happened to her.* These rational, sensible conclusions did little to comfort Rina. She could tell herself that the precaution wasn't necessary, but still she felt a need to take action—any action—to relieve the tension inside her.

As the men worked, the shrill sound of a power drill drowned out the ticking of the clock. Rina ran upstairs and checked again to make sure all the windows were locked. Perhaps she would see about having shutters put in so that she could close them tightly over the windows at night. In a way, she realized, Chelsea was the least of her worries. It was very possible she was focusing on her fear of Chelsea to keep from thinking about things that frightened her even more.

The ground seemed to be shifting under her feet. She had thought she wanted James to be a vampire. But when he had come to her and asked her to drink his blood, she hadn't been able to suck the life from him. Something was dreadfully wrong with her. She couldn't trust herself anymore. A strange tenderness had touched her soul, and she was terrified that it was making her weak.

When she had shown up at school that first day, she had been focused like a laser on a single goal—to win James as her own. But as a single beam of white light is shattered by a prism into an infinite and dazzling fan of colors, she had found herself losing focus over the days that followed. Now her jeans were soaking in bleach in the bathtub because she wanted them to look like those the other kids wore. She had even found herself wondering how she would score on the new SATs!

Jeans and SATs had nothing to do with vampires! The ominous thing was that whole moments passed at school when she forgot she was a vampire. Sometimes the sudden recollection of what she was hit her like a bucket of cold water.

She stared at her pale face in her bedroom mirror. "Give it up," she said out loud. "It's not for you. You're different, remember?"

When she went downstairs, the men were carrying their tools to the car. The lawn out front was deep green with moving shadows and Rina could hear the wind in the trees. "Looks like we may get some rain," commented the man.

Rina wrote a check. When the men had gone, she locked the door and leaned against it, breathing heavily. A clap of thunder sounded in the distance. What was happening to her? she wondered. Suddenly it seemed as if everything that mattered most was spinning out of her control.

When night fell, Rina could no longer contain herself. She grabbed her cape and left the house on foot. A fresh breeze stirred her dark curls. She reached back and lifted her hair free of her collar. Still warm from feasting on Chelsea's blood, she could feel her supernatural strength springing in the tense arches of her feet as if she were about to be launched to the stars. She flexed her hands, conscious of their growing power. How could she have doubted that she was a vampire? She had both the vampire's bitter strength and the unnatural hunger that fed that strength.

She unclasped the cape and tossed it negligently over the banister of the gazebo. The grass did not bend under her feet as she slipped out of the yard. She made her mind blank to try to wipe out the painful thoughts that had troubled her, and she felt herself fade and grow wispy. She became a dark and formless figure blending into the night.

In a twinkling, she found herself at the graveyard. Distant lightning flashed in the sky just above the trees that bordered the cemetery, and the air crackled with electricity. In the fresh dampness she could smell the mold that worked its way in the crumbling tombstones. She willed herself back to a solid human shape and soon she felt the rough surface of the iron palings under her fingers. The crossbar pressed against the instep of her slippers. In a quick, nervous gesture, she touched her cheek, to reassure herself of her own solidity. Wind rattled the leaves of the big old oak.

Hundreds of brass plates lay in the grass beyond her, each of them marking the end of a life. Each life was like a poem. It reached its end and came to a full stop in a silence that seemed inevitable and right. This was the peace and order she had disturbed when she had made Chelsea into a vampire. She had done a terrible thing.

Letting herself lean back, she tightened her grip on the iron palings so that she wouldn't fall and she let one foot dangle free. She had once swung on the churchyard gate with her foot dangling this way. Remembering her human childhood, she felt a hot stab of regret. *You're a vampire*, she reminded herself viciously. *Face it. You can pass as a human being, but no power on earth can make you human. You have never been able to find the spell for it because a spell like that DOESN'T EXIST.*

Remembering the first time she had seen James in this very place, she turned her head toward the new grave and gasped suddenly. He was there! A flash of lightning bleached him white like an overexposed photograph. Then he was plunged once more into darkness. A loud crack of thunder sounded and Rina felt the iron fence shudder in her palms.

"Rina!" James yelled suddenly.

He had seen her. She stepped down from her perch. As if her feet had a will of their own, she stumbled out the open gate and ran to him. He held his arms out and as she ran into his embrace she felt a sudden rush of feeling. She wanted to melt into him and to know nothing but the warmth of his embrace.

"You shouldn't be out on a night like this." He threw an anxious glance at the sky. "That last one was pretty close. But then, I shouldn't be out here, either. I guess I'm crazy."

Rina drew away from him a little. "No," she said, "you aren't crazy. I understand why you are here. You came here to talk to your sister."

"I *am* crazy, then," he said, his voice hardening. "Because Susan's dead. Chelsea's dead, too."

James flinched as lightning flashed. The sudden light bleached his face so that for an instant he looked as if he had been carved from marble. "We're going to end up dead ourselves if the next bolt hits us."

Rina let her hand rest lightly on his head, willing him to accept what she must tell him. He had to know, but everything in her shrank from telling him. She didn't think she could bear it if he turned away from her in disgust. She fixed him in her anguished gaze. "I cannot die,

James," she whispered. "I am one of the *nosfe-ratu,* the undead."

James's head jerked suddenly as if she had slapped him. "You mean you're a vampire, don't you?"

She nodded.

James laughed harshly. "Why does that make sense to me?"

"Because it's the truth," Rina said in a small voice.

"When you came into my bedroom those nights you were drinking my blood, weren't you?"

"I'm sorry," she whispered. Suddenly she felt too ashamed to meet his eyes.

"You did it to the janitor, too, didn't you?"

Rina nodded miserably.

He gripped her shoulders. "Why didn't you kill me, Rina? Vampires kill people, don't they? Isn't that what they do?"

"I want you to live!" Rina felt hot tears fill her eyes.

He laughed shortly. "Well, right now I don't see much point in it." Releasing her, he sat down suddenly on the grass.

A fresh breeze whipped Rina's hair. "Life will be sweet for you again, James," she murmured. "It will."

"If what I've seen so far is any sample, I'm not holding my breath."

In the darkness, his pale coloring gave the impression of a faint luminescence. It was this ghostly color and the scent of grave dust that had drawn her to him on the night that seemed so many lifetimes ago.

Now in some odd way they had become friends. It wasn't exactly what she had expected. But it was good. Rina could hear rain, a soft swooshing sound drawing closer. She sank to the grass beside him.

"Maybe I should try being a vampire like you," said James ironically. "Could you make me into one? It seems to work out okay for you."

Rina shook her head sadly. Being a vampire was a terrible thing. She didn't know how to explain that.

He closed his eyes and smiled. "What I remember about your bite was that after that, for a minute, nothing seemed to matter. I felt peaceful. Is that what being a vampire is like?" He glanced at her.

"No," she gulped. "That's what death is like."

"I liked it," he said simply.

Rina heard the raindrops on the oak coming faster and more urgently. Cold rain pelted her head. "You're upset about Chelsea," said Rina. "You don't know what you're saying."

"I wonder if they're ever going to find her," James said wearily. "Sometimes they don't find people, you know. Maybe just a few bones surface years later and nobody knows who it was." He hugged his knees. "I never realized before how awful it would be not knowing for sure—wondering if she could still be alive out there somewhere. I keep thinking maybe some creep is holding her prisoner in a cabin, torturing her. She could get away. Or maybe she's already dead and her body's rotting under a pile of leaves somewhere. If I just knew what happened I feel like I could deal with it." He clenched his fists.

"I know what happened to her," Rina said quietly.

"How can you?" James stared at her. His breath was coming in short gasps, which alarmed her, but she knew she had to go on. "Does this have something to do with your being a vampire?"

Rina nodded unhappily.

"What did you do to her, Rina?" James grabbed her wrist. Wisps of his wet hair were plastered to his face. He pulled Rina to her feet and they stood facing each other.

"I think I made her into a vampire." It seemed as if her words were acid burning away the trust between them. She felt a pulse pounding in her temples when she met his gaze. Though she had willed him to understand, she saw no answering sympathy there, and her throat clogged suddenly with tears.

"It was an accident," she cried. "I didn't mean to do it. I went back to the mall and looked for her where I left her, but she was gone. I got hurt in the fight and somehow she must have drunk some of my blood. I didn't mean for that to happen. I only meant to kill her."

"You tried to *kill* her?" yelled James.

"I'm sorry!" cried Rina.

"It's a little late for that now, isn't it?" shouted James. He grabbed her arm and jerked her along beside him.

"Where are we going?" She stumbled along at his side.

"We can't talk here," he said savagely. "I don't know if you vampires die when lightning strikes, but I sure will."

As they hurried through the driving rain, Rina was cold with apprehension. Her spell had not been strong enough after all to make him accept what she had done.

It would have been easy for her to tear herself free of his grasp, but she didn't want to. She would rather be near him, she realized, even when he was furious at her, than to go home to her lonely house.

They reached James's white Toyota. He jerked its door open and pushed her in. Through the pouring rain she could see his dark figure passing before the car. Overhead a streetlight drowned in the downpour, shedding only enough illumination to show shapes in the rain. The inside light of the car flashed on when he opened the driver's side door and she saw his face, stretched tight and unreal, like a mask. He slid in and slammed the door. When he shook his head, a shower of drops struck her.

"Is this your car?" Rina asked.

James's short laugh was harsh. "Yeah, it's my car. I did not steal it. We aren't all criminals like you."

"I'm not a criminal!" Rina gulped. "I'm a vampire. It's just the way I am. It's not my fault."

"I can't believe this." He pushed his wet hair out of his eyes with his hands and she heard that he was gasping for breath as if he had been running.

"You don't believe that I'm a vampire?" she asked.

He looked at her and suddenly laughed. "Oh, I believe that, all right."

When Rina saw the expression on his face, she felt sick. She shouldn't have told him the truth, she thought. She couldn't stand for him to hate her. "I thought you were just saying that being a vampire wouldn't be so bad," she said in a small voice.

"That was just talk," he said savagely. "But this is real, Rina. Chelsea has disappeared. Where is she? What have you done with her?"

"That's just it!" she cried. "I don't know! She's

disappeared! When I went looking for her, she wasn't there and her car was gone. What if she comes after me and tries to kill me?"

He interrupted her. "She can't kill you," he said impatiently. "You just told me you're one of the undead, right? So she can't kill you."

"There are ways," Rina said, wincing at the thought of stakes of wood and consuming fires. She resolutely pushed those dangers out of her mind and grabbed James's arm. "If she can get me out of the way, she'll probably try to make *you* into a vampire next because she'll want for you to be together. That's why I had to warn you. Oh, James! Can you forgive me?"

He gently removed her hand from his arm. The windshield was blurred with rain. "It's not up to me to forgive you," he said grimly. "It's up to Chelsea now, isn't it?"

Rina hugged herself and shivered. "I know you're mad at me. It's an awful thing I did." She shot him a quick glance. "But I think Chelsea might like being a vampire."

15

Chelsea decided she adored flying first class. She glanced at the apple-cheeked boy in the seat beside her and giggled.

He surreptitiously ran his tongue across his front teeth and then reddened. "Do I have something stuck between my teeth?"

"No." She settled back in the seat. "I'm in a good mood, that's all. I'm on a winning streak."

"Oh, right!" he said. "You got on this flight at Las Vegas, didn't you?"

"Yeah." Chelsea sighed. "It was the first time I'd played roulette. Somehow I just *knew* what number was going to come up. The slot machine was the same. I couldn't seem to lose. I think I'll buy a lot of new clothes with my winnings when I get home. I want to really knock out my friends when I see them."

"I'm flying to North Carolina for a college interview," he confided. "And I'm kind of nervous. Have you decided yet where you want to go to college?"

"Actually," Chelsea began. Suddenly she realized she didn't want to lose status by confessing that she was dropping out of high school. "Harvard," she said airily.

The boy looked impressed. "You must have a lot of self-confidence."

"I do." Chelsea grinned. She glanced across the aisle to where Vlad was. His eyes were closed and his face was faintly green. Chelsea couldn't understand how somebody could be so weak-willed as to let motion sickness get to them like that.

She pulled a fashion magazine out of the elastic pocket on the seat ahead of her and leafed through it with interest. She could wear anything she wanted now, she realized. The familiar refrain, "You aren't going out of the house in *that*, young lady," was history. No more parents bugging her.

The plane touched down with a bump. "Please remain in your seats until the plane has come to a complete stop," said the loudspeaker. As if this was the cue to leap up, passengers immediately began groping in the overhead compartments for their luggage. Vlad struggled to his feet just as a falling bag hit his head. He fell into his seat and groaned. "I'm so sorry," cried a blonde, bending to pick up her bulging bag. It had a tennis racket strapped to its side. Somewhere in back a baby shrieked.

Chelsea smiled to herself. No carry-on luggage for her. But then she had had her own reasons for urging Vlad to check their two slender bags. She stood up, offered Vlad a hand, and helped him to his feet.

A man in a suit tried to squeeze by. "Can I just get by here?" he said impatiently. "I've got a connection to make."

Vlad whipped around suddenly and snarled.

The man fell back and sat down in the aisle. He looked stunned.

A flight attendant bent over him solicitously. "Are you all right, sir? Do you need me to call ahead for a wheelchair?"

He wiped his red face with a handkerchief. "I shouldn't have had that second drink," he choked.

Chelsea hurried Vlad off the plane. "Don't keep pulling at me," he snarled.

She bent her head close to him and whispered, "Did you *have* to show that man your fangs?"

"I won't be trampled by a foul-smelling bore," snarled Vlad. "I'd have him for dinner," he expelled his breath sharply, "but I hate airline food."

Chelsea glanced around as they made their way down the covered flexible corridor to the gate. A group of men carrying briefcases were staggering along behind them.

Ahead of them a girl with her hair in neat

French braids rushed into her father's out-stretched arms.

"Are we there yet?" A child tugged at his mother's clothes. "I want ice cream."

Chelsea wondered why she had never noticed before how stupid human beings looked. All those pink and shiny faces. Most of them could stand to get some exercise, too. She herself felt amazingly fit now that she was a vampire.

"You go get the bags," she suggested. "I'll get the car. The long-term parking is too far for you to walk, the way you're feeling."

Vlad glanced up at the arrow that said BAGGAGE CLAIM and obediently moved in that direction.

Chelsea smiled as he disappeared into the elevator. Taking two steps at a time, she ran up the escalator, then trotted across the ticketing area. The glass doors swung open and she could see that evening had darkened the parking decks that stood directly ahead. She raised her hand. "Taxi!" she shrieked.

The taxi skidded to a stop in front of her and she got in. Inside it smelled of stale cigarette smoke and she wrinkled her nose distastefully as it sped away.

A mile or so down the road stood the sign LONG-TERM PARKING. The taxi pulled up at the entrance of the parking lot and Chelsea got out. She tipped the driver lavishly and ran to her car.

She was making good time, and with any luck, she would be out of the airport before Vlad had even claimed the luggage.

Chelsea hummed as she followed the signs saying AIRPORT EXIT. Soon she was speeding down the open highway toward Tyler Falls. It was funny to think that Rina had done her a favor by turning her into a vampire. Chelsea's face darkened. Not that that was any excuse. It was pretty clear that Rina hadn't intended to make her into a vampire—she had meant to kill her. And now, Chelsea was determined to pay her back.

An hour later, Chelsea had reached the familiar streets of her hometown. She let her car glide silently past the darkened high school. A few low lights burned inside, but the overwhelming effect was both dank and depressing. The buildings might have belonged to sightless cave dwellers, she decided, so insistent was their ugliness. *It's no Las Vegas*, she thought, casting a critical glance over the school grounds. She was glad she was finished with school. She had never liked it much to begin with. The only problem was she knew she would miss her friends.

Chelsea made a face thinking of how complicated her situation had become. She was anxious to see her friends again, but it was awkward. She had been away at Vegas for days, so everyone must be wondering what had happened to her. In fact, the police were bound to have been notified. She decided it would be better to case the situation before she let anyone find out she had returned. Particularly since she had already decided not to go home and not to go back to school. That part was kind of tricky. The last thing she wanted was for her parents to find out she was back in town. Even if she did have all the powers of a vampire now, she couldn't exactly see herself using them on her mother. It was best, she decided, to steer clear of her folks.

Chelsea sped toward James's house. She knew the tree-lined streets of that area well and drove at once to the lake and grassy common at its center. She and James had often parked on the circular drive that ran around the lake. She pulled her car up there under a tree, slipped the keys in her pockets, got out and faded into the shadows, giggling as she felt herself go vague and formless. A minute later the giggle sounded from a shadow as Chelsea let herself slide like melting gelatin from one puddle of darkness to another. Hearing the ultrasonic squeak of a bat as it glided over her head, she instinctively reached the tendrils of her hands up and plucked it from the air. Her molecules jelled suddenly into the recognizable form of Chelsea. The change was so sudden, her head rang and she had to pause a moment to collect her thoughts. She remembered now that she had caught a bat. She could feel the tiny creature's wings frantically struggling in her cupped palms. It was so small its bones must be delicate, like a sardine's, and for a moment she considered eating it whole. Her grip tightened until it could no longer squirm at all. She could feel it, warm and throbbing with fear as she lifted it to her lips and bit off its head. She sipped the blood delicately from the corpse and then tossed the dry bit of brown fur to the ground. *Nice*, she thought, licking her lips. It reminded her of the tiny chocolates left on hotel pillows.

She stretched out her arms luxuriously. Already she could actually become formless faster than Vlad himself: He had gibed that she was good at it because her mind was empty to begin with, but Chelsea chalked that up to jealousy. It was so good to be away from him. *Soo* . . . But as her mind tried to form the next vague thought she began to slip into formlessness again and she let herself go with a sigh. She slid through the night to James's house, more a beam of intention than any sort of recognizable being. Suddenly she was simply there, hovering, no more than a vapor, at the back window that overlooked the kitchen. The vapor cast a vague and shifting shadow when the light from the kitchen window shone on it. But when Chelsea's consciousness strained to understand the voices coming from the kitchen, the mist at once began to take shape. In seconds, it was recognizable as Chelsea.

Glancing down, she saw the new shoes she had bought in Vegas and the gleaming expanse of perfect legs under a short, rayon skirt. She had to cover her mouth quickly to stifle her giggle. *What a lucky thing,* she thought, *that whatever I'm wearing dematerialized with me.* It could have gotten embarrassing if she had materialized suddenly not wearing a stitch.

"Still no word about Chelsea," said Mr. Ryder's voice. Chelsea peered in the window and saw that the family was seated around the kitchen table. It pleased her to think they were talking about her. It was cool—like getting to go to your own funeral and hearing all the nice things people said about you after you were dead.

"Her poor parents," said Mrs. Ryder. "They must be half crazy with grief. If only they knew for sure what had happened to her—but not to know! I can't imagine anything worse." She sighed.

"Everybody knows she was carjacked," said Danny in a froggy ten-year-old voice. "They haven't found the car—that proves it!"

"I have to hope she's okay," said Mrs. Ryder, blowing her nose noisily.

I'm fine. Chelsea smiled in the darkness.

"Everybody at school is sure she's dead," said James.

Chelsea jumped in surprise. His voice

sounded so strained that she didn't recognize it at first. She peeked in the window, but his back was to her and all she could see was the stretch of his shoulders under his shirt and his sleek blond hair. He sounded upset, and that gave her a warm and satisfied feeling. He was crazy about her, obviously. Only now, perhaps, did he realize the deep and abiding love he had felt for her. She remembered reading a book like that once. A wreath of roses had framed the sweethearts pictured on its cover.

"Molly Haggerty is going to have a séance tomorrow night. She's trying to get in touch with Chelsea's spirit," James said. "Her idea is that the spirit can tell us where Chelsea's body is hidden. Molly figures the more of Chelsea's friends are there, the more likely it is that the spirit will show up."

"Honestly!" exclaimed Mrs. Ryder. "Of course, you're not going, James."

"We're all going," said James.

Chelsea covered her mouth firmly to keep her laughter from giving her away. What a break! She saw now how she could do it! She could slip into Molly's den under cover of darkness and grab James without anyone's even seeing her. He was the one she most wanted to make into a vampire anyway.

She frowned. The only problem was that he was a little bit straitlaced about things that weren't strictly on the up-and-up, and she wasn't sure how he would react to being a vampire. It was probably better to make him into one first and then talk over the fine points later. Her fangs slipped out of their sheaths.

What fun it would be to suck James dry and have him white and helpless at her feet until she poured her own life-giving blood down his throat. Once he'd tried being a vampire, he'd see what a good deal it was. And then they could talk about who else they wanted to get to join them. Trip, of course, but after that she wasn't so sure. It would be like having a special sort of secret club.

Chelsea shook with silent laughter. She had never been able to get James to do what she wanted before, but after this everything would be different. When he was a trembling, new vampire, he would need her desperately.

Chelsea's shapely legs compressed like an accordion. Her pale skin grew velvety and black and she swelled to a plump roundness. Her nose turned up and her lips rolled into her mouth, leaving only the black bony ridge of her mouth. Inside the kitchen, the Ryder family talked earnestly, unaware that a velvet-furred creature as large as a St. Bernard clung to their back stoop. The huge hulk was shrinking with such speed that it gave the impression of a black blur. When the blur of motion stopped, only a small mouse-like creature with tiny velvety ears remained. It grasped the porch pillar and began climbing up it, arm over arm, its sharp, hooklike nails digging into the wood. When it had reached the top of the pillar, it stretched out bony arms and uttered a tiny squeak. Its bones were no heavier than matchsticks and black membranes hung loosely between them. The small furry head turned a bit, then bat wings spread and the creature glided to a nearby tree. It dipped over a tall woodpile, catching an updraft. Only a dog raised his head as the bat passed, and its head quickly sank again in sleep.

The small bat winged into the night, looping and dipping near the streetlight as if to catch the insects drawn by its glow. Its tiny eyes glowed with a strange green intelligence in the snub-nosed furry face, and when it opened its mouth, it showed a flash of white fangs. "Chelsea," it hissed softly. On the whole, she decided, she preferred being a bat to turning to mist. As a bat she could think straight and she never had to worry about forgetting her name.

16

Partives *Partners in crime,* thought James as he stared out the classroom window. Wasn't he being as bad as Rina if he didn't tell anybody what she had done? She had turned him into her accomplice. The problem was he couldn't very well announce that Chelsea was a vampire. People were already giving him strange looks. He didn't know if they were trying to figure out whether he was cracking up or if they actually suspected him of murdering Chelsea. But he was pretty sure that if he told anybody that Rina had made Chelsea into a vampire, he would fast find himself staring at the blank wall of a psychiatric hospital.

The bell rang. James stood up and moved wearily toward the door. Mr. Butler beckoned to him, and reluctantly James went over to the teacher's desk. He vaguely remembered that he used to get depressed thinking that someday he might end up looking as bad as Mr. B. Now that thought seemed amusing. He couldn't imagine himself getting old and fat, his pants peppered with chalk dust. He could scarcely imagine getting as far as next week, much less twenty years ahead.

"I just wanted to say, James, that it's fine if you need to hand in your paper late," said Mr. Butler. "In fact, if you want to hand it in at the end of the term, that's okay. Don't worry about it."

James nodded, not trusting himself to speak. Mr. Butler clasped his hand on James's shoulder and for a second James was afraid they were both going to burst into tears, but the moment passed, and James left the classroom with an uncomfortable constriction in his throat.

He winced to see that Rina was waiting for him.

"James," she pleaded, "we've got to talk."

James could not stop himself from glancing to either side to check if anyone was watching them. He felt guilty, he realized, and it made him act guilty. He took her hand. "Not here," he said.

He led her down the hall and out the door until they found themselves behind the building. All the rush and noise of changing classes was only an uneasy murmur from here, and he felt himself relax. If he could only live in the sensations of the moment and not think about what had happened, then maybe he wouldn't crack up.

He backed up against the brick wall and slid down to a sitting position. If he looked up he could see the blank blue of the sky. He wished he could stare at it the way he had when he was little, his mind a blank. Instead he was uncomfortably conscious that Rina was settling down beside him. Dry grass bristled between his outspread fingers as he leaned back and closed his eyes.

"I'm afraid this is going to make us late to class," said Rina.

"Rina," James exploded, "I'm not worrying about being late to class. I've got bigger things on my mind."

"I heard about Molly's séance," she said.

James let his head fall back against the wall. "Yeah," he said. "Want to come along? The more the merrier."

"Don't go!" she cried. "It's not safe."

"I've got to. It'd look pretty weird if I didn't show up." He shrugged. "Everybody else is going."

"You ought not to go out at night, James," she cried. "You're being careful to lock your bedroom window, aren't you?"

"You bet. I just wished I'd locked it in the first place." He met her gaze unflinching, but she didn't seem to realize how angry he was.

"You aren't going to the cemetery anymore, are you?" she asked.

James sighed. "No." The cemetery had grown less attractive to him now that he associated it as much with Rina as with Susan. The odd thing was that when he was sure she wasn't looking, he found himself stealing glimpses of Rina. His gaze was still drawn to her in the old, wondering way. He was dazzled by the sight of her and something in him shrank from hurting her, even now. He took a deep breath. "Look," he said, "has it occurred to you that Chelsea might actually show up at that séance?"

Rina clutched her hands together tightly. "You're right! It's the kind of thing she would do! Maybe she's just been waiting for this chance to snatch you when all the lights are out."

"No," James said gently. "I mean she might come back as a spirit."

"You mean—her ghost?" Rina's eyes were wide.

"I don't know why you have to be so surprised about that. It's not a bit weirder than her being a vampire."

"But Chelsea's not dead! So how can she be a ghost?"

"The fact is we don't know for sure what happened to Chelsea."

"I guess that's true," Rina agreed reluctantly. "But I'm sure—"

"We don't know," James insisted. "All kinds of things are possible. I'm going to Molly's séance.

I figure I don't have anything to lose." He shrugged. "Maybe I'll even find out something."

Rina's chin jutted dangerously. "I'm going with you, then."

"I can't stop you."

She choked on a sob. "I hate it that you're mad at me."

James shook his head helplessly. Rina couldn't seem to grasp that what had happened between them was darker than an ordinary fight. He saw now that there was something lacking in her. She wasn't human! She looked human. She acted human. But something important was missing.

The building behind them had fallen quiet, and James realized he hadn't even heard the second bell when it rang. He struggled to his feet. "Oh, forget it," he said. "Let's go get a hamburger."

"Together? You mean skip classes?" asked Rina, looking at him anxiously.

James laughed. "Yeah. That's living dangerously, huh?"

In a funny way going off with Rina made a kind of sense, he thought. She seemed to be the only one he could talk to now. He looked up as a truck loaded with tied bunches of tobacco leaves lumbered noisily past the school. Bright sun struck the line of parked cars in the student lot, so that their taillights glowed and the parking decals made a monotonous row of purple squares on their bumpers. Rina was subdued as they got in James's car and he slipped the key into the ignition. "Pizza okay?" he asked.

"I don't usually—eat much," she stuttered.

"No." He sighed. "Of course you don't. Who was your last square meal—Chelsea?"

"James! Don't!" Her eyelashes were beaded with tears.

"Forget it," he said curtly. He slammed the door, and his car roared out of the parking lot. Part of what bothered him most was the queasy feeling that Rina had gone after Chelsea just so she could have a clear field with him. Those encounters in his bedroom—he still was uncomfortable thinking about them. Hadn't he told Rina she had to get out of his life because he was in love with Chelsea? How could he have been so stupid? It was as if he had set Chelsea up to be murdered.

He glanced over at Rina and caught his breath at her heartbreaking beauty. He recalled the day she had eaten a raw hamburger at lunch. Blood had dripped down her chin. Why hadn't he seen then that something wasn't right? Did he need to be hit over the head? But even now when he looked at her, it was hard for him to believe she was a killer. He found himself still wanting to protect her. It was completely crazy.

The parking lot of the pizza restaurant was all

but empty on this midafternoon. Inside, the place had a shuttered, closed feeling. The waitresses behind the counter looked up, startled when James opened the door. "Bring us a small cheese pizza and a couple of soft drinks," he said. "We'll be in the back corner."

He took Rina's arm and led her to a dark booth well away from the windows. He realized that he'd prefer that nobody saw them together.

They slid in the booth. "Rina, what made you come to high school to begin with?" His hands fell helplessly to the table. "I mean, it's not like you want to get a regular job or go to college, is it? Why go to high school?"

Her amber eyes shifted and he sensed she was about to lie to him, but suddenly she met his gaze directly. "I wanted to try having a normal life. I'm not really sorry I came. I like school. It's fun to be one of the bunch."

"One of the bunch." James smiled tightly, almost overcome by the black comedy of it. "Sure. We all like to fit in, don't we? But what made you go after Chelsea? I've never been very clear about that." He was afraid to hear the answer, but suddenly he had to ask.

Rina's eyes shifted. "She made me mad."

James reflected that it was really pretty conceited of him to think he was behind everything that had happened, and the thought cheered him up a little. He had seen that Chelsea had her needle into Rina. She could have made anybody mad.

"She made fun of my clothes," Rina went on, her eyes flickering to his face. "She said I ought to hang out with kids who were c-clueless."

James smiled in spite of himself. He could almost hear Chelsea saying it. And suddenly he could see it as a tabloid headline—VAMPIRE KILLING—"SHE WOULDN'T LET ME JOIN HER CLIQUE," SAYS BEAUTIFUL DRACULETTE. He coughed. Maybe it was a sign he was cracking up that he could see the funny side of it.

"She made me real mad," Rina repeated.

"That was no good reason to try to kill her," James pointed out.

"I know." Rina rested her chin in her fist and gazed at him wistfully. "I was bad."

James sighed. "I don't think you even know what bad is, Rina."

The waitress slid their order onto the table.

James stared at the pizza. It seemed to him his life could be measured out in pizza slices. It had been in this very restaurant that it had first hit him that he and Chelsea had become a couple. They had gone places together, had fun. And somehow, gradually, they had become a couple. People began to expect to see them together. Then one night at the pizzeria it had dawned on him that she had a claim on him. Chelsea had come to seem like an unchangeable part of his life.

But a few weeks ago, he had been in a booth with Trip and Chelsea when he realized that something had changed. He had met Rina and quickly Chelsea slipped to the sidelines of his life.

Something tickled him, and when he glanced up he saw that Rina was stroking his arm. He went rigid. "Don't do that."

Her hand pulled away suddenly. "It's not okay?" she asked, her eyes anxious. "I thought touching was okay as long as I didn't bite."

It was hard to know where to begin. James closed his eyes. "Don't touch me," he said. "Leave it at that."

"It's because you're mad at me, isn't it?" A tear trickled down her pale cheek.

James rested his head on his hands and sighed heavily. People who thought they had troubles with their girlfriends, he thought, didn't know what real troubles were.

That night on his way to Molly's, James felt exposed, as if his skin had been stripped off him leaving the nerves bare. A truck pulled ahead of him. Its air brakes sighed and James jumped. Rina had warned him not to go out at night. His mouth was dry and a muscle twitched nervously under his eye. He was glad to pull up in Molly's driveway and see that the house was brightly lit. Cars were parked along the curb. He must be one of the last to arrive. Nobody answered his knock at the front door, so James stepped inside and moved toward the hum of voices from the den. If he hadn't been so preoccupied he would have remembered that nobody came in the front door at Molly's. Everyone came in at the side door near the garage. James stepped into the bathroom, thinking he'd get a swig of water out of the spigot. Glancing at his face in the mirror, he saw it had a sheen of perspiration. *Cold sweat,* he thought grimly.

"Are you okay?" Molly was at the door when he came out.

James cleared his throat. "Sure."

"We're all in the den," she explained. "That's where we're going to have the séance."

It was two steps down to the dimly lit den with its green shag carpeting and the Tiffany lamp hanging over the bar. The den was a big room and friends of Chelsea's were everywhere, sprawled on the hearth, perched on hassocks, sitting cross-legged on the floor. They mostly looked embarrassed. Trip took up much of the couch. He lifted one paw in a weary salute as James came in.

"I've been reading up on how to do a séance," Molly announced. "But would anybody like some brownies first?"

James felt a curious sense of unreality as Molly passed around a plate of brownies. In the corner a couple of girls were giggling. They glanced at James and fell into embarrassed silence.

"We have to keep the room dark so the spirits feel comfortable," explained Molly. "We'll all hold hands—I think we'd better get in a circle—so that way we know nobody will try to play any tricks." She glared at Trip as if she expected him to pull out a fake ghost.

It was hard for James to imagine Trip could be up to anything tonight. He stared ahead in mute misery, his big hands hanging between his knees.

"Okay," said Molly, "if we're all finished eating, let's stand up and join hands. Now remember, the books all say that it may take a long time for the spirit to show itself. Your fingers may get numb while we're waiting. We have to be patient."

James heard the side door open. Rina came in. Her face was pale and starkly framed by wild dark hair that fell to her shoulders. She seemed to bring the night inside with her, and James felt a chill run up his back. Faded jeans and a T-shirt looked odd on her. She should have been trailing loose streamers of linen as if she were an Egyptian queen who had just risen from her tomb.

"We're just about to start," said Molly. "Here, you can come in the circle between James and me. Mom!" Molly raised her voice. "Will you cut the lights?"

A moment later they were plunged into darkness. The darkness was so complete that for a second James had the panicky sensation that he had been swallowed alive.

"Good," said Molly. "That's nice and dark. Now let's all concentrate real hard on thinking about Chelsea."

The stereo came on and James jumped as he realized it was playing one of Chelsea's favorite songs. She loved that country-and-western stuff about love affairs gone wrong. The twang of the guitar and the nasal whining of the singer brought a lump to James's throat. He could almost see her twirling a strand of her long blond hair around her finger and crying, "Don't you *love* it?"

"Chelsea," Molly said aloud, "you know we miss you. If you have something to say to us, speak now!" A moment of silence passed and then Molly hissed. "This may take quite a while. Think hard about Chelsea, you guys."

James felt tears well up in his eyes. Thinking about Chelsea was easy. It was not thinking about her that was tough. He felt a breath of cold hit the hair at the back of his neck.

"Something touched me!" someone cried.

"I'm here," cried Chelsea's voice.

James realized then that he smelled the scent Chelsea wore and the floor seemed to pitch under his feet. He was afraid he was going to pass out. "Chelsea?" he whispered.

Confused voices rose around him and he heard a soft thud and then a crash with someone swearing.

"Be still, everybody. What do you want to say to us, Chelsea?" peeped Molly, her voice shaking a little.

"I love you!" the familiar voice cried exuberantly. "This is great. All my friends are here! Thanks for coming, guys."

James couldn't tell where the voice was coming from. It seemed to be moving. Rina held tight to his hand.

"What's going on?" cried Trip's anguished voice.

Another crash sounded, and there was the sound of thin glass crunching underfoot.

"Stay still! And don't anybody turn on the lights!" cried Molly in excitement. "The séance is working! Where are you, Chelsea? Tell us! Where can we find your body?"

Suddenly James felt cold arms clasp and lift him. "Hey!" he protested.

James heard confused voices and crashing as he felt himself hoisted roughly. A door closed and he fell and hit his head on something hard. He was rubbing his head, overcome almost with the sweet smell of roses. A confused part of his consciousness told him he must be in the bathroom. He scrambled awkwardly to his feet and groped along the wall for the light. He was dimly aware of the sound of wild confusion outside as he flicked the light on. James wrenched at the door, but it seemed to be stuck. Grunting, he pulled at it with all his strength but couldn't make it budge. He kicked it and swore. Great, he thought, he was trapped! All hell was breaking loose outside and he might as well be locked in a closet. He couldn't figure out what had happened. Whoever grabbed him had picked him up so easily he felt like a paper doll. It must have been Trip. But why?

He glanced around at the vapid prettiness of the tiny room. Hearts and flowers. Tiny pink soap in the shape of roses. A bowl of potpourri. Pink tissue. It was like being trapped in a powder puff. Hopelessly, he kicked the door.

17

Chelsea could have screamed in exasperation. It was pitch black and even with her vampire vision, she was having trouble making out what was happening. The sound of her voice seemed to have panicked people. She could hear things crashing all over the room.

"Turn the lights on, somebody," Trip bellowed.

Chelsea turned toward the familiar voice in relief. "Trip?" she said, stepping over a fallen hassock to get to him. She touched his shoulder, astonished at how hot he felt. He stiffened. "Chelsea?" he said in a strange voice.

"Turn on the lights, Mom!" screeched Molly. "Somebody's going to get hurt. Keep still, everybody!"

Chelsea grabbed Trip and dragged him off the couch, kicking the hassock aside as she pulled him along. She could hear his heavy heels dragging on the carpet and feel that he had gone limp. She knew Molly's house well and could have found her way out the side door in her sleep. She groped for the doorknob and a minute later they were out of the house. The window shot out a fan of light. Someone had turned the lights on inside—she had got out just in time.

She dragged Trip into the toolshed. Already his eyelids were fluttering. Somewhere a dog howled plaintively. Even though she had gotten out before anybody saw her, she had to hurry. People might come looking for Trip any minute. Inside the shed, Chelsea could feel the lawn mower pressing against her knee. It was a tight squeeze with both of them in there, and the place smelled of oil. The aluminum-seamed structure let in cracks of light and Chelsea could see perfectly. She touched Trip's neck gently, but he didn't respond. Suddenly she bent over him and bit. The surge of blood that shot into her throat made her weak with pleasure. She closed her eyes as his warmth filled her. She could feel his heart beating, its pulse shooting blood into her mouth. Slowly she became conscious that his heart was fluttering uncertainly and a message of alarm reached her brain. She lifted herself up abruptly. Reaching for his hand, she pressed her fingers against his pulse point. He was still alive. Now was the time to make him into a vampire. She ran her sharp fingernail down her arm until her blood welled up in the flesh, a thin ribbon of red.

His eyes flew open. "Chelsea!" His eyes rolled up in his head like a doll's eyes and she thought he might pass out again, but he only gulped a couple of times. His gaze was unfocused. "You're dead," he whispered.

"Sort of." She grinned. She pressed her wrist insistently against his mouth. "Drink it!" she commanded.

He turned his head away. "What?" he mumbled. He closed his eyes.

"Just do what I say," she said sharply. "Drink my blood and you'll feel great."

He groaned. "I feel sick and I got practice tomorrow."

"Just do it and I promise you you'll play better football than you ever dreamed." Chelsea laughed. "You'll eat 'em alive. And any injuries you get will heal up right away. Trust me, this stuff is great."

Trip blinked at her in confusion. "I don't do steroids."

"This isn't steroids," she said impatiently. "It's vampire blood. I'm getting pretty sick of holding my arm out, Trip. Do me a favor and get on with it, huh?"

He didn't speak or move. She decided he must have lost a dangerous amount of blood. "Hurry up," she urged. "If you don't do it now, it may be too late."

"I'll try anything once," he muttered.

Chelsea grinned as she pressed her torn flesh to his mouth. He swallowed, and she felt him shudder. She felt a tremor of sympathetic excitement. "Drink all you want," she murmured.

He grabbed her arm, and Chelsea could feel his teeth and his tongue against her flesh. It was like nursing a piranha. "I think you're going to make a good vampire," she said.

"What did you say?" Trip's eyes flew open in astonishment.

"Vampire," repeated Chelsea. "You're a vampire now." She threw back her head and laughed.

The door to the bathroom opened and James saw Rina peer at him anxiously. "You aren't mad at me, are you?"

"Yes, I'm mad," snapped James. "How did you—" But he remembered suddenly that Rina was a vampire and his voice trailed off. That was why she could pick him up so easily and pitch him in here. He could feel himself reddening. He felt stupid being locked in a bathroom by a girl.

"I was scared," said Rina. "Chelsea was here and I was afraid she would grab you."

"Chelsea," he said numbly. "I heard her voice plain as anything. What's going on?"

When he went back to the den, the lights were on but signs of confusion were everywhere. A lamp shade was askew. The hassock had over-turned and rolled in front of the fireplace. Fragments of a lightbulb glittered in the carpet and pieces of a broken plate had been picked up and carefully laid on the hearth. James looked down and saw that he had stepped on a brownie. He scuffed his shoe on the carpet to get off the crumbs. Molly threw her arms around him. "James!" she cried. "I thought you had disap-peared, too."

"What do you mean?" he asked, jolted. "Who's disappeared?"

"Trip!" cried Molly. "When the lights came on, you were both gone!"

James's heart sank.

"Oh, you know Trip," a blond girl sniffed. "He's probably trying to scare us."

"This is no joke!" Candi cried. "Chelsea was here! She really was."

Molly's fingers worked nervously in the folds of her skirt. "I wasn't sure we would raise her spirit. Boy, the séance sure did work!"

"No, I mean she was *really* here," insisted Candi. "I touched her. She was solid, wasn't she, Laura? You were standing right next to me. Tell them."

Laura agreed. "I brushed against her and I could smell her perfume. I've never heard of a spirit wearing perfume, have you?"

"Look!" cried Candi. She bent over, and when

she straightened up, something gold glittered between her thumb and forefinger.

James found himself crowding forward with the others to see. He leaned over someone's shoulder and made out that Candi was holding a little earring in the shape of a horse. She held it out toward him in her palm. "Do you recognize it, James?"

"Recognize it?" he said. "I gave it to her." He fell onto the couch.

Chelsea had snatched Trip. It was the only thing that made sense. *I should have warned him!* James thought in dismay.

"I can't figure it out," said Molly. "If Chelsea is alive, why is she hiding from us? We're her friends! Why would she run away from us?"

Candi's eyes widened. "Maybe she's being controlled by whoever kidnapped her. Maybe she can't help herself."

"But she sounded so happy!" protested Molly. "Didn't you think she sounded happy?"

"Mind control," muttered Candi darkly. "You know, there's this thing called the Stockholm syndrome where the prisoner starts to think like the kidnapper. It's very strange."

"We'd better call the police," said Tom Schwartzkoff. "Whatever's going on, it's not okay, that's for sure."

"Do you think they'll believe us when we say Chelsea showed up?" Laura put in. "Maybe they'll think we're just imagining things." She glanced around the room at the wreckage. "They'll think we were expecting to see Chelsea and we just worked ourselves up into a state until we convinced ourselves we saw her."

"We've got witnesses!" protested Candi.

"None of us really saw anything," Laura pointed out. "It was dark."

"We sure heard something, and what about the earring?" Tom put in.

Molly shook her head miserably. "It could have been in the rug for weeks. For months, even. I found a Christmas tree ornament hanger in the carpet just the other day."

They all began talking about Chelsea's earrings—when she had last worn them, whether anyone had seen her wearing them lately.

Tom spoke up. "I still say that we should call the police."

Everyone seemed to have forgotten that Trip was missing. Maybe they figured this was another of his famous jokes. James touched Molly's arm. "I'm taking off," he muttered. "I feel pretty rotten."

She turned to him with quick sympathy. "Sure," she said. "Are you okay to drive, James?"

James nodded.

But when he got outside the house he stood still a moment, unable to move, he was so overcome with remorse. He should have warned Trip. He should never have gotten mixed up with

Rina. Slowly he realized that she was standing beside him. "How did you get out here without me hearing you?" he asked.

"My footsteps are light. I don't weigh much," she hesitated, then added, "at night."

A groan escaped James as he reached out to open his car door.

"Wait!" said Rina sharply. "Did you hear something?"

James froze and listened. He half expected to hear Trip screaming. "No," he said finally. "Just that dog howling."

"I'd better stay with you."

James felt he was looking at Rina through a red haze. "Don't do me any favors," he said in a stifled voice. He jumped in his car and sped away.

When he got home, he was relieved none of his family was around. He would have hated to explain what had just happened. He felt sick to his stomach as he went up to his room.

James paced the floor of his room restlessly. Could Trip have possibly gone with Chelsea willingly? Impulsively, James dialed his friend's number. It rang three times and then the answering machine kicked in. Trip's voice said, "We cannot come to the phone right now, but if you will leave a message . . ." James slammed the receiver back in the cradle. His fists were clenched as he strode to the window. He parted the curtain and peered out at the night. Across the street he saw a gray Lincoln, and his hand jerked in surprise. Rina was parked outside, watching his house!

Something dark flew past the closed window. James drew back suddenly, letting the curtain fall closed. He wasn't sure why, but suddenly he felt frightened.

18

The morning was heavily overcast with clouds that looked like smoke. When James got to school the next morning, he found he had a splitting headache. He had scarcely slept at all.

Trina Hartley ran up to him and said breathlessly, "Oh, James, I heard about the séance. Aren't you just so relieved that Chelsea is alive?"

"Sure," he said woodenly. "I'm real relieved."

"What do you think is going on? I've said to everybody that if she could get in touch with *anybody*, she would be bound to get in touch with *you*. She hasn't called or anything?" Trina's eyes were bright with curiosity.

James shook his head. "I don't know what's going on, Trina."

He got away from Trina somehow, but all morning people kept coming up to him, wanting to hear what had happened. He had the sensation they were watching him closely, as if they wanted to gauge his reaction. He felt like a zoo exhibit. Nobody even mentioned Trip.

In class he found himself stealing longing looks at Rina. He wished he could get her aside and talk to her. He imagined himself blurting out the truth to the next person he met—"Chelsea is a vampire now, and I'm afraid she's made Trip into a vampire, too." The thought made him laugh harshly. He could see the way that would go down. Whoever he was talking to would take a step backward, blink, and say, "Oh. That's very interesting. How long have you felt this way, James?" By lunch the grapevine would be humming with word that he had completely cracked.

The morning stretched out interminably.

When it was time for lunch, James stood indecisively in the hall. What was the point of going to the cafeteria where everybody he saw would only give him the third degree?

"Jim-bo, buddy!"

James whirled around, feeling the blood rush to his feet with sudden shock. It was Trip! He looked awful, but he was alive! James closed his eyes. "Man, you'll never know how glad I am to see you."

Trip clapped him on the shoulder. "Let's get out of this place," he said. "I can't face the cafeteria, can you? We can go get a burger."

"Great," said James. But he found himself casting an uneasy glance at his friend as they left the building and walked toward the parking lot. "Are you okay?" he asked. "Why'd you take off last night? You look kind of . . ." His voice trailed off. "Anyway, are you okay?"

Trip clapped his hand to his belly. "Felt sick to my stomach," he growled. "Twenty-four-hour virus or something. Figured I'd better get out of there fast."

He did look as if he'd had the flu. He was pale and gaunt and James noticed that his hands were trembling. "Maybe you got out of bed too soon."

"Nah, I'm okay," Trip said. He glanced up at the dark sky and opened his car door.

"You had me worried," said James. "I called your house, but all I got was your answering machine."

"No call to worry about me. I'm in great shape. Better than ever." Trip slid in behind the wheel, then reached over to unlock the door on the other side.

"I'll follow you in my car," James said quickly. He walked back to where he was parked. He wasn't really sure what impulse made him want to have his own wheels. Maybe it was because of the odd sinking sensation in his stomach.

Trip's car puffed black exhaust as it pulled out of the lot. James followed behind, keeping Trip's old Chevy in sight. *It's funny,* he thought. *You don't look at guys the way you look at girls. I'd hate*

*to fill out a missing person report on Trip. It's not
like I really LOOK at him that often. But I somehow thought his eyes were a different color. Darker.*

Trip pulled up in the parking lot of T.R.'s
Steak and Burger. James pulled beside the Chevy
and got out.

"I like this place," said Trip. They climbed the
stairs together. "You can get the burger just exactly the way you want it here."

The diner was a converted railway car.
Underscoring the theme, a wooden railway
crossing sign with flashing lights stood by the
front door. When James opened the door, a
warning whistle tooted overhead. "I could do
without the sound effects," James said uneasily.

Small tables were by the windows, each with
a tiny vase of flowers. At the larger table at the
back a group of businesspeople were laughing. A
harassed-looking waitress showed up at James's
side. "A burger with extra onions," said Trip.
"And make it really rare. If it can still moo, it's
just right."

James folded his menu. "Fries and a milk
shake," he said. As soon the waitress had left, he
asked, "What did you make of what happened
last night? I can't figure it out."

Trip took out his wallet and counted his bills.
James had the impression his friend was purposely avoiding looking at him.

"Have you talked to Chelsea, Trip?" James insisted. "Is that where you were last night? With her? Tell me the truth. Heck, I won't be mad. What's she up to?"

"Okay, yeah, I've talked to her." Trip lowered his voice. "She's run away from home, see? And she kind of wants to keep a low profile."

"Making a big splash at the séance last night wasn't too smart, then, was it?" James found himself looking closely at Trip's face. His flesh had begun to creep.

"She wants to see her friends," Trip explained. "That's why she showed up. In fact, she really wants to see you, James."

James wondered if he'd stopped breathing. But Trip did not seem to notice that anything was wrong. He went on talking. "She's got a proposition she'd like to put to you," he said.

James sucked in his breath. "What kind of proposition?"

"What she's got in mind is a kind of commune. All her friends together. It's not a bad deal, really. If you sign on there are all kinds of fringe benefits."

The waitress put their plates down before them and bustled off.

"Like me, for example," Trip went on. "Now that I've signed on with Chelsea, I expect to have my best football season ever." He paused thoughtfully. "I may play another position. I'm not sure tackle is the best place to use my potential." He lifted his burger, and when he opened his mouth, James saw long white fangs.

James leapt up suddenly, knocking over his chair. He wrenched open the door to the restaurant. Trip's voice was calling his name. As he ran, the restaurant's warning whistle sounded overhead.

James wasn't sure how long he drove around in a daze. He couldn't go home, he decided—when he was able to think at all. Home was the first place Chelsea and Trip would go to look for him. He decided to take refuge in the public library. The trees planted in front of the library cast shadows that told him it was late afternoon. He glanced at his gas gauge and saw that his tank was almost empty. He had no idea where he had been. Driving aimlessly was probably not a bad way to stay out of Trip's and Chelsea's reach. But he knew he couldn't do it forever. He pulled his car up where it would be half hidden, behind the bookmobile. Then he got out and went inside. The windows of the library were high overhead, which made it impossible to see in or out of the building. The quiet, the dim light, even the slow movements of the workers at the circulation desk, calmed him. It was hard to believe anything really bad could happen here. The library had another advantage, he realized. He had never known either Trip or Chelsea to show up there willingly.

He went in the rest room and tossed cold water on his face. A kind of commune! Trip had said. James stared in the mirror at his ashen face. He wondered why he had not realized before how desperately he wanted to hold on to the life he had, no matter how painful it was. How could Trip sit there talking coolly about having a good football season as if turning into a vampire was nothing more than a new training technique? Shuddering, James wondered what Trip had in mind for the poor suckers he tackled.

In the reading room, he leafed through newspapers, staring sightlessly at the headlines. He could hardly bear to think of Chelsea, pale and gaunt like Trip and with long teeth. First one and then another of his friends had been sucked into the dark world Rina had brought to them. It was like a chain-reaction wreck on the highway, James thought. He felt stunned by the disaster. All he could think of was that somehow he had to steer a careful course and escape. He gripped his head in his hands. *I could go live with Grandma Fenner,* he thought. *My parents would understand that I might want to get away for a while.* It seemed like a good idea to gas up his car and drive to the mountains to visit Grandma Fenner, but somehow James knew he wasn't

going to do it. Not yet. He had to talk to Rina.
Somehow he couldn't bear the idea that Trip and
Chelsea might gang up on Rina and hurt her. He
just wanted to see for himself that she was all
right and warn her what she was up against.
Then he would leave town.

When James pulled into Rina's driveway, he
could see the gray Lincoln in the garage. But the
house was spookily silent and he found himself
holding his breath as he mounted the front steps
of the porch and knocked. Maybe Trip and
Chelsea had already gotten to her.

The door opened, and in spite of himself
James smiled in relief when he saw her.

"Oh, James!" she cried. She threw her arms
around his neck. "I was so worried. I called your
house and when you weren't there—"

He stepped in. "I've seen Trip, Rina. It's happened. He's a vampire."

Her hand flew to her mouth.

James moved into the living room and sank
onto the brocade couch. The big black clock's
tick was unnervingly loud. James wished he
could shut it up. He glanced at the window,
checking to make sure it was locked.

"Did you talk to Trip?" Rina cried. "What did
he say?"

James closed his eyes. "Let's see, how did he
put it? I think he mentioned 'signing on with

Chelsea.' You know, as if it were a cruise. And then he said it was 'sort of like a commune.' Chelsea wants all her friends to join."

"It's all my fault," cried Rina.

James took a deep breath. "You're right about that."

"You're mad at me, aren't you?"

"Would you quit asking if I'm mad at you?" James leapt up, strode to the window, parted the curtains, and peered out. No sign of any other cars. "Do all vampires travel in cars like you do, Rina?" His voice was tight.

She shook her head. "Vlad, this vampire I used to know, never would get in a car because he got carsick."

James shot her a questioning glance.

"Sometimes he rode a demon horse," she said. "But later, when people weren't riding horses so much, he learned how to turn into a fly. Not a housefly, but what they call a blowfly, the kind that grows in dead and decaying things." She looked embarrassed. "A vampire's molecules can be rearranged any number of ways, you see. Even into a mist."

James swore and strode across the hall to the dining room. He tried that window and was relieved to find that it was locked. "Have you got every window in the house locked? You know, now that Trip's a vampire there are two of them, and both of them are bigger than you."

"I know," said Rina. "I had a new front door put in. Without a mail slot. I already thought of that."

"I don't know what they'll try, but I thought I'd better not go home because they'll look for me there."

"You can stay here," said Rina. "This place is as safe as any."

James felt a shiver of apprehension when she put her hand on his arm. He wasn't sure exactly what sort of invitation Rina was extending, and he drew away. "I'm not sure that's a good idea."

"I would never hurt you," she said in a small voice. "I l-love you."

James laughed. "I don't think you even know what love is."

"Yes," she said, gulping. "I do. I didn't mean to fall in love with you. But I did. I love you! Do you love me?" She hesitated. "Even a little?"

James stared at her a moment in silence. "How can I, Rina? Look at what you've done."

"But you came here to be near me and to warn me," she insisted. "You must—like me a little."

James couldn't speak, because he couldn't bear to cause her pain. You're a vampire! he wanted to scream.

Yet in some crazy way he wanted to take care of her. He couldn't take his eyes off her, and he supposed he must be drawn to her, because even his fear had not been enough to keep him away.

But that wasn't love. A person couldn't be in love with a vampire.

"Kiss me!" she pleaded.

James stepped back. "I can't do that, Rina." He could feel sweat beading on his forehead. "Now that I've seen what happened to Trip—I can't take any chances."

"No!" Her eyes pleaded with him. "I mean a kiss. A real kiss. Like people do. That's all. I promise."

I am out of my mind, James thought confusedly. But he drew her into his arms and crushed her close to him. He had wanted to do it for a long time, and somehow he couldn't stop himself. The world grew smaller as they clung to each other, until it seemed it contained nothing but the two of them when they kissed.

Tears glistened in Rina's eyes and James drew back from her. "What's wrong?" he asked.

"Everything," she whispered. "I want to be alive. Really alive."

James held her close again, feeling her beating heart against his. *What a mess,* he thought. *This is a hopeless situation. I ought to get the heck out of here.* But he found himself stroking her silky hair and murmuring, "It's all right. It's going to be okay."

He was startled by a scraping sound like metal hitting metal, and he stiffened. "Have you got a cat?"

"Of course not." She smiled as she wiped the tears from her eyes. "Cats are afraid of vampires."

"Then what's that noise?" It had come from the kitchen. James was almost sure. What was even more eerie was he felt he smelled a familiar perfume. He grabbed Rina's hand. "Did you have the space sealed around the pipes?"

She looked puzzled. "What are you talking about? What space?"

"When houses are built the plumbers cut holes in the walls and subflooring for the pipes to come in, and there's almost always space around them. Sometimes an inch all around."

Rina gasped.

"Let's get out of here," he whispered. Holding hands, they crept toward the hallway.

Suddenly the kitchen door flew open and Chelsea was standing there. She was pale; her legs looked as if they were sheathed in white stockings. Her blond hair flowed freely to her shoulders and her eyes gleamed. She put her hands on her hips and smiled. "Hi there, James. Cheating on me?"

"Run, James!" cried Rina.

Chelsea was coming toward him. She licked her lips so that they shone, and James heard the light tap of her heels on the floor as she walked. In the parlor, the clock ticked an ominous counterpoint, as if to tell him that his time was running out.

He felt frozen. Suddenly Rina screamed, "No!"

James grabbed Rina's hand and they ran. But when he threw the front door open, Trip faced him, his huge hulk blocking the way. "Hi, Jimbo." He cracked his knuckles. "I guess we're going to be just one happy family, huh?" He grinned widely, and James saw that blood was dripping from his fangs.

Don't miss the conclusion to this
terrifying mini-series:

VAMPIRE'S
Love
2: BLOOD SPELL

James heard a movement and spun around. "Rina?" he whispered anxiously. "Is that you?"

Rina smoothed her black hair as she stepped out of the shadows into the clearing where he stood. "I wish you wouldn't stare like that," she complained. "When I'm changing, I get self-conscious."

"I couldn't see where you had gone to," he said. "I was worried." He eyed her uneasily. "What's so embarrassing? I thought you were just going to sneak up close to the house and listen."

Her face darkened with a blush. "I changed into a bat," she confessed.

James gulped. Looking at Rina now, he found himself thinking that maybe her hair was bat-colored. He shut his eyes. "Could you hear what they were saying? What did you find out?"

Rina's expression changed. "I've got bad news, James."

He grabbed her arms. "What happened? Tell me!"

"Trip is dead."

James staggered several steps backward. "But he's a vampire now!" he gasped. "Vampires can't die!"

Rina licked her lips. "Remember I told you there are ways for us to die? Well, Chelsea set him on fire. I think they were fighting over my ruby bracelet. Chelsea wanted to wear it, and Trip wanted to sell it and buy a Corvette."

James stared at her blankly.

"I guess you haven't seen my bracelet." Rina took a deep breath. "I don't wear it anymore because I have very bad memories connected with it. The guy who gave it to me is the one who made me into a vampire. Chelsea can have the stupid thing. I don't want it. It certainly wasn't worth killing Trip over."

James was struggling to understand. "What happened, Rina?"

"Chelsea dropped a cigarette onto Trip's shirt. Well, technically, he dropped it, but she made it happen."

"And that killed him?" asked James, bewildered.

"Flames destroy vampires almost instantly. I guess Trip didn't realize."

"Rina—" James hesitated "—are you *sure* he's dead?"

Rina nodded. "I could hear his screams. I flew by and saw he was on fire, and when the fire sputtered out a minute later, I heard Chelsea say that it wasn't her fault."

"That's Chelsea, all right," said James. "Whatever happens, it's never her fault." A breeze stirred the tree branches. "Maybe Chelsea figures she can sell the rubies to make a getaway," he added. "Maybe she wants to go to South America or someplace. She never did like North Carolina. She was always saying she hated living in a dinky little town where there's nothing to do."

Rina glanced over her shoulder at the brightly lit house visible through the trees. "Maybe it's a lot more interesting for her, now that she's become a vampire."

James shuddered.

"I wish I could say she's leaving town," said Rina, "but she's not. I heard her say she's going to tell her parents she has amnesia. That way they can't ask her any questions about what happened while she was missing."

James ran his fingers through his hair. "You mean to tell me she's going to go back to school as if nothing happened? She hates school. You're saying that after she's become a vampire and murdered Trip, she's going to go back to taking algebra tests? Is she figuring she can lure kids over to the pencil sharpener and suck their blood?" He became uncomfortably aware that he was spouting off wildly. He hoped he hadn't said something that hurt Rina's feelings. "It's such a shock," he said apologetically. "I don't know—I keep expecting to find out it's all a mistake."

The moonlight filtering into the clearing seemed threatening, as if it were trying to steal his reason. Trip dead! It was hard to believe that a guy who had been his friend, a two-hundred-pound football tackle, had vanished in a puff of smoke. Or that Chelsea had killed him.

James took a deep breath. "What are we going to do now, Rina?"

About the Author

Janice Harrell lives in North Carolina. She has written numerous books for young adults and adults.

Point Horror

Are you hooked on horror? Thrilled by fear? Then these are the books for you. A powerful series of horror fiction designed to keep you quaking in your shoes.

Point Horror

Dare you read

NIGHTMARE HALL

Where college is a
scream!

High on a hill overlooking Salem University
hidden in shadows and shrouded in mystery, sits
Nightingale Hall.

Nightmare Hall, the students call it.
Because that's where the terror began...
Don't miss these spine-tingling thrillers:

The Silent Scream
The Roommate
Deadly Attraction
The Wish
The Scream Team
Guilty
Pretty Please
The Experiment
The Nightwalker

P●INT CRiME

If you like Point Horror, you'll love Point Crime!

A murder has been committed ... Whodunnit? Was it the arch rival, the mystery stranger or the best friend? An exciting series of crime novels, with tortuous plots and lots of suspects, designed to keep the reader guessing till the very last page.

Fatal Secrets

Stunned, Ryan realized she'd reached a corner, and she squeezed herself into it, trying to be invisible. She sank to the floor and felt a tiny breath of cold air seeping in under the door.

"Help me," she murmured, and in that split instant she realized something was near her – beside her in the dark – she could *feel* it –the darkness pulsating with its *presence*, its *danger*– "Oh, God..." She put out her hand and felt heavy, wet fabric ... damp human skin ... icy cold...

Something slimy coiled around her neck...

Shrieking, Ryan's head snapped back and hit the wall, and through the insane darkness, she saw a soft explosion of stars.

Look out for:

Point Horror

FATAL
SECRETS

Richie Tankersley Cusick

SCHOLASTIC

Scholastic Children's Books,
Commonwealth House,
1-9 New Oxford Street,
London WC1A 1NU, UK
a division of Scholastic Ltd
London ~ New York ~ Toronto ~ Sydney ~ Auckland

First published in the US by Simon & Schuster Inc., 1992
First published in the UK by Scholastic Ltd, 1995

Copyright © Richie Tankersley Cusick, 1992

ISBN 0 590 13274 1

Printed by Cox and Wyman Ltd, Reading, Berks.

10 9 8 7 6 5 4 3 2 1

For Mom and Dad
on your 50th anniversary
for all your love and faith

Prologue

If I die out here in the cold, it'll be all your fault," Marissa snapped, burrowing deeper into her jacket. She glanced up at the sky and tugged impatiently on her necklace. "Look—it's snowing harder, and we're miles from anywhere. I could be home smelling the turkey bake, instead of out here in the woods with you, looking for stuff to make stupid garlands with and—what was that? Did you hear something?"

"Hear what?" Ryan McCauley frowned over at her older sister, then redirected her gaze to the softly piling drifts around them. In the darkening maze of gnarled trees, her voice sounded almost eerie. "What's the matter with you? You've been jumpy ever since you drove in from school last night."

Marissa carefully avoided Ryan's eyes. "The trip upset me, that's all. Some jerk stayed on my tail practically the whole way home."

"Oh, right. A half-hour drive, and you're nervous. Maybe you wouldn't be so nervous if you drove it a little more often and came home to see Mom. If Steve didn't teach there at the same college, we wouldn't even know you're alive. At least he sees you on campus once in a while."

Marissa pressed her lips together and ducked her head. Ryan had the distinct feeling that her sister was about to say something but changed her mind.

"Anyway, I thought you'd like coming along with me—we've never been all the way up here to North Woods before, and I thought it'd be fun to get out of the house awhile and do some exploring." She waited for a reply, but when none came, she sighed and turned away. "Come on . . . I need some more pinecones."

"Your boss said a *few,* didn't he? I'm sure he didn't mean to clean up the whole forest—hey, where are you going?" Marissa cast an uneasy glance behind them but followed as Ryan ducked beneath some tangled limbs and came out into a snow-covered clearing. "And it's just the perfect job for you, too, isn't it?" she muttered. "Working in a toyshop, for God's sake."

"It's not just a toyshop," Ryan said indignantly. "Mr. Partini is a dear, sweet man, and he makes practically all the toys himself."

"Then if he's so sweet, let *him* come out here and freeze *his* butt off—"

"Marissa, he's old! He can barely walk around as it is! We've been making store decorations for weeks now—Mr. Partini's even been working on them at night! You know how busy shopping will be tomorrow —the day after Thanksgiving! I told him to be sure and call me if he needed more greenery or anything, so—" Ryan broke off and stared at Marissa, whose eyes were fixed on the surrounding trees.

"Ryan . . . I know I heard something move—do you see anything?" Ryan followed her sister's gaze and tried to shake off a sudden chill that had nothing to do with the weather. "How could you see through all this snow anyway? It's probably just the wind. Or a deer or something."

"I want to leave, Ryan. I want to leave now." Marissa jerked one hand through her hair, red ribbons tangling in her long blond curls. "We need to drop that film off before the drugstore closes."

"Film?" Ryan stopped and brushed snow from her mittens, her face puzzled. "Did you give it to me already?"

"You put it in your purse!" Marissa's voice sharpened. "Ryan, I mean it. We have to get that film developed—"

"Okay, okay, just a few more branches, and then we'll go. And if we'd just split up, like Mom suggested in the first place, instead of you following me everywhere, we'd be done a whole lot faster! I don't know what your big fat hurry is anyway—they won't even pick the film up till tomorrow—"

"I told you—I have to get those pictures before I go back to school—Ryan, what was that?"

This time Ryan stood and looked where Marissa was pointing. Between the swirling snow and the fading light of late afternoon, the woods and shadows ran together in one ghostly blur. Marissa, poised statuelike, was clutching a tree trunk and trying to peer deeper into the gloom. Ryan walked up behind her and stopped. She listened for a long time, then finally gave an exasperated sigh.

"Marissa, I don't hear anything—what is—ouch!"

To her surprise, Marissa suddenly whirled and grabbed her by the shoulders, shaking her, staring wide into her eyes.

"Ryan," she said, her face grave, "if I tell you something, will you promise not to tell a soul? Not a single soul? You *swear?*"

"Well . . . yeah, I guess so—"

"Don't *guess* so!" Marissa's vehemence startled her. "Ryan, I'm not kidding around—*swear!*"

For a long moment Ryan looked back at her sister. She could feel her own heart racing, and there was a knot tightening in her stomach. "I swear," she whispered.

"I think I'm in trouble," Marissa said. "Serious trouble."

It took a few seconds to register. "What . . . kind of trouble?"

As Ryan watched, Marissa gazed off into the woods again, twisting her necklace distractedly. "It's a long story, and I don't want to go into all of it right now."

"Wait a minute. Is this something you should tell Mom—"

"No!" Marissa's voice raised, and she tightened her grip. "Especially not Mom! Not yet!"

"Okay, okay, don't get so upset—I won't tell her!" Ryan was growing more alarmed by the second, and

4

she tried to pull away. "Marissa . . . you're really scaring me. What's *wrong?*"

"I'm not sure—not a hundred percent anyway—but I'm *pretty* sure." As Ryan squirmed free, Marissa put her hands to her head, then let them drop. She leaned back against a tree and closed her eyes.

"Sure about what?" Ryan stepped closer. "When will you know?"

"In a few days. Then I'll have to decide what to do. Oh, Ryan, it's just too complicated, I don't even know where to start!" For a minute Marissa looked as if she might cry. "I just never thought he'd do something like this—"

"Oh, God. Oh, God, Marissa, it's some guy, isn't it? What have you done now?" Ryan was fighting to stay calm, and she took another step closer. "I mean it, this better not be a joke—"

"I swear it's no joke!"

"Then who's *'he'*? Have you told him about your . . . problem?"

Marissa shook her head. "I think he might suspect something—but sooner or later I'll have to go to him with the truth—"

"Oh, Marissa . . ."

"That's why I had to talk to you—and why you have to *promise!* This *has* to be our secret till—oh, God, what was that?"

Ryan nearly jumped out of her skin as Marissa grabbed her again. "What is *wrong?* What are you—"

"Was that something moving? I thought I saw—"

"This *is* a joke, isn't it? You're just trying to scare me into leaving! I *hate* when you do stuff like this!" Angrily Ryan plowed into the woods again, only half conscious of Marissa's rapid breathing as her sister tried to keep up. "Okay—*I'm* going right over here up this hill—and *you* go straight ahead over there—see—there's another clearing way off through those trees—and finish getting the pinecones! I'll meet you back at the car!"

"Ryan—wait!"

"No!"

"You're such a brat, Ryan! Come back here!"

"No! I'm sick of your stupid games, Marissa! Now, just hurry up so we can go *home!*" She watched as Marissa threw her a hateful glare and flounced off into the woods.

Grumbling, Ryan turned and went in the opposite direction.

She was on her knees, digging holly from underneath a fallen log, when she heard Marissa's screams.

In the soft, white stillness the terrified sounds ripped through her heart, and Ryan dropped everything and began to run back.

"Marissa! Where are you?"

As the screams came again, Ryan crashed through the forest and fought her way through, shouting her sister's name. She could hear Marissa's cries growing closer—only now there was something else—something so horribly out of place in this picture-perfect countryside—

Water.

6

Churning . . . splashing . . . *water*.

"Oh, God—*Marissa!*"

As Ryan tore free of the trees, she saw the snowbank lying so deceptively just a few yards away, its surface broken, big chunks of ice upended, revealing a dark, jagged hole and black water beneath. And as Ryan spotted Marissa's head—Marissa's arms thrashing—she raced toward her sister in a haze of terror.

"Marissa!" she shrieked. "Hang on!"

"Ryan! Help me!" Marissa's cries gurgled as she went under, and as Ryan started across the snow, the ground suddenly began breaking up around her, splitting apart with a slow, steady groan—

Oh, my God—it's not a clearing at all—there's water everywhere—"No!" Ryan was on her stomach, sliding, crawling, and she could see Marissa's face again, Marissa's fingers, blue, blue, and the wide, frantic eyes, the arms reaching—

"—ian!" and it *sounded* like her own name, but Ryan couldn't be sure. *Ryan?—dying?—*

"I'm here, Marissa! I'm coming!"

"—ian!" But Marissa's head was underwater, and Ryan couldn't hear.

"—elp! *Help* me! My hand—*sleeve*—" And Ryan was trying to understand Marissa's shouts as the water choked them off again and again. With a sob she grabbed out for Marissa's sleeve and hung on with all her strength.

"I've got you! Come on—I've got—"

Marissa's arm jerked, nearly pulling Ryan into the water. She felt herself slip helplessly toward the edge of the hole. She looked down and saw Marissa's sleeve still in her grasp, part of Marissa's jacket, floating . . .

"No, Marissa—please—hang on—hang—"

The hole was empty.

"Oh, God, no—"

As Ryan watched in horror, she saw the smooth patch of snow-cleared ice, and beneath it, Marissa's face, eyes bulging, mouth gaping in a soundless scream.

And then . . . Marissa was gone.

Chapter I

Three Weeks Later

There it was again—that feeling of being watched.

Ryan paused at the edge of the school parking lot, oblivious to the horde of students around her. As her heart raced uneasily, she glanced back at Fadiman High and squared her shoulders. "It's Christmastime," she mumbled to herself. "And no more bad things can happen, because it's my favorite time of year."

"There you go again," a familiar voice said with a sigh, so close behind her that she jumped.

"Oh, Phoebe, you scared me to death! I didn't hear you!"

"Didn't hear me?" Phoebe's mouth twitched, and she nodded at the jostling crowds around them. "You mean, standing here in the middle of a wild stampede, and you didn't hear me coming?" She smiled then, showing her dimples, but it quickly faded as she watched Ryan solemnly scanning the rows of cars, the laughing groups of kids. "Ryan . . . did you hear me? Hey, are you—"

"Fine," the other girl finished mechanically. The lot held only the usual faces and voices, and she flashed

Phoebe a look that was almost guilty. "For a minute—I don't know . . ."

"Someone following you again?" Phoebe giggled. "I keep telling you, it's probably just some guy trying to get up his nerve to ask you to the New Year's dance!"

"No . . . I don't think so. Oh, well, it's probably nothing. Just the season. You know how I get this time of year."

"Yeah, more like a little kid than usual," Phoebe responded fondly, falling into step beside her. "Believing in everything. Magic and wishes and Santa Claus and—"

"Well, why not? It's just as easy to believe as not to."

Phoebe studied her a moment, then added softly, "Even though this Christmas will be so . . . different?"

Again Ryan studied the leaden sky, her heart feeling suddenly as heavy. "You can say her name, Phoebe. I'd rather you say her name than just act like she never existed or something." She saw the flush on her friend's face and immediately took Phoebe's hand. "I'm sorry. It's just that . . . it still doesn't seem real that Marissa's dead. I keep thinking I see her every time I turn around. . . . I think I hear her calling me when I'm home. And people still stare at me—"

"You're imagining it," Phoebe broke in. "And even if they *are* looking, it's just because . . . you know . . . they're sorry."

"No. I know what they're thinking."

Phoebe took a deep breath and patted Ryan gently on the back. "Come on. You told me you weren't going to start all this again."

"I can't help it. I know when Mom looks at me, she's seeing Marissa and wishing things were all switched around—"

"Ryan . . . please don't keep doing this to yourself. I can't stand to see you so unhappy." Phoebe stopped and stared earnestly into her friend's face. "You've got to stop feeling responsible for what happened. There wasn't anything you could do—it was just a freaky thing."

"But I didn't save her." Ryan's eyes teared up. "And we'd been fighting—"

"Sisters fight all the time, Ryan, *please*—and you couldn't have known there was water underneath that snow—"

"If only we hadn't gone up there . . . if only she hadn't gone with me." Ryan closed her eyes, trying to shut out the regrets she'd gone over so many, many times before. She didn't feel Phoebe take her shoulders and give her a gentle shake.

"It wasn't anybody's fault," Phoebe insisted. "Think about it, Ryan, how many people you could blame for what happened that day. You told me yourself, Mr. Partini's still never gotten over it. And your mom's the one who made Marissa go with you. And poor Steve—he suggested you check out North Woods. And *I* had to help my mom, so *I* couldn't go with you. Maybe if I had, Marissa wouldn't have died.

11

Maybe if I'd gone, we *both* could have saved her. Do you blame *me* for what happened?"

"Of course not," Ryan said in a tight voice. "But I'm the one who left her. And one second I had ahold of her—and—then—" She raised haunted brown eyes to Phoebe's clear blue ones. "She was gone, Phoebe. She was trying so hard—and then she was just gone."

"Oh, Ryan"—Phoebe looked like she was going to cry herself—"it was just a horrible accident. It's awful, and it's tragic, but it *happened*, and it *wasn't your fault!*"

"If only I hadn't gotten mad at her—I was so mean—"

"Ryan, you couldn't be mean to anybody." Phoebe thought a moment, then gave Ryan her let's-be-logical look. "Think about me and Jinx! We're *always* at each other's throats, and I really *am* mean to him because I *like* to be, and *nothing* bad ever happens to him! Am I making sense?"

"No." Ryan stared at her a long moment and, in spite of herself, had to smile. "It's not the same. You'd be *glad* if something awful happened to Jinx."

"You're right. I would." As Phoebe pretended to wistfully consider the possibility, Ryan gave her a shove.

"You're terrible."

"I know I am. That's why I have you—to balance me out." Phoebe nodded, and then her face went serious again. "Ryan, you've got to get on with your own life. I swear I'm not trying to minimize what's happened, but you're going to make yourself crazy if you keep on like this."

Ryan sighed. "Come on, you can walk me to work." She did smile then, much to Phoebe's relief, and they headed away from school and started through town. "Remember that red shirt I got Marissa last Christmas? You and I got it at that discount store and it was on sale, and we thought it was so glamorous?"

Phoebe tilted back her head and laughed out loud. "And she wore it out that night without a coat, and it rained—"

"And it was her first date with that weird guy she'd been drooling over for so long—"

"And the blouse got all wet—"

"And the color ran out all over everything—"

"The poor guy thought she was bleeding to death—"

"And she was so mad at us, she wouldn't talk to us for weeks!"

They were roaring with laughter now, and it felt so good, washing over the deep, deep pain, soothing it away. Phoebe linked her arm through Ryan's and tugged her down the sidewalk.

"You get a tree yet?"

"No. I keep bringing it up, and Mom keeps ignoring me. All she does is drag herself to work, come home, and sit in Marissa's room. She still keeps the door closed . . . sometimes she even locks it. It's like a shrine or something."

"Tell Steve," Phoebe said helpfully.

"I guess I'll have to. He's the only one in her life these days."

"Ooh." Phoebe winced. "I know a nasty when I hear one."

"Well, it's true," Ryan said defensively. "And the thing about you is—"

"I'm so smart."

"You *think* you are," Ryan corrected, trying not to smile. "Just because you've known me since first grade—"

"And we were best friends from day one—"

"Doesn't give you the right—"

"To know you so well," Phoebe finished triumphantly. "Come on, Ryan, you might as well accept the fact that your mom's going to marry Steve someday—she's crazy about him! As a matter of fact, *I'm* crazy about him."

"You're crazy about every guy. In fact, you're just crazy."

Phoebe thought a moment, then nodded. "So I have a very healthy attitude about the opposite sex. Why couldn't Steve have just met me first?"

Ryan shook her head indulgently. "I thought you were all *for* him and Mom."

"I am! I think it's cute. And I think *he's* cute. That smile of his—and he's so funny—the way his hair's a little thin on top—and that mole on his—"

"God, Phoebe, what have you been doing, watching our house with binoculars?"

"I also like the fact that he has a sports car and a"

boat and likes to treat you and me to dinner a lot. Face it—not every widow gets a second chance at love—and it's a good idea for your mom to think of financial security."

Ryan couldn't help chuckling. "You sound like a commercial. And the money must be in his family because I know college professors don't make that much."

"A college professor," Phoebe said dreamily. "He's so intelligent, too."

"Forget it, Phoebe, you'd make a terrible professor's wife." Ryan ducked her head as a cold blast of wind rushed at them along the sidewalk. "And anyway, he's going to interview for a department chairman's position at another university, so he might be moving away."

"No! You didn't tell me! When?"

"In a few days. Mom's already starting to mope."

"So if they *do* get married, maybe your mom'll have a brand-new start in a brand-new place." Phoebe looked pleased. "That's good for her. Now we just have to worry about you."

Ryan sighed. "Don't worry about me."

"You need a boyfriend," Phoebe said stubbornly.

"I don't want one."

"Yes, you do, and especially now. Steve and your mom are a twosome. And . . . well . . . you're not."

Ryan felt arguments welling up inside her, but as Phoebe held her in a steady gaze, she sighed again and gave in.

"Why are you doing this to me?"

"Because you need a *guy!* Ryan, you are the most giving, the most caring person in the whole world! Except to me, that is. It's just that you and your mom both lost someone you love, and now your mom's got Steve and you don't have anyone. Life's not fair, but that's the way it is." She nodded for emphasis, then cast Ryan a sly look. "I'm *still* in love with Steve, you understand, but I don't think life's fair."

"Well, if life were fair, Marissa wouldn't have died." *If life were fair, it would have been me who fell through the ice, not Marissa, and Mom would be happier and things would seem more normal and right. . . .*

"If life were fair, I wouldn't have Jinx. Little brothers would be against the law. Especially ones who are only a year younger." Phoebe rolled her eyes. "If life were fair, I'd be an only child. Or the trolls would have stolen him at birth."

"So what's Jinx done now?" Ryan asked, amused. Through all their growing-up years together, she couldn't remember a time when Jinx hadn't been a constant source of irritation to her friend.

"What's he *done?*" Phoebe echoed. "He hasn't done anything. He doesn't *have* to do anything except exist. He doesn't have to do *anything* except be his own obnoxious self. Isn't that bad enough?" She looked slightly incredulous. "Can you believe girls actually *call* him? He gets phone calls all the *time* at home. Carla Smith called—and she's a senior! Girls think he's cute! *And"*—she paused for effect—"I have my suspicions that he's got his heart set on Tiffany Taylor! Seriously!"

Ryan chuckled. "You're kidding—that little sopho-more cheerleader who walks like this and giggles all the time? I thought she was interested in what's-his-name—that nerdy guy in Jinx's class—"

"That's what I heard, too—the junior class vice president. Wow. Tiffany and Jinx—can you even imagine? Or that anyone in her right mind would think Jinx is *cute!*"

"Well . . ." Ryan said generously, "he *can* be kind of cute when he wants to be. With that baby face of his."

"Yeah, when he thinks he's in trouble, or when he wants something. You can have him. I'll give him to you. For free! If life were really fair, you'd take him."

"And if I had a dollar for every single time you've threatened to give him to me—"

"See?" Phoebe shot her an accusing look. "You don't want him, either! If life were *really* fair, my parents would lock him up someplace and throw away the key. And . . . I'd have naturally curly hair." She laughed, looking pleased with herself as Ryan re-garded her in disbelief.

"You are so impossible! I'd give *anything* to have hair like yours. Look at this—brown hair, brown eyes—*dull!* If life were fair, I'd be blond. And I'd have a million dollars."

"Well . . . you're rich in friendship. You have me!"

"Oooh . . . bad."

Phoebe laughed and started to hug her, then suddenly shook her arm. "Look over there—on that corner by the bus stop—isn't that Winchester Stone?"

As Ryan followed Phoebe's stare, she felt a strange flutter go through her chest, and she quickly ducked her head. "Yes, that's him. Come on, don't look, let's just keep walking."

"He is the most *gorgeous* guy I have ever seen—"

"Come on, Phoebe, quit looking at him. Just hurry up—"

"I mean it, Ryan, he is *so* sexy. And to think your sister actually went out with him."

"You know she only did it so all her friends would be jealous. She used him. After a couple dates she lost interest."

"Oh," Phoebe moaned, "I wish he hadn't graduated last year—maybe I'd have had a chance, now that we're finally seniors."

"From what I hear, he doesn't have a girlfriend," Ryan said casually. "Why don't you get Jinx to fix you up? He's always down at the garage."

"Oh, him and his creepy little friends—and Winchester's teaching them all to work on cars—God!" Phoebe made a fist and beat on her forehead. "Working with Winchester practically every day! Can you imagine being that close to Winchester *every day!*"

Ryan toyed with the thought, then pushed it firmly away. "What does Jinx say about him?"

"Nothing. *Nobody* knows anything about Winchester. You never see him with friends . . . you never see him with girls—not that every female I've ever talked to wouldn't sell her *soul* to go out with him! You have to admit he's gorgeous. You *have* to have noticed—"

"Well, of course I've noticed. He used to come by for Marissa—how could I help but notice?"

"Ha! And I bet you were hiding, I bet you never even came down to talk to him in person!"

"Well"—Ryan shrugged, her voice defensive—"he *did* come to see Marissa, after all. He didn't come to see me."

"Oh, Ryan, it's no wonder you never have a date. They're all afraid they'll give you a heart attack if they come near you!" Phoebe groaned in frustration. "Look at him. He has that shy look, but he's always in those tight jeans—"

"Phoebe, honestly!" Ryan shook her head, then shot a hasty glance back at the figure on the corner. "He's kind of a loner, I guess. Maybe he doesn't like having friends."

"Doesn't he ever come around to see you? To talk to your mom or anything?"

"No, why should he? I told you Marissa didn't care about him."

Phoebe couldn't resist looking back at the bus stop one more time. "Well, I still think it's strange, that a guy that great looking should be alone so much." She sighed, falling into step with Ryan once more. "I'd love to just talk to him. Just be alone with him and"—she shivered—"oh, I bet he's a great kisser. And other things—"

"Phoebe, will you quit looking at him!" Ryan tugged on the other girl's arm, and Phoebe immediately tripped over the curb. "You don't want him noticing us, but you keep looking back at him. Just stop it and try to walk like a normal person!"

At some unspoken signal, the girls began to run, not stopping again until they had turned a corner onto a dingy side street. As they slowed down and tried to catch their breath, Phoebe grinned and pointed to the brightly lit store window several feet ahead of them.

"Well, here we are! Cold weather and Christmas coming and this great job waiting for you! What more could you ask for?"

"A best friend with half a brain." Ryan grinned back. "An A on my history test tomorrow."

"Oh, darn, I forgot about that stupid test!"

"I *have* to make a good grade. I'm really doing awful in my classes."

Phoebe looked concerned. "But I thought the teachers were being really understanding."

"They are, but they can only be *so* understanding. I feel like I'm really losing it . . . I can't concentrate . . . I can't study . . . I don't hear things in class . . . sometimes I come to and realize time's passed, and it's like I've just blanked out."

"Give yourself time," Phoebe said. "It's only been a few weeks, and you've been through a lot. The teachers know that. Hey—I'll be by later to study, okay?"

"Okay. I'll make sure there's plenty of popcorn."

They paused on the sidewalk in front of a shabby brick building, smiling as they peered through the frost on the front window. Beyond a quaint sign reading PARTINI'S TOYSHOP, a Santa Claus doll super-

vised his workshop. In caps and aprons, amidst pots
and wood shavings and sleepy-eyed reindeer, mechanical elves measured and cut, hammered and sawed,
assembling toys while Christmas carols sang out from
a hidden speaker. Ryan felt a rush of emotions go
through her—an ache for her childhood, an emptiness for Marissa—and she gave Phoebe a playful
shove to keep the tears from coming.

"See you tonight. Thanks for the escort."

"You're not still walking all the way home from
here, are you?" Phoebe's eyes went worriedly back
and forth across the little alleyway, and she frowned.
"I never have liked this place after dark, way back here
by itself."

"What do you mean?" Ryan teased. "This is the
artsy section of town. This is where us creative types
work."

"Well, it just doesn't seem safe to me," Phoebe
grumbled. "And it's getting dark so early now."

"It's better than waiting for Mom to come and get
me. She always forgets anyway. Look—it's safe."
Ryan steered Phoebe back to the curb, pointing out
more rundown shopfronts. "See? The art gallery? The
bakery? The used bookstore? The Coffeehouse? All
these antique shops?" Her voice sounded confident,
but as she suddenly remembered her strange feeling
back at school, a shiver went through her. "And Mr.
Partini wouldn't let anything happen to me." She
smiled now, thinking of the toy shop owner and the
friendship they'd developed over the past six months
she'd been employed.

"This place is creepy enough, but you still have to walk out on that old road," Phoebe said stubbornly.

"I've walked that old road hundreds of times. Since I was old enough to walk home from school."

"Well, I still don't like it. Just please be careful, okay?"

"I promise. See you later."

Ryan waved until Phoebe had disappeared, and as she finally stepped through the door, the fragrant warmth of the shop enveloped her like a welcoming hug.

It had started as a temporary job, a way to make extra money, but even after all these months, Ryan still hadn't grown tired of the toy shop. It wasn't like any other place she'd ever known, with its dark musty corners and cobwebbed ceiling, its dusty shelves and creaking, uneven floorboards. What had at one time been a showroom for antique furniture had become through the years a hopelessly cluttered wonderland of handmade toys, with Mr. Partini's workshop at the back. Tiny locomotives trundled through the rooms on ledges along the walls. There were dolls of all sizes and kites shaped like animals; tins and tops and windup toys. From shadowy corners carousel horses watched with painted eyes that seemed to move. There was even a magnificent dollhouse with a back-yard pond where the dollhouse family enjoyed seasonal outings. Ryan loved them all, and now as she sniffed the fresh evergreen from the decorated Christmas tree, she felt all her concerns melting away.

"Mr. Partini!" she called. "Mr. Partini, it's me!"

Of course he'd be at his workbench, and of course he'd pretend he hadn't heard her so he could act surprised when she poked her head through the curtain at the rear of the store. It was a game they always played, and as Ryan shrugged out of her coat, she began to pick her way carefully through the maze of toys and furniture.

And then she felt it again.

That strange tingly sensation of eyes boring into her back.

She had told Mr. Partini time and again how easy it was to overlook customers in the hopeless disarray, and now, as she slowly turned, her eyes swept each corner, expecting to find some customer browsing half hidden in the gloom.

"Hello?" Ryan called. "Is anyone there?"

No answer. As her eyes continued around the shop, she suddenly noticed a movement from the front window.

It was hard to see the figure clearly from its place out on the sidewalk; all Ryan could make out was a lumpy coat, a black ski mask with holes for eyes, and a cap pulled low on the head. One of the train whistles screeched, startling her, and when she looked again, the window was empty.

"You *are* a mess," she scolded herself and continued on to the back. As she entered the work area, she saw the toymaker's empty stool, where he should have been sitting, and uneasily she took down her apron from its hook on the wall. From behind her the bell tinkled over the front door, and she hurriedly walked out into the shop.

"Merry Christmas! If I can help you find anything, please—"

The cheery greeting died on her lips.

The shop was empty.

Funny . . . I could have sworn I heard that bell. . . .

Frowning, Ryan let her gaze wander once more over each crowded, shadowy corner, but when she didn't hear anything else unusual, she sighed and got to work.

"Okay, family, everybody out—the maid's here to dust!"

Ryan leaned in at the back of the dollhouse, where all the rooms lay open to view, but though she peered into the parlor, where the family should have been, it was deserted.

"It's no use hiding," Ryan joked, "I see *everything!*" But as she took a quick survey of all the other rooms, she stepped back, puzzled. *I know I left them in the parlor . . . maybe some kid moved them . . . maybe some kid stole them. . . .* She moved to one rear corner of the house and suddenly spotted the little dolls in their backyard, apparently enjoying some winter game as they clustered around the glass-mirror pond. "So there you are! What is this—a skating party and I wasn't—"

Ryan froze, her eyes riveted on the artificial water. From somewhere far away she heard screams . . . screams for help . . . but the room was deathly silent.

FATAL SECRETS

The mirror was broken, shiny shards of glass in scattered silvery pieces, and trapped there, far out from shore, was one of the dolls.

Only her head was visible . . . and her arms, reaching for help . . .

And the bright red ribbon that streamed from her hair onto the soft white cotton snow.

Chapter 2

Mr. Partini!"

As Ryan stumbled backward, a display of wooden blocks clattered down around her, and she screamed and ran for the back room.

"Mr. Partini! Where are you!"

"Yes, yes, *Bambalina!* I hear you! The whole street —it hears you, too, eh?"

To Ryan's relief, the back door opened and a bushy white head poked through, faded blue eyes twinkling behind round spectacles.

"What you so excited about, *Bambalina?* You just see Santa Claus? And he promised to bring you a nice young man for Christmas?" The heavy Italian accent gave way to a chuckle, but as Mr. Partini closed the door behind him, he finally focused in on Ryan's pale face. "What happened to you? Why you look so scared?"

"The . . . the dollhouse!" Ryan tried to steady herself with a deep breath. "The pond—it's broken—"

"What?" Mr. Partini lifted his head and made a disgusted sound in his throat. "You mean somebody busted up the mirror? Seven years' bad luck!"

"But the doll—you've got to come—"

"Yes, Ryan, I come—ah! There go my tools on the floor—clumsy me! Yes, yes, just let me pick them up. . . ."

Ryan could hear herself babbling as she flung the tools back onto his table, as she grabbed his arm and pulled him into the front. "She's drowning—in the pond—in the ice—" She could see confusion all over Mr. Partini's face, and as she got to the dollhouse, she gestured wildly. "See? The pond—"

"Yes, yes, I see the pond." Mr. Partini's head nodded rapidly up and down. "Yes, yes, but nobody drowning."

"Look—there—" Ryan's words choked in her throat, and she stared at the broken pond in the miniature backyard. The mirror still lay in slivers, but the doll was gone. Stunned, she leaned in close to the dollhouse. The family was back in the parlor. The drowning doll sat in a chair and wore no ribbon.

"No," Ryan murmured, stepping back again. "No . . . you don't understand . . ."

"Then you tell me, eh?" The old man shuffled forward, his kindly, wrinkled face full of concern. "You tell me, *Bambalina,* so I understand."

Ryan shook her head slowly. "She was in the pond."

"And you move her back inside?"

"No. I didn't move her."

"But . . ." Mr. Partini spread his hands, his face completely baffled. "How can that be? These no walking dolls—are sitting dolls!"

"But she *was* there," Ryan insisted, her voice

beginning to tremble. "She was in the pond, and no one would help her—"

"Ahhh . . . what you say to me, *Bambalina?*" He looked earnestly into her face, his confusion growing. "What—you think she need help, this little doll? Maybe she wanna go outside in the snow, eh? Yes, yes, is okay!" He nodded, pleased that he'd figured it out. "You help her! Put her outside! Whatever you want!"

"No . . . I . . ." Ryan's voice faded, and she bowed her head. "It . . . made me think of my sister."

She hadn't wanted to say it, but she couldn't help it. And now, seeing the look on Mr. Partini's face, she hated herself.

"Ah . . . Ryan . . ." His hand fluttered over her head, settled shakily on her hair. "Is much too sad. My worst heartache . . ."

"I'm sorry," Ryan whispered. "I didn't mean to bring it up." She watched the old man sink down onto a wooden trunk, and she sat on the floor beside him.

"Is very hard, losing someone." Mr. Partini sighed. "Like my Rosa . . . twenty-five years now . . . but I never forget."

A long silence drifted by. Mr. Partini closed his eyes and rocked gently, lost in thought. After a while he spoke again.

"I say to myself, is a good idea to put fresh things, green things in the toyshop. Nice for customers . . . nice for you and me . . ." He shook his head sadly. "No. Was bad idea."

"No, Mr. Partini, it wasn't a bad idea. It didn't have anything to do with what happened." She smiled wryly, hearing Phoebe's own words coming out of her mouth. *Why is it always easier to comfort everyone else instead of me?*

"Twenty-five years," Mr. Partini murmured. "My Rosa . . . my love . . ."

"Mr. Partini"—Ryan nudged him gently, and he looked at her as if he'd forgotten where he was—"Mr. Partini, *someone* broke that mirror."

"Aah . . . not your fault," he said kindly, patting her cheek with one blue-veined hand. "I no blame you—you not worry, eh?" He got up and gathered the broken pieces of the mirror, shuffled over, and dropped them into a wastebasket. "No more worry. Everything okay now. I get a new mirror. Everybody happy."

"Someone moved the doll, Mr. Partini," Ryan said, trying her best to be patient. "Between the time I found it and you came in. Someone must have been here, and I didn't know it—"

"You have other things on your mind." Mr. Partini patted her shoulder, smiling. "Crazy things up here sometimes, just like me!" He tapped one finger to his forehead, his smile spreading, lighting up his whole face. "Is normal, eh? I hear voices—they say, 'Work harder, Guido Partini, you way too slow, even for an old man!'" He laughed heartily, catching Ryan in a hug. "You okay, *Bambalina*. You go home now. Rest. Come back tomorrow . . . feel better, eh?"

"I shouldn't leave, Mr. Partini. I'm here to work—"

"Yes, yes, and all these customers need help!" He flapped his arms at the empty room and tried to look serious. "Go away, all of you! My little friend here needs to go home, and I can only wait on fifty of you at one time!"

In spite of everything Ryan began to feel better. "Well, I hope all the customers don't start looking like that weird one in the window."

Mr. Partini turned and stared at his front window display, then back to Ryan, his expression more blank than ever.

"You make a joke with me." He shrugged his shoulders good-naturedly. "But I don't get it!"

"No joke, Mr. Partini." Ryan couldn't help smiling. "He was out on the sidewalk in a big fat coat with his face all covered up."

"I no see this big fat guy." Mr. Partini shook his head. "Maybe he fat with money, eh? Maybe he come in sometime and buy all my toys for his fat babies!"

Shaking her head in amusement, Ryan followed him back to the workshop and got out of her apron.

"Where were you when I got here?"

"Is a funny thing! I hear knock on door. I say, who's there?" Ryan chuckled as the old man counted out the events on his fingers. "Voice say 'Delivery.' I say 'I no expect delivery.' Voice say 'Delivery.' I go out, eh? Nobody there. Nobody in whole alley." He stared at Ryan, dismissing the whole incident with a wave of his hand. "So maybe another joke on me. Bad boys playing around."

Ryan considered it, nodding. "Well . . . I suppose it could have been a joke. . . ."

"Or maybe shop is haunted!" Mr. Partini slapped

his leg and gave a laugh. "They break mirror—they call me outside! Those bad, bad toys, eh? Causing trouble!" He laughed again, ushering her to the front door, then regarded her thoughtfully as she put on her coat. "You bundle up warm, *Bambalina*—no catch cold in the snow." Gently he reached out and patted her cheek, then closed the door after her as she went outside.

It was nearly dark. Ryan usually enjoyed the shorter days of winter, but now it looked ominous outside, and she was thankful for the dim light from the other shops.

That doll . . . reaching for help . . .

A raw wind gusted out from an alleyway, twisting old newspapers around Ryan's ankles. Catching her breath, she tore them away, then watched them scatter out into the street.

The doll . . . with the red ribbon . . .

"It was my fault," Ryan whispered now, walking faster, head bent against the wind, "my fault that you're dead, Marissa—"

An earsplitting squeal made her look up in alarm— she saw the headlights only inches away and felt a crushing jolt as she spun backward and sprawled facedown onto the curb.

"Hey, are you okay?"

Stunned, Ryan lay there on the pavement and gave in to the strong hands that took her shoulders and gently eased her over.

"Are you hurt? Say something—can you talk?"

As Ryan gazed up into the young man's face, she

felt her breath catch in her throat. Winchester Stone was staring down at her, silhouetted against the slate-gray twilight.

"Can you hear me? Can you move?"

At long last Ryan found her voice, though it came out little more than a croak. "I . . . I think so."

"Try, then. Move your arms."

Ryan gingerly did so, relieved when nothing seemed to be broken.

"Now your legs."

Again she did as she was told. She could feel his arm beneath her shoulders, propping her up. His other hand moved to her right ankle, and then to her left, carefully testing for broken bones. Flustered, she struggled to sit up.

"I'm fine. Really. I just need to get up now."

"You sure?"

"Yes. I'm really okay. Just . . . surprised."

"Surprised." As he echoed her words in his soft, slow voice, Ryan could see the fear on his face relaxing a little. "Surprised," he said again. "You stepped out right in front of me—I didn't even have time to honk the horn. You're lucky I didn't kill you."

Ryan got clumsily to her feet, avoiding his eyes. He picked up her things and handed them to her.

"I'm sorry," she said. "I've just had my mind on other things lately."

His glance was quick and curious. His eyes shifted back to the street.

"Forget it," he said quietly.

"I'm . . . I'm Ryan McCauley," she stammered.

"I know."

"You do?" She bit her lip, embarrassed, and tried to be casual about brushing herself off.

"I went out with your sister," he said, and his eyes swung back to her again. "But I never saw you at your house."

Because Phoebe was right, I was always hiding upstairs.

Ryan shrugged and tried to smile. "Well, I was—you know, around somewhere probably."

Without warning Winchester turned back to his truck, but stopped after only a few steps. He kept his back to her, one hand resting on his hip.

"I'm sorry about her," he said.

Ryan stared at his tall, lean frame, his thick black mane of hair hanging just below the collar of his denim jacket.

"You helped look for her. I never thanked you."

There was a long silence.

"I guess . . . you haven't heard anything," he said at last. He sounded uncomfortable, and Ryan shook her head, forgetting that he couldn't see her.

"They still haven't found her body. They told us they might never find her. . . . I hate to think that."

"It's the river," he said quietly. "The current's so strong . . ." He turned around and looked at her, but his face was in shadow. "Do you need a ride somewhere?"

"I'm going home," she said, then added quickly, "but really, I'm used to the walk."

"It's dark. That's a pretty long way to go." He

33

moved to his truck and opened the passenger door.
"Get in."

She felt that curious fluttering in her chest again and
glanced back in the direction of the toyshop. *Maybe I
only thought the doll was in the pond . . . like when I
blank out at school and then realize half the class is
over. . . .*

"—the door?"

"What?" Ryan's mind snapped back, and she saw
Winchester staring in her window.

"I need to close your door."

"Oh, yes—yes—sorry."

She watched as he slammed the door and climbed
in the other side. The pickup was old and battered,
and it was all she could manage, not to bounce off the
seat at every bump. She tried to study Winchester
from the corner of her eye and sensed great calm and
strength behind his handsome features. When he
suddenly turned off the main road to her house, she
realized that somehow she'd missed the whole trip.

"Well . . . thanks a lot." Ryan pushed on the door
handle, but it wouldn't budge. She pushed again. "I
really appreciate the ride—" She was shaking the
handle now, and nothing was happening, and he was
just sitting there staring at her while she made a total
fool of herself. "It really was nice of you—"

"You have to unlock it," Winchester said. To Ryan's
embarrassment, he reached across her, pulled up on
the lock, and shoved the door open.

"I-I—thanks," Ryan murmured. She scrambled
out and headed straight across the yard to the front

door. As she reached the porch, she couldn't resist one last backward glance. Winchester was leaning out his window watching her, and as she bolted inside, she heard the truck's engine fading down the road.

"Mom?" she called. "You home?"

"Up here," came the toneless answer, and Ryan's heart sank. When she looked in Marissa's room, Mrs. McCauley was sitting listlessly on the edge of the bed.

"Come on, Mom," Ryan coaxed. "Let's go downstairs, and I'll make hot chocolate."

"I missed her today," Mrs. McCauley murmured. "Even more than usual." When Ryan didn't answer, she roused a little, her eyes searching for Marissa's clock. "Are you home already? It must be late—"

"No, I'm early." Ryan peeled off her coat, relieved when her mother finally faced her.

"Are you sick?"

"Sort of. Not really."

Her mother nodded and turned away. "That's so like you, Ryan. Can't you decide? So different from your sister. . . ."

Ryan sat down but couldn't bring herself to touch her mother's shoulder. "Maybe I'm trying to catch the flu. It's going around school."

Mrs. McCauley held a thin hand to Ryan's forehead. "No fever. Maybe you're just tired. I've told you a hundred times, you shouldn't stay up so late to study."

I stay up late because I can't sleep, and when you see my grades, you'll find out that all the studying hasn't helped. "I know—let's go out for dinner."

"I can't, Ryan. Steve flies in tonight, and I promised to pick him up."

"God, Mom, he has his own boat, can't he even afford a taxi?" The words were out before she could stop them, and her mother's face grew even more remote. "I'm sorry." Ryan reached for her mother's arm . . . hesitated . . . drew her hand away. "That was a rotten thing to say."

"Yes, it was. Especially since Steve thinks so much of you."

"Well, anyway"—Ryan sighed—"I forgot Phoebe's coming by later to study and—" She broke off, following her mother's gaze to the windowsill, where a smiling photo of Marissa stared back. "Mom?"

"When I'm in here," Mrs. McCauley murmured, "it's like it used to be. I can feel her . . . she's alive."

Ryan's eyes swept the room, and she suppressed a shiver. Nothing in the room had been changed or removed or rearranged since the day of Marissa's death. Ryan didn't like the strange feeling the room gave her. She only came in here when she had to drag her mother out into the world of the living.

"Just like today," her mother went on. "Like today when I just started missing her so much, I thought I couldn't bear it. I thought, my beautiful daughter is dead, and the pain is more than I can stand—"

"Mom . . . please . . ." *You still have me . . . doesn't that help . . . even a little?*

Her mother's eyes swung reluctantly back to Ryan's face, and an ironic smile quivered at the corners of her mouth. "I know I'm being silly. Everyone's told me it's impossible she could have survived. Maybe . . . with the spring thaw—"

"Mom—"

"It's just that I keep thinking of her, lost out there somewhere, and all alone, and wondering why we haven't found her and brought her home. . . ."

Ryan was shaking. She made it to the hallway and stood there looking back.

"I know I'm being morbid," Mrs. McCauley went on, her voice breaking, the tears coming, yet still she stared at Marissa's photograph, still her eyes never moved. "Morbid and completely illogical, but maybe she really *did* survive somehow, maybe she's sick somewhere and confused and someone's taking care of her and she can't remember who she is or what happened. Maybe it'll suddenly come back to her, and we'll hear a knock at the door and—"

The doorbell pealed through the silent house, and Ryan jumped as her mother turned frightened eyes toward the hall.

"It's probably Phoebe." Ryan backed gratefully toward the stairs. "Mom? Did you hear me? I'm going now."

Hurrying down, Ryan breathed deeply, trying to rid herself of the stale stench of Marissa's room. The porch light was on, and through the frosted glass at the top of the door, she could make out an indistinct form, someone standing there, head lowered.

"Phoebe, you silly," Ryan scolded, jerking open the door. "What'd you do, forget your key again—"

But it wasn't Phoebe standing there on the porch,

arms heaped with gaily wrapped packages. As Ryan stared, the young man looked up, his wide, full mouth relaxing in a polite smile, the presents shifting slightly as he stepped forward.

"Is this the McCauley residence?"

"Yes," Ryan mumbled. In the glow of the light she saw dark blond hair brushed back from a high forehead, and narrowed blue eyes that swept over her without so much as a blink.

"I'm delivering these presents. From Marissa."

Ryan knew she was staring, but she couldn't help it. In the sudden quiet her voice sounded unnaturally loud. "From . . . I'm afraid there must be a mistake—"

"No mistake," he interrupted, stepping closer, the smile fixed on his lips. "I know Marissa's dead."

"You . . . then . . ."

"You must be Ryan," he said, and in that instant she saw something flicker behind his eyes, something tighten in his smile.

"Yes. Yes, I am."

He bent his head, his chin deep in the collar of his jacket. His voice sounded muffled, but Ryan could still hear each word.

"You're the one who let her drown."

Chapter 3

Ryan had a strange feeling of being suspended in time. She saw the smile on the stranger's face, and she heard footsteps descending the stairs behind her, but she couldn't seem to make herself move or speak.

"Ryan?" It was her mother's voice, fearful, on the staircase, and as Ryan mentally shook herself, her mother spoke again. "It isn't Marissa, is it? Tell me it's—"

"Charles Eastman." The young man peered around Ryan, his smile open and friendly as Mrs. McCauley hovered at Ryan's back.

For a moment Mrs. McCauley looked as confused as Ryan felt. "I'm . . . I'm afraid I don't—"

"I was a friend of Marissa's," he said quietly. "A very good friend."

"Marissa?" Mrs. McCauley echoed, and the longing in her voice stirred Ryan at last. "You knew Marissa?"

"We had classes together. We'd been going out awhile."

"Charles . . . Charles . . ." Ryan could see her mother struggling to think back, to place him somewhere in Marissa's interrupted life. "I'm sorry, I . . ."

"You mean Marissa never mentioned me?" He chuckled. "Isn't that just like her—with her string of boyfriends, I'm not surprised. But that's okay." He smiled understandingly. "There's no reason you should know me. Actually, I've been wanting to come and see you for a long time—ever since I heard about . . ." His voice trailed away, and his face went serious. "Well, I was cleaning out some stuff last week, and I found these." He held the packages out and took a step closer. "We used to go antique hunting together, and I guess some of her things got mixed up with mine. I knew she meant to give these to you for Christmas." His voice softened, his eyes suddenly sad. "Anyway, I wrapped them and decided to bring them myself. I know it's what she would have wanted."

Throughout his whole speech, Ryan had been watching, listening, feeling as if she were invisible. *"You're the one who let her drown."* He *had* said that, hadn't he, as she'd stood there holding the door? Yet the charming young man before her now *couldn't* have said those horrible words—and through a slowly clearing fog, Ryan heard her mother's voice taking control at last.

"Come in, Charles, come in—Ryan, don't leave him freezing out there on the porch! Close the door."

Ryan felt him move past her into the hall. She closed the door and watched as her mother led Charles into the living room and gestured to a chair.

"Ryan, take the packages and his coat. You can stay

for a while, can't you, Charles? Wouldn't you like something hot to drink? Coffee? Tea?"

"Coffee'd be great, but only if it's already made." He smiled at Ryan and draped his coat across her arm. She hadn't remembered following them into the room.

I'm scaring myself. First I was seeing things that weren't there . . . and now I'm hearing things that nobody said. . . .

"Ryan!" Mom's voice, firm. "The coffee?"

She felt herself nod and was glad to escape to the kitchen, glad to be doing something she didn't have to think about. *Pot . . . filter . . . coffee . . .* Her hands moved slowly, but her mind was racing. *"You're the one who let her drown."*

He didn't really say that. He couldn't have.

Ryan slipped back to the hallway, positioning herself so she could watch Charles without being seen. He was sitting forward in his chair, hands clasped together on his knees, his expression intense as if determined not to miss anything her mother might say. From time to time he slowly flexed his fingers, reminding Ryan of a contented cat. She moved closer, propping herself in the doorway, and was surprised when Charles turned and gave her a winning smile.

"I wish you'd sit down. I didn't want you to go to any trouble on my account."

"It's no trouble," Mrs. McCauley assured him and gestured toward Ryan. "I'm so sorry, Charles, I didn't even introduce—"

"Oh, I'd know Ryan anywhere," Charles broke in smoothly. "From the way Marissa described her. She talked about you a lot, Ryan. You must have been so close."

He was staring at her intently. Something about his expression seemed almost mocking, but Mrs. McCauley didn't seem to notice.

"Marissa's—accident—has been pretty hard on Ryan. She was with Marissa when it happened, you see—"

"So I heard," Charles said softly. His eyes brushed over Ryan, leaving a peculiar coldness in their wake. "I'm sure it's something . . . she'll never forget."

You did say it . . . when I opened the door, you said what I thought you did—"I'm going to Phoebe's," Ryan burst out, and she could see the disapproval on her mother's face as Mrs. McCauley motioned toward the kitchen.

"Ryan, I wish you wouldn't run off. I thought Phoebe was coming here to study. Isn't that coffee ready yet?"

"I forgot. She *was* coming here, but we decided to go there, instead. I just forgot."

"Ryan's always forgetting things." Mrs. McCauley gave Charles a strained smile. "Not like Marissa. Marissa never had trouble making up her mind—"

"It doesn't look very Christmasy in here," Charles broke in pleasantly. "You decorate about as much as I do."

"Oh, we *used* to decorate . . . I just . . ." Mrs.

McCauley's eyes flicked to the mantel, more photos of Marissa, more painful reminders. "It just didn't seem right somehow. . . ."

To Ryan's surprise, Charles said, "But what about Ryan? It must be hard on her, your not going ahead with family traditions. If it were me"—his eyes slid to Ryan's puzzled face and then shifted away—"I guess I'd feel like I was being . . . you know . . . punished."

Ryan stared at him, but he kept his gaze averted. "I'm going to Phoebe's," she said again, but her mother didn't seem to hear.

"I suppose you're looking forward to Christmas," Mrs. McCauley said to Charles. "Being home from college, spending time with your family—"

"Actually, I'm not." Charles shook his head politely. "My parents are divorced. My dad's in Europe on business, and my mom's remarried, living out on the West Coast. I've been hanging out at school, but it's so dead around there, I decided to just get in my car and drive."

"And you don't have friends to stay with anywhere?"

"No, I'm heading out again in the morning." He laughed softly. "I booked myself a room at that motel outside of town."

"But that's a terrible place to stay! There aren't even any decent restaurants nearby!"

"Really?" Charles looked surprised. "Marissa's the one who gave me the name of that place—in case I ever got here over the holidays."

"Did she?" Mrs. McCauley leaned forward, her face wistful and sad. "Tell me how you knew her. What you remember about her."

Charles's voice was barely a whisper. "I really miss her."

"Oh, I do, too. More than anyone can understand—"

"Goodbye," Ryan broke in. "I'm going." But nobody seemed to care, and she escaped out the kitchen door.

What kind of a creep had Marissa met up with this time! Ryan thrust her hands in her jacket and trudged off across the yard, down the slope behind the house. It was a shortcut she often took to Phoebe's, one that ran through fields and woods instead of along the main road into town. The air was nippy, but she welcomed the sting of it against her cheeks. She couldn't have stood another minute in the same room with Charles Eastman.

It was a good twenty minutes' walk to the Evanses' house at the south edge of town. As Ryan wiped her feet on the welcome mat, she noticed both cars gone from the driveway, but she could hear loud music blaring from upstairs, which meant Jinx was home.

"Phoebe!"

The music kept going, and Ryan shouted again as she climbed the stairs to Phoebe's room.

"Phoebe, it's me! Let's study here tonight, okay?"

"Go home, McCauley, who invited you?"

As Ryan neared the landing, Jinx suddenly appeared in the upstairs hall, lounging lazily against the railing. There was something about Jinx that always made her smile, even though she and Phoebe usually felt like strangling him, and she hid a smile now as he purposely blocked her way to Phoebe's room. He was a year younger, but every bit as tall as she was, and Ryan guessed that if he ever decided to unfold his body from its perpetual slouch, he'd be even taller. She and Phoebe had come to the conclusion long ago that Jinx had been born in tattered jeans and dirty sneakers—trading off seasonally between holey T-shirts and stained sweatshirts. The jeans he wore tonight had a torn back pocket and rips in both knees, and his hair, as usual, looked like he'd just gotten up and forgotten to comb it. His quick brown eyes never missed a thing, though most of the time they looked deceptively bored.

Ryan stared at his ear and frowned. "So that's where Phoebe's earring went. She'll really kill you this time."

"Like I'm worried." His thin body slouched itself forward over the banister.

"And new laces in your shoes. Fuchsia. How sweet."

"Yeah. I thought so." A slow, disarming grin crept across his face, showing the one dimple in his cheek, the only similarity to Phoebe. Ryan wondered how he could often look so cuddly and be such a holy terror.

"Don't tell me she's not here."

"She's not here."

"But we were supposed to study—"

"Forget that. Some guy called, and she went out."

"Really?" Ryan brightened. "Was it Michael Kilmer? Did he finally ask her to the dance?"

Jinx shrugged. "Her eyes glazed over. That's all I know."

Ryan sighed. "Well, I wish she'd at least called me."

"She did call you. She called you lots of things. But I stuck up for you."

"I meant on the phone. You know what I meant—"

"She left a message with your mom."

"Well, that explains it." Ryan grimaced. "Do you know when she'll be back?"

"What do I look like—a secretary?" He snorted and started back down the hall to his room. "I got things to do."

"Important, I'm sure." Ryan heard the thump of a basketball hitting the wall, and she trailed along, following the sound. Jinx's room was a perfect reflection of his personality, and she paused in the doorway, shaking her head.

"How can you live in here? Where's your bed?"

Totally unbothered, Jinx yanked his headphones down over his ears and promptly flopped down amidst pillows, tangled covers, books, dirty clothes, car magazines, cassettes, and baseball cards. "Don't you have something to do?" he yelled. "Besides standing around adoring me, I mean?"

Ryan sighed and went down to the kitchen, stopping to admire the Christmas tree along the way. She'd always loved the Evanses' house—its cozy atmosphere always encouraged warm visits and heart-to-heart talks. Helping herself to a ham sandwich, she sat down and opened her history book. *I have to study . . . I have to concentrate.* But every time she closed her eyes to memorize something, Charles Eastman's face popped into her mind and spoke to her. *"You're the one who let her drown."*

"I didn't," Ryan whispered, pressing her hands over her eyes. "I didn't let Marissa drown. You didn't say that . . . why did you say that?"

A sudden noise made her jump. Jinx was propped in the doorway staring at her.

"There's a guy at my house," Ryan said stupidly.

"So what'd you do, kidnap him?" Jinx sauntered in, opened the pantry, shrugged, left the door open. "You're gonna have to think up new ways to get a date, McCauley."

"I'm serious."

Jinx stood at the sink with his back to her. After a moment he glanced over his shoulder.

"What guy?"

"He just showed up. Just tonight, out of the blue. With Christmas presents he said Marissa'd bought for us. He was at school with her. I guess they went out."

"So?"

"So . . . I think he's weird."

"You should know." Jinx turned his attention back to the countertop. He took an apple from a bowl and bit into it with a loud, intentional crunch.

"I shouldn't have gone off like that," Ryan mumbled. "I shouldn't have left Mom there alone with him. I shouldn't even be here." She stared down at her book and frowned. "I should go. I don't know why I even came here in the first place."

"Well, when you finish this fascinating conversation with yourself, let me know what one of you decides to do."

"Maybe I should call the police." Ryan sat straighter, her frown deepening. "Do you think I should call the police? I mean, we don't know anything about this guy—do we?"

Jinx shrugged. "I give up. Do we?"

"Then maybe I *should* call the police—"

"No, no"—Jinx reached toward the phone—"let *me* call them. They have places for people like you who go around arguing with themselves."

Ryan closed her eyes for a moment. When she opened them again, Jinx was staring at her curiously.

"Hey, McCauley . . . you okay?"

"He said I let Marissa drown," Ryan murmured.

"What?" Jinx's face hovered between skepticism and surprise, and he took another bite of apple, continuing to talk around it. "That's dumb. He didn't say that. Why'd you think he said that?"

"Because . . ." Ryan's mind went back . . . the front door opening . . . Charles Eastman's face peering over the packages . . . "I just did. That's what it sounded like."

"That's really dumb," Jinx said again. "Tell me how he said it. How you *thought* he said it."

"'You're . . .'" Ryan took a deep breath. "'You're the one . . . who let her drown.' That's how it was."

"Your mom heard him say it?"

"No, she wasn't there. She came down right after."

"Then you must have gotten it all messed up in your head." Jinx looked annoyed now, and he spit some seeds into the sink. "He probably said, 'I'm new in town' . . . or . . . or maybe 'I'll hang around.' Something like that."

"No, I don't think so."

"You don't *think*—that's the whole problem with you," Jinx snorted. "I mean, why would a total stranger ring your doorbell and say something dumb like that? Hey—where you going?"

"Home." Ryan gathered her things and paused by the front door to put on her coat. "Tell Phoebe to call me the minute she gets home. Okay? No matter how late."

"Yeah, yeah." Jinx waved impatiently, following her onto the porch. "Man, it is *cold* out here . . . and you *walked* over? What a loony."

"Mom needed the car to pick up Steve. Anyway, it's not that bad."

"Anyway, like I'd trust your judgment." He shivered and thrust his hands into his jeans pockets. "How come you never drive Marissa's car?"

"You know why," Ryan retorted. "It's part of the shrine. Sacred. Can't be touched."

"So touch it. What's your mom gonna do?"

Ryan considered a moment. "Cry. Mope. Sulk."

"Ah. The usual."

"I hate it there, Jinx. It's like a funeral home. I want a Christmas tree."

"So *get* a Christmas tree."

"I want to be happy again."

"Then stop making yourself unhappy. Only you can."

She looked at him in mild surprise, and he shrugged his shoulders with a lopsided grin.

"See you around, McCauley. Don't talk to strangers —or yourself—on the way home."

Ryan stood there a moment after Jinx had gone inside. She watched the Christmas tree glowing in the front window . . . she breathed in the sweet aroma of winter and woodsmoke and pine trees that lined the drive. The air felt heavy and wet with the promise of snow, and she walked quickly, slowing down only when she reached the frozen creek near her house.

Stopping, Ryan felt the hair prickle along her scalp. The woods were full of silence, and then the cold, cold sigh of the wind.

Ryan frowned, her hands making fists in her pockets.

She listened, and the night listened back.

She started walking again, her ears straining through the deep winter night. She thought she heard a rustle of leaves . . . the soft sucking of mud. A raccoon, she tried to tell herself, or maybe a deer . . . Annoyed with herself, she started to duck under a fence.

It's back . . . something . . . watching me . . .

With a gasp Ryan spun around, challenging the empty fields with wide, frightened eyes. *No, I'm only imagining it, just like the doll in the pond, just like*

Charles's speech at the door, just like I've started imagining lots of things since Marissa died—yet she began to run, across the fields, up the last slope to the house, her breath ragged in her throat as she fell into the kitchen, as she sagged against the door—

"Mom! Mom, where are you?"

But of course Mom wasn't there, Ryan remembered now, she'd gone after Steve and they'd eat out afterward and *thank God I'm home safe, and Charles is gone*—

Ryan felt weak as she dragged herself upstairs. She left the switch on in the hall, and she left her door open, and then she turned on every lamp in her room, flooding herself with bright, safe light. She took hold of the sweater she was wearing and began pulling it up over her head.

"I'd close the door if I were you."

Gasping, Ryan whirled around, her arms tangling in her sweater as she tried to jerk it back down again.

Charles Eastman was standing in her doorway.

Smiling.

"I knocked, but I guess you didn't hear me," he said. "Sorry about that."

Ryan stared at him and felt her cheeks burn as his eyes moved from her sweater to her face. "What are you doing here? What are you doing in my house?" She took a step toward the phone on the nightstand by her bed. "Get out of here right now."

"But didn't you know?" And his mouth fell open in mock surprise. "Your mom asked me to stay."

"She . . . what!"

"She invited me to stay. To spend Christmas. I was just going to the motel to get my stuff."

Ryan saw the smile widen across his lips and the way he took another casual step into her room. She heard her own voice, and it sounded strange and hollow.

"But . . . she couldn't have. We don't even know you."

"Your mom likes me." He smiled again and came closer, hesitating at the foot of the bed. "And Marissa liked me," he said softly. He leaned toward her.

His smile was gone.

"But *you* don't like me. Do you, Ryan."

As Ryan stared back at him, she saw Charles lift his hand . . . felt his fingertips trace lightly down one side of her face . . . across her shoulder . . . down her arm . . .

"Well, who knows?" He shrugged, and again something flickered behind his smile, behind his eyes, that made Ryan's skin turn cold. "I just might surprise you."

Chapter 4

How could you?" Ryan demanded before her mother could get in the back door. "I can't believe this!"

Mrs. McCauley dropped her purse on the counter but didn't turn around right away. "Ryan, I don't think I need to explain myself to you—I'm still the head of this house—"

"Welcome home, Steve!" Steve said with forced brightness behind her. "Gosh, Steve, it sure wasn't the same with you gone! Come on, ladies, it's too late for an argument tonight, okay?"

"Steve, do something!" Ryan looked at him as he poured himself a cup of coffee and sat down at the table. "Can't you make her listen?"

"It's not his decision to make," Mrs. McCauley said. "I *want* Charles to stay—and Ryan, keep your voice down, I don't want him to hear you."

"He won't. He went to get his things."

"Have a nice trip, Steve?" Steve nodded in answer to his own question. "Hey, I sure did! And thanks for asking!"

"You don't even know him!" Ryan went on. "You don't know anything about him! He could be—"

"He and Marissa were good friends," Mrs. McCauley said softly. She braced herself against the counter, her hands trembling. "If Marissa cared about him, then he's welcome here."

"Did you ever hear her mention him?" Ryan persisted. "Did you ever hear his name around here a single time?"

"I'm sure there were lots of friends we never heard about. You know how popular Marissa was."

"Leslie, I think what Ryan's trying to say," Steve began, clearing his throat, "I mean, she's really got a valid point, I think—"

"I want him here," Mrs. McCauley said, her voice beginning to quiver. "He was a part of Marissa's life. I want him here."

"Oh, Mom!"

"We don't have Marissa this Christmas, and Charles doesn't have his family. The least we can do is share our holidays with him. For Marissa's sake."

Ryan stared at Steve, who silently mouthed a warning to let the subject drop. Ryan ignored him.

"*What* holidays? A couple hours ago you couldn't have cared less whether Christmas came or not. Now all of a sudden—" She broke off as her mother's shoulders began to shake, as the quiet sobbing filled the silent kitchen. Steve got up and motioned Ryan away, and she slipped dejectedly up to her room.

I don't even belong here. I'm an outcast in my own house. As Ryan stretched out across her bed, the telephone rang, and she was relieved to hear Phoebe's giggle on the other end of the line.

"Ryan—I'm in love."

"Again?" Ryan sighed. "Phoebe, something terrible—"

"Michael Kilmer called tonight and—you'll never guess—he asked me to the dance! He's been working up his nerve all this *time!* He thought I was going with *Randy*—I can't believe it—Michael Kilmer! I nearly fainted! No—no—I nearly died!"

"Was that before or after your eyes glazed over?" Ryan shook her head indulgently. "Phoebe, listen—"

"We went to the Coffeehouse and talked and talked —do you think I talked too much? I hate that, Ryan, I always worry—"

"Phoebe—"

"Anyway, a bunch of kids are getting together tomorrow night to go caroling, and I said you'd come—"

"Will you listen? I have to tell you—"

"We'll meet in front of school at seven. Then we'll go back to Michael's afterward for a party—"

"Phoebe—"

"—and I bet when you're there, someone'll ask you to the dance—"

"Stop—"

"I put the word out that you're still available—and I'm so sorry about studying tonight, but I really *did* try to call and—"

"Wait—I have—"

"Mom's giving me the evil eye. She needs to use the phone, so I have to go, okay? See you tomorrow— bye!"

Ryan heard the click and stared at the dead receiver in her hand. Slowly she replaced it on the stand, then sat up as a knock sounded at the door.

"What is it?"

Steve's head poked in, his smile cautious. "Truce?"

"I'm not upset with you. Come on in."

Steve nodded and closed the door behind him, leaning back against it as he surveyed Ryan sitting cross-legged on her bed.

"I know, I know," he said at last. "She's being weird again."

"You can't let her do this," Ryan said flatly. "It's totally insane, and you're the only one she'll listen to."

"Okay, I'll try. But she seems to have her mind—*and* her heart—set on this. Ryan . . ." Steve grew quiet for a moment, pursed his lips, looked at the ceiling. "Your mom's going through a really bad time right now—which isn't to say you're not, too"—his smile was sympathetic—"only she's not thinking about anyone but herself. It's not so unusual, you know, these crazy things she's doing. She's reacting to her grief and trying to work it all out in her mind."

"So we'll all get our throats slashed in the process," Ryan said gloomily. "While she's working out her grief, I mean."

Steve looked surprised, then laughed. "Boy, you really *don't* like Charles, do you? What's with all the hostility? You just met the guy."

"Nothing. I don't know." Ryan flopped down on

her stomach and propped her chin in her hands. "Okay. I know that look. What'd I say?"

A chuckle sounded low in Steve's throat, and he shook his head, giving in to a grin. "You're too much, Ryan."

"Don't give me that. You're wondering something. Out with it."

"Okay, then. I'm wondering why you're down on this poor guy. I know I haven't met him yet, but I have to trust your mother's judgment, at least a little! We don't have any reason to doubt he's a friend of Marissa's, and you're already accusing him of throat-slashing! Do you know something about him maybe the rest of us don't know?"

"How could I know anything about him?" *Except he accused me of killing my sister.* "Marissa never mentioned him. What about you? Haven't you ever had him in one of your classes or something?"

"Come on, Ryan, the campus is bigger than this whole town! I don't know *everybody*. Though he does seem kind of familiar."

"So is he telling the truth or not?"

"Well"—Steve shrugged—"his story sounds believable enough to me. And since this isn't my house, I can't very well throw him out if your mom wants him here."

"That's the trouble. She doesn't know what she wants," Ryan said irritably. "I don't trust him. He's too . . ." She spread her arms in frustration. "Too nice to Mom."

"Thanks," Steve said, deadpan. "Not like me, who's a real jerk, huh? Thanks a lot, Ryan."

"I didn't mean that. You *are* nice to Mom," Ryan said quickly as Steve laughed.

"Tell you what. The least we can do is find out if he's really going to school where he says he is."

"How will you do that?"

"Look through my directory. And if he's not there, call the admissions office."

"But will they tell you? Is that confidential or something?"

Steve shook his head. "The only problem will be finding someone in the office over the holidays."

"You won't forget, will you?" Ryan was relieved when he smiled.

"Not if it'll make you feel better. Just let's not talk about this in front of your mom, okay? I don't want to upset her any more."

Ryan sighed. "Just don't tell me I have to be nice to him." She put a hand to her forehead as the doorbell rang. "That's probably him now. We better not let Mom catch us talking."

"Right." Steve opened the door and peered cautiously out into the hall. He gave Ryan a thumbs-up sign and left.

I really am going to flunk that history test tomorrow. Once more Ryan opened her textbook, but before she could tackle her notes again, another knock sounded on her door. This time it was Mrs. McCauley who looked in, and Ryan could tell from the expression on her mother's face that she wasn't going to like whatever was about to happen.

"Ryan, I want you to let Charles have your room."

"What!"

"He's going to be here for a few days, at least, and—"

"At least! Mom, are you—"

"And I can't put him on the couch. If it were for a night, that'd be different, but he'll need some privacy."

"What about me?" Ryan sat up, her voice thin and tight. "It's *my* room—I don't see why I have to give it up for—"

"You can sleep in Marissa's room," Mrs. McCauley said quickly, and Ryan stared at her as she rushed on. "It makes perfect sense to do things this way, and you'll be just across the—"

"Why don't you put *him* in Marissa's room? He was *her* friend!"

"No!" Mrs. McCauley burst out. She put her hand on the wall to steady herself, and Ryan could see her fingers clenching. "I don't want some stranger sleeping in there, do you hear me? I don't want some stranger in Marissa's bedroom—"

"But it's okay for some stranger to be in *my* room." Ryan looked at her accusingly. "It's okay for some stranger to be in our house."

"Hey," a voice in the doorway startled them both. Charles was standing there, a regretful smile on his face. "Hey, look, the last thing I want is to cause problems. I think it'd be best for all of us if I just leave."

"You can't!" Mrs. McCauley caught him by the shoulders, recovered herself, then pretended to straighten his collar. "No, Charles, please"—her eyes swung to Ryan . . . pleading—"I want you to stay. We all do. Don't we, Ryan?"

For an endless moment Ryan locked eyes with her mother. Then she looked at Charles. His expression was politely unreadable, yet somehow she sensed cunning watchfulness just below the surface. Very slowly she closed her book and got up.

"I'll move my things," she said. *But I won't stay in Marissa's room, I'll pack a suitcase and go over to Phoebe's, and I'll live there till this creep is out of our house. . . .*

But deep inside she knew she wouldn't.

She could never go off and leave her mother alone with him.

Chapter 5

So he's really staying in your room?" Phoebe's mouth opened in disbelief, and she leaned against her locker, blue eyes wide. "And you slept in Marissa's room last night?"

"No." Ryan sighed. She put one hand to her mouth to stifle a yawn, then rubbed her forehead. "I slept on the couch. I watched TV and studied till I fell asleep."

"Oooh." Phoebe gave a shiver. "I don't blame you. I'd feel really creepy sleeping in there . . . you know . . . where she used to be. So what else about this guy? What's his name—Charlie?"

"Charles. Eastman. And that's all I know about him—*nothing*. Oh, Phoebe, what am I going to do?"

"Well, what does Steve think about it?"

"He's going to try and find out if Charles really went to school with Marissa. Steve doesn't like the idea of him being with us, either"—Ryan shrugged—"but what can he do? He can't *force* Mom to listen. She's really determined about this."

"What's he look like? Charles, I mean. Is he cute?"

"You'd probably think he is." Ryan sighed again

and shot her friend a look. "Don't get any ideas, Phoebe, okay?"

"Well, he does sound intriguing." Phoebe grinned. She pulled some books from her locker and slammed the door. "I think you're way too paranoid. Let's just analyze it. Maybe this is a sign. Maybe you're looking at it all wrong."

"Whatever you mean, I don't think I'm going to like it." Ryan looked suspicious as Phoebe locked arms with her and maneuvered along the crowded hallways. "I know that gleam in your eye, and it usually means trouble for me."

"Okay, just listen." Phoebe talked fast, knowing they were already late for class. "There's no reason that I can see for you to be nervous. Charles *has* to be a friend of Marissa's. What other possible reason could he have for wanting to bring presents and stay with you for the holidays? I think it's really sweet that he liked Marissa so much, he'd want to get to know her family better. He's probably thinking it will help somehow, if he's there to cheer up your Christmas."

Ryan frowned, still skeptical. "Well . . ."

"And it's a real compliment to you and your mom that he'd feel so comfortable, he'd even want to stay."

"But he's not the same to me as he is to Mom," Ryan argued.

"How?"

They paused outside their classroom door. Ryan could see Miss Potter inside glancing from the clock to the bundle of papers in her hands.

"I . . . I don't know how to explain it. He's just different."

"Are you sure you're not imagining things?"

"Phoebe—he practically accused me of killing Marissa!"

"Oh, Ryan, honestly, you *must* have heard him wrong! What a horrible thing to say!" Phoebe almost laughed. "I mean, why would someone come on a mission of mercy and say something so outrageous? It just doesn't make sense! I'm *sure* you misunderstood him—like you've been getting your assignments wrong all week. You're not listening very well these days. You said so yourself."

Ryan saw Miss Potter's frown deepen as she gestured for them to hurry. Phoebe took Ryan's arm and shook it.

"It's a *sign,* Ryan. Charles Eastman came into your life to take you to the New Year's dance."

As Ryan gaped at her, Phoebe turned and hurried to her desk, leaving Ryan to trail behind.

"So glad you could spare some time for us, ladies," Miss Potter greeted them. And as Ryan slid miserably into her seat, she could already see the big fat F slashed across the top of her history test.

"Mr. Partini!" Ryan paused in the workshop doorway, relieved when the toymaker grinned up at her from his bench.

"Ah! You sneak up on me, *Bambalina!* You feel better, eh?" He held up a grinning marionette, squint-

ing at it from behind his spectacles. "This customer—
he wants it *delivered!* Today! So now Guido Partini is a
taxi again!"

"You've got to stop making all those deliveries for
people," Ryan scolded him lovingly. "They have just
as much time in their day as you have. It wouldn't
hurt them one bit to get themselves over here and save
you some trouble!"

"Ah, no, *Bambalina,* no trouble!" Mr. Partini
shook his head, catching his glasses as they slid down
his nose. "Is a little thing for me. I help them out, eh?
No bother!"

"Then let me do it for you. I'd like to."

"You do plenty. Too much sometimes. I no deserve
you."

"And you're too nice." Ryan tried to frown but felt
the corners of her mouth turning up. "If I've told you
once, I've told you a hundred times. You've got to quit
being so nice!"

"Then I be mean to you!" He tried to put on his
fiercest expression, but his twinkling eyes gave him
away. "I be mean to the toys! I tear down the
dollhouse! We punish those bad dolls for giving you
such a scare!"

Ryan laughed and went out into the shop. The
afternoon went quickly, with a steady flow of customers to keep her busy, and she was totally absorbed in
demonstrating a jack-in-the-box when Mr. Partini
politely excused himself and took her aside.

"I go now to deliver the puppet, *Bambalina.* You
can watch the shop, eh? Lock up when you go home?"

"I think I can handle that," Ryan teased. "But I still wish you wouldn't go running all over town. You look tired."

"Ah, is such a little thing," he protested, waving her back to her customer. "Just a little way to say thank you for buying my toys, eh? I see you in the morning!" Laughing delightedly, Mr. Partini went out the back door, leaving Ryan to tend the shop alone.

She was exhausted when six o'clock came. Her lack of sleep the night before was catching up with her, and the last customer was a picky, rude woman who couldn't make up her mind. As Ryan's eyes went impatiently to the window, she suddenly stiffened and gripped the counter with both hands.

She saw the lumpy coat and the black ski mask. She couldn't see the eyes, but she knew they were looking at her, could *feel* them as if they were only inches away.

"—please?" The woman stepped between Ryan and the window, waving a doll under Ryan's nose. Startled, Ryan jumped back.

"Excuse me?" She was craning her neck, trying to see around her customer, but the woman kept side-stepping, blocking Ryan's view.

"Too expensive." As the woman turned to leave, Ryan saw that the window was empty.

"Wait!" she called, hurrying around the counter, but the woman stomped out the door. Ryan stood for a moment peering out at the street. Unsettled, she put her hand on the latch to lock it, but a shadow suddenly filled the doorway, and she screamed as the door burst open.

"God, McCauley!" Jinx stood there, looking just as startled. "What'd you do—see your own reflection?"

"Come in here!" Ryan yanked him out of the way so she could lock the door. She glanced outside again, but the street was empty. "We're closed, Jinx. Go home. No! Stay here."

"I love a girl who knows her own mind."

"Did you see that man a minute ago?" Ryan looked again, half expecting the strange figure to materialize at the window.

"What man?"

"Big coat. Ski mask. At the window."

"Yeah. He robbed the place next door and took off." Ryan gave him a withering look. "I'm serious."

"You're seriously demented. No, I didn't see anyone. Why?"

"He was there yesterday, too. Just looking."

"Uh-oh," Jinx said gravely. "A compulsive window-shopper. Quick! I'll call nine-one-one—"

"No, you jerk, he was watching *me.*"

"Even worse. The guy is desperate beyond hope."

"Don't you have someone else to bother?" Ryan headed for the back room, sighing as Jinx followed.

"I have to get Phoebe something for Christmas," he announced.

"Well, that's nice of you for a change."

"Yeah, Dad's making me."

"If you really want to make her happy, why don't you move out?"

"Suffering gives her character." Jinx grinned. "Dad said there was something here she wanted."

"That teddy bear over there." Ryan began turning off lights in the back room. "I was going to get it for her, but you can if you want."

"Why does she want this dumb thing anyway?" Jinx picked it up and studied it, frowning. "How much?"

"There's a price tag on it. I thought you finally learned how to read last year."

"Kind of touchy tonight, aren't you?" Jinx gave a slow grin. "Couldn't be that new guy, could it? Got your fantasies working overtime?"

Ryan bristled. "The only fantasy I have of Charles is him getting in his car and leaving."

"Right. After the New Year's dance, you mean."

"I mean now. The sooner the better. I can't stand the guy."

"That's not what Phoebe said."

"Phoebe's too wrapped up in Michael Kilmer to know *what* she's saying." Ryan gave a last look around the shop. "Are you buying that or not?"

"Yeah, okay. You don't have to bite my head off." Jinx sauntered over to the counter as Ryan rang up the sale. "Can you wrap it for me?"

"Now?"

"Well . . . sometime before Christmas."

Ryan made a point of sighing loudly. "Just leave it here, and I'll wrap it tomorrow when I come in."

"Could you hide it, too? She might find it at home."

"Jinx, *no* one could find it if you hid it in your bedroom."

"Okay, then, if she's not surprised, it'll be *your* fault—"

"Well, she spends as much time at *my* house as she does *yours!*" Ryan slammed the drawer into the register. "Okay"—she sighed again—"I'll put it somewhere." She pushed past him to the door and stood staring out. "Oh, great—"

"What?"

"It's snowing."

"I coulda told you that. I thought you liked snow."

"I do. I just don't feel like walking home in it right now."

"Come on . . ." Now Jinx sighed loudly. "I'll give you a ride."

"In *your* car? The last time I saw your car, it looked like your room. There's probably something contagious in there."

"Relax." Jinx grinned and reached above her, holding open the door just wide enough for her to squeeze through. "You're so ugly, nothing in my car would jump on you anyway."

He managed to sidestep Ryan's fist, keeping his distance as they started down the sidewalk. Huge wet flakes fell lazily from the darkened sky, and as Jinx brushed them from his hair, Ryan stretched out one hand to catch a few on her mitten.

"Phoebe's wrong about Charles," she said again.

Jinx had a ready retort, but her troubled expression stopped him. "You're still all hung up about what you thought he said to you. About Marissa, right?"

Ryan nodded, falling into step beside him. They walked slowly, and she turned her face up, loving the feel of snow on her cheeks.

"To tell you the truth, I'm not even sure now if he really said it or not. I keep thinking what you told me—"

"Me? What *did* I tell you? Something wise, I'm sure."

Ryan nodded absently. "Well, why *would* he have said something so awful to me? It's such a . . . *cruel* thing to do." She thought a minute, glancing up at him. "He really is nice to Mom. Sweet and polite. It's so weird . . . part of me wants to think he's just a nice guy. And part of me keeps having this feeling he's up to something."

"Yeah? Like what?"

"That's just it, I don't know."

Jinx nodded amicably. "So what's your plan?"

"What plan?"

"To get this guy out of your house."

"I don't have a plan." Ryan made a face. "Mom wants him to stay, so I guess he's staying."

"Well, don't blow this, McCauley. If you're really nice to this guy, maybe you'll end up at the dance after all."

Ryan threw him an exasperated look. "And has it ever occurred to you that maybe I don't even *want* to go to the dance?"

"Yeah." Jinx gave a solemn nod. "Girls always say that when they haven't been asked."

Ryan tapped her foot impatiently as he opened her car door. "And I suppose you've got girls *begging* you to take them?"

"As a matter of fact—" Jinx began, but Ryan slid in and slammed the door. After going around to the other side, he climbed in and fixed her with a smug look. "As a matter of fact—"

"You can't fool me," Ryan said primly. "No girl in the whole school would be desperate enough to go out with you or your goofy friends."

"You're just jealous." He stuck the key in the ignition and gave it a turn. "'Cause I'm popular, and you're not."

"Popular?" Ryan stared at him. "Excuse me, Jinx, I thought you said *popular.*"

Jinx managed to keep a straight face as he stared back at her. "Mystique, McCauley. It's called 'mystique,' what I have."

"It's called 'mistake,' what you have," Ryan corrected. "And besides, I hear little Tiffany Taylor has her eye on the junior class vice president."

"So who cares about Tiffany Taylor anyway?" Jinx snorted.

"*You* do. So maybe I should talk to her, huh? And tell her what you're *really* like—all the little things about you that I've known for years and years. . . ."

This time she got to him, as she knew she would.

"You know your problem, McCauley? You're still mad 'cause I pulled your stupid doll's head off when you were six years old."

"And you're still brain-damaged 'cause Phoebe and

I held you down and tickled you till you cried and told your mom." Ryan chuckled as he tried to ignore her. "I bet Tiffany would like to know about *that*. I bet she'd think it's cute—"

"Cut it out, McCauley, you're not—"

"Does she know how ticklish you *still* are? Maybe I should tell her *that*, hmmm?"

"Come on, now, quit fooling a—"

Too late Jinx tried to defend himself, but Ryan cornered him up against his door and mercilessly attacked his ribs.

"Cut it out, McCauley—I'm stronger than you—"

"Not when you're laughing, you're not—and—uh-oh—look at this—you're *blushing*—"

"I am *not!* Come on, Ryan, stop it!"

"So much for mystique." Ryan laughed as Jinx finally managed to grab her hands and shove her away. As he fumbled to put the car in gear, she settled back against the seat, enjoying his efforts to regain his dignity.

"No more favors for you," he scowled, cool and in control again. "You're too dangerous to ride with."

"Your face is still red."

"Shut up."

By the time they reached the house, Jinx still wasn't speaking to her, but Ryan finally coaxed a grudging wave from him as she ran up to the door. The house stood dark and silent against the wintry sky, and as Ryan let herself inside, she wondered where everyone had gone. Marissa's room seemed even spookier as she paused in the doorway, as if every personal possession were waiting for its owner's return. Ryan crossed to the window and looked out, resting her forehead on the cold, smooth glass. She took a deep breath and closed her eyes.

From somewhere outside came the honking of a car horn—not intermittently, but constant—as if someone was leaning on it and not letting up.

Jinx? Has he forgotten something and come back? Puzzled, Ryan scanned the yard below and the drive along the house. There were no cars that she could see, yet the honking continued, setting her nerves on edge. Irritated, she hurried downstairs and out onto the front porch, halting in dismay.

The front yard was deserted. There were no cars near the house or in the driveway leading to the road.

Ryan rubbed a chill from her arms and went back to the kitchen. *Maybe I just missed it, maybe it was driving around back when I looked from upstairs—*

After grabbing a flashlight, she stood nervously out on the back stoop and put shaking hands to her ears. She could still hear the monotonous honking—on and on—*but there's nobody here, I can hear it, but there's absolutely nobody here—* Slowly she followed the driveway behind the house, and as she quickened her pace, she suddenly *knew* where the sound was coming from.

The garage. *And it's coming from Marissa's car.*

With numb fingers Ryan scrabbled at the latch, then heaved the heavy door upward. In the darkness she could just barely see Marissa's car along the far wall, and as she groped for the light cord which hung from the ceiling, she felt her heart turn to ice.

Is that someone bent over in the front seat? Leaning facedown on the steering wheel . . .

Ryan found the cord at last and gave it a jerk.

Nothing happened.

She yanked it again—again—but still the garage lay in darkness.

Like a statue, she stood rooted to the spot, her heart pounding, the sound of the horn going on and on, shrieking through her, every nerve ready to explode. She found the switch on the flashlight . . . felt her feet stumbling forward . . . saw the car getting closer . . . Her eyes slowly adjusted to the gloom, and she tried to make out the shape on the front seat of Marissa's car. . . .

The beam of her flashlight skittered over the windshield, casting pale, eerie shadows into the black interior. . . .

She saw the stiff upholstery . . . the dust on the dashboard . . . and it looks like a coffin, Ryan thought wildly, *a gray-lined coffin all musty and stale and sealed tightly away. . . .*

And then she saw the body.

Through a haze of disbelief, Ryan aimed the flashlight onto the driver's side and saw the human figure slumped forward . . . the head propped on the steering wheel, its face hidden . . .

The long blond hair streaming over its back . . .

Wet hair—

And the red, red ribbons tangled in the matted curls—

Ryan tried to scream, but no sound came out. The weak beam of the flashlight began to tremble violently, crazy shadows in a macabre dance over the slumped body in Marissa's car—

The body began to move.

Horrified, Ryan saw the shoulders pull slowly back . . . the head begin to lift sluggishly from the wheel—

"No!"

Springing back, Ryan heard the flashlight hit the floor, saw the crazy spin of light and shadow as it rolled under the car. As she whirled around, the garage door crashed to the ground, leaving her in total darkness. Sobbing, she stumbled forward, running her hands frantically over the door, mindless of the splinters and cuts as she searched desperately for the latch. As her fingers closed over it at last, she gave a shove but nothing happened. Slamming her shoulder against it, she moaned and staggered sideways.

The car door squeaked slowly . . . slowly open.

Oh, no . . . God, no . . . help me—

In absolute terror Ryan flattened herself against the garage door. She could hear the footsteps now . . . dragging toward her across the floor . . . like something heavy . . . dead . . .

Like something inhuman.

"Marissa," Ryan whispered, and she began inching along the door, praying the thing couldn't hear her, wouldn't find her, the relentless blare of the horn filling her head, disorienting her in the terrible darkness—

"Marissa," she whispered again, "I didn't mean it . . . I tried to hang on—I—"

From the other side of the garage Marissa's car started up.

Stunned, Ryan realized she'd reached a corner, and she squeezed herself into it, trying to be invisible. She sank to the floor and felt a tiny breath of cold air seeping in under the door.

"Help me," she murmured, and in that split instant she realized that something was near her—beside her in the dark—she could *feel* it—the darkness pulsating with its *presence,* its *danger*—

"Oh, God . . ." She put out her hand and felt heavy, wet fabric . . . damp human skin . . . icy cold . . .

Something slimy coiled around her neck . . .

Shrieking, Ryan's head snapped back and hit the wall, and through the insane darkness, she saw a soft explosion of stars.

Chapter 6

Ryan? Can you hear me? Come on, open your eyes!"

As Ryan gasped and began to cough, she recognized Charles Eastman's face bending over her. She was lying in the driveway, and as another fit of coughing seized her, Charles began thumping her back and rubbing her face with snow.

"Stop it!" Ryan could hardly speak for choking. "Stop doing that! Let me go!"

"Of course I'm not going to let you go," Charles said patiently. "You'll probably just fall down again."

"What happened? What am I doing out here?"

"Why don't you tell me? I opened the garage door, and you fell out. What'd you do—lock yourself in?"

"The car! Did you turn off the car?"

"What car? My car?"

"No—Marissa's car! The motor—" Ryan struggled to sit up, and Charles obligingly slipped an arm beneath her back. "Someone was in there! Marissa! And she started the motor and I couldn't breathe and she came after me—"

"Whoa, hold on a minute. You're saying someone was in the garage with you?"

"I don't know, I don't know!" Ryan shook her head desperately. "There was a body in the front seat, but it was her! I saw her hair and her ribbons—Oh, God!"

"What's the matter?"

"She came after me—her clothes were wet—she put her ribbon around my neck—"

"There's nothing around your neck."

"But I felt it! Did you look for it? Did you look around?"

"Well, no." Charles looked baffled. "Come on, Ryan, let's get you inside. Lucky for you I started to put my car in here—"

"Lucky for me?" Ryan stared at him. "Lucky for me?" She struggled to push him away, then got clumsily to her feet, falling immediately into his outstretched arms. "Leave me alone!"

"Don't be stupid. If you don't let me help, then I'll have to carry you."

Ryan had no choice. She leaned heavily on Charles as he guided her back to the house, then she collapsed on the couch as he stood back to appraise the situation.

"You stay right here," he ordered. "I'm going to fix you some good strong coffee."

Ryan nodded vacantly, looking past him to one corner of the living room. "You got a tree," she mumbled.

Charles shrugged, brushing it off. "I thought the place needed brightening up. I thought *you* needed brightening up."

Ryan stared at him. "I didn't imagine what happened out there."

"I'll get the coffee," Charles said. "Then we'll talk."

Ryan must have dozed. When she opened her eyes again, Charles was standing over her with two steaming mugs, and she wondered how long he'd been watching her.

"Feel better?" he asked politely.

She gave a halfhearted nod, then ran her fingers cautiously back over her hair. "I hit my head against the door, I think. I was so scared—"

"What happened, did you lock yourself in? When I got there, the door was closed, and when I opened it, you fell right out." Charles gave a grim smile. "Surprised *me*, I'll tell you that."

"Then you must have turned off the horn." Ryan sighed, trying hard to think back, to remember every detail of what had happened.

"What horn?"

"The horn on Marissa's car. It was stuck—that's why I went out there. It was stuck, and when I looked in her car, I saw . . ." She hesitated, swallowing fear. It sounded so preposterous now, she could hardly bring herself to say it. "I saw . . . Marissa."

"Marissa?" Charles's glance was skeptical.

"Yes . . . I mean . . . it looked like her . . . her hair —her ribbons—"

"You saw her face?"

"No . . . the door fell and everything was so black —but she started to get up—I *saw* her! She started to raise her head and—and—"

78

"Take it easy." Charles regarded her thoughtfully. "She *started* to, but you never actually saw anything."

Ryan shook her head. "No. But she walked toward me. I felt her wet clothes . . . and her skin—"

"She touched you?"

"Well . . . not exactly. I sort of . . . touched her. Accidentally."

"I see."

"But the motor was running by then, and I was all confused—" Ryan was talking fast and Charles was just staring at her, saying nothing. "The horn wouldn't stop, and I hit my head—" She broke off as he got up from his chair and walked slowly over to the tree. "You don't believe me."

He reached out and slowly stroked a branch. "When I got here, I brought the tree inside. Then I went to the garage. There wasn't any horn honking . . . there wasn't any car running. There wasn't anyone—or anything—in there. Except you."

Ryan stared at the cup in her hand. "It was real," she whispered. "I couldn't imagine something that horrible . . . could I?"

"Well . . ." Charles hesitated, his fingers caressing another branch. "It seems to be all tied up with Marissa somehow, doesn't it? Maybe . . . if you talked about her, you'd feel better."

Ryan's voice grew defensive. "Talk about her how?"

"You know." Charles sounded deliberately casual. "Your relationship, for example. Or . . . what you remember most about her. Or . . . what you remember about the time you spent with her before she died."

Ryan's throat closed up and she looked away. "There's nothing to tell. We were . . . you know . . . just sisters."

There was a long silence. Charles sat down on the floor beside the tree and looked at her. "So what's it like, being just sisters? I'm an only child, so it's always seemed special to me. You share a lot? Private jokes? Secrets?"

Ryan nodded. "Yes. Both. Sometimes."

"And she probably confided in you a lot, I bet. Told you stuff she probably wouldn't tell anyone else. . . ."

A flash of memory hit Ryan—that last day in the woods—the secret she'd sworn to keep but never knew—and her eyes brimmed. "Sometimes," she murmured.

"She told me stuff, too," Charles said, and Ryan glanced at him in surprise as he nodded. "Yes, she really did. We were really close friends. She told me lots of things about you."

Ryan glanced away again, feeling suddenly uncomfortable. She didn't want Charles to know anything about her. It made her feel violated somehow.

"She told me about your mom's favoritism." Charles leaned back against the wall and shook his head sadly as Ryan stared at him in disbelief. "I think she really knew you were always being overlooked, that she always got her way, while you just—"

"That's not true!" Ryan said hotly. "Marissa was just the oldest, that's all, she—"

"Ryan," Charles said smoothly, his smile sympathetic, "you don't have to pretend with me, Marissa told me everything. She thought you were really special, you know."

Ryan felt trapped. She shifted on the couch and spilled coffee on her sweater. She dabbed at it with her sleeve.

"Your turn," Charles said from his corner.

"My turn what?" Ryan said jumpily.

"I've told you things Marissa told *me*—now why don't you tell me something she told *you?* We'll trade."

"I don't want to trade." Ryan set her mug down on the floor. "I want to go upstairs."

"It might help, you know," Charles said softly. When Ryan didn't answer, he tried again. "Whatever happened out there tonight—maybe if you talked about her, all the ghosts would go away."

"I don't want to." Ryan shook her head fiercely. "I don't need to."

She was almost to the door when his voice stopped her.

"But *I* need to."

Surprised, Ryan faced him. He was gazing down into his cup, and his lips were pressed in a troubled frown.

"I need to, Ryan," he said again, avoiding her eyes. "I need to know what her last day was like . . . her last hours. What she did . . . what she talked about . . ." His eyes raised at last as his voice lowered. "If she was happy."

Again the memory came back—Marissa's voice, her odd behavior. *"I think I'm in trouble . . . serious trouble—"*

"But it doesn't matter now," Ryan mumbled. "It doesn't matter because she's gone, and I'll never know what she was talking about—"

"What?"

She frowned, not realizing she'd spoken aloud or that Charles had heard. "Nothing."

"You said she was talking about something . . ." Charles spoke carefully. "Don't shut me out, Ryan. I care about her, too."

"I can't." Ryan turned again and started for the hall. "I can't talk about her. Maybe someday. But not now."

She jumped as Charles grabbed her elbow. She hadn't even heard him get up or cross the room.

"When you *do* feel like it," he said, "talk to me, Ryan."

She stared into his face, saw his half smile, winced as his fingers tightened on her arm.

"I'm here for you," Charles whispered. "It would mean so *much* to me."

Chapter 7

So," Mrs. McCauley said. "Do you want to tell me what happened?"

Ryan sat up, blinking against the light, and saw her mother standing rigidly beside the bed. A quick glance at the clock told her she'd only been napping an hour, but her head felt like it had been in a coma for weeks.

"I fell in the garage," she mumbled.

"And hit your head. Charles told me." Mrs. McCauley sighed.

Then why bother to ask? "I'm okay now," Ryan added.

"I'd hardly call hallucinating okay." Mrs. McCauley bowed her head, her fingers plucking at the hem of her skirt. "Actually, I'm glad we're talking. There's something I think you should know about."

"What?"

"I had a talk with Mrs. Corbett this afternoon—"

"The school counselor? Why?"

"Don't get upset, Ryan, everything is *all right*. She called and asked if I had a minute, so I went by." Mrs.

83

McCauley's fingers twisted more tightly, but Ryan couldn't see her expression. "She's . . . disturbed about you."

She's disturbed . . . that's really funny . . . I'm losing my mind, and she's disturbed . . . "What'd she say?" Ryan was apprehensive.

"It's about school," Mrs. McCauley said slowly. "Your grades . . . how you're so distracted . . . depressed . . ." Her voice trailed away. "I told her it hasn't been easy for any of us. That you have all this . . . this"—she made a frustrated gesture —*"guilt.* And of course she understands, but she thinks maybe it would help—"

"Guilt?" Ryan echoed as her mother glanced at her. "And what do you say, Mom, about this *guilt* of mine?"

"Mrs. Corbett says it's normal, your having these lapses in class, perfectly normal, after what happened to Marissa—"

"I didn't let her drown," Ryan whispered, and she hated her mother in that split second for tearing her eyes away, for not looking at her, for letting seconds go by before she answered.

"Of course you didn't, Ryan, for God's sake, nobody thinks—"

Mrs. McCauley jumped as there was a knock on the door and Steve peered in.

"Phoebe's here. She says you're supposed to go caroling."

"I don't want to go." Ryan threw back the covers and moved past both of them into the hall.

"You're going!" Phoebe's voice carried up from downstairs. "I'm not going if you don't go!"

"Then stay home!" Ryan yelled down.

"You can't do this to me! I told you we're all going to Michael Kilmer's afterward." Phoebe bounded up the stairs and confronted Ryan with her most desperate look. "You've *got* to go! My whole *future* depends on it!"

"Oh, go on, Ryan." Steve grinned. "I'm driving your mom over to Morrisville to see her friends, anyway. And you wouldn't want Phoebe's tragic future on your conscience. . . ." His voice trailed off as his grin faded. Carefully he reached out and touched Ryan's head, giving a long, low whistle. "Wow . . . is this where you hit yourself?"

"Yes," Ryan grumbled. "When I fell."

"Well, you must have fallen awful hard." Steve looked concerned. "If I didn't know better, I'd say someone hit—"

"Well, hello!" interrupted a cheery voice. "Am I missing something exciting?"

Grouped at the head of the stairs, they all turned as Ryan's bedroom door opened and Charles peered out in surprise. Ryan saw the gleam in Phoebe's eyes and gave an inward groan.

"Maybe." Phoebe dimpled. "You must be Charles."

"Ah, so you've heard of me." He cast Ryan an amused look. "And you're undoubtedly the one and only Phoebe I've heard so much about."

Great, Mom, what else have you told him about our lives? Ryan closed her eyes. *No, Phoebe, don't—*

"We're going caroling. Want to come?"

"He'd be bored," Ryan said.

"I don't think he would." Mrs. McCauley smiled. "I think it's a fine idea. Go ahead, Charles, it'll be fun."

"Michael's not expecting another guest," Ryan broke in.

"Oh, he won't care!" Phoebe's dimples deepened as Charles reached out to shake her hand. "Lots of kids are coming. Dad even loaned me the van. Please come. You can be Ryan's date!"

"No," Ryan said.

"Well . . . I was going to ask Ryan to show me around town tonight, but . . . sure. I'd love to." Charles smiled, casting Ryan a sly glance. "Come on, Ryan, we're practically old friends. Don't be shy."

"This isn't a date thing," Ryan said quickly and saw Steve throw her a sympathetic look. "It's just a bunch of kids getting together. No dates."

"Don't wait up for Ryan, Mrs. McCauley! She can spend the night at my house!" Phoebe's hand was still locked in Charles's, and she began to pull him downstairs. "Oh, I'm so glad you said yes!"

"Me, too," Charles said smoothly. "I haven't been caroling since I was a kid. I probably won't even remember the songs."

"We'll teach you." Phoebe nodded eagerly. "Won't we, Ryan?"

"You can," Ryan tossed back. "You're so good at stuff like that."

"Okay. I don't mind a bit!"

As the threesome bundled up and trooped outside,

Ryan cast a miserable look back at the porch. Mom looked happy, but Steve had an uneasy expression that matched the way Ryan felt.

"I just love this time of year, don't you?" Phoebe chattered as she headed the van through town. "All the Christmas decorations—everything's so beautiful. Especially in the snow."

Ryan huddled in the back, where she didn't have to talk to Charles. It startled her when he reached back and patted her shoulder, then turned around to smile.

"I love the snow, too. So clean and pure."

"I don't even mind driving in it. Not like ice," Phoebe babbled. "I hate driving on ice."

"Ice," Charles murmured. "It's so dangerous, ice. So scary."

"Let's not talk about ice," Phoebe said quickly. "Let's talk about you."

"There's nothing to tell, really. I lead an extremely boring life."

"You don't look boring," Phoebe's glance was coy. "What do you like to do?"

"The unexpected." Charles's smile broadened. "I'm a great believer in surprises."

"Ooh, I like that!" Phoebe giggled. "Most guys are so predictable."

"Are they?" Charles shrugged. "I like to think I'm not like other guys."

"Oh, look!" Phoebe honked the horn and waved. "There's everybody over there!" In her excitement the van went too quickly around a corner, and Phoebe slid into Charles.

"Hey, it's okay." He grinned. "It's a nice change having a girl throw herself at me." As Phoebe laughed, Charles glanced back at Ryan, but she looked away.

The evening should have been fun, but to Ryan it was only an endless blur. As she listlessly trailed the merry group of carolers up and down neighborhood streets, she felt conspicuously separate from everyone else. Phoebe and Michael were snuggled up together, singing offkey harmony, and every time Ryan looked up, Charles was watching her with a concerned smile. She tried to beg off from the party, but Phoebe wouldn't hear of it, and once they'd reached Michael's house miles out in the country, she resigned herself to being trapped. With the party in full swing around her, Ryan finally managed to find an empty room and settled herself down to wait.

"So there you are," a voice greeted her from the doorway, and her heart sank as Charles sat beside her. "You're missing out on all the fun."

"I want to miss the fun." Ryan leaned back and shut her eyes. "I don't feel much like fun right now."

When he didn't answer, she opened her eyes and looked at him. He was smiling and holding out a cup.

"No, thank you," she said.

"Oh, go on, drink it. It's only hot cider."

"I don't want it."

Charles sighed and set the cup down on the table in front of her. "I'll leave it here in case you change your mind."

He had started back toward the door, but now he

stopped and faced her, and the hurt on his face caught her off-guard.

"You know," Charles said slowly, "if I hadn't shown up when I did at the house earlier, you might have frozen to death. At the very least, you could have ended up with pneumonia." A muscle moved in his jaw, and his voice lowered. "I don't understand why you're acting this way. I don't think I deserve it."

As Ryan stared, Charles opened his mouth as if to say more, then seemed to change his mind. He let himself out, closing the door behind him.

Taken aback, Ryan sat there, her mind in a whirl. She could still see the expression on his face, hear the confusion in his voice. *I've been acting so mean to him.* She remembered him offering to change rooms with her . . . talking so sweetly about Marissa . . . bringing the Christmas tree . . . *"I thought you needed brightening up. . . ."*

"Oh, Ryan, you're such a bitch sometimes," she groaned. So what if Charles seemed a little self-centered—maybe he was really insecure and that was his way of covering up. *Maybe he really is hurting about Marissa—just as much as me. . . .*

Ryan picked up the cider and sipped it. No matter how different Charles seemed, that didn't give her the right to be rude. *Especially when he really might have saved my life tonight.* Not wanting to think any more about her close call, Ryan downed the rest of her drink and went out to join the others.

The party was getting wilder by the minute. Charles

didn't seem to be anywhere around, and Ryan caught up with Phoebe in the kitchen.

"Phoebe, have you seen Charles?"

"He was here a minute ago, and I wondered why you weren't with him. Okay, what happened?"

"Nothing. I told you before, he's not my date."

"Well, you'd better get smart and latch on to him. He's *cute!* And he has nice manners, unlike most of the heathens around here."

"Are you speaking of Michael, too?" Ryan teased.

"If *you're* not interested in Charles, *I* could be," Phoebe retorted. "All that beautiful blond hair—and that smile—"

"Look, Phoebe, if you see Charles, just tell him I'm looking for him, okay?"

Phoebe pretended to be deep in thought. "Hmmm . . . this sounds almost promising—"

"Just do it." Ryan chuckled. She started through the doorway when the room suddenly tilted around her.

Shocked, Ryan grabbed at the doorframe, her stomach lurching, her heart pounding in a frantic race. Above her the ceiling turned upside down, and around her the furniture went topsy-turvy. Her legs turned to rubber, and she sat down hard on the floor.

"Phoebe"—she tried to shout, but her mouth was all cottony—"Phoebe—oh!"

If she hadn't felt so dizzy, she would have laughed at herself hugging the wall, even though she'd already fallen onto the floor. She *wanted* to laugh, it was so ridiculous, and as she tried to boost herself up, she heard Phoebe's voice close to her ear.

"Oh, Charles, what's *wrong* with her? Is she okay?"

"She's fine. Come on, now, Ryan, I've got you, up you go—"

"Ryan, what's wrong?" And there was Phoebe's face, all distorted like a funny mask, and Charles's face blurry beside it. "Oh, don't let anyone see her like this, she'd be so embarrassed!"

"Phoebe." Ryan reached for her friend's arm, but her own hand fell uselessly away. "I really need to go home, okay?"

"What did you do, Ryan? Did you drink something? Did you eat something bad? Are you sick?"

"No, I always look like this!" Ryan heard herself laughing and saw Phoebe and Charles exchange looks. "Oh—oh—the room's going again. I'm going with it—"

"Catch her!" Phoebe yelled at Charles. "Oh, God, Ryan, I've got to get you home. Did you take something? Medicine? What's *wrong* with her, Charles?"

Ryan tugged on her sleeve. "You'll have to drive me home."

Phoebe nodded, helping Charles hold Ryan up. "Okay, wait just a second while I tell Michael—"

"Come on, Phoebe, there's no reason for you to leave," Charles broke in. "I'm ready to call it a night anyway. I can borrow your car and bring it back."

"No, just keep it. Take Ryan home, and I'll get a ride and pick up the van tomorrow." Phoebe glanced worriedly at Ryan's glazed expression. "Do you think she'll be okay?"

Charles accepted the keys Phoebe handed him. "She didn't feel too good earlier. This is probably just a delayed reaction. Don't worry—she probably just needs some sleep."

Ryan felt chilled to the bone and could hardly feel herself walking to the van. She leaned against Charles as Phoebe gave him directions and hurriedly piled blankets on the floor.

"You lie down and bundle up back here, Ryan," Phoebe insisted. "Then you can sleep on the way."

"Good thinking," Charles said admiringly. "Everyone should have such a good friend."

"That's what I keep telling her." Phoebe chuckled and waved as they took off.

Ryan felt like a sack of lead. She was conscious of the hard floor beneath her and the mountain of blankets on top of her, but her mind was too fuzzy to comprehend more. The only sounds were the motor's hum, the whine of the heater, and the tick of the wipers brushing snow. As she gave in to the rocking motion of the van, her eyes grew unbearably heavy. When she came to, it was because of something sensed rather than known, and as she struggled to sit up, she saw Charles leaning forward, squinting through the windshield.

"What's the matter?" Ryan mumbled. "Where are we?"

Charles's look was concerned but calm. "To tell you the truth, I'm not sure. I think we might be lost."

"What? We can't be."

Ryan strained to see through the fogged-up windows. It was snowing again—even harder than before—and nothing in the landscape looked even remotely familiar.

"What'd you do?" She turned accusing eyes on him, and he gave a sheepish shrug.

"I don't know. I must've taken a wrong turn somewhere. Stop looking at me like that—you act like I did it on purpose."

"There weren't any turns to take until we hit town. Stop the car." Her heart was racing now, danger signals coursing through her body.

"But—"

"Stop the car! I mean it, Charles, stop it right—"

Her sentence was jolted from her as Charles yanked the wheel and the van slid sideways. Ryan hit the floor and felt the van fishtail, straighten out, then skid. There was a heavy thud as they stopped, and then she heard Charles cursing as he threw off his seat belt and shoved open the door.

"Stay here," he ordered, even as Ryan struggled to follow.

"I will not," she said groggily. "You're crazy, you know that? People like you shouldn't be allowed out on the road."

"A dog ran right in front of me. What'd you expect me to do—kill it?"

"Did you hit it?" Ryan asked anxiously. She was so dizzy, she could hardly hold her head up. *I feel like I've been drugged.* . . . "Where are you going?"

"To check the van." Charles disappeared for several minutes, then his face reappeared in the window, his expression tense. "This is great. I think we have a flat. *And* a missing hubcap."

"What about the dog?"

"What do I care about a damn dog? I've got to get us out of here."

"Well, what are you going to do?"

"I'm going to try and find that hubcap, and then I'm going to try and fix the tire, if the tools are here to do it with."

"Oh, they're probably not." Ryan groaned, and fell back onto the blankets. "Jinx is always using them, and Mr. Evans is always yelling at him to put them back, and he's always forgetting."

"Well, just stay put." She could hear him walking away, and she pulled herself up to the front and tried to yell at him.

"Why don't you see if you can find that dog?"

"Ryan, I mean it—stay inside and keep the window up. And get under those blankets. It's freezing out here."

Ryan listened for several minutes more. She could hear him muttering, and as she craned her neck through the window, she saw him walking farther and farther from the car, his head lowered, searching the ground. With all her strength she managed to inch open the door and get out. *I wonder if he really did hit that dog. The poor thing could be lying out here in the cold. . . .*

The temperature had dropped a lot in the past few

hours. Ryan gasped as the first icy blast hit her and she started walking unsteadily. *If we skidded from over there, then the dog must be around here.* . . .

The snow was heavy and wet, already changing the landscape with deceptive drifts. Ryan blinked snow from her lashes and shielded her face with one hand, scanning the white fields for some sign of movement. *Maybe it was just a shadow Charles saw.* . . . *Maybe there really wasn't a dog at all, and he just thought he hit something.* . . . She couldn't bear to think of any creature lying out here, hurt and frightened and alone in the dark. She cupped her hands and whistled softly.

"Here, dog! Come on—good dog!"

Straining her ears, Ryan heard deep, heavy silence. . . .

And then something that made her heart stop.

"Oh, no," Ryan whispered, "oh, no, oh, no—" and she began to run, painfully slow motion in the suffocating snow, gasping, trying to scream "Charles! Charles!" over and over again, her cries swallowed in a swirling white fog. . . .

It wasn't the dog she heard . . . that whining sound growing fainter and fainter in the distance . . .

It was the van as it drove away into the snowy night.

Chapter 8

My God, he's left me here. . . .

In slow realization Ryan reached out and anchored herself against a sturdy tree.

I don't believe this . . . he's left me here to freeze to death.

She had no idea where she was. As her frightened eyes tried to see past the thickening snow, she searched desperately for a light . . . a sign of chimney smoke against the pale sky . . . some small sign of hope. *The tire tracks . . . I'll just follow the tracks—*

Her legs took over then, mechanically, steering her along. *Someone will miss me and worry about me and come looking for me and—*She suddenly remembered that no one would even notice her absence till morning—Phoebe thought she'd gone home for the night, and Mom thought she'd be at Phoebe's and *what will Charles be doing in the meantime, what story will he be making up about how he managed to lose me out in the middle of nowhere . . . ?*

Ryan stopped, staring helplessly at the white terrain stretching ahead of her, the van's tire tracks covered in fresh snow as if they had never existed. "Damn you, Charles Eastman!" she sobbed. *"Damn you!"*

For a split second she was so consumed by panic that she had to forcibly restrain herself from just dashing off into the whirling white oblivion. *Try to think, Ryan, try to think . . . think and keep walking . . . don't stop moving . . .* She remembered reading somewhere that snow could actually keep you warm, and as she kept doggedly on, she tried to concentrate on the millions of tiny flakes, imagining them as little white coals, surrounding her with heat. She thought of Phoebe's kitchen . . . the Evanses' Christmas tree . . . her own room safe at home—*No, Charles is there*— and Mr. Partini's toy shop—*Someone was watching at the window, someone tried to scare me with the dollhouse*—and suddenly she was thinking of Marissa and that last day—

"Ryan," a voice called softly, "Ryaaaan . . . come to me . . ."

Ryan stopped so suddenly that she nearly fell. A shiver went up her spine, far more chilling than the cold.

"Hello?" she called shakily. "Is someone there?"

The wind gusted through the bare trees, sending a flurry into her eyes. Ryan's hand went slowly to her face, and she tried to blink the snow away.

"Ryaaan . . ." And there it was again, that strange, lifeless voice, calling . . .

Ryan's lips moved but made no sound. As she stared off into the swirling darkness, a white, filmy shape began to gather itself from the snow. . . .

It was floating toward her.

She saw the long, flowing hair . . . the fluttering clothes . . . the arms lifting . . . reaching out . . .

"Ryaaan," the voice wept, "why did you let me drown?"

And even from this distance Ryan could see the flickering light it gave out, the dying light that surrounded it—

"I can't come home for Christmas, Ryan . . . I'm dead. . . ."

"No!" Ryan shrieked. *"Marissa! No!"*

She ran in a directionless frenzy until her body refused to run anymore. Without warning she slid headfirst down an embankment into shallow, icy water and lay there, stunned, as the snow covered her.

She didn't hear the heavy boots stirring the drifts around her, stopping beside her face.

She didn't even try to look up.

She only knew she was warm now.

Chapter 9

The first things Ryan saw were orange and red shadows flickering in quiet patterns up a wall. Then she heard a soft crackle of firewood . . . a sputter of flame . . . and the hiss of falling ashes. She felt layers of thick blankets upon her and soft pillows beneath her head, and she realized she was lying in a bed she didn't recognize, in a room she didn't know. She also realized her clothes were gone.

"So you're awake."

A soft voice startled her from the shadows, and she clutched the blankets tightly to her chin.

"You need to rest," the voice said again. "You should sleep as much as you can."

It was someone she knew but couldn't quite place. She stared apprehensively toward the sound and at last was able to pick out a figure kneeling in front of a fireplace. Shadowy hands snapped twigs and fed them into the flames, and a face turned into the light.

"Don't be afraid," Winchester said. "I won't hurt you."

Ryan felt numb. All she could do was stare.

"Do you remember anything?" he asked softly. "I found you outside about half a mile from here. You were soaking wet and practically frozen. Pretty cut up, too."

"My . . . clothes," she mumbled.

"They'll be dry by morning." He nodded toward the fireplace, where her things were draped neatly over a screen. "Are you warm enough?"

Ryan continued to stare at him in disbelief, and he went on.

"My dog came home hurt—looked like he might have been hit by a car. We don't get much traffic back here—mostly people who end up lost and can't find their way to the main road. Anyway, I went out to see if anyone might be in trouble."

"A . . . car?" Ryan finally said. "Your dog?"

"Oh, he's okay," Winchester assured her. "Just a few scratches. Better than I can say for you." As if to reassure her, he gestured to a corner near the fire. Ryan hadn't noticed the dog before, but now the big shepherd thumped his tail amicably and regarded her with sleepy eyes.

"Then . . . he really did hit a dog," she whispered.

"What?" Winchester moved closer. "What is it?"

Ryan lowered her eyes, shaking her head slowly. "I hurt all over. I don't understand. . . . How did you—"

"Then you *do* remember me." His smile was shy and slow, like his voice. He stopped several feet from the bed, as if afraid of frightening her.

"Of course I remember you." Ryan chanced a quick look at him. "But I still don't—"

"I live here," he said quietly. *"We* live here. My dad, my brothers and sisters—and—" He nodded to the dog.

"Your dad has the garage in town," Ryan said stupidly.

"That's right."

"And you . . . live here?"

"We're so far out from town—on nights like this, Dad usually just sleeps at the station."

"So . . . he's not here?"

Winchester shook his head, firelight gleaming on his hair, black as ravens' wings. "I have to watch the kids tonight," he said after a moment. "They're upstairs asleep."

"And your mom . . . she's not home, either?"

He glanced away. "She died two years ago."

"Oh . . . I'm sorry."

Ryan scanned the dimly lit room and noticed several closed doors. "How old are the kids?"

"All of them?" He squinted, doing a tabulation in his head. "Three to ten. They don't mind staying alone when I have to help Dad, but a couple of them came down sick tonight."

Again Ryan took a quick inventory of the room. It looked like a big log cabin, with wood walls and Indian rugs and old comfortable chairs around the hearth. She could hear the wind whining outside, and a stray gust whooshed down the chimney, scattering sparks. Winchester bent over and crushed them calmly beneath the toe of his boot.

"I'm sorry about your brothers and sisters," Ryan said.

He shrugged philosophically. "Probably the flu. I just hope you don't catch it."

"I . . . I guess you're wondering what I was doing out here." Ryan watched as Winchester came closer and put one hand gently to her forehead. "I know this is going to sound really crazy."

His hand slid away. He straightened the covers around her shoulders. "All that matters is that you're okay."

Ryan regarded him for a long time, but he kept his eyes on the blankets. "I'd like to go home," she said and was surprised when he shook his head.

"I wish I could take you, but I'm stranded here without a car. And I can't call anyone for you because the line's out." He looked softly troubled. "Your mom's going to have a sleepless night worrying about you."

"She doesn't even know . . ." Ryan began, and suddenly tears filled her eyes, spilling down her cheeks. She felt the bed move slightly as Winchester sat down on the edge.

"Don't cry," he said gently. "I promise you'll be safe here. And I'll take you home in the morning as soon as my dad gets back with the truck."

"It's not that," Ryan choked. "It doesn't matter about that . . . only . . ."

"Only what?"

"I saw my sister out there tonight. I saw Marissa."

For a long moment there was silence.

"Your sister," Winchester said at last, and he stared hard into the flames.

"I know it sounds crazy. But she was there in the woods—before you found me—" She broke off as his eyes fell full upon her face.

"Come sit by the fire," he said quietly. He wiped her tears with one corner of the blanket. "Pull these tight around you—I'll carry you."

Before she could protest, Ryan felt herself being lifted into his arms, being carried across the floor as if she were weightless. Winchester lowered her gently onto the rug beside the hearth and put pillows at her back so she could rest but still see the fire.

"Are you comfortable?" He tucked the covers around her once more, and when she nodded, he stretched out on his side, crossing his long legs. "Now. Tell me what happened."

"I saw Marissa tonight. In the woods." Ryan hesitated. "The guy I was riding with drove off and left me after he hit your dog."

Winchester's eyes were calm, intent on the fire. He roused himself slightly but didn't look at her.

"Then you weren't alone?"

"No. We'd been to a party, and I got sick, and he was supposed to take me home. He just left me! And then Marissa came. . . ."

There was an uneasy silence. Finally Winchester shook his head.

"There's no way Marissa could have survived in

that river under the ice. The current's too strong . . . the water's too cold." He leaned forward so slowly that she didn't actually see him move at all, just felt the sudden warmth of his body against hers. "You'll never see her again, Ryan. She's gone."

Ryan ducked her head but immediately felt his fingers beneath her chin, forcing her to look up at him. His eyes were compassionate, and they seemed to peer into her soul.

"I thought I saw her in my garage today." Ryan forced a laugh. "Can you imagine? It's like I can't get away from her. Like she won't stay out of my mind."

"Then maybe you should talk about her," Winchester said slowly. "Maybe there's something bothering you that you need to let go of."

Ryan swallowed tears. "I just wish that last day had been different, you know? I was mad at her." She closed her eyes, trying to shut out the memories. "She was so upset—"

"About what?"

"I don't know! She never told me! I thought she was joking, so I walked away and left her, and she—she started screaming. . . ." Ryan twisted her face from his grasp. "Oh, what does it matter anyway? I wish I could forget about it—but I *can't!*"

Winchester pulled away . . . stared into the fire. "So . . . you really believe now that something was bothering her?"

"Maybe if I'd taken her seriously, she would have told me. I swore I'd keep it a secret, but I never knew what it was." Ryan leaned back and closed her eyes. "I don't even know why I'm telling you this."

A log fell in the fireplace with a muffled thud. Golden light danced over Winchester's hair.

Ryan sighed. "I'm so tired."

She felt Winchester's arms go around her once more, lifting her, carrying her across the room, placing her carefully back into bed. She held the covers close as he stood back.

"Thank you," she murmured, "for finding me."

"Sleep now."

She watched him, wanting to say more, not knowing how. She glanced over at her clothes on the fireguard and felt a blush spread over her cheeks.

Winchester followed the direction of her stare, and a faint smile played at the corners of his mouth.

"I kept my eyes closed," he said quietly. "Good night."

Chapter 10

Ryan awoke to pale gray light and the smell of bacon and coffee. Rubbing her eyes, she started to sit up, then dived back under the covers as the door opened and Winchester appeared with his arms full of firewood, stamping snow off his boots. He nodded and kicked the door shut.

"I thought you might be hungry."

"Is your father home?"

"He's out in the shed."

"I guess he must be thinking who-knows-what—"

"He thinks I rescued you from the snowstorm." Winchester dropped the logs into the woodbox by the hearth. "Which is exactly what happened, isn't it?"

Ryan stared at him as he knelt on the rug and busied himself stirring the fire. He shrugged out of his denim jacket and shook his windblown hair from his eyes.

"I'd really like to go home now," she said.

"Sure. As soon as you eat something."

"Could you hand me my clothes?"

He tossed her jeans and sweater onto the bed, hardly looking at her. Without a word he got up and went outside again, leaving Ryan in a brief moment of privacy.

Pain swept through her body the moment her feet touched the floor. She dressed as quickly as she could, then limped over and knelt in front of the fireplace. She held her hands to the coals, savoring their delicious warmth, and was startled when Winchester leaned in beside her to pitch in another log.

"Oh! I didn't hear you come in!"

"You're still cold." He sounded concerned and in a moment had coaxed the flames to a crackling inferno. "Stay right here. I'll bring your food."

Ryan made a face as she examined the scrapes on her hands and arms, as she gingerly touched the scratches on her cheeks. "I really am a mess, aren't I?" she grumbled.

Winchester gave a half smile. "Not to me, you're not." As he began buttering toast, one of the doors opened, and a child's tousled head poked through.

"Hi," the little girl said, her huge eyes on Ryan.

"Hi, yourself." Ryan smiled back.

"I'm Katy," the child said, looking from Ryan to Winchester, then back again.

"Go back to bed," Winchester said softly.

Katy looked at him as if trying to decide how much leeway she had with his instructions. She stared at Ryan. "Did you sleep here last night?"

"Yes." Ryan nodded.

"Where?"

"There." Ryan pointed, and the child giggled.

"With Winchester?"

"No!" Ryan's face reddened, and Winchester's voice sounded again.

"Bed, Katy. Now." This time there was no mistaking the orders. Katy waved and promptly disappeared.

Ryan sighed as Winchester handed her a plate. "I guess . . . there's some explaining to do."

Winchester seemed amused. "That *is* my bed."

"Your bed!"

"Well, we're pretty cramped for space here." He sat on the floor and balanced a cup of coffee on one knee. "Her comment was perfectly innocent."

Smiling, Ryan tackled her food. There were muffled thumps from the ceiling, and Winchester went to the door where Katy had been, his voice firm but calm.

"I better not have to come up there! Stay in bed!"

Ryan chuckled. "How are they this morning?"

"Bored." Winchester closed the door again and shook his head. "When you're finished, we can go."

The snow had stopped, but the sky threatened more. As Ryan followed Winchester out to the shed, she sank up to her knees several times in deep drifts and had to be rescued. The last time Winchester pulled her out, she ended up against his chest with his arms around her to keep her from falling. She didn't pull back right away, and he didn't let her go until a cheery voice boomed out from the shed.

"Well! Hello, there, young lady! I hear you need yourself a lift home!"

Flustered, Ryan disentangled herself from Winchester's arms and saw Mr. Stone grinning at them.

"I'm really sorry about this," she began, but he pumped both her hands easily in one big paw.

"No bother at all! Just as soon as I finish up here, we'll be ready to hit the road. I brought Mrs. Larsen to look after the kids"—he winked—"but don't worry—I sent her in the back way, and she'll never know you've been here!"

"As if Katy will keep her mouth shut," Winchester said in mock seriousness, and Ryan looked away, flustered.

Ten minutes later, with the three of them squeezed tightly into the tow truck, Ryan tried to ignore Winchester's arm resting along the top of the seat over her shoulders.

"I hope you fed this pretty little thing some breakfast." Mr. Stone chuckled, glancing at his son.

Winchester nodded and stared out the window.

"I went back down to the field and had me a look around," Mr. Stone went on, smiling broadly out the windshield. "Damn, it's a beautiful morning! Didn't see a thing out there—no tire tracks, nothing busted. 'Course, wouldn't expect to find anything after a snow like this." He took a deep breath of crisp morning air. "Still, doesn't hurt to check it out."

Ryan glanced sharply at Winchester.

"What's he talking about?"

"And if you *had* a car, I sure couldn't find it." Mr. Stone glanced over, his smile widening, and covered one of her hands with his huge one. "You know, sometimes when we've had a little too much to handle, we can dream all kinds of things—"

"What?" Ryan looked from Winchester to his father and back again. "Are you saying I was drinking?"

"Shoot, you kids just don't realize what it can do—"

"But—but—I don't even *drink* and—"

"Just drop it, Dad, okay?" Winchester sighed. He'd never taken his eyes from the window, and now Ryan grabbed his arm.

"Do you think I made it all up? Do you think—"

"We're just trying to find out what really happened to you. That's all, little lady, that's all it is." Mr. Stone smiled again.

"But I told you! The guy I was with just drove away and left me—"

"And you saw Marissa. I remember. She came out of the woods and you ran." Winchester finally looked at her, and Ryan felt herself redden.

"That's what happened. Yes."

"We just want to make sure you didn't have a car out here somewhere," Mr. Stone said, trying to soothe her. "That you didn't have yourself a wreck and wandered away and forgot it."

Ryan didn't speak the rest of the way home. As Winchester climbed out to help her down, Ryan pulled out of his grasp.

"Thanks for the ride," she said stiffly. "Thanks for everything."

She tried to slam the door, but he was blocking it. "Ryan—wait—"

"You don't believe a single thing I told you! You think I was drunk and lost my car!"

"That's not true—I don't think that—"

"I can't believe I trusted you! And let me tell you something else—it wasn't a joke, either, me being left out there—he did it on purpose!"

Ryan ran for the house, but she could tell before she even got inside that no one was home. Her mind spun in a hundred directions, and she could feel her fears going out of control. *What should I do? Call the police? Run away? What's Charles going to do when he sees me? Why won't anyone believe me—*

Something stirred on the floor above.

Ryan froze at the foot of the stairs, her heart racing.

"Mom?" she whispered. "Is that you?"

There was no one in her mother's bedroom. As Ryan peered in fearfully, she saw the curtains billowing against the wall, and she felt weak with relief.

She walked slowly to Marissa's room and took a deep, steadying breath.

The door swung open easily, yet Ryan stood where she was.

The room was cold and full of shadows. Ryan rubbed the chill from her arms and suddenly noticed something on the bed.

A package.

As she frowned and picked it up, she saw that it was wrapped in Christmas paper and that the tag had her name on it. *It must be one of the things Charles brought. Mom must have put it in here for me to open in private. . . .*

Sitting down on the bed, Ryan began unwrapping the small, square box. She lay the paper aside and tried to smooth out the wrinkles. Then she held her breath and lifted the lid.

And at first she wasn't sure what she was seeing— the little gold chain lying on shiny black satin—but as she kept staring at it, she realized what it was, that she had seen it so many times before, and that she *shouldn't* be seeing it now—

"Marissa's necklace," Ryan whispered. "No—it's not possible—"

The box shook violently in her hands, and her thoughts spun back to that last fatal day, and *Marissa with her necklace on . . . the necklace she always wore —and my God, it was around her neck that day. . . . How can it be here now—*

With a horrified cry, Ryan dropped the box and ran. And as she flung open the front door and saw Charles standing there, she felt his arms clamp around her like a steel trap.

Chapter 11

Ryan!" Charles gasped. "My God—you're alive!"

As Ryan stared into his shocked face, she gave him a shove and dashed past him out across the yard.

"Ryan! Come back here!"

She could hear him shouting, and she tried to run faster, but the deep snow slowed her down. She heard his breathing, and she began to scream.

"No! Get away from me!"

Something grabbed her ankles, and as she pitched forward, his body pinned her to the ground.

"Stop it, Ryan!" Charles shouted. "I don't blame you for being upset—but listen to me, will you?"

"I will *not!*" She was beside herself with panic. "You tried to *kill* me! I'm calling the *police!*"

He slammed her shoulders down. "Fine! Call them! They'll be glad to know you finally showed up! Where have you *been?*"

"Stop it! You're just disappointed I'm not a corpse by now!"

She struggled to free herself, but he was too strong. As his face bent closer, his eyes bored into hers with a chilling intensity.

"I've been up . . . all . . . night . . . long," he said slowly, each word hissing between clenched teeth. "I have been scared out of my *mind!* I finally got back here last night, and you weren't in the van! I didn't even know how to get back to where I'd lost you!"

"You're a liar," Ryan said. "I don't believe you."

"Just shut up and listen." Charles was really angry, and she winced from his pressure on her arms. "I don't know when—or from where—you decided to hitchhike home. All I know is that I thought you were buried under all those blankets, only you weren't in the van when I got back last night! I couldn't remember where we'd gone off the road—I drove around for hours—I got stuck in the snow—I slid into things— not to mention all the times I got lost all over again!"

His eyes glittered fiercely, and Ryan stared back in confusion.

"I finally came home and waited for the storm to let up. Then I had to wait for the roads to be cleared. And *then* I finally *did* find the road again, but you weren't *anywhere!* So I got out and *walked* . . . and *called* . . . but you were *gone!* Dammit, Ryan, I thought you were dead!"

Ryan gazed at him helplessly. "And . . . you really called the police?"

"What kind of person do you think I am, anyway?" he shot back. "No . . . never mind. Don't answer that." He released her and straightened up. "You've been wanting to build a case against me ever since I got here. Come on, Ryan, I want to know what your problem is. All I wanted to do was bring Marissa's presents, and it's turned into a visit to hell! I don't blame you for being mad about last night—but how do you think *I* felt! I've been in a *panic,* wondering what to do, wondering what I could tell your mother and Steve—"

"Where are they?" Ryan mumbled. "Where's Mom?"

"She had to stay over at her friend's house last night because of the snow."

"How do you know that?"

"There was a message on the machine. She tried to call Steve at his house to tell him the roads were closed, and not to come and get her, but she couldn't get him there, so she left a message for him on the machine here."

"So you listened in on our phone calls?"

"I thought it might be you! Or the police! God, I was—" He broke off abruptly, running one hand through his hair. Ryan heard him make a disgusted sound in his throat as he got up and yanked her roughly to her feet. "Forget it, Ryan, it's no use talking to you, since you already have some twisted idea about me in your head. Whatever that idea is." Charles turned and started away, and Ryan hurried after him.

"Wait! Where are you going?"

"To call the police. To let them know you're home safe, however the hell that happened—"

"Charles!" Ryan was hurrying to keep up with his long strides, but he wouldn't slow down. "Charles, wait! I'm sorry!"

He did slow down then. As she covered the last few feet to his side, he looked back at her, his eyes so . . . so *hurt*, Ryan thought with a shock—*I've hurt his feelings, and all this time—*

"I'm sorry," she said again. She reached slowly for his hand, and he stared down as her fingers closed around his. "It's just that . . ." Tears welled in her throat, and she took a long moment to bring her voice under control. "It's just that I've been so scared and . . . and . . . so—" She glanced toward the house and tried to suppress a shudder. "I'm really scared, Charles. I don't know what to think—"

His expression hovered between bewilderment and concern. She could tell he didn't want to give in to her apology, but then she felt him squeezing her fingers.

"Ryan . . . what's wrong? You look so—"

"It's Marissa."

"Marissa?"

"That package you brought—it doesn't make sense! Her necklace was in it, but it couldn't have been, don't you see? She was *wearing* that necklace the day she died—she *never* took it off—"

"Whoa, whoa, whoa, slow down here," Charles was muttering, and Ryan felt her hand caught between both of his as he rubbed her fingers, trying to warm her up. "Just back up a minute. I don't know what package you're talking about—"

"Yes, the one you brought. That Marissa got for me when you went shopping for antiques, remember? The one on the bed in Marissa's room just now—"

"No." Charles shook his head. "No, the present I

brought for you is down in the living room. I stuck it under the tree."

"No," Ryan argued, pulling away, making the size of the box with her hands. "The little box—"

"Big box," Charles corrected. "Ryan, I know what she got you. I wrapped it myself, remember? It's a big box. And it's under the tree where I put it. I just saw it—just now—when you ran out of the house—"

Ryan looked at him helplessly. "Then who left that box on the bed for me? Did someone come in the house while everyone was gone?" Her voice rose, working its way toward hysteria. "Charles, her *necklace* was in that box! How could her *necklace* be in that box when she drowned with it? And *where* did that box come from? Oh, my God—"

Her head jerked up as a car pulled into the driveway. She looked at Charles and heard herself whisper, "Oh, no, I can't let Mom see that necklace!"

"Where is it?"

"In Marissa's room—I threw it somewhere on the floor."

She saw Charles run ahead of her into the house . . . she heard her mother and Steve calling to her . . . she watched them as they struggled through the snowdrifts up to the porch.

"Looks like I'll have a lot of shoveling to do." Steve grinned, helping Mrs. McCauley up the steps. "You're out awful early, aren't you? How was the caroling last night? Did you manage to salvage Phoebe's future?"

Mrs. McCauley gave her a weary glance. "I called Phoebe's last night, but you two weren't home yet. I wanted you to know I'd been stranded. Where's Charles? Did you two have a good time?"

For once Ryan was glad her mother wasn't really listening. "It was okay. What's in the box?"

"A plaque." Mrs. McCauley smiled sadly, lifting off the lid so Ryan could see. "Glenda gave it to me as a reminder of Marissa. I'm going right upstairs and hang it in her room."

"No, don't!" Ryan grabbed her mother's arm, and Mrs. McCauley winced.

"Ryan, that hurt. What on earth is wrong with you now?"

"Nothing. Nothing at all." Ryan loosened her grip, but began pulling her mother toward the kitchen, all the while trying to signal Steve with her eyes. "I just want to hear all about your visit, that's all. I'll make us some coffee."

"But we can talk about it as soon as I— Ryan, what is the *matter?*" Mrs. McCauley firmly pushed Ryan's hand from her arm and stared at her daughter. "You look terrible this morning. I bet you and Phoebe didn't get a wink of sleep all night, as usual. Just look at her, Steve. You won't be happy until you *do* get sick, will you, Ryan?"

Steve was looking at her, and as Mrs. McCauley suddenly turned to face him, he managed to twist his face into an instant smile while trying to interpret Ryan's frantic gestures behind her mother's back.

"Honestly, Steve, what are you looking so silly about?" Mrs. McCauley said irritably. "Everyone's acting so peculiar around here this morning. . . ."

"Maybe we *should* have coffee first," Steve said quickly, his smile wavering uncertainly as Ryan glanced up the stairs and back to him again. "I'll help you hang the plaque up later. Uh . . . where's Charles?"

"Still asleep, I think." Ryan stepped aside to let her mother pass, and Steve gave an amused grin.

"Welcome to the asylum, Steve." He looked good-naturedly perplexed. "Well, I'm glad to see nothing's changed much since I was last here. Ryan, would you mind telling me what's going—"

Ryan thought fast. "It's Charles. He's not feeling too well this morning—you know, the party last night and all—well, you know how Mom can be if she found out—"

"Morning everyone. Some storm last night, huh?"

Steve and Ryan glanced up as Charles came down the stairs. Mrs. McCauley peered around the kitchen door and smiled.

"There you are, Charles. Did you have a good time last night?"

"Great, thanks." Charles paused on the bottom step, his eyes brushing casually over Ryan as he even more casually patted one pocket of his jeans. "Nothing like caroling to put you in the Christmas spirit, right, Ryan?"

Ryan gave him a desperate look, her mind spinning. *You found it, didn't you? Tell me you found it—don't tell me I imagined that, too—*

"Well, I think Ryan looks terrible this morning." Mrs. McCauley seemed annoyed. "She's much too pale, and she's got those dark circles under her eyes that always mean she's coming down with something. And how'd you get all these scratches? I think you should lie down, Ryan. Maybe I should call the doctor."

"I don't need a doctor—" Ryan began, but Charles cut her off.

"Good idea. I'll go back up with you, Ryan—I need to get some stuff out of my bag."

Ryan felt Charles's hand close around her elbow, guiding her up to the second floor. *I'm going to explode, I'm going to start screaming, any minute, any second, I'm just going to go completely crazy. . . .* She snapped back to attention as Charles squeezed her arm.

"It's okay, Ryan, I found it. Come on, let's talk."

They were in the hallway now, and Charles was steering her toward Marissa's room.

"No—I don't want to go back in there—"

"We have to. They're less likely to hear us in there."

As the door closed behind them, Ryan perched uneasily on the window seat and watched Charles listen several minutes to make sure that Mom and Steve had really stayed downstairs. Satisfied, he turned to face her and fished into his pocket. Ryan's heart clutched as she recognized the chain dangling from his fingers.

"It's hers," she said shakily.

"Are you sure?" He looked doubtful. "It *looks* like the one she always wore, but that doesn't make any sense."

Ryan began rocking, stiff, jerky movements, her body one giant knot. "This is impossible—you know that, don't you? *Impossible!* She had it on that day—I *saw* her—she was fooling with it. She had it on when she—"

"Are you . . . positive?" Charles asked again quietly, and Ryan nearly screamed at him.

"Of course I am! Don't you think I know what happened that day!" As Charles lowered his eyes, she wrapped her arms around herself and fought for composure. "Okay . . . okay, I'm sorry—but what does this *mean?* Is Marissa still alive? Did *she* put it here? I keep *seeing* her—I don't even know what's *happening* anymore. . . . Charles, *how did this get here?*"

Ryan stopped, her whole body weak and shaking. She felt sick and bent her head, taking deep breaths. When Charles spoke, his voice sounded hollow and distant.

"You know she's not alive. You *know* that. There has to be some explanation. Some logical reason."

"Well, then, what is it?" Ryan gave a nervous laugh, shocked that she could find it even remotely amusing. "If Marissa's really gone . . . then why isn't her necklace with her?"

Chapter 12

Ryan?"

As Mrs. McCauley's voice sounded from the hall-way, Ryan nearly jumped out of her skin. She stared fearfully as Charles opened the door with an easy smile.

"Oh, good, Charles, I'm glad you're here. Maybe *you* can talk some sense into her. Ryan, I *insist* that you lie down. I called Mr. Partini and told him you wouldn't be in today."

"Mom—I—"

"He was very understanding," Mrs. McCauley said firmly. "Now, I want you to rest. Dr. Wilson's calling in a prescription for you—just something to help you relax."

"But I don't need to—"

"You're entirely too high strung." Her mother glanced apologetically at Charles. "She's not usually this bad—she's been under a great strain. She hasn't been herself."

"Can I pick up that prescription for you?" Charles offered. "I'd like to do something to make myself useful."

"I'll go," Steve volunteered. He came up behind Mrs. McCauley and winked at Ryan over her mother's head. "The roads are pretty well cleared off by now, and I need to stop at home for a minute, anyway. Got a little bit of packing to do before my trip." He smiled down at Mrs. McCauley and gave her shoulder a squeeze as her face fell. "Only a couple days! It's *good* I'm going away—you guys will appreciate me so much more when I come back!"

"Oh, I just hate to think of you gone," Mrs. McCauley said sadly. "The house will be so empty.

"You have Ryan," Steve reminded her. "And now you have Charles. Okay, Ryan, get to bed. I'll be back as soon as I can." And then we'll talk, his eyes communicated to Ryan.

"Then would you take me to the grocery store, Charles?" Mrs. McCauley motioned Ryan toward the bed and pulled an extra blanket from a closet shelf. "I'm running low on just about everything. Do you mind?"

"My pleasure." Charles gave a sweeping bow. "I hope you feel better, Ryan."

Ryan turned her face away, not looking at the door again until she heard everyone leave. In the heavy quiet she lay motionless, but she could feel her mind slowly and steadily crumbling.

I have to make some sense out of this. . . . I have to talk to somebody—

She grabbed the phone and dialed Phoebe's number. After seven endless rings, she was finally answered by a blast of rock music.

"Jinx!" she tried to shout but barely managed a croak. "Is Phoebe there?"

"What?"

"Turn down the—" Ryan took a deep breath. *Come on, Ryan, get a grip. . . .* "Jinx, turn that down and get Phoebe!"

"She's not here!"

"When will she be back?"

"When she wants to. Get lost, McCauley—I'm not a social director—"

"I'm not kidding, Jinx—it's a matter of life and death!"

"Huh?"

"I said—" Ryan shook so violently that she had to hold the receiver with both hands to keep from dropping it.

"I heard that party last night was wild," Jinx said. "I heard someone spiked the cider."

The cider! So I wasn't drugged after all. . . . Charles wasn't trying to get rid of me . . . he really did hit the dog . . . he really did leave me there by mistake—
"Jinx—"

There was a thud as the phone was thrown down, and then the volume of the music took an unexpected plunge.

"Okay." Jinx sighed. "What do you want me to tell her?"

"Tell her I have to talk to her. Tell her I need her to come and get me as soon as she can!"

"You might have a long wait. She and that Michael guy went out early this morning. She *must* be in love to have her eyes open before noon on a Saturday."

"You don't understand how important this is! I *have* to come over there—"

"So fly. Jeez, McCauley, you sound terrible. You have a hangover or what?"

"Can your mom or dad come and get me?"

"They're down at Aunt Agnes's. They won't be back till late tomorrow night."

"Jinx, *please*—"

"Oh, no, you don't. I just took a nice big pizza out of the oven, and I'm *very* comfortable here on the couch."

"I'll pay for your gas."

"With what, your looks? That wouldn't even get me out of my driveway."

Ryan slammed down the phone and sat stiffly on the edge of the bed.

How did that necklace get away from Marissa?

How did it get in the bedroom?

Ryan's head came up, her blood going icy in her veins. *What was that?* For just a second she thought she'd heard something downstairs . . . a door creaking open . . . a footstep . . .

"Steve?"

Ryan went to the top of the stairs and peered down. The house held its breath around her. She went back to Marissa's room and crawled into bed, feeling cold all over.

Someone was in this house . . . someone knew where Marissa's room was . . .

A car door slammed outside, and as someone came in and started up the stairs, Ryan scooted back against the headboard and watched the door with frightened eyes.

"Steve?" she called fearfully.

"No. Me." Jinx poked his head in and scowled. "Don't worry, McCauley, your secret's safe with me."

"What secret? Oh, I'm so glad you're here!" Ryan threw off the covers, and Jinx quickly turned his back. "You don't have to be so polite, Jinx—I'm dressed."

"I'm not being polite. I just didn't want to throw up on the rug when I saw your body."

"I can't believe you came." Ryan slipped up behind him and tried to give him a hug, but he wiggled out of her arms. "I didn't think you really would."

"Yeah, well, that's obvious. So who is he, anyway? I probably know him, right?"

Ryan frowned. "Who?"

"No, that's what *I* asked *you*. Pay attention and try to get it right this time."

"Jinx . . ." Ryan sighed. "What are you talking about?"

"Oh, come on, I've already seen him, so you don't have to play dumb." Jinx snapped his fingers. "Oops, sorry . . . I forgot you weren't playing."

"You're making even less sense than usual," Ryan said, annoyed. "Will you please tell me what you're—"

Jinx sighed. "The guy, McCauley. The boyfriend. The secret admirer. I saw him just now sneaking out the back door, so quit pretending . . ." His words faded as he watched the reaction on her face. "The guy," he said again and tapped Ryan on the forehead. "Hello? Anyone home?"

"What guy?" Ryan whispered.

"I told you, he—" Jinx broke off as Ryan sagged back against the wall.

"You're teasing me, right? Please say you're—"

"He was coming out the back door when I drove up—I could see him through the trees. By the time I hit the driveway, I guess he'd taken off through the woods."

"Oh, Jinx, nobody was here—I mean, nobody I knew about—"

"You mean you've been here alone? You didn't see him?" Jinx was already out in the hall, racing down the stairs. "Stay here—I'll take a look!"

That noise I thought I heard downstairs . . . someone must have been in the house with me. . . . On shaky legs Ryan stood at Marissa's window with its clear view of the backyard. She saw Jinx searching the area, and she saw prints in the snow leading down the slope and into the woods. Jinx looked back toward the house, and she raised the window to call down to him.

"Jinx, come back inside!"

"Want me to see where these footprints go?"

"No! Just please come back in here!"

"Should I call the police?"

"Jinx!"

"Okay, okay, I'm coming."

Ryan went downstairs and was holding the kitchen door when he came back inside.

"Did you see anyone?"

"Not a soul. You sure you weren't expecting anyone?"

"Positive. When you saw this person—"

"Guy," Jinx corrected. "He was a guy."

"Are you *sure* he was coming out of the house?"

"Well, he was on the kitchen steps, with his back to the door. I just figured he was."

"Maybe you scared him off, and he never *got* inside. What'd he look like, could you tell?"

Jinx shook his head. "I wasn't close enough—but he looked pretty big. Hey, you better sit down or something." Dragging her to a chair, he forced her into it, then ran cold water on the dishrag and dabbed clumsily at her face.

"I need to talk to Phoebe," she whispered.

"Not unless your name is Michael. Only Michael's got her attention this weekend."

"Oh, Jinx, please . . . I've got to tell her what's going on. . . ." Ryan closed her eyes wearily. When she opened them again, Jinx was squatting on his heels in front of her.

"Maybe it was a hunter," he said helpfully. "You know how they're always wandering onto your property. Maybe he wanted to use your phone, and you didn't hear him knock."

"No . . . not a hunter . . ." she mumbled, and Jinx tried again.

"A delivery man."

"I didn't order anything. And anyway, where was his car?"

"A delivery man on foot." Jinx rocked back on his heels, holding on to the rungs of her chair for balance. "You look terrible. Even more than usual, I mean."

"I feel terrible. I . . ." Her eyes misted, and she stared down at him, her voice small and frightened. "Jinx . . . do you think I'm crazy?"

She'd expected the usual insults, delivered in the usual quick-fire manner. What she hadn't expected were his hands reaching out to hers, grasping them tightly, and the way his eyes looked suddenly serious and sad.

"Come on, McCauley," he whispered. "Talk to me."

She told him everything—all that had happened, all her fears and suspicions—and the whole time she talked, Jinx never said a word, just crouched there, holding her hands.

"I don't know what to believe anymore," she ended. "I don't know what to think."

Jinx was silent a minute. "You really spent the night with Winchester?"

"Jinx!" Ryan looked indignant. "That hardly seems very important compared to the rest of this mess."

Jinx looked a little embarrassed. "Yeah, okay. You're right. So how come you never told anyone Marissa might be in some kind of trouble?"

"She made me promise not to. At first I thought she was just joking. And then . . ." She caught herself, feeling disloyal.

"Yeah." Jinx nodded. "Some guy."

"But then she was gone, and whatever it was didn't

matter anymore anyway," Ryan said miserably. "And I swore I wouldn't tell. I shouldn't even have told you."

"Ryan, Marissa's dead. I really don't think she'd care."

"But I promised. It was our secret. The last secret we ever shared." Ryan groaned. "I think something terrible is happening. Or going to happen. To me, maybe. I don't want to think that. Talk me out of thinking that."

"Okay. Nothing bad's happening, and nothing bad's gonna happen."

"Promise?"

"Look—" Jinx rubbed his chin and began pacing. "What if everything's just the way it seems?"

"What do you mean?"

"Some kid just messed up the dollhouse. Coincidence. Some fat guy likes to window-shop. Coincidence. Charles really *is* a friend of Marissa's . . . he really *has* just come here out of the goodness of his heart . . . he *wants* to be your friend—" Jinx glanced up. "Obviously, the guy must be *desperate* for friends, but that's his problem." Jinx kept pacing. "He didn't know you got out of the van, and you nearly gave him a heart attack, and Winchester saved your life, and you slept there."

"Jinx"—Ryan shot him a chilly glance that he chose to ignore—"what about the necklace?"

"I'm thinking."

"What about the garage? The body in the car?"

"That door's always jamming, you know that."

"The body," Ryan repeated impatiently. "The ghost in the woods."

"Both times it was dark, right? It could have been shadows—"

"Shadows don't honk. Shadows don't talk."

"Come on, McCauley, you already said you felt weird at the party—"

Ryan gave an exasperated sigh. "I only had one cup of cider!"

"Then it was probably some farmer. He didn't see you, and he was"—Jinx thought quickly—"talking to his buddy. He said, 'I can't come home for Christmas, I'm staying here instead.'"

"No." Ryan thought a moment. "That wasn't it."

"'I can't come home for Christmas . . . I'll be sick in bed.'"

Ryan gave him a scathing look.

"'I can't come home for Christmas . . . I'm Fred.'"

"Fred!"

"Ed?"

"Jinx—"

"Well, you said talk you out of it!" Jinx said crossly. "You're not being very cooperative."

"Don't you understand this is really serious!"

"What's serious is that you spent all night in a cabin with Winchester Stone! That's what's serious."

Ryan stared at him, her anger rising. "He was a perfect gentleman! And anyway, why do *you* care so much about it?"

"I don't," Jinx said quickly, shrugging his shoulders, looking away. "I don't care at all."

"A perfect gentleman," Ryan reiterated. "I trusted him completely."

"Right. This coming from Miss Approachable of Fadiman High. Face it, McCauley, any guy who even *looks* at you is a criminal, as far as you're concerned. You don't trust anything male, and you've got about as much self-confidence as a rabbit. There're lots of guys who'd grab you up if—" Abruptly he broke off, then busied himself at the sink filling a glass of water.

"If what?" Ryan said, embarrassed. "How would you know?"

"Trust me on this one. I know."

"Who, then? Who's interested in me?"

"You wouldn't catch on if they looked you right in the face." Jinx scowled. "Which no one could do and live, 'cause you're so ugly."

"We're way off the subject here—quit being a jerk."

"Well, excuse me! Going over all the ways you're being terrorized just happens to put me in a bad mood, okay?"

"Then . . . you believe me? That someone's after me?"

"I didn't say that. I believe you're paranoid as hell, but what's new?"

"Should we go to the police?"

"With what? All your concrete evidence? The ghosts you've seen? A four-inch tall victim of doll abuse?"

Furious tears filled Ryan's eyes. "It's not funny, Jinx—I'm so scared!"

"Am I laughing?" he challenged her. "Do you see

me laughing at all this, McCauley? I'm just telling you that if you go to the cops with these wild stories of yours, they're really gonna wonder about some things—"

"Like *what* things?"

"Like what you had to drink at that party—and all your problems at school—and where you spent the night last night—"

"But—well—I know it all sounds kind of funny—"

"Right, and that's what the cops'll think, too. Just listen to what you've been telling me! You said yourself Mrs. Corbett had a conference with your mom— they think you should see a shrink!"

"But that's not fair! I'm telling the truth!"

"Okay, then, where's the necklace? Let me see it."

Ryan stared at him. She hung her head and shook it slowly. "I don't have it. I guess Charles still does."

"I rest my case."

"Look, Jinx, someone might have been in the house a little while ago—he could be the one following me all this time!"

"Following you? You've actually *seen* someone following you?"

"Well . . . no . . . I . . ." Her voice sank. "I've just felt it." She raised her eyes again, imploring him. "Oh, Jinx, what am I going to do? You've got to believe me! Say you believe me—*please!*"

"I believe you."

"You're just saying that!"

"Oh, hell . . ." He glanced at her quickly, then

toward the hallway. "You're giving me the creeps, McCauley. Let's get outta here."

"You're the only one I've told," Ryan said, following him downstairs. "I'm not crazy. . . . I'm not imagining things—"

"And I gave up pizza for this," Jinx grumbled. "I gave up pizza and my nice soft couch for this. I gave up pizza and my couch and the football game for—"

"I'll buy you a new pizza. We can stop on the way."

"And gas."

"Yes." Ryan sighed. "And gas. Just let me leave a note."

"Terrific, McCauley. Now they'll come to *my* house and terrorize *me!*"

Ryan felt drained. She sat stiffly in the car and scarcely even realized when they pulled into the service station. She reached into her purse and handed Jinx a wad of bills, watching vacantly as he hopped out to pump gas. A tapping sound startled her, and she looked up to see Winchester's father smiling in at her through the window. She rolled it down, and he leaned partway in.

"How you doing there, little lady? After what you been through last night, you should take it easy."

Ryan couldn't help smiling back. "I wanted to thank you again. I could have died out there."

"Hey, now, no thanks necessary. I'm just glad Winchester was there to help. Hope your folks weren't worried, though, wondering about you."

"No," Ryan fibbed. "They understood about the phone and all."

Mr. Stone fixed her with a puzzled grin. "What about the phone?"

"The storm knocking out the lines," Ryan said. "I hope you got it fixed okay."

"Nothin' to fix." And Winchester's father was shaking his head while something cold snaked up Ryan's spine.

"Oh, I must have misunderstood . . ."

"Must have," Mr. Stone said cheerfully. "Far as I know, that phone worked just fine last night."

Chapter 13

As Jinx slid in and started the car, he eyed her skeptically. "You okay?"

"I just want to sleep, that's all."

"Well, do it in Phoebe's room. I got friends coming over."

"Not those slimy little guys you always hang around with."

"Well, who asked you? Like it's even your house." Jinx took a corner too fast, and the car skidded on some ice.

"If you're not careful, I won't even live long enough to get to your house." *Winchester lied to me . . . and I just said I trusted him. . . .*"Why are we stopping?"

Jinx looked at her in amazement. "I swear, McCauley, you've got a brain like a slug. Pizza. Remember?"

He held out his hand, and Ryan dug through her wallet for more money. Not finding any, she searched through her purse, then emptied the contents on her lap.

"Terrific," Jinx grumbled. "So I starve."

"Oh, just wait a minute," Ryan grumbled back.

"The lining's loose on the bottom—sometimes I find all kinds of money under there." As she pulled out a twenty, her look of triumph turned to surprise. "Look —some film!"

"Big deal. Declare a holiday."

"No . . ." Ryan shook her head. "No, I remember —Marissa gave this to me. The day of the accident. God . . . it's been buried under here all this time. . . ."

"With your brain. Come *on,* I'm hungry—"

"Oh, Jinx, can we stop and drop this off at the drugstore? Please—"

"Yeah, yeah, just give me the money before I'm too weak to walk!" He disappeared into the building, and Ryan leaned back with a groan.

Maybe he didn't know about the phone—you really want to believe that, don't you, because he was so nice and—

Someone's watching me.

Ryan jerked upright, her hands slamming flat against her window. She could see the whole parking lot and the street beyond, but there weren't any people anywhere. *Come on, Jinx, hurry up. . . .*

Taking a deep breath, Ryan started to sit back.

She never saw the shadow beside her door. The huge thud on the glass rocked the car, and as she screamed, the black ski mask stared in at her, filling the window.

She saw the door shake as the handle moved and held—

My God, he's trying to get in—

She threw herself across the seat, falling out onto the slippery pavement. She tried to stand up, but she couldn't get a foothold. Panic-stricken, she looked back over her shoulder.

He was coming around the car after her.

As Ryan scrambled up at last, she saw Jinx coming out of the building, and she screamed again as the bulky figure closed the distance behind her.

"Jinx! Help me!"

Ryan saw the pizza box fly into the air as Jinx hurtled toward her attacker. There was a hoarse cry and a thud as Jinx and the man went down together on the ground.

"Run, Ryan!" Jinx yelled. "Get inside! Hurry—call the—"

"Hey, buddy, will you wait a minute? *Wait a minute!*" The voice from the ski mask was muffled, yet instead of sounding dangerous, it only sounded annoyed. "Get off me, will you? What are you, crazy?"

As Jinx gaped at him, his opponent groaned and gave Jinx a shove. Jinx promptly landed in the snow.

"Don't try anything," he said angrily.

"Hey, don't worry"—the stranger held up his hands—"I'm just trying to get up!"

And as the large man finally stumbled to his feet, he worked off the ski mask.

Ryan had never seen him before, but he looked totally unthreatening and totally put out.

"Hey, buddy, I appreciate you trying to defend your

little girlfriend here—I really do—but I just want you to move your car, okay?"

Jinx's mouth fell open. "You . . . want—"

"Your car." The man sighed. "Look, I got deliveries to make. You got me blocked in!"

As one, Ryan and Jinx turned their heads. Now they could see the pizza delivery truck idling in a little alleyway that Jinx's car had barricaded.

Ryan gulped. Jinx closed his eyes for a long moment, as if gathering every ounce of control.

"I'm really sorry," Jinx mumbled, starting forward, but the man shook his head and backed away.

"Hey, pal, forget about it. As a matter of fact, I admire your nerve. I mean, look at you! Look at *me!*" He patted his wide stomach. "I coulda squashed you like a bug!"

Again Jinx closed his eyes. Ryan could see him taking deep breaths. She hurried back to the car and got in, careful to look straight ahead as he finally slid in beside her.

"Jinx—"

"Don't look at me, McCauley."

"I'm not. I just wanted—"

"Don't talk to me, either. You've ruined my day. You've ruined my weekend."

"But see? You were ready to help me, so that proves you *must* believe some of what I told you back at the house—"

"You're ruining my life."

"What about the . . . pizza?"

139

In answer Jinx hit the accelerator and aimed his car for the take-out box upside down in the snow. She heard a soft crunch as they ran over it.

"Can we still leave the film?" she asked timidly.

"Only if I can leave you with it."

Jinx did stop at the drugstore but stayed silent all the way home. Ryan went straight to Phoebe's room to lie down, and when she woke up, it was nearly eleven. She found Jinx asleep on the couch in the den, the TV blaring away, and she stood there a long time watching him. She was the one who had given him his nickname when they were little—Jinx instead of Jimmy—because, as she'd explained to an agreeable Phoebe, something bad always happened when he was around. Now, however, he didn't look so little anymore, and Ryan was surprised at the changes she'd never noticed till now. The baby face had grown more angular and strong, somehow, and she could see the curve of muscles beneath his sleeves. No wonder girls are calling him, she thought with a small shock. She reached out and gently touched his hair, knowing he'd either kill her or die of embarrassment if he ever found out. When he stirred slightly, she made a quick retreat to the kitchen and was just sitting down to eat something when Phoebe came home, wearing a familiarly dreamy expression.

"Don't tell me," Ryan greeted her. "You're in love."

"To my deepest depths. To my innermost soul." Phoebe pressed her hands to her heart. "This is it, Ryan. This is the big one."

"They're all big ones," Ryan reminded her. "And even bigger ones when they end."

"Oh, but this one won't." Phoebe draped her scarf over her shoulders and shimmied. "He can't resist me."

"Phoebe"—Ryan sighed—"no one can resist you."

"I guess I was born that way."

"I guess."

"So how's your life since I saw you last?"

Ryan stared at her. It seemed like months since she and Phoebe had talked, but now, with the chance right in front of her, Ryan didn't even know where to begin.

Phoebe clapped her hands. "Let's go get cappuccinos at the Coffeehouse!"

"Phoebe, I really don't feel like—"

"It's only eight blocks—we can walk—"

"No, I'm exhausted. All day I've felt like I'm catching a bad cold."

"We *have* to walk. When Dad saw the scratches on the van, he blew a fuse. I can't drive for a week. And I can't tell him Charles did it, 'cause he said no one could drive it but me."

"Why didn't you say something?"

"'Cause I wanted Michael to bring me home. Where's Jinx?"

"Asleep."

"Great. Then we'll take *his* car."

"Phoebe—"

"Dad said I couldn't drive *my* car—he didn't say anything about Jinx's."

"Jinx will kill you."

"He won't know! By the time he wakes up, we'll be gone!"

"We still have to come back sometime."

"I'll tell him *you* drove!"

Ryan groaned and felt herself being pulled out the door. "That's probably the *worst* thing you could tell him tonight."

The Coffeehouse was noisy and crowded, but they managed to find a booth in back. After ordering, Phoebe proceeded to tell Ryan all about her day with Michael Kilmer, including the three future dates they'd scheduled before he brought her home tonight. She didn't seem to notice that Ryan wasn't listening.

"So I'm going to the dance!" she finished triumphantly. "And you are, too."

"I am?" The stifling heat was making it hard for Ryan to concentrate. *Jinx is right ... everything is just a coincidence ... but what about the necklace ... ?*

"With Charles Eastman."

"What!" Coffee spewed out of Ryan's mouth, and Phoebe hurriedly grabbed a napkin and dabbed at Ryan's chin. "Have you totally lost your—"

"I had a feeling you'd take it like this," Phoebe fussed, creasing her napkin primly, folding her arms on the tabletop.

"I don't even want to discuss this," Ryan said.

"Maybe my timing is all wrong—"

"Phoebe, you *have* no timing."

"Oh, Ryan, *please*—just ask him?"

"No."

"I want us to go to the dance together. We'd have such a wonderful time!"

"No."

"I know he'd take you if you asked him! Your mom thinks so, too—"

"My mom? You asked my mom?"

"Well, when Michael and I stopped at your house to pick up the van, I just mentioned—"

"Oh, God, Phoebe, you didn't mention it to Charles—"

"Not exactly. But your mom thinks it'd be good for you to go. I know Charles would think so, too."

"Phoebe, you make me sound like a charity case! Don't you understand? I just can't think about the dance at this particular time of my life." *I'm too busy thinking about coincidences. . . .*

"Oh, Ryan, you're just shy. I bet deep down you're just the tiniest bit interested in him—"

"No, I'm not."

"Well, will you at least think about it?"

"No. Phoebe, leave me alone. I don't want to talk about the dance or Charles Eastman anymore."

"Oh, Ryan, you're breaking my heart." Phoebe looked miserably down at the table. "I was counting on us going together. You're really and truly breaking my heart—it's our absolute *last* New Year's dance together. . . ."

"Phoebe, you'll be having such a fantastic time with Michael, you won't even miss me."

"Yes, I will."

"No, you won't. I promise you won't."

"Yes, I will. Pleeeeeeease?"

"No! And that's final!" *Thank God I didn't tell her—she'd never take me seriously—*

"Well, then, we might as well just go home, I'm so sad now." Phoebe gave Ryan her most pitiful look. "I don't know what you're in such a bad mood about anyway."

They walked back to the car without talking. The streets were empty, except for one Santa Claus standing on a corner, slowly ringing a bell.

"Isn't it a little late for him to be out?" Phoebe nudged Ryan, laughing, then suddenly stopped and let out a groan.

"Oh, my God! Jinx'll have a stroke!"

Frowning, Ryan knelt and examined the front tire. "It looks like someone cut it. Look—*all* the tires are slashed."

"Dammit, who would do such a mean thing! And all the stores are closed!"

Ryan looked down the street and shivered. The Santa Claus had disappeared. "I don't have my key to the toy shop with me, either. Come on, we can call from the Coffeehouse."

Returning to the restaurant, the girls found someone already using the phone, and as the minutes dragged by, Phoebe grew impatient.

"I could have been to the gas station and back again by now," she fretted. "Look, they're getting ready to close—"

"Let's just go, then."

"No—I'll go. It's my fault we're in this mess. You stay here where it's warm and wait for me."

"Phoebe, don't be silly, I'm not letting you go alone."

"You're the one who's getting sick." Phoebe shook her finger under Ryan's runny nose. "You stay here and get us coffee to go, and I'll try to find another phone."

"I think the drugstore has a payphone—try there."

"It's probably quicker if I just walk to the station myself," Phoebe grumbled, digging in her purse. "You got change?"

"What is it with your family? I'm always handing out money."

"I'll be back in a second. You stay warm. If they run you out, just stand under the awning—at least you won't feel the wind."

"Yes, Mother." Ryan watched Phoebe disappear around the corner, then she ordered their drinks and waited.

She waited a long time.

As the restaurant began to empty, Ryan wondered what was taking Phoebe so long. She could feel the coffee getting cold in her sack. She drank one, but when Phoebe still didn't reappear, she drank the other. *I bet that dumb phone wasn't working. . . . I bet she had to walk to the station after all.*

Frowning, Ryan stepped outside and looked up the

street. It was starting to snow again, and she tried to ignore the growing fear in her heart. *She's stopped to talk to someone . . . typical Phoebe, she's forgotten all about me and Jinx's car. . . .*

Thrusting her hands into her pockets, Ryan started up the street, averting her eyes from the alleyways she had to pass. She tried to imagine Phoebe safe in the gas station. She glanced up through a flitter of snow and stopped and stared.

At first she thought she'd imagined it, the Santa Claus standing there ahead of her on the corner. He looked like the one they'd seen near the car—huge and jolly in his fur-trimmed suit—and Christmas lights twinkling from a nearby window sparkled off his heavy black boots. He was stamping his feet as if he was cold, his curly white beard flowing down over his chest.

He was ringing a bell.

Ryan stood there, strangely mesmerized by the magical Santa in the dead of night.

And then she began walking.

He was ringing the bell in time to her footsteps.

She walked faster.

The bell went faster, too, echoing each stab of fear in her heart.

Phoebe . . . I've got to find Phoebe. . . .

Through the softly sprinkling snow Ryan saw Santa standing there on the corner—*just standing there*—like one of Mr. Partini's mechanical dolls, arm up, arm down, ringing, ringing, just standing there, waiting for her to pass—

She swung wide out into the street, rushing away from him up the sidewalk—

Behind her she heard the bell clang as it fell into the snow.

She heard the footsteps coming after her.

"Help, somebody! Please help me!"

The buildings loomed lifelessly around her. As she turned the next corner, she cast a wild glance over her shoulder.

He was plodding through the snow, his head down, unhurried. Ryan could see his boots lifting in long, crushing strides. Without warning she suddenly slipped and fell, and the footsteps began to run.

Oh, no . . . oh, God . . . As Ryan struggled to her hands and knees, her eyes made a terrified sweep of the street—

But now it was empty.

Chapter 14

Ryan!" a voice shouted. "Ryan—what are you doing!"

As Ryan got to her feet, dazed, she saw the tow truck coming toward her with Phoebe hanging out one window.

"Ryan, I told you to wait for me! What happened?"

Ryan stepped back as the truck pulled up beside her, as Mr. Stone leaned out the other side with a grin.

"You must really like being out in the cold, little lady," he teased.

Phoebe opened her door impatiently. "For heaven's sake, Ryan, get in here. What were you doing down on all fours in the snow?"

"I fell," Ryan mumbled. "Santa Claus."

"No, it's Phoebe." Phoebe regarded her friend apprehensively. "Oh, Mr. Stone, I think she's delirious!"

"Stop it, Phoebe, I know who you are, I'm not delirious," Ryan said sharply. "Didn't you see him? He was chasing me—"

"Santa Claus was chasing you?"

"You *must* have seen him—"

"We didn't see anyone," Mr. Stone said. "Lucky for you I came along when I did. Come on—hop in."

"Did you get mugged?" Phoebe asked worriedly, and Mr. Stone looked disgusted.

"You mean, now they're even dressing up like Santa Claus? What if some little kids had seen that—that's terrible!"

"Should we call the police?" Phoebe asked.

"I doubt they'd do anything about it." Mr. Stone sighed. "That mugger's long gone by now."

"But it wasn't a mugger," Ryan protested. "Look— I've still got my purse."

"Well, I musta scared him off." Mr. Stone motioned her to close the door. "You girls better stay at the station, and I'll go take a look at that car of yours."

The girls drank hot chocolate while they waited for Mr. Stone to get back. Ryan was trying to pay attention to the night clerk's fourth boring story when she felt Phoebe nudge her and saw Winchester come through the door. He looked tired, Ryan thought, and he glanced away as he recognized her.

"You need some help?" he asked softly, but it was Phoebe he spoke to, not Ryan.

Phoebe promptly bestowed him a dimpled smile. "Well, actually, we have four flat tires, but your father went to fix them." When he nodded and started to walk away, she nudged Ryan again and added, "He said we could stay here and wait."

"Sure. Make yourself comfortable."

"I'm Phoebe." Phoebe held out her hand, and after an awkward pause Winchester shook it. "You probably know my brother, Jinx? And this is my friend Ryan."

His eyes swept over Ryan but didn't stop. "We've met."

"Oh, that's right." Phoebe's smile widened. "You went out with Marissa, didn't you?"

Oh, Phoebe, stop. Ryan looked down at the floor, at Winchester's black workboots dripping over the old linoleum. *Why did he lie to me about the phone . . . ?*

"My friend Ryan got mugged," Phoebe said proudly.

"Phoebe!" Ryan hissed.

"Right down the street. Your father probably saved her life."

"Did he?" At last Winchester's eyes settled on Ryan's face. Ryan tried to step on Phoebe's toe, but Phoebe slyly moved her foot away.

"Yes, it was terrible. Somebody chased her, but then your father came. Oh, look, there he is now." Phoebe waved out the window as the tow truck pulled in, dragging Jinx's car behind. "So I guess this means I'll have to leave the car, right? Could you keep this kind of quiet? Till I think of something to tell my brother?"

Before Winchester could answer, Mr. Stone came in, and Phoebe went over to talk to him, leaving Ryan standing there.

Winchester poured some coffee . . . raised the cup to his lips, squinting through the steam. "So . . . you're okay."

Ryan nodded. Behind her Mr. Stone told Winchester to take the girls home. Ryan stepped forward and blocked his way.

"You lied about the phone," she said quietly. She watched his face, and the surprise it registered. "Your father said it was working."

"Not when I tried it." He frowned and lowered his eyes. "Maybe one of the kids did it . . . took it off upstairs, and I didn't know."

He looked down for a long time. She could see him swallowing . . . she could see a muscle clench in his jaw.

"I'm sorry if you think I lied to you," he whispered. "But I'm not sorry you stayed."

This time his eyes met hers, holding them, and something fluttered in her chest as he took a step toward her.

"Winchester," Mr. Stone said, "come on now, and get these ladies home—we got work to do."

The three of them rode to Phoebe's in a tow truck, Ryan trapped in the middle. There wasn't much room in the front seat, and again she was all too aware of Winchester's body against hers. She could feel his eyes upon her as she got out, and once inside the house she felt curiously weak.

Phoebe peered cautiously into the kitchen and made a face. "Oh, *damn*—Jinx is on the phone, and I think he's talking to Mom and Dad." She glanced again and looked worried. "What am I going to tell him about his car? I'll have to tell him you—" She broke off as Jinx swung around the doorframe and blocked her path.

"You're dead." Jinx looked decidedly smug. "Dad wants to talk to you."

"Dad?" Phoebe's voice quivered. "Dad's on the phone?"

"Yeah. He called right after the garage did."

"The garage? You mean that stupid night clerk?"

"You really screwed up this time, Phoebe. You know you're grounded, and you're *never* supposed to touch my car unless it's an emergency."

"You told Dad?" Phoebe was shocked. "You actually *told* him? I don't believe it—"

"Get in there." Jinx jerked his thumb toward the kitchen. "He's really mad. You are in *deep* trouble."

"You jerk!" Phoebe sounded tearful. "I can't believe you *told* him—I would have paid for your stupid car—"

"He's grounding you for good this time." Jinx leaned back, looking pleased with himself. "He says no New Year's dance."

Even Ryan looked shocked. As Phoebe stared at Jinx, the silence seemed to grow and grow until the room was unbearable.

"No . . ." Phoebe mumbled. "He wouldn't . . ."

"Think again," Jinx said. "You shouldn't have tried to be so sneaky."

Phoebe disappeared into the kitchen. Ryan could hear her babbling, then pleading, and finally the crash as the receiver came down.

"I *hate* you!" Phoebe came into the hallway and went for Jinx, but he managed to make it to the stairs. "You've ruined my *life!* You've absolutely ruined my *life!* I can't believe you *did* this to me!"

"Hey, *I* didn't do it," Jinx said, his voice rising. He looked indignant but took another step away from her. "You *knew* better—don't blame *me!*"

"This is the most horrible thing you've ever done!" Phoebe was crying now, and as Ryan reached for her, Phoebe pushed her away.

"Well, what am *I* gonna do for a car now, huh?" Jinx threw back. "They didn't just slash my tires— they ripped out half the *insides!* What am *I* gonna do about getting to the dance!"

"Who *cares* about your stupid car?" Phoebe screamed at him. "Why don't you just ask Ryan to go with you like you've *wanted* to do all along, and maybe *she* can drive you!"

Ryan stared from Phoebe to Jinx. Jinx had taken another step back, but his face looked peculiarly drained of color.

"Oh, right"—his laugh sounded forced—"like I'd trust her with my life—"

"Oh, stop it, Jinx, just why not let her hear it? I'm sure she'll be so *flattered* that the jerkiest little guy in the whole *town* has had a *crush* on her his whole *life!*"

Ryan's mouth dropped open, and she stared at Jinx. His face was still pale, but his look had gone defiant. He gave her a grim smile and started up the stairs.

"Yeah, stupid, in her dreams . . ."

"Okay, then, why don't we tell her about the *pictures* you've got, huh? In that box with all your most private stuff?"

Jinx froze. He whirled round and slowly began shaking his head.

"You're crazy, Phoebe. You don't know anything about my stuff—"

"Like hell I don't! That box you keep in your closet—and all those pictures of Ryan—from the time she was little all the way up till now—and what about that *letter* you wrote her but you never mailed —how did it go? 'It's so hard for me to tell you what I'm feeling, because I think you're so—'"

"Shut up, Phoebe!"

"Oh, you don't like it, do you, when *you're* the one who's unhappy." Phoebe gave him her most superior big-sister sneer. "And what else did it say—'I'd love for us to be alone together sometime and—'"

"Phoebe . . ." Jinx's voice had dropped. He was still shaking his head, but the paleness had turned into a creeping, helpless red. "Don't . . ." he whispered.

"And I love the part that—"

"Phoebe, stop it!" Ryan said. As her friend looked at her in surprise, Ryan started toward her, but Phoebe gave a sob and ran past Jinx up to her room. Ryan heard the door slam. She lifted her eyes reluctantly to Jinx, but he was staring at the floor and wouldn't look at her.

"Oh, there she goes again. . . ." Ryan laughed, a phony, nervous sound. "Don't pay any attention to her—*I* never do when she does that to me. She's so upset, she doesn't even know what she's saying—you know how she gets—"

Flustered, Ryan broke off. Jinx hadn't moved, and she could hear Phoebe wailing upstairs.

"Wow, look at the time!" Ryan exclaimed. "I better call Mom to come and get me!"

After escaping into the kitchen, she dialed her number with shaking hands. *Oh, Phoebe, what have you done—*

"Steve? Can you pick me up? I'm at Phoebe's—"

"Hey, kiddo, what's the matter? You crying?"

"It's just . . . Jinx and Phoebe had a fight."

"With you caught in the middle?"

"You could say that. Please hurry."

Ryan didn't have long to wait. As they drove away from the house, she looked up and saw Jinx watching from his window. She waved, but the curtains fell shut.

"Well, you can stop worrying about Charles Eastman," Steve told her. "Looks like all his intentions are as noble as he said they were. 'A' student. And now I know where I thought I'd heard his name—he's assistant editor of the paper—*very* well respected."

Ryan scarcely heard him. She could still see Jinx frozen on the stairs . . . the look on his face . . .

"What's wrong?" Steve asked kindly. "You look beat. And your mom's not too happy about you flying the coop. Just a friendly warning." He winked at her.

"So what else is new?" Ryan sighed. "I wish things could just be normal again."

"Me, too, Ryan."

There was a long moment of silence. Ryan forced a smile.

"So what about that important interview? You been practicing?"

Steve gave an exaggerated grimace. "Department chair—pretty scary, huh?"

"Probably not as scary as the interview will be. Once that's over, piece of cake." Ryan patted his arm. "You'll get the job. We all know you will. Mom's going to be so proud."

"Well, I don't have it yet, so recruit some finger-crossers for me, will you?"

"You got it. So when do you leave?"

"Tomorrow night. I hate going at a time like this, but at least Charles is here to help out."

I hate you leaving, too, because it's Christmas, because I'm so unhappy, because you're fun to have around, because . . . because everything—

"Ryan," Steve broke into her thoughts. "Your mom really loves you, you know."

Ryan said nothing. A dozen emotions choked her, and she stared out the window.

"She does," Steve said again. "Even though I know she doesn't show it much these days."

Ryan had a hazy image of her mother's face, superimposed with Marissa's . . . and then without warning, Jinx's expression came again, hurt and embarrassed and helpless—and she shoved it away.

"So what was Mom doing when you left?"

"Sleeping. I don't know where Charles was. Last I

heard, he'd taken the car over to get gas. And by the way, he might not be so bad to have around after all," Steve teased. "I've already got him shoveling snow!"

He let Ryan off and she tiptoed upstairs, thankful to be alone with her thoughts at last. There were so many confused emotions whirling through her brain that she felt numb, and as she let herself into Marissa's room, it didn't register right away that the bedside lamp was already on, that the closet was open, that a tall shadow was leaning over the desk . . .

And as Charles Eastman turned and looked straight at her, Ryan saw the knife in his hand, aimed at the lock on one desk drawer.

Chapter 15

What are you doing!"

As Ryan burst into the room, something went across Charles's face—some fleeting emotion that Ryan couldn't identify—that melted immediately into a sheepish smile.

"God, Ryan, I didn't hear you come home!"

"What are you— Get away from there!"

"Well . . . sure. Hey, I didn't mean any—"

"You don't have *any* right to be in here. When Mom finds out about this—"

"There's no need to tell her." Charles backed away. "You wouldn't want to upset her, and I didn't hurt anything."

"How dare you come in here!"

Charles nodded contritely as he tucked the knife into his belt. "I guess I did get a little carried away. But if you'd just listen and let me explain—"

"Start explaining. And while you're at it, where's the necklace?"

In answer, Charles reached into one pocket and dangled the chain between his fingers. Ryan took it from him slowly, staring down at it in her open palm.

"It *is* hers, I know it. What's going on, Charles?"

When he didn't answer, she looked up at him. His eyes looked worried, and he sank down onto the end of the bed.

"I didn't want to tell you, Ryan. I didn't want you to worry after everything you've been through. But I'm going crazy keeping it to myself . . . and you've got a right to know."

Ryan stared at him, her whole body going cold. "My God," she whispered. "Charles . . . what is it?"

"How strong are you, Ryan?" Charles asked tightly. "I mean, really—how strong?"

Something in his tone alarmed her, and she put one hand to her throat. "What do you mean—what—"

"The necklace." He gave a curt nod. "I haven't been able to quit thinking about it—or about something else that happened at school about a month ago."

"Marissa?" Ryan murmured.

He paused, as if searching for words, then went on slowly. "She and I worked on the paper together; she had the gossip column. Marissa loved her job, and she was good at it—enthusiastic . . . talented at sniffing out rumors. Right before Thanksgiving she started acting . . . I don't know . . . preoccupied. Distracted. Like she was bothered about something. Or . . . scared."

Ryan looked at him in surprise. "That's how she acted with me, too—she seemed different from the minute she got home from school."

"She told me she was pretty sure she'd uncovered something big," Charles said solemnly. "She said it was an accident, that she'd just stumbled onto it, but that it was real scandal material if she could prove anything."

"She didn't say what it was?"

Charles shook his head. "It was weird—she seemed half excited about it, half terrified."

Ryan let out a long sigh and sat on the window seat, facing him. She put the necklace on the cushion beside her.

"She told me she was in trouble." Ryan gulped. "Maybe even serious. That last day we were together —she was so nervous and jumpy, and she kept saying she didn't want to go into it, but maybe she'd know something when she got back to school."

"That's what she told me, too!" Charles leaned forward eagerly. "She said she had some evidence— that she was taking it home with her and—"

"Oh, my God!" Ryan jumped up, her hands to her mouth.

"Ryan, what's the—"

"Oh, my God, Charles—the *film!* Marissa wanted me to drop off some film that day. She needed to take the pictures back to school with her! Do you think—"

"Film . . ." Charles was staring at her, his mouth open, his head shaking in amazement. "Then there really *was* something. . . . So this film . . . you still have it?"

"Yes! I mean, no! I mean, I forgot about it till today! I dropped it off this afternoon!"

"Where? You're sure the film was hers?"

"Yes! Yes! At the drugstore—only they were closing —they said it'd be ready Monday morning—"

"Because tomorrow's Sunday." Charles groaned. He shook his head and then, to Ryan's surprise, reached for her hand. "Ryan, do you realize what this means?"

Her voice was shaking so that she could hardly speak. "That . . . that Marissa might have been . . ."

She couldn't say the word. She closed her eyes and leaned against him.

"If she really *was* on to some scandal," Charles said gravely, "and if someone knew about that film, they could have followed her. They could have been following her for a long time, waiting to get her alone—"

"She said someone tailed her home from school"— Ryan's voice was trembling—"but I never dreamed . . ."

Charles looked pale. He jumped up and thrust his hands into his pockets. "If someone brought that necklace here, then that someone—"

"Must be the . . . killer," Ryan finished.

Charles avoided her eyes. "Maybe he doesn't know how much *you* know about it, Ryan. How much you saw that day."

"Then that means someone really is after me." Her eyes widened and her voice came out the faintest whisper. "If someone murdered Marissa . . . oh, Charles—are they going to kill me, too?"

Chapter 16

Charles offered to drive Ryan to work the next day, and she eagerly accepted.

"I didn't sleep a wink," she told him as they came into town. "I had bad dreams all night."

"Me, too," Charles admitted. "It seems so—so—impossible! We were jumping to an awful lot of conclusions last night. It's not like we have any proof, either. We can't very well go to the police and say anything. At least, not without those pictures."

Ryan looked troubled. "I thought about that, too. But how else can you explain the necklace unless someone took it from her?"

"I can't." Charles shrugged, glancing over at her. "I guess someone could have picked it up later in the woods. Maybe she dropped it before she fell."

"But then whoever found it had to have known it was hers. In order to give it back, I mean."

"Maybe someone saw her fall through the ice." Charles thought a moment. "Maybe they didn't have anything to do with it, but they saw it happen."

"I'd rather believe that than think someone's after me."

"Why do you keep saying that? I wish you'd stop—"

"Sometimes"—Ryan ducked her head—"I really think I *am* going crazy."

Charles lapsed into silence, and as he pulled up near the toyshop, Ryan forced a smile in his direction.

"Do you want to come in? Just don't mind Mr. Partini. When he sees you, he'll probably make a fuss."

No sooner had they stepped inside, than Ryan's prediction came true.

"Ah, *Bambalina,* you surprise me! Here I think you feel sick, and all the time you be *love*sick, eh? With this new fella of yours?"

Ryan made a helpless gesture to Charles, who seemed amused by the whole thing. "He's just a friend, Mr. Partini. He was a friend of my— Oh, never mind. But I really didn't feel well yesterday," she said.

"And I believe you!" The old man nodded in exaggerated seriousness and patted her shoulder. "I *like* this fella—"

"Mr. Partini—"

"You bring him anytime! Anytime!"

"But Mr. Partini, he's not—"

"You bad girl, hiding him from me, Ryan." He shook his finger, then caught Ryan in a hug. "But I'm so happy for you, I gonna forgive you, eh?"

Ryan could hardly stand to look at Charles, but Charles only winked. After a personal tour of the toyshop, he took off, leaving Ryan to spend her busiest Sunday ever.

By five o'clock Ryan was exhausted and eager to go home. As she waited for her mother's car, she heard the phone ring in the back of the shop, and after a brief conversation, Mr. Partini appeared behind her in the doorway.

"Your mother's gonna be late, *Bambalina*. She says for you to meet her on the corner in half an hour, eh?"

Ryan nodded and saw the way he tried to glance discreetly at the clock. "It's all right, Mr. Partini, I know you have some toys to deliver tonight. Why don't you go on—I'll lock up."

"Oh, you caught me looking! Is okay? You don't mind?" He looked so grateful that Ryan smiled.

"Of course not. I'll see you tomorrow."

He patted her cheek with one soft hand. "You a good girl, Ryan—what would I do without you? And hey"—he winked—"that's one cute fella!"

He shuffled back to the workshop, and Ryan heard him lock the door as he left. Minutes later his old car chugged off into the darkness, and silence settled softly over the shop.

Ryan leaned against the wall and tried to think. Her mind had been in such a turmoil that she'd finally resigned herself to a perpetual headache. *Marissa . . . the necklace . . . the film . . . Am I in danger or just caught up in coincidences? Charles . . . Winchester . . . Jinx*— her cheeks flamed, even though she'd tried so hard not to think about last night. *I don't know what to feel about anything anymore—*

Suddenly her mind went blank. She was staring at the front of the store, and something was staring back in at the window—someone—in a lumpy coat and ski mask—huge gloves cupped around black knit eyeholes . . . the head rotating slowly from side to side . . .

Ryan's breath caught in her throat. Very slowly she flattened herself against the wall and tried to slide down onto the floor. Because of her position, the stranger hadn't seen her yet, but she knew it was only a matter of seconds . . .

She huddled there, scarcely daring to breathe, and tried to draw back into the shadows. She didn't have to see the eyes to know they were making a slow, careful sweep of the shop. She could *feel* them.

They were frighteningly cold.

She saw the head tilt slightly, as if thinking. She heard feet scraping pavement . . .

The doorknob began to turn . . .

Oh, my God, I forgot to lock it!

As the front door groaned slowly inward, the bell tinkled spookily overhead, and Ryan slid along the wall and underneath a desk. Icy trickles of sweat chilled her, and she wrapped her arms around herself to keep from shaking.

The silence went on . . . on . . .

And then the feet began to move. Slow, deliberate steps upon the creaking floorboards.

They passed right beside her hiding place.

Terrified, she saw his boots, not ten inches from where she crouched.

And then the voice came . . .

One she knew . . .

"Hi, this is Marissa . . ." And it *was* Marissa, *her* voice—real and laughing, fuzzy and faraway—"but I'm not here . . ."

"Marissa," Ryan whimpered, and she clapped her hand over her mouth, not sure if she'd spoken aloud or only in her fear-crazed mind—

The footsteps stopped.

He can hear me, I know he can, he must be able to—

And then . . . in the deathly quiet . . . the trains started up . . . slowly at first . . . then faster . . . faster . . . little engines chugging . . . tiny whistles blowing . . . around and around—

From some forgotten corner a baby doll cried in a tinny, mournful wail—"Ma . . . ma . . . ma . . . ma . . ."

The mechanical Santa Claus burst into insane laughter.

Ryan could see the wild eyes of the carousel horses —nostrils flaring—*My God, they're alive, they're moving, I can't get out—*

Sick with terror, Ryan clamped her hands over her ears and curled herself into a ball. They were coming closer now, all the toys . . . skates crashing into the wall . . . a top spinning crazily past the desk . . .

If I try for the door, maybe I can make it—maybe he won't hear me—

Ryan took a deep breath and ran.

She never expected the door to be jammed.

Oh, God—something's wrong with the lock—

As she frantically twisted the handle, she cast a desperate look back over her shoulder. *Is that him—moving in the corner? By the dollhouse? Near the tree?* She couldn't see anything now—just black, murky shadows—but he seemed to be everywhere—*everywhere*—and *nowhere*—the trains faster and faster—the Santa laughing and laughing—

Without warning the elves started singing their Christmas carols . . . but on low speed, demons' voices . . .

"Help! Let me out!"

She hammered on the glass and screamed, trying to shut out the unearthly sound of Marissa's voice—*"I'm not here . . . I'm not here—"*

The tree lights blinked on.

A baby carriage started rolling toward her across the floor.

Glass shattered as Ryan's fists went through. Her hands were slippery on the latch, and as it finally gave, she stumbled out onto the sidewalk.

She never looked back . . .

Just raced widly toward the corner, leaving a trail of blood behind her in the snow.

Chapter 17

Her mother wasn't waiting for her.

As Ryan looked frantically up and down the empty sidewalks, she thought she heard the bell over the toy shop door.

"No—no—"

She felt as if she were trapped in a recurring nightmare—running once again through the dark streets, snow clouds covering the stars. The only light came from a few sputtering streetlamps and the sign in the Coffeehouse window—CLOSED.

If I can just get to the gas station—Winchester— how many more blocks? Four? Five? She began to think she'd gone the wrong way when she suddenly saw it up ahead—the pumps, the group of boys hanging around the garage—

"Jinx!" she gasped. She saw the faces turn toward her as one, Jinx looking up from under the hood of a car, his cheeks stained with dirt.

"Get outta here," he said gruffly. "Don't you ever get tired of chasing after me?"

She heard the snickers around him, and she saw him

start to grin, but as she stepped forward into the light, everyone seemed to freeze.

"Jinx—" she began, and *why is he looking at me that way, why are they all staring at me like that*—

"Somebody call the cops," one of them said, and for the first time Ryan looked down.

There was blood everywhere.

She didn't have a jacket on, and there was blood on her sleeves, on her white sweater, on her jeans. Blood was running down her wrists, and there were dark red spatters around her feet.

"Holy sh—" Jinx came around the car. "Does somebody have a rag? Quick, someone, bring me a rag!"

"You better get her to a doctor or something," someone else spoke up, and Ryan realized they all sounded so scared, as scared as she suddenly felt—

"I . . . I did this," she said stupidly, holding up her hands, and as the boys exchanged wary looks, Jinx was suddenly grabbing her arms, binding them together in a towel.

"God, McCauley," he murmured, "get in the car."

She felt him shoving her into a front seat, heard him slamming a door—

"You've got to go back there!" Ryan told him. "I left the door open—Mr. Partini trusted me—"

"What are you *talking* about?"

"The toyshop! The toys were after me, but *he* was there—*he* did it—"

"Who? Mr. Partini? Who did what?"

"No, I couldn't see him—I couldn't see anyone, I just heard Marissa—"

"She's nuts," someone said and snickered, and Jinx leaned out the window.

"You shut up! And you—" He turned back to Ryan and stared.

"She said she wasn't here—but it was her voice— What's *wrong* with you?" Ryan broke off. "Why are you looking at me that way?"

"Just quit talking," Jinx said. "Here." He tossed her his jacket and hit the gas. "And don't bleed all over the seat—it's not my car."

As streets and intersections whizzed by, Ryan realized they were running lights and stop signs, and she looked over at Jinx's stony profile.

"You know you can't afford to get any more tickets," she scolded weakly. "You better slow down."

"Don't talk to me, McCauley."

"I couldn't stand it, Jinx, I just couldn't stand it anymore—I was so scared—"

"Okay, okay, I hear you—but—but did you have to do *this?"*

"I didn't realize—it was the only way out—I couldn't go back—"

"Just be quiet. Look—here's the hospital."

Ryan reached for her door, but Jinx already had it open, and he rushed her into the emergency room. In the bright, clean light, Ryan was surprised to see dark stains oozing through her towel, and as a nurse whisked her away, Jinx stood there, looking lost and confused.

"I'll call your mom, okay?"

Ryan could see him waving at her, but the pain was starting now, and she felt as if someone else's hands had gotten mixed up with hers. "No, don't call her! Don't leave me!"

"I'll be right here!"

What followed was a blur—white uniforms . . . questions . . . more pain—and through it all Ryan kept trying to *tell* them, to make them *listen,* but they just kept looking at her hands and then at each other with secretive looks, making her be quiet, making her sleep. . . .

"But you don't understand," she kept telling them. "It was the only way—nobody would help me—"

And the nods . . . the reassurances . . . the slipping away of time . . .

"Ryan? Honey, can you hear me? We can go home now."

Ryan stared at the pale green ceiling, and it seemed she'd been staring at it forever. She knew her thoughts had wandered, even though her eyes had been open all this time. She turned her head and saw Steve's and her mother's anxious faces.

"Why'd you do it?" Mrs. McCauley asked, her voice rising, but Steve put a hand on her shoulder, and she cut off with a guilty look.

"I had to get out," Ryan said. Her voice was thick, and she wanted to sleep. "I had to get out. That's all. It was the only way." *Why does everyone keep asking me that? I keep telling them, but they're not listening. . . .*

"It's my fault," Mrs. McCauley whispered, and she reached for Ryan's hand.

"No, it's not," Ryan mumbled. "I was just waiting like you said."

She saw her mother and Steve exchange blank looks.

"What's she talking about?" Mrs. McCauley whispered again, and again Steve patted her shoulder.

"Come on, Leslie, save it for another time."

Ryan stared at them, frowning. Strong arms helped her into a sitting position, and her head spun.

"How about a little ride?" Steve smiled.

"Only if I don't have to drive." Ryan got into the wheelchair, and Steve pushed her out into the lobby. To her surprise Jinx was still there—and with him Phoebe, Charles, and Winchester, who all stopped talking and stood up when they saw her. She stared at them in confusion. She suddenly felt angry, but wasn't sure why.

"Why are you all here?" she asked. *They're still doing it . . . everyone's still looking at me so funny. . . .*

"Oh, Ryan," Phoebe whispered, her eyes filling with tears. "Oh, I'm so sorry, I—"

"Phoebe, I'm fine, really, just a scratch." For the first time Ryan looked down and saw the bandages on her hands and wrists.

"Come on, Ryan," Mrs. McCauley said softly. "Let's just get you home."

And then, without warning, Ryan's anger turned to fear, and she grabbed Steve's hand and tried to stand up.

"But I don't need to go home! I'm fine! As a matter of fact, I'm hungry! Can't we all go out and get pizza or something? Jinx?" She looked wildly from face to face, each pair of eyes lowering in turn, refusing to meet her accusing stare. "Jinx?" she said again. "What's going on? What's wrong with everyone? What's—"

"You can see everyone later," Mrs. McCauley said, and Steve gently forced Ryan down again. "After you're better—after you've had a chance to—"

"Leslie," Steve interrupted. "Let's not talk about it now, okay? We agreed . . ."

Ryan tried to look back as Steve and her mother settled her into the car. "Where's Charles?"

"He had his car, and we came in mine," Mrs. McCauley said, trying to calm her.

"But why—why didn't he come with you?"

"He was supposed to pick you up. He was going to bring home hamburgers for dinner, and Steve asked if he'd mind getting you at work on the way."

"But *you* called. Why weren't *you* there?"

Her mother was looking at her as if she expected Ryan to attack her at any minute. "But I didn't call. I asked Charles to call. Ryan, what does it matter who came in which car or who called—"

"You weren't there. Charles wasn't there."

"Charles said he waited for you, but you never showed up. So he went to the shop and found the glass in the door broken. He was afraid there'd been a robbery, and he couldn't find you, so he called the police—"

"And in the meantime Jinx had called us," Steve picked up, "so we called the police, too, and the police called Mr. Partini—"

"Was the man in the store when Charles went in?" Ryan sat forward, her voice tight, pleading.

"Ryan, please, you've got to calm down—"

"The *man*, Mom—"

"What man? Ryan, what are you—"

"I need Charles," Ryan mumbled. She could see him standing outside the hospital talking to the others, and she lunged across her mother's lap to the window.

"Charles! Did you see the man! When you went into the toy shop, did you see the—"

"Ryan." Steve tried to pull her away. "Come on, kiddo, get back in the car—"

"No! Charles! Did you see him! Tell me you saw him!"

"Ryan, stop it!" Mrs. McCauley grabbed her and blocked the window. Steve hurriedly backed the car up and drove away.

"I need to ask him," Ryan whispered. "I need to talk to Charles . . . you don't understand . . ."

"Yes, yes, as soon as we get you home. Hush, now."

Ryan felt sick. She could see her mother and Steve exchanging looks over her head, and she choked on hot, burning tears.

"Almost there," Steve said cheerfully. "Almost home now, Ryan."

"A nice warm bed, won't that be nice?" Mrs. McCauley sounded peculiar, too cheerful, too strained. "I'll bring you some broth, you'll like that, won't you?"

"Why are you doing this?" Ryan murmured. "Why are you being so nice to me? I'm perfectly all right."

"Of course you are," her mother said quickly. "We know that, don't we, Steve? And you'll be even better once you see—"

"Leslie." Steve shook his head warningly, and Ryan stared at him. Something in the back of her mind sensed a change that she wasn't going to like, but she was too exhausted to care.

Mrs. McCauley and Steve got her upstairs into her mother's bed, and though Ryan kept protesting, nobody seemed to hear.

"You just take this medicine," Mrs. McCauley kept saying, "and when you wake up, we'll talk. When you feel better, we'll talk."

"I feel fine," Ryan insisted unhappily. "I want to sleep in my own room."

"You'll be fine in here," Mrs. McCauley said anxiously, smoothing Ryan's hair back from her forehead. It was something she hadn't done in a long, long time, and Ryan suddenly felt like crying. "And Charles is in your room, don't you remember?"

"Of course I remember. And where *is* Charles? I've got to ask him about the man. . . ." Ryan's eyelids drooped, and Steve and her mother shimmered, ghostly shadows. She tried to tell them, but they seemed to be growing dimmer, fading away from her. "Tried . . . to kill me," she mumbled.

"But we know you didn't mean it, Ryan. . . ." Her

mother's voice, down a long, dark tunnel. "We know you didn't, honey."

Mean what? Ryan's brain was all fuzzy, and she couldn't seem to concentrate. *Mean what—to get away from that horrible stranger—to break down the door so I wouldn't die in there?*

"Yes, I did," Ryan murmured. "Yes, I did mean to do it."

She thought she heard her mother crying, and then she slept—a fitful slumber of painful memories and haunted nightmares. Wild-eyed Santas chased her through streets that led nowhere, and every time she turned a corner, there stood Marissa, with blue skin and wide eyes, one arm pointing accusingly—*"I'm not here . . . I'm dead . . ."*

In the dream Ryan screamed and finally managed to wake herself up. She was drenched with sweat, and as she reached up to pull back her hair, she realized her hands wouldn't work, and she couldn't remember what had happened. Squinting into the dark, she tried to focus and saw a movement by the window.

"Marissa?" she murmured. "Marissa, what are you doing in my room?"

The figure barely stirred. Ryan thought it whispered to her, and she tried to sit up.

"Marissa . . . what is it? Why won't you talk to me?"

She leaned forward, her eyes widening, and the phantom moved again, coming nearer the bed.

"Don't scare me like that, Marissa, *don't scare me like that!*"

Ryan flung back the covers and blinked as the light came on, as her mother came into the room and pushed her gently back into bed.

"It's only a dream, honey, you're safe, don't be afraid—"

"Something moved there, Mom, by the window—"

"Curtains, that's all it is—ssh—"

"But my curtains don't look like that—"

"I know, honey, you're in my room, remember?"

And she did remember then, about everything that had happened, and she fell back upon the pillows with a groan.

"My hands hurt, Mom."

"I know, but they'll be better soon. Here—take this medicine. Try to sleep now."

"No—Marissa's here, Mom, in the room with me—"

"You only dreamed it, Ryan. Marissa's not here."

"No . . . I remember . . . Marissa's dead. I killed her."

"Oh, Ryan . . ."

The darkness hid Mrs. McCauley's face, but Ryan could tell her mother was crying. She heard the door click shut and then a lowered exchange of voices just outside in the hall.

"I really don't think I should leave you like this," Steve's voice, serious and concerned. "The doctor said she's just about over the edge as it is."

"Of course you have to leave. It's so important for you—"

"Not as important as you and Ryan. Come on,

Leslie, there'll be other chances. Suppose something happens and you need me—"

"No." Mrs. McCauley's voice, firm and stubborn. "You've been praying for this opportunity, Steve—we both have. It may not come again. I *want* you to go. I know Ryan would, too."

"I'm not leaving. It's a terrible time to even think—"

"If you don't, I'll never speak to you again. I mean it. Look, Charles is here if I need anything. And I have lots of friends to help. For goodness' sake, you'll only be gone a few days—how much can happen in a day or two?"

"It looks to me like a hell of a lot has happened already." There was a guilty pause, and Steve's voice grew quieter. "Then at least let me change my flight. Let me wait till tomorrow."

"Absolutely not. You know we can't depend on the fog in the morning—and you need to get there on time!"

"I'm only thinking of Ryan . . . of what she's been through—"

"And I'm thinking of Ryan, too," her mother said sadly. "How's she going to feel when this gets out?"

Ryan frowned, straining her ears to hear. *What's she talking about?*

Steve sighed. "There must be something we can do."

"Nothing we can say is going to stop all the gossip. Especially this kind." Her mother sounded hurt. "There she is, lying in there confused and in pain, and

I'm not helping her. I've only been thinking of myself!"

"Come on, Leslie . . . you've both been through a hell of a lot."

"Yes, but I've had you to lean on through all this, and she's been alone. I just didn't realize she was so fragile!" Mom's voice broke, and she began to cry again. "And by tomorrow it'll be all over town . . . everyone will know that Ryan tried to kill herself."

Chapter 18

*K*ill *myself!*

Ryan's brain reeled, and she grabbed the edge of the bed.

Kill myself! What's she talking about . . . ?

As Steve's and her mother's voices faded out of earshot, Ryan held her hands in front of her face, her eyes piercing the darkness. She could feel the pain now, dull and throbbing, *and so it must be real, I haven't imagined the pain, so I must not be crazy, they just don't know, they couldn't know because they weren't there. . . .*

Trying not to make any noise, Ryan fumbled with the phone on the nightstand and torturously dialed Phoebe's number. The phone rang and rang, and just as she was about to give up, Ryan heard Mrs. Evans's cheery hello.

"Mrs. Evans"—her voice shook—"Mrs. Evans . . . this is Ryan."

Something was wrong. She could tell immediately from the long uncomfortable silence, and then the careful calmness of Mrs. Evans's voice when she finally spoke again.

"Yes, Ryan. How are you feeling, dear? We heard you had . . . an accident."

She knows. . . . Ryan closed her eyes and fought back tears. *She thinks she knows what's happened, but she's wrong*—"May I speak to Phoebe, please?"

"Phoebe?" There was an awkward pause. Ryan had the distinct feeling that Mrs. Evans had covered the mouthpiece and was whispering to someone. When she spoke again, she sounded strained. "Well . . . Ryan . . . this really isn't a . . . a good time right now. Could Phoebe—"

"Why won't she talk to me, Mrs. Evans?" Ryan demanded. She was trying not to raise her voice, trying not to cry, and she *knew* Phoebe was there, she *knew* it—"Why won't she come to the phone? It's not what you think—why won't you believe—"

Surprised, she heard the dial tone and looked down to see her own hand on the telephone. *I hung it up myself. Who needs Phoebe, anyway? I don't need anyone*—

Sick at heart, Ryan crawled back under the covers, and tried to sleep. She could hear the clock ticking . . . minutes dragging by into endless hours. She heard Steve and Mom saying their goodbyes in the downstairs hall, then a little while later, her mother's heartbroken sobs from the living room. She wouldn't cry for long, Ryan knew—it would only take a couple of the usual sleeping pills, and her mother would be oblivious till morning. Ryan wondered where Charles was, and what he'd been doing all evening—she hadn't heard him in the house, but maybe he'd been making himself inconspicuous throughout all this tragedy she'd seemed to cause. *My fault again . . . everything's always my fault . . .*

It started to snow. She could see it from the bed, laciness drifting past the window. She dozed . . . woke . . . dozed again. The night waned, and she never knew when the snow let up, and she never knew what woke her, bringing her up from terrible dreams, tapping softly against her window. . . .

Ryan opened her eyes. She saw the pewter sky of early morning and, upon the windowpane, dribbles of clinging snow. Lying there, she tried to slip back into her twilight state, but as she gazed through half-open lids at the window, something hit the glass and came apart in soft flurries.

A snowball?

Puzzled, Ryan tried to raise herself on her elbows. Almost at once the pain stabbed through her hands and wrists, and she bit her lip to keep from crying out. She didn't want to remember yesterday or what she'd have to face today—

Splat! The windowpane rattled as more white softness exploded against the glass. Ryan frowned and pushed back the covers. It *was* a snowball—but who would be out throwing snowballs at this hour?

The world was bathed in shadowy light as she pressed her face to the glass and peered down into the backyard. Fresh wet snow clung everywhere, giving the lawn a surreal appearance that Ryan found unsettling. Her breath fogged up the glass, and she winced as she tried to rub clumsily at the pane . . .

And then she saw it.

There on the lawn, just beneath her window, a huge, three-tiered snowman, at least six feet tall.

As Ryan gazed in wonder, she saw its long stick arms, reaching toward the sky . . . the ends branched out, like fingers, desperately clawing . . .

She saw the round oversize head . . .

She saw the face—not on the *front* of the head looking outward, but rather on *top* of the head, so that it looked straight up at her window.

From where Ryan stood, the eyes were empty black holes.

The mouth formed a silent scream.

And fluttering around its head in the morning breeze were long, red ribbons.

Chapter 19

No!"

Ryan raced to the kitchen and out the back door, her screams exploding with unbearable fury. She didn't even feel the cold as she raced into the yard and attacked the snowman, tearing it apart. She didn't hear the running footsteps on the porch behind her, didn't even know anyone was there until she fell down, exhausted, and saw her mother and Charles huddled together on the steps. In the gray morning Mrs. McCauley's voice carried across the lawn, and it sounded terrified.

"Ryan . . . my God . . . what are you—"

"Make it stop!" Ryan screamed, and she pointed to the snow heaped around her. "Please, Mom—*please!*"

"Oh . . . oh, Ryan . . ."

"This isn't the first time!" Ryan shouted, and she tried to stand, but her legs wouldn't hold her. "I've seen Marissa before—"

Mrs. McCauley looked frantically at Charles, who started forward slowly, as if afraid of making a wrong move.

"I know I'm not crazy!" Ryan babbled. "I tried to hold her—I wouldn't have left her there! If I'd known she was serious, I wouldn't have gone off—"

"What's she talking about, Charles? Oh, Ryan, come here to me—"

"I wish it'd been me!" And suddenly Ryan was laughing uncontrollably, digging through the snow, holding up lumps of charcoal and long strings of curly Christmas ribbon. "I don't know what's happening! I'm so sick of all this, I just wish I were *dead!*"

Mrs. McCauley covered her face with her hands, and Charles moved past her, reaching Ryan in four long strides, trying to coax her gently to her feet. Ryan pushed him and sent him sprawling.

"We have to tell her! No, don't tell her—get away from me! I wish you'd never come!"

"I'm calling the doctor." Mrs. McCauley headed into the house, but not before Ryan had time to fling a final comment.

"Yes! Call him! I'm not the sick one here—I'm the *alive* one! Remember me? I'm the one you'd rather have dead, only I'm still here!"

Charles managed to grab her at last, and as Ryan kicked and fought him, he dragged her back into the house. At the foot of the staircase he lifted her into his arms and started up.

"Put her in my room, Charles." Mrs. McCauley was following them, wringing her hands, and after another brief struggle, Ryan went limp. She didn't resist as Charles lowered her into bed; she lay there calmly and closed her eyes to shut out their stares.

"Ryan—"

Mrs. McCauley's hand lingered on her forehead, but Ryan jerked her head away. She wished they would go away and leave her alone. She felt like that snowman down there—crushed and crumpled and flat.

"Ryan"—her mother sat down on the bed, talking fast—"it's going to be okay, honey—you're going to start seeing a very nice doctor."

"You're sending me to a psychiatrist. And then you're locking me up."

"Locking you up! Of course we're not locking you up! Where would you ever get such an idea?"

"Please lock me up." Without warning Ryan sat up and grabbed her mother's shoulders, her eyes pleading. "Please lock me up, Mom, I want you to. Then maybe all these scary things will stop happening to me—"

"Ryan, no one is going to lock you up—"

"Just leave me alone, then." She saw Charles framed in the doorway, and she hated the look on his face, so sad, so sorry—"Just go away."

The phone rang, but Mrs. McCauley ignored the one on her nightstand. Nodding to Charles, she went out into the hallway, and he followed, closing the door behind them. Ryan could barely hear her mother talking in the kitchen, and then someone turned the radio on, and she couldn't hear anymore. She lay there and watched the sky change from gray to pearl, more snow clouds piling up, quilting the sky, and the bedside clock ticking toward schooltime. Ryan had no intention of going to school today—or any day from now on. She knew she'd never be able to face anyone there—the stares and whispers, the phony, sympathetic smiles . . .

Someone's after me, and I'm all alone. Charles knows, but he can't stop what's happening.

Mrs. McCauley didn't want to go to work—Ryan could hear Charles offering to drive her, promising to come right back. Ryan was glad when they'd gone, yet she was also terrified to be alone in the house. She groped her way carefully downstairs and checked all the doors. She made herself some hot tea, then sat down at the table to think. *For a while I was the only one who thought I was going crazy . . . but now everyone else thinks so, too, so I really must be. . . .*

The tea warmed her a little. She could feel her nerves relaxing and her mind began to calm and clear. She thought about last night—her terror in the toyshop—the patronizing way everyone had looked at her at the hospital. . . . She knew she had to stop going over it before she started crying again. She went upstairs to Marissa's room and stood in the doorway and stared.

The aching in her heart was almost more than she could stand, and she pictured Marissa on the window seat, the way she'd be staring back with a smug smile.

It's normal for everyone to miss you so much . . . you were the pretty one, the popular one . . . you were everything Mom always wanted in a daughter—

The room seemed to hurt around her, the silence long and grieving.

"But still," Ryan whispered, "still . . . I know we fought . . . I know sometimes we even hated each other—but—I never would have left if I thought you were in danger." Tears burned her throat, and she could hardly speak. "You know that, don't you . . . you know I wouldn't have let anything happen to you. And now . . . I could be next . . ."

As Ryan gazed at the windowpane, the sun struggled free of the clouds, and in that instant a ray of light shimmered on the glass, slanting down across one photograph on the crowded sill.

Marissa.

She was sitting in a chair, going through a pile of things in her lap, and someone had obviously surprised her into looking up. She was smiling straight at Ryan, and in the picture she was holding a bunch of photographs.

Photographs . . .

As Ryan stared at the golden shaft of light, it vanished.

She walked over to Marissa's desk and rummaged through the phone book. She picked up the phone and called the number of the drugstore.

"Good morning, may I help you?"

She took a deep breath and leaned against the desk. "I'd like to see if my pictures are ready, please."

"Sure. Your name?"

"McCauley. Ryan."

"Just a minute."

Ryan could hear voices laughing. Drawers opened and papers rustled. Someone picked up the receiver again.

"McCauley, you said?"

"Yes."

"Sorry. There's nothing here."

Ryan stared, seeing nothing. Pain crept slowly up her arms.

"But there has to be. They said I could pick them up today."

"When did you bring them in?"

"Saturday. Late afternoon."

"Hmmm . . . okay. Hang on a minute."

More rummaging, then finally the voice back again, apologetic.

"One of the girls says someone picked them up earlier."

"Are you sure?" Ryan asked. "Who was it? Who picked them up?"

"She says it was a guy," the voice said. "She was at the counter, but she didn't wait on him."

"What'd he look like?"

The voice mumbled, then came back. "She wasn't really paying attention, but she heard him give his name—Ryan McCauley."

"No, I'm—" Ryan broke off, shaking her head impatiently. "Never mind. Thanks."

She walked slowly to the window, staring out at the wintry day, a feeling of dread washing over her.

Charles must have gone by and picked them up, and as soon as he brings them home, then we'll know for sure, we'll finally know the truth one way or the other—

The telephone shrilled into the silence. Heart pounding, Ryan picked it up.

"Hello?"

"Mrs. McCauley?"

"No, she's not here right now. Can I take a message?"

"Well . . ." The voice sounded businesslike, but now it hesitated. "This is Officer John Henley from the sheriff's department. I need to speak to Mrs. McCauley—it's in regard to the death of Marissa McCauley."

Ryan went icy all over. "Yes! This is Ryan! I'm Mrs. McCauley's daughter! What is it?"

"Well, ma'am . . ." Another long pause, then a burst of static. Ryan clutched the receiver, wincing.

"Are you there? What *is* it? Are you there?"

The voice came back, even more solemn than before. "The truth is, ma'am, we've located a body over near Platt Valley. A farmer discovered it about an hour ago, and we think it might be—"

"Oh, God, oh, God, where is she? Where are you?"

"—could come down here to make a positive identification—"

"Yes! Yes! Where are you again?" Ryan was trying to get through the door, the cord stretching as far as it could.

"Platt Valley," the voice said again. "Are you familiar with—"

"I think so, yes! I think I know where it is—"

"Ten Mile Road . . . you take the northeast turnoff, about twenty miles to a farm—"

"Yes, I'll find it, I'm coming right now. Wait for me—will you wait for me?"

"Yes, ma'am," the voice said soberly. "We'll be right here."

Ryan hurtled down the stairs and through the kitchen, grabbing up her jacket and purse as she ran. Mom's car was in the garage, but the keys that were usually in the ignition weren't there.

"Damn!" Racing back to the kitchen, Ryan pulled open a drawer so fast that it flew off its rollers, spilling all its contents onto the floor. She fell to her knees, digging through all the junk until she found an extra set of keys. She was halfway out the door when the phone rang again.

She wasn't going to answer it, but as Ryan hesitated the thought suddenly came to her that it might be her mother. Making a split-second decision, she raced back and snatched up the receiver.

"Hello?"

"It wasn't my idea to call—Mom wants to know if—"

"Jinx—I can't talk—I have to go—oh, Jinx—"

"Oh, McCauley."

"They found Marissa—I mean, I think they found Marissa—"

"What? Wait a minute, where?"

"I have to go! Down at Platt Valley out on Ten Mile Road—I have to go identify her—"

"Ryan, wait a minute—is your mom there?"

"No, it's just me, I have to go!"

She took off at a run, dropping the receiver, leaving the phone cord banging against the wall.

She didn't hear Jinx calling after her.

She didn't hear the concern in his voice or the way it suddenly turned to fear.

"But they wouldn't have you identify it there, would they?" he shouted. "Wouldn't you go to the morgue?"

Chapter 20

Out on the road Ryan racked her brain, trying to remember exactly where her turnoff was. The sky seemed to press down on all sides, and she grimaced as the first spatter of snow and ice slid down the windshield.

She urged the car to go faster, hanging on painfully to the steering wheel. Within minutes what had started as a flurry became a slushy downpour. Ryan turned on the wipers and hunched forward, squinting. She could already feel slick spots beneath the tires. *This is unbelievable . . . I can hardly see the road. . . .*

She flipped on the radio and groaned as she heard the winter storm warning. *I can't have a wreck . . . I have to get to Marissa. . . .* She tried to find a familiar landmark, but the snowy fields were changing shape before her eyes. Nervously watching ice build up on her wiper blades, she passed the turnoff before she realized and tried to brake on the icy blacktop. Heart pounding, she slammed into reverse and whipped onto the side road.

I wonder what she'll look like. . . . Horrified, Ryan tried to stop her mind from its imaginings, but she couldn't seem to turn it off. *Will her skin be blue—stop it stop it stop it!* Tears blurred her eyes, and as she blinked them away, she missed a curve and slid toward a tree. She turned into the skid and managed to straighten the car in time. The wind was blowing so hard, it was like driving into a swirling tunnel.

Ryan tasted blood and realized she'd bitten her lip. The wipers were barely moving now, they were so encrusted with ice. How much farther? Ten miles? Fifteen? She had no idea how far she'd come. She rubbed hard at the windshield, trying to clear away the fog. As the wheels gave a sudden jerk, the car plowed into a snowbank.

Ryan floored the gas pedal, but the wheels spun helplessly on ice. Fighting off a wave of panic, she shut off the engine and opened her door.

Miraculously she thought she saw a rooftop in the distance, and she started toward it. As the roof materialized into a building, Ryan called out and saw a vague human form suddenly appear through the snow. For just a moment it seemed to be listening, but then it disappeared.

Ryan could see the barn clearly now, not ten yards ahead. As she called again, she noticed the open doorway, and the human figure framed there, as though it were waiting for her.

"Hello! I'm stuck in the snow! I'm trying to find—"

The words caught in her throat. As she looked up in horror, she saw the lumpy coat . . . the black ski mask . . . the eyeholes staring back—

"No!" Ryan tried to run, but she was no match for

his uncanny speed. Dragging her into the barn, he chuckled softly and barred the doors behind her.

At first she couldn't see a thing. The darkness yawned emptily around her, smelling of damp wood and straw. As Ryan picked herself up from the floor, a dim light began to focus in one far corner, and a lantern threw ghostly shadows up the drafty walls.

"Oh, God, who are you? Where's the police?"

Helplessly she felt her arms twisted behind her as he forced her to the back of the barn. She didn't even have time to brace herself for the fall—as the yawning hole appeared without warning in the floor, she hurtled through it and landed on a cushion of cold, prickly straw. Dazed, she scooted back into a corner and blinked against the gloom. She could see the ski mask, floating in the hole above her head, and as she felt a movement near her feet, she realized she wasn't alone. Terrified, she watched as a human shadow pulled itself from the darkness and began to glide toward her, a flickering lantern held high above its head.

"Ryan McCauley"—the voice sounded amused, echoing through the blackness, sending chills up her spine—"so glad you could join us."

"Who—who are you? Where's Marissa?" Her voice shook uncontrollably, filling the space with her fear.

"Marissa?" The shadow moved closer, pulsing up the damp stone walls. "Well . . . of course she's not here . . . but I'll take you to her."

"The police," Ryan murmured. "Where are they? They called and—" She froze as the approaching figure stepped out at last into a sickly pool of yellow light. "Oh, my God . . . Charles . . ."

"You do want to see her, don't you?" he asked smoothly, a faint smile creeping over his face. "Just to be together again . . ."

"What are you doing here? How did you know about Marissa? How—" She broke off as her eyes probed her shadowy surroundings . . . as they swept over the piles and piles of clear plastic bags . . . the snowy drifts of powder inside . . . "What—"

"Come on, now, Ryan, surely you've watched enough TV to recognize drugs when you see them." Charles laughed softly. "Marissa recognized them. She even took pictures of . . . shall we say . . . a business transaction?" He set the lantern down carefully on the floor, but his smile never wavered. "Thank goodness I picked up that film in time. Thank goodness I believed her when she said she'd uncovered a scandal. Otherwise . . . a lot of people would have been in a whole lot of trouble."

Ryan's mouth fell open. *"You!* You were selling drugs on campus and Marissa found out! You're the one she took pictures of—it was you all—"

"No, no, no." Another chuckle, as if the whole matter were unbearably comical. "I'm too smart to be photographed, Ryan. It's just too bad everyone isn't as smart as me."

"Then . . . who . . ."

"It was a perfect little setup, you have to admit." Charles crossed his arms and leaned back against the wall. "Basing the whole operation right here in this boring little town—who would have thought it would be so easy? We couldn't let Marissa ruin it, now, could we? Not with all the millions at stake. It was only fair . . . she tried to stop us . . . so naturally . . . we had to stop *her*."

"You killed her!" Ryan screamed. "You killed my sister!"

Charles's face registered exaggerated distaste. "Ryan, I'm surprised at you! I have more class than to dirty my hands with something so unpleasant—especially when there are other people around who are so good at it!"

She saw him staring into the space above their heads . . . she saw his smile widening . . . and as she looked up, she saw the lumpy coat fall away . . . the ski mask peeling back from the shadowed face. And suddenly she was back again, back at the river that horrible day, trying to rescue Marissa, Marissa's terrified screams echoing over and over in her head—*"sleeve—sleeve"*—and Ryan had tried so hard to hang on, had tried so hard to keep hold of Marissa's sleeve . . .

Only she hadn't been saying *sleeve*.

Swallowing water, fighting for her life, Marissa hadn't been saying *sleeve* at all . . .

And now, as the black ski mask fell through the air and landed at her feet, Ryan saw Steve grinning down at her.

Chapter 21

No . . ." Ryan murmured, "no . . . I don't believe this . . ."

As the shadows swayed around her, she strained against the wall and fought for air. Sobs caught in her throat, and she choked them back down again as she saw Charles and Steve exchange satisfied glances.

"Do you think I could have had a life," Steve said reasonably, "wondering just how much Marissa knew? I thought I saw her that day with her camera, but I couldn't be sure . . . not till she told Charles she had evidence of something that was so important. We were talking about my whole future . . . my reputation . . . all my new prospects . . . even my bank accounts. I couldn't let her destroy what I'd worked so hard for. There was too much tied up in everything . . . way too much at stake."

As Ryan stared at him numbly, he shook his head and shrugged.

"But it wasn't just me. She would have ruined a lot of people's lives. So you have to weigh the consequences . . . one life for all that money. All that freedom. There's really no decision when you look at it that way, is there? We did the only thing we could do."

Charles shook a finger condescendingly. "And then Marissa got you into it, Ryan. How were we supposed to know how much she'd told you? Steve went through as many of her things as he could after she died . . . as many of *your* things as he could when no one was in the house . . . but how could we really know what you knew? Maybe there were things you repressed about Marissa's accident . . . maybe you would have remembered them later on. . . . How could we live under that shadow, always waiting for you to remember? You wouldn't talk to anyone about it. You wouldn't confide in anyone. So I decided to come for a little visit. But you didn't trust me, either, did you? Not until you got really scared. . . ."

"And you were so easy to scare." Steve sighed. "It takes time to drive someone right out of her mind . . . to make it believable. You felt so guilty about Marissa, it was almost too easy. A few unfortunate accidents . . . a tape from Marissa's answering machine at school . . . some great disguises . . . and then that necklace I grabbed at the last minute . . . an afterthought, really. The game's not nearly so much fun when there's no challenge. And you were so good at helping us, too . . . everyone thinks you tried to do yourself in. Charles and your mother *heard* you say you wanted to die. . . ." He bit his lip and tried to hold back a smile. "So no one will really be surprised when you kill yourself . . . for real this time."

"It was the film." Charles patted his coat pocket.

"These photos. We couldn't really be sure Marissa had proof until you remembered the film. And now, of course, we can't afford to keep you around."

Ryan made a desperate move toward the ladder, but Charles caught her and pushed her back down.

"Uh-uh, now, Ryan, don't be a bad girl. You wanted for it all to be over, didn't you? So we're really doing you a favor. We're helping you be with Marissa again."

"You can't do this," Ryan choked. "Think about Mom—"

"But I am thinking of her." Steve looked perfectly at ease. "I'm thinking what a wonderful life we'll have with all that money . . . her being so destroyed by the untimely deaths of her two daughters, that she'll be the perfect little wife . . . always do what I say . . . always depend on me and please me so I don't leave her. She's my perfect cover. I should really thank you, Ryan. Sacrificing yourself for our happiness. But then, you always were such a good girl." He stretched languorously and flexed his fingers. "Well, I better get to work. There can't be a suicide till we cut through that ice." He started to say something more when there was a series of thuds behind him, as if someone were pounding on the barn door. As Steve disappeared from view, Ryan lunged at Charles. The struggle lasted only a minute—as she fell back once more into the corner, Charles pointed his gun at her and cocked the hammer.

"Come on, Ryan, don't be stupid. It'll be so much

more romantic to fling yourself into the river than to shoot yourself in the head. . . ."

"Please let me go," she begged. "I won't say anything, I swear! You'll never have to worry—we can pretend none of this ever hap—" She broke off at the sudden disturbance of voices overhead. It sounded as though there was an argument going on, and as the voices came nearer, she cringed back into the shadows and tried not to look at Charles's pistol.

"Where is she?" a stern voice demanded, and as Ryan gazed up fearfully, another face hung there, disembodied, in the empty blackness, caught in a feeble web of lantern light.

Ryan's heart turned to ice. She felt tears on her cheeks, and a cry lodged in her throat.

"Ah, *Bambalina,*" Mr. Partini said gently, "why couldn't you mind your own business, eh?"

"Oh, my God—Mr.—oh, my God—"

"I never want to hurt you"—he spread his hands helplessly—"but there's no other way! Ah, why you hurt me so much, Ryan—another bad, bad heartache!"

Over the toymaker's shoulder Steve looked anxious. "We better get to work—we have appointments—"

"I try to keep you out of it," Mr. Partini said sadly. "The toys . . . you want to deliver . . . I always say no. You never find out they hide the cocaine . . . you and me, we stay good friends. Who would ever think this sister of yours would be snooping around? That she could cause so much trouble for all of us?" He shook his head—"No, *Bambalina* . . ."—I never think this will happen, eh?"

"Mr. Partini, *please!* You've *got* to help me! You've got to *do* some—"

"Take care of her." He nodded to Steve, then motioned to Charles with one frail hand. "I no like my friends to suffer."

He and Steve both twisted around as a flurry of snow and ice swept through the barn . . . as raised voices shouted from the front.

"Now what?" Mr. Partini snapped, and as Charles started up the ladder, the old man looked down with an amused smile. "How nice to have so many visitors today!"

Before Ryan could even scream, a body plummeted down through the trapdoor and lay motionless in the straw.

Chapter 22

Jinx! Oh, Jinx—what have you *done* to him!"

Ryan knelt beside the still figure . . . saw blood smeared over the dirty straw. "You'll never get away with this! I'll make *all* of you pay—I swear—"

"Ah, poor Ryan." Mr. Partini shook his head. "Why didn't you just kill the boy outside, eh, if it make her so upset—"

"What! Did you say Ryan!" And as Mr. Partini was pushed roughly aside, Winchester peered down, stricken. "Ryan—my God—what are you—"

"I hate you!" Ryan screamed. "How could you do this! How—"

"What is she doing here?" Winchester demanded. He was staring at Charles, and even in the dim light his face was unnaturally pale. "What are you doing to her? Why is she down here—"

"There, there, delivery boy, calm down." Mr. Partini chuckled softly. "You got lots to do—customers are waiting, eh?"

"You can't do anything to her—" Winchester turned to the old man, his voice bewildered. "She doesn't know anything about anything—she told me so—"

"Yes, yes, and of course you believed her." Mr. Partini nodded patiently, waving one hand. "But now we know different, eh? And so . . ."

"You can't," Winchester whispered. "You never said anything about this . . . you promised no one would get hurt. . . ."

"But Marissa got hurt." Charles gave a derisive laugh. "How did you think that happened so conveniently?"

"She fell." Winchester's voice was numb. "She had an accident and fell . . . through . . . the . . ." As his voice trailed away, he shook his head slowly. "No. No . . . I don't believe you. . . ."

"Is a matter of survival." Mr. Partini shrugged. "Survival of the fittest. When you became one of us, I thought you understood—"

"I made those deliveries for you because I didn't know what they were at first," Winchester said flatly. "I only thought they were toys—"

"But you stayed. And your loyalty is touching." The old man put a hand to his heart. "Don't you agree, boys."

"Loyalty had nothing to do with it. You threatened to hurt my family. To burn down my father's business. I didn't have a choice."

"And you don't have one now, as far as I can see." Charles raised his eyebrows and met Steve's expression with a smug smile. "Your job is to take orders. So take them."

Winchester was staring from one to the other, as if he couldn't believe what was happening. "Look . . . I've done everything you wanted . . . but you can't hurt her, do you understand? You can't—"

"Poor little brothers and sisters . . ." Mr. Partini shook his head solemnly, wiping invisible tears from his eyes. "Poor little ones . . . such nasty accidents that kids can fall into—"

Charles climbed up and handed the gun to Winchester. "We'll be back in a few minutes, so keep them nice and quiet. Oh . . . and Winchester . . . don't screw up."

The voices faded eerily into the black cavern of the barn. There was a shriek of wind . . . and then . . . deathly quiet.

Ryan gazed up at Winchester through a blur of tears. She could feel Jinx rousing, trying to lift his head. As he moaned and turned over, she looked down and wiped the stream of blood from his nose.

"Jinx—are you all right?" It seemed such a hopeless thing to say as she put one hand to his cheek. "Did you break anything?"

"Dammit, McCauley," Jinx mumbled, pressing a fist to his gushing nose, "what the hell have you gotten us into this time?"

"They're going to kill me," Ryan said, surprised at how calm and resigned she sounded. "They're going to throw me in the river and make it look like suicide—they're going—"

She jumped back with a scream as Winchester

landed lightly beside them. He started to lean over Jinx, but Ryan shoved him away.

"No! Don't you touch him! You leave him alone!"

"There's a back way," Winchester said quietly, motioning them to hold their voices down. "Mr. Partini's gone, and Charles and Steve are on the other side of the barn, so they won't see you. Here're my keys. I want you to take my truck and—"

"Your truck?" Jinx murmured. "That old thing'll never make it—"

"Use the radio to call the police. Don't hang around, understand? Just get out of here!"

"But—but what about you?" Jinx had sat up now and was trying to get his bearings. "We can't just leave you—when they find out you let us go—"

"No." Winchester gave a faint smile, shaking his head. "They're going to kill me anyway. Now, hurry —we can't waste any more time."

"It was all planned, wasn't it?" Ryan peered miserably into his face, "that night when Charles let me out of the van. He really was trying to kill me—"

"I was supposed to find you—to get you to trust me—so maybe you'd talk and tell me what you knew. Steve and Charles had both tried to get you to open up to them, and they thought you might confide in me. . . ." Winchester's face darkened. "I never wanted to hurt you, Ryan. You have to believe that. And I didn't lie about wanting you to stay that night. I've liked you for a long time. The only reason I ever went out with Marissa in the first place was to try to meet you."

Ryan swallowed a lump in her throat. She looked at Jinx in panic. "We can't just leave him—"

"It'll be safer for you if I can distract them. Go on." Winchester grabbed her elbow and jerked her to her feet. "They'll be back any second—hurry—"

They got up the ladder and raced to the other end of the barn. As Winchester held the lantern high, Ryan spotted a door camouflaged in the rear wall of one of the stalls, and she reached nervously for Jinx while Winchester struggled with the rusted latch. Without warning the door blew open on a blast of icy wind.

"This way!" Winchester herded them through. "Keep running—whatever you do, don't stop! Don't come back!"

As Ryan saw the door closing, she was seized with a sudden premonition of tragedy. "No!" She tried to wedge herself in the doorway. "Come with us! You've got to come with us—"

She felt Jinx pulling her, saw the quick flash of tenderness in Winchester's eyes as he thrust her away from the door.

"Take care of her, Jinx!" he said. "Now, run!"

Ryan couldn't even see where they were going. The wind tore at them from all sides, pelting them ruthlessly with ice and snow. As she slipped and stumbled, Jinx forced her to her feet and dragged her on.

"I think I see the truck!"

"Where?"

"We're almost there—come on, Ryan—just a little more—"

As tow truck suddenly appeared through the

white, swirling eddies, Ryan flung open the door and fell inside.

"We're going to make it!" she said breathlessly. "Oh, hurry, Jinx—hurry!"

Beside her Jinx fumbled the key into the ignition and gave it a turn. Nothing happened. Casting a wild look at Ryan, he slammed his fist against the dashboard and turned the key again. The engine ground slowly several times, then stopped.

"Damn!" Jinx pumped the accelerator . . . jiggled the key. "Try the radio!"

Ryan looked at him helplessly. "I don't know how to work it!"

She saw him start to lean toward the dashboard— she saw his door suddenly burst open—but before she could scream, Charles had Jinx around the neck, bending him backward out the door.

"Bad idea," he sneered at them. "Tricks like that make me very . . . very angry—"

"Get out of there!" Outside Ryan's window Steve pounded the roof with his gun and put his other hand on the door. "I'm going to enjoy this, Ryan"—he pushed his face to the glass, his features grotesquely distorted—"even more than I enjoyed killing Marissa —even more than—"

"Shut up! Look at the barn!" As Charles broke in excitedly, his grip loosened around Jinx's neck, and Steve straightened with a look of alarm.

"What's wrong?"

"The damn thing's on fire!"

Jinx moved so quickly that Ryan scarcely realized what happened. Twisting out of Charles's grasp, Jinx shoved him backward into the snow and slammed the door, flooring the gas pedal as he thrust the key in one last time. With a hoarse groan the engine sputtered, tried to die, then turned over at last—and the truck lurched into action, fishtailing through the snow as Jinx tried desperately to find the road.

Something ricocheted against the roof. As the truck shook violently, Jinx glanced in the rearview mirror and reached out for Ryan.

"Get down! They're shooting at us!"

As another bullet struck, he swerved, flinging Ryan hard into her door. She tried to sit back up again, but the truck spun wildly, and she hit the dashboard before she could catch herself.

"Get down!" Jinx yelled again. "Get down on the—"

His words were drowned out by the crash of breaking glass. Ryan screamed as she saw the back window come apart—as she felt sharp slivers spray across the side of her head and her shoulders. Jinx was shouting to her, trying to steer the truck, trying to push her down onto the seat.

"Are you okay?"

"I don't know—I think I might have gotten hit—"

The truck slowed down . . . slid the last few feet to a stop. As Jinx grabbed her, she shook uncontrollably and pulled her hand away from her head, staring down in amazement at the fresh smear of blood.

"You're okay, Ryan, you hear me? It's just the glass—you're not shot—you're just cut—"

Ryan shrieked in terror. As Jinx swung around, Charles's gun exploded through the window in a hail of flying glass. Jinx slammed back against the seat, and as Ryan screamed again, Charles thrust his gun against Jinx's face and tightened on the trigger.

"Merry Christmas, Ryan," he snarled.

The gun exploded, a deafening roar that went on and on, spattering the seat, the dash, the windows with blood. As Ryan stared in paralyzed horror, Charles's body twisted crazily, then went limp, hanging half inside the truck like a disfigured doll. She saw his head lift slowly as he stared at her with wild, glazed eyes, and then suddenly his whole body jerked, falling away as the door burst open.

"Get out of here!" Winchester shouted, hanging on to the door. "Steve's right behind me! *Go!*"

To Ryan's dismay, the truck roared back into action. She could see Jinx sagging over the steering wheel, blood gushing down his face, and Winchester against the side of the truck, yelling directions as he tried to dodge bullets and balance on the running board.

It seemed they drove through the snow forever.

From some remote corner of her mind, Ryan realized they were slowing down at last . . . stopping in an unfamiliar place where everything was quiet and hidden. She saw Winchester's haggard face beside her . . . she heard the pain in Jinx's voice as he kept his head turned away.

"I'll take you," Jinx whispered. "Wherever you say . . . wherever you want to go . . ."

The silence went on and on.

"To town, then," Winchester said softly. "To the police."

Ryan closed her eyes and cried.

Chapter 23

He's turning state's witness," Jinx said. "He'll testify against Steve and Mr. Partini . . . the police promised it'd go easier on him, and he wants to do it."

Ryan looked up from the bench in the hallway, trying to ignore the uniformed officers hurrying by.

"Then . . . Charles is . . ."

"He was already dead when the police got there," Jinx said, his voice lowering. "Winchester saw the whole thing—Steve trying to shoot him *and* us. He's going to tell them all about the toyshop and the deliveries, too. All the evidence probably burned up when he set fire to the barn, but he's pretty sure where all the other drugs are hidden. He knows about some of the things they did to scare you. And with you and me to tell how Winchester saved our lives . . ."

Ryan's voice shook. "But it wasn't his fault. They threatened his family. . . . Did you say how they threatened to hurt his family and how he was just trying to protect the people he loves?"

Jinx stared at her as she bent her head and tried to regain her composure. "I guess they're finally through talking to me—how about you?" At her nod he added, "I told my mom she didn't have to hang around. The snow's stopped now, and I kinda feel like walking home. How's *your* mom?"

"Still in there talking to the police." Ryan sighed. As she pressed a soggy tissue to her lashes, she felt Jinx awkwardly touch her shoulder. "Oh, God, Jinx, my poor mom . . . first Marissa and now Steve. I can't imagine how she must feel."

"Pretty lucky," Jinx said. "'Cause she's got you."

Ryan looked up at him, her eyes brimming. "Some luck. Everyone thinks I'm crazy. Everyone thinks I tried to kill myself. I'll never be able to show my face at school again. I don't even have a best friend anymore—the last time I tried to call Phoebe, she wouldn't even talk to me."

Jinx shook his head. "Not true. She was really upset about you going to the hospital—she was crying so hard, Mom wouldn't let her talk on the phone when you called. Hey, I was there. I know. Phoebe felt like she'd let you down."

Ryan's eyes widened. "Really?" She sniffled. "You're not just saying that?"

"I'm not just saying that."

"Well . . ." She cast him an accusing look. *"You* thought I was crazy."

"I've always thought you're crazy. I *know* you're crazy."

In spite of everything Ryan had to smile. "Well, that certainly makes me feel better."

"Don't mention it." Jinx glanced down at her, cleared his throat, looked away. "So . . . you hungry or something?"

"Not really."

He nodded, started to say more, turned toward the door instead. "Well . . . see you around."

Ryan watched him go out the front door of the police station and head down the sidewalk. She took a final wipe at her eyes, then hurried after him, pulling on her jacket as she burst through the door.

"Jinx!"

He turned then, and for just the briefest moment Ryan thought he actually seemed glad to see her. She paused beside him, searching for words.

"Will you . . . tell Phoebe I said hi?"

"Like I don't have better things to do than deliver your messages." He scowled and hunched his shoulders. "Oh, and don't worry about your stupid dance —she's gonna get to go."

"You're kidding—how did she manage that?"

Jinx gave an exasperated sigh. "I told Dad to *let* her, okay?"

"Did you really?" Ryan stepped toward him, but he backed away. "Jinx, that was so sweet of you—"

"Self-defense," he said quickly. "That's all. She was crying so loud, I couldn't get any sleep." He moved away, but Ryan caught his sleeve.

"Jinx—wait."

Again he looked at her. This time she put one hand cautiously to his cheek, feeling it harden beneath her touch.

"You're going to have a scar here, aren't you?" she said quietly. "Where that bullet grazed you."

"Big deal."

"I think it's kind of sexy."

A muscle twitched in his jaw. He lowered his head, and she could swear he blushed a little.

"Oh, Jinx—" She shook her head and sighed. "That's not really what I came out here to say."

He was staring at her, getting that suspicious expression on his face, and she hurried before she lost her nerve.

"I just wanted to thank you. If you hadn't called and followed me this morning—"

"Hey"—he shrugged—"it was better than going to school—"

"No, it's for more than that. It's for everything. For always being there every time I was scared and confused and needed someone."

Jinx looked away quickly, staring at the sidewalk as if he suddenly found it intensely fascinating.

"And I just want you to know that I didn't believe a word of what Phoebe said that night," Ryan rushed on. "I mean, I know she was upset and it wasn't *true*, all those things she said—" She broke off and took a deep breath. "Was it?"

Jinx's head came up, startled.

"Right, McCauley. You should be so lucky."

He glanced away, but then his eyes came back again . . . reluctant but curious.

"So . . ." Ryan said casually, "are you going to the New Year's dance?"

"Well, yeah." Jinx shrugged. "Yeah, as soon as I decide which girl deserves the honor."

"How about me?"

He looked so taken aback that she almost laughed but managed to catch herself in time.

"Yeah, sure," he said gruffly. "How about you what?"

"I'm serious. How about me? Going with you to the dance?"

This time there was no mistaking it. As he ducked his head, a blush worked its way slowly up over his cheekbones, and Ryan wondered why she'd never realized before how irresistible it made him look.

"Well," he said, taking his time, as if considering hundreds of possibilities, "there'll be a lot of really disappointed girls . . ."

"But one really happy one."

Jinx gave a loud sigh. "Look, McCauley—"

"So?"

"So what?"

"So are you going to ask me?"

He started to grin, his head nodding slyly. "Yeah, okay. But only on one condition."

"What's that?"

"You gotta promise to wear a bag over your head."

As she took a swing at him, he caught her hand in one of his own, and they started walking.

Point Horror

Are you hooked on horror? Are you thrilled by fear? Then these are the books for you. A powerful series of horror fiction designed to keep you quaking in your shoes.

POINT FANTASY